MONIKA

Titles available in this series

Yannis
Anna
Giovanni
Joseph
Christabelle
Saffron
Manolis
Cathy
Nicola
Vasi
Alecos
John
Tassos
Ronnie
Maria
Sofia
Babbis
Stelios
Kyriakos
Monika

Greek Translations

Anna

published by Livanis 2011

MONIKA

Beryl Darby

JACH

ISBN 978-1-9997176-0-5

Printed and bound in the UK by
CPI Group (UK) Ltd, Croydon, CR0 4YY

First published in the UK in 2017 by

JACH Publishing
92 Upper North Street, Brighton, East Sussex, England BN1 3FJ

website: www.beryldarby.co.uk

For John McDonald of Eklektos bookshop.
You will be missed by all who knew you.
Stay strong, Lynne.

Author's Note

My friend, Monique Brooimans, asked me to write a book using her name as the title. She and her husband have the gift shop 'Plaka's Ilios' in Plaka. I agreed to do this on the proviso that she had her photograph on the front cover.

This is certainly not Monique's life story, but totally a product of my imagination.

All the characters in this novel are entirely fictitious. Any resemblance to actual persons, living or dead is entirely coincidental.

Rhodes 1975 - 1980

Litsa walked back from school with her friend, Rebekah. Having passed through the San Francisco Gate they parted company and Rebekah walked down the wide cobbled street to where she lived in the Jewish quarter of the Old Town whilst Litsa turned into the narrow street that would lead to her mother's general store.

She detested Fridays. She would happily sit in the back room behind her mother's shop and concentrate on her homework until her father returned from working on the roads. His face, hands and clothes speckled with flecks of tar, and her mother would have the tin bath down in the kitchen and water heating ready for him. All the other evenings when he came in from work he would just strip off his dirty shirt and wash down to his waist, but on a Friday he would have a bath. His working trousers and shirt would be left on the floor for her mother to scrub the following day and it was her job to scour the bath clean, removing the sticky residue of tar that would cling to the sides. The following evening she and her mother would bath so they were clean ready for church on the Sunday morning.

Each morning, on her way to school, she took a short cut from the shop to the San Francisco Gate. The shutters on all the houses along there would be closed. When she passed by on her way home the girls who lived in the street were sitting outside, their hair brushed, their faces made up and always dressed in low necked blouses and short skirts during the warm weather. They would wave and call out a greeting to her which she would return. Litsa decided they must all have very rich husbands to be able to rise late and sit outside doing nothing during the day.

When it turned colder they would sit inside by their window, the curtains drawn back and the room would be lit with a soft pink glow from the electric light giving it an inviting, warm look. Litsa wished they had a pink light in their living room. Today the girls were not sitting outside and the street was completely deserted; their shutters were open, but their doors closed. In the distance she could hear the sound of women wailing and she shuddered at their keening, but at the same time she was curious. This only happened when someone had died. Litsa walked a little more quickly and when she rounded the corner she saw the girls and other neighbours gathered outside her mother's shop along with the priest. Had something awful happened to her mother?

Eleni saw her coming and left the group, placing her arm around Litsa.

'Your poor Mamma. You must be brave, Litsa, for her sake.'

'What do you mean?' Litsa felt herself go cold and her body trembled beneath Eleni's arm.

'Your Pappa has had an accident.'

'An accident? But he was at work.'

'The steam roller ran into him.'

'Is he hurt, badly hurt?'

Eleni nodded. 'That is why the priest is here. Your Pappa has died.'

Litsa looked at the woman in disbelief. 'Pappa, dead? He can't be. Mamma will be getting his bath ready for him.'

'Not tonight, Litsa. He will not be coming home. Go and try to comfort your mother. She's beside herself with grief.'

Litsa stood still and Eleni gave her a gentle push. 'Go along. I know it's difficult for you, but your Mamma needs you.'

'So I won't have to wash the bath?'

Eleni looked at the young girl in bewilderment. It was very unlikely that Monique would consider taking a bath that night.

Monique clasped her daughter closely to her. 'Your Pappa. Your Pappa.' she repeated over and over again whilst Litsa could feel her mother's tears dripping onto her hair. Litsa stood there unresisting, not knowing how she was expected to react. Should she join in with the women who were wailing or cry with her mother?

Father Gianni patted her shoulder. 'This is a sad day, Litsa. You will need to comfort your mother.'

'What happened?'

'The handbrake on the steam roller gave way. The men continued working not realising it was gradually rolling towards them until it was too late for them to jump out of the way. Three men were hurt, but your Pappa was the one who lost his life.'

'Why my Pappa?'

'No one can answer that question for you. All I can suggest is that in your prayers you ask for comfort for yourself and your mother and pray for your father's soul.'

Litsa nodded. No amount of praying on her part would bring her father back.

Monique kept Litsa home from school from school for over a week, unable to let her out of her sight. Each night she took her daughter into the bed she had previously shared with her husband, holding her tightly, her tears dripping onto Litsa's cheeks. Litsa hated it and wished she could return to her mattress in the small back room. She felt sorry for her mother but had no idea how she could comfort her.

Father Gianni was a frequent visitor and he persuaded Monique to allow her daughter to return to school. 'I know it is hard for you, but the girl must continue her schooling and meet with her friends. I am sure she is feeling the loss of her father deeply, but she has to accept his passing. It will be easier for her if she is away

11

from the house for a few hours each day and has other things to occupy her mind.'

Reluctantly Monique succumbed to the priest's persuasive words. Now she was over the initial shock she knew she must open up the shop again. As her husband was no longer there to provide them with a weekly wage she was dependent upon the meagre income that she gleaned from the nearby residents.

Litsa walked to school nervously. Would the girls still be friendly towards her now she had no father? Had she missed so much work that she would be behind the others in the class and made to feel foolish? As she reached the San Francisco Gate she heard footsteps and her name being called. Looking behind her she saw Rebekah hurrying to catch her up.

Rebekah stood in front of her, but then seemed at a loss for words. 'I'm sorry, Litsa,' she finally managed to utter.

Litsa nodded and shrugged at the same time. Rebekah linked her arm in Litsa's and they walked along together in a companionable silence until Litsa spoke.

'Does everyone at school know why I haven't been there?'

'I think so. Your priest came along one day. I saw him talking to Mr Sfyrakos and later that day Mrs Mavrikanos told the class. I'm not sure if everyone knows, but most of them certainly do.'

Litsa nodded. 'I don't want to have to talk about it to them.'

'Of course not. What happened?' Rebekah could not contain her curiosity.

'Pappa was squashed by the steam roller.'

Rebekah stopped. 'Squashed? You mean like a fly is squashed when you hit it?'

'I expect so. I was only allowed to see his face. The roller went over his legs and chest.'

Rebekah shuddered. 'That's awful. Were any of the other men hurt?'

'Two others had their legs crushed and were burnt by the hot tar they were spreading.'

'You don't expect accidents like that to happen. I mean, people die when they get old, not when they are out working. How is your Mamma?'

'Very unhappy.' Litsa felt slightly impatient with Rebekah. How was her mother expected to be feeling? 'She's opened up the shop again today.'

The girls stood together on the kerb, waiting for a lull in the traffic that would allow them to cross safely. 'I'm glad you've come back to school; I've missed you,' said Rebekah. 'After all, you are my best friend.'

'Really?' Litsa's earlier annoyance with Rebekah disappeared. 'I've hated being at home just with Mamma. She hardly speaks; she just sits in her chair rocking herself backwards and forwards. I hope now the shop is open again she'll be better.'

'I'm sure she will. Come on, we'll walk into class together and if anyone isn't kind to you they'll have to deal with me.'

Litsa was happy to have returned to school and for a few hours each day she was able to put the loss of her father to the back of her mind. She was catching up on the school work she had missed and although they had looked at her curiously her class mates had not asked questions about her father's accident. Mrs Mavrikanos called her to one side at the end of the day and explained that she had told the children about the tragedy that had befallen Litsa. She had reminded them that they should treat Litsa as they had in the past, not asking her for details about her father's demise or showering her with excessive sympathy.

As she returned from school each day the girls who lived in the street close to the shop were often chatting amongst themselves or sitting outside their houses. They would smile and encourage her to sit beside them whilst they gave her a sweet or some nuts until she felt they were also her friends. Finally she felt she could ask them the question that had been nagging at her for some time.

'Are your husbands very rich so you do not have to go out to work?'

'Husbands! You hear that girls? Are our husbands rich?' The girls who heard her laughed.

'We don't have husbands. We work at night.'

Litsa nodded. That explained why they were there during the daytime and their shutters closed in the morning. They were working in the tavernas and bars until the early hours of the morning. She hoped she would be able to find that kind of work when she left school. It would be so nice to stay in bed as late as she wished each day. She would be able to help her mother in the shop during the afternoon although there were rarely more than two customers at a time and they always seemed to have plenty of time to chat. It was only a Saturday that was difficult.

On a Saturday her father had always visited the warehouse down by the commercial port and returned carrying a sack of flour, rice or lentils on his back. Now she was expected to collect the goods as her mother needed them. Unable to carry a heavy sack, she would take two large shopping bags and make numerous trips back and forth until she had collected and delivered the required amount to her mother. By the end of the day she felt exhausted and her arms, shoulders and back ached.

Without the additional regular income that her father had brought home each week, money was short. Her mother let down the hems of her skirts as she grew taller, but they were faded and washed out. Now Monique always wore black and she had taken tucks in the white blouses that had belonged to her and passed those down to her daughter. Litsa felt embarrassed when she saw how drab she looked in the old clothes. She consoled herself with the thought that when she was old enough to go to work in a taverna or bar, as the girls who lived in the street did, she would be able to afford to buy new clothes and look as smart as them. Then she would be able to attract a young man and when they were married she would have a house of her own and children to care for.

Litsa knew she would be leaving school that summer and decided it was time she approached the girls and asked if there would be a position available in any of the establishments where they worked. She was aware that she would be given the most menial of tasks to begin with, but she was willing to learn how to take an order from a customer correctly and serve them without spilling a plate of food in their lap.

As she walked home she saw Anna leaning against Eleni's wall as they talked together. It could be an ideal opportunity.

'Hi, Eleni, Anna. Can I ask you about your work?'

The girls raised their eyebrows and exchanged looks. 'What did you want to know?'

'I wondered if any extra staff were needed during the summer season? I finish school in three weeks and I need to find some work. I know I haven't any experience, but I'm willing to learn.'

Eleni gasped and Anna gave a giggle that she tried to stifle.

'Where do you think we work?' asked Eleni.

'In the bars or tavernas. I wouldn't mind which I worked in provided I could earn some money,' said Litsa earnestly.

'What gave you that idea?'

'When I come past in the morning your shutters are closed where you are sleeping in. In the afternoon you're around and you all look so smart and well dressed that you must be earning good money.'

Anna shook her head. 'We work from home.'

'But these are not bars or tavernas.' Litsa waved her hand indicating the row of houses.

Eleni sighed. 'I've nothing personal against you, Litsa, but if a young girl like you joined us you'd steal all our regular customers away.'

'What difference would it make to the customers who served them?'

'A lot. We all have regular patrons and we know what they like and expect us to do for them. Whenever a new girl joins us they always try her out a few times to see what she has to offer. Some stay with her and some return to the girl they know. If you were here they'd be queuing up to be served by you and we would be losing money for weeks.'

Litsa frowned. 'I don't understand.'

Ann sniggered. 'You're going to have to spell it out for her, Eleni. She really hasn't got a clue.'

'Litsa,' said Eleni patiently, 'We are members of the oldest profession in the world. Men come to us for the pleasure they are unable to get elsewhere. They pay us well, some have special requests and they pay double for those favours. We can earn more in one night than we would earn in a week at a bar or taverna.'

'Oh.' Litsa was nonplussed. 'I hadn't realised.'

'Well, now you know I don't expect you want to join us.'

'Is it unpleasant?'

Anna shrugged. 'You soon get used to it. It's a job like any other.'

'Suppose you meet someone you really like?'

'You don't become friends with your customers, particularly the regulars. If you do they'll expect to have you for nothing.'

'What happens if they refuse to pay you?' Litsa asked curiously.

'You take their money first.'

Litsa frowned. 'How much do you charge?'

'Depends what they want and how long they want to stay. A straight forward job lasting no more than fifteen minutes is twenty drachmas. If they need more time then half an hour is forty drachmas. A rough calculation would be a hundred and twenty an hour, but you need a bit of time in between customers to clean up. Two an hour is about the usual. An all night job would be six hundred, but we don't get many of those.'

Litsa gasped. Six hundred drachmas earned in one night. 'What happens if they say they're not satisfied and want their money back?'

'Our customers are always satisfied,' replied Anna smugly. 'If they do turn nasty we tell Mr Pavlides and he very soon sorts them out.'

'Who's Mr Pavlides?'

'He owns these cottages. We pay him the rent each week and he makes sure that trouble makers are dealt with.'

Litsa was calculating rapidly in her head. If the girls spoke truly when they said the men would be queuing up for her due to her youth and inexperience she should be able to make at least two hundred drachmas a night and that would be over a thousand drachmas by the end of a week.

'How much rent does he charge?'

'A hundred a week.'

'Does he let out just a room?'

'You'd have to ask if you could use one of ours on a week when we're not working. If he agrees you'll have to pay him rent for that week.'

'Are you serious, Litsa?' asked Eleni. 'What is your mother going to think?'

'I would only do it for a few weeks, just to get some money together for some new clothes; then I'd look for a proper job in the town. I wouldn't need to tell my mother.'

Eleni shrugged. She had only intended to work for a few months to have some money during the winter months when casual work was scarce. When she had realised just how much more she could make by selling her body she had decided to continue until she was too old or unattractive to be patronised. By then she should have a sizable amount of savings and be able to move to a different area and look for some acceptable occupation.

'Think about it carefully, Litsa. It's a big step for a young girl like you to take.'

Litsa nodded. 'I will. Could you ask Mr Pavlides if he would allow me to use a room?'

'He'll probably want to be first to inspect the goods,' sniggered

Anna. 'If he's happy with what he gets he'll probably expect to have you for free until someone else takes his fancy.'

'Stasia will be pleased,' added Eleni. 'She's fed up with his inventive ideas and wobbly stomach.'

Litsa felt a moment of foreboding. 'What kind of ideas does he have?'

Anna rolled her eyes. 'All sorts. He even managed to surprise me with one or two of them. Tell him that you only do it straight to start with. You don't have the experience to experiment as you're new to the game.'

Litsa hated Lakkis Pavlides. He would study her with his cruel, green eyes, lick his lips and say 'I have thought of something we could find amusing.'

Litsa knew by now that she would not find it amusing. Lakkis appeared to get his pleasure in the most perverse ways, but she dared not complain. She was grateful he allowed her to use a room when one of the girls was unable to work for a few days. He would charge her a hundred drachmas but would still expect the full rent from whichever girl was not working.

At the end of each week Litsa would give her mother fifty drachmas and say it was half her earnings from the late night bar where she was working. The other money she earned, having paid Lakkis, she would spend on a new item of clothing, assuring her mother that she had bought it cheaply from the market stalls, and always making sure she was able to place some money into the shoe box under her bed. Monique accepted the money her daughter gave her gratefully and did not urge her to rise early in the morning. Litsa was a good girl. Having been out until the early hours she was still willing to help in the shop during the afternoon or prepare a meal for them both. Monique missed the presence of her daughter in her bed, but Litsa had insisted that now she was arriving home in the early hours it was not fair to disturb her mother and would creep in quietly to her mattress in the small back room.

The only thing Litsa was no longer willing to do was collect the flour, rice or lentils from the warehouse. She had found a boy with a cart who would deliver the sacks to the shop for twenty drachmas and persuaded Monique that it was money well spent.

'You can give him a list of anything that you need and he says he's willing to bring those goods at the same time. He'll still only charge you twenty drachmas.'

Monique considered the idea and finally agreed that it would be helpful to have a little more stock in the shop in the hope of attracting more customers.

Had it not been for Lakkis Pavlides, Litsa realised that she would be quite enjoying the camaraderie she experienced with the other girls. They had been correct when they said that their customers would want to visit her whilst she was fresh and new. Some had returned a second time, willing to wait until she had satisfied the man she was with.

When the naval ships docked the girls were particularly busy, the sailors hurrying to their houses as soon as they were given shore leave. Litsa found she was in demand from late afternoon and told her mother she was working extra hours due to one of the girls at the bar being unwell.

'I hope they'll be paying you extra. You're beginning to look very tired. You'll be off sick next if you keep working at this rate,' warned Monique.

'I'm sure she'll soon be back. I'm able to give you some extra money this week. You could buy yourself a new skirt or shoes.'

Monique accepted the additional money gratefully. She felt guilty about taking money from her daughter, but consoled herself with the fact that for the previous six years since her husband had died she had fed and clothed Litsa to the best of her ability whilst often going without herself.

Litsa smiled at the handsome young sailor as he walked down the road looking at the girls who were standing in their doorways.

'Are you looking for anyone special?' she called to him as she thrust her chest out and lifted her skirt an alluring few inches.

His smile widened. 'You're new, aren't you? I don't remember seeing you the last time I was in port.'

'I was probably busy. I'm sorry I missed you. Maybe we could make up for the lost opportunity now?' Litsa stood to one side as he walked into the room and threw his hat on the chair.

'How much do you charge?' he asked.

'That depends upon your requirements and the time you spend with me. My rate is the same as the other girls. Payment in advance.'

He drew some notes from his pocket and handed them to Litsa. 'We'll say half an hour to start with.'

Litsa sighed as she unlaced her blouse and hung it over the back of the chair, followed by her skirt. If he wanted half an hour it would mean she had to spend half that time encouraging him. She was far happier when a customer arrived eager and ready and all she had to do was moan occasionally and pretend she was in ecstasy. She set the alarm clock so that she would know when his half an hour was over and she could either ask for more money or tell him to leave.

To her surprise the sailor only stopped to remove his trousers before thrusting into her, not needing any encouragement at all from her. Finally he gave a deep groan and collapsed on top of her.

He gave a sheepish grin. 'We've been at sea for a month,' he said by way of explanation. He knelt astride her and removed his top, before settling himself beside her. 'I hope I wasn't too rough. That was necessity, now I can have pleasure. Let me look at you. Once I was inside you could have been an eighty year old hag. I only had one thing on my mind.'

'I hope you didn't think I was that old when I first spoke to you.'

'I thought you were the most beautiful woman I had ever seen.'

'And if I hadn't invited you in you would have gone to the

girl next door and thought she was the most beautiful woman in the world.'

He shook his head. 'No, I've been to this street before and never seen a girl here who looks as good as you. How long have you been working?'

'Long enough to know what a man wants.' Litsa reached out her hand and stroked the inside of his thigh. He gave a quick intake of breath and moved her hand to his member which was already hardening.

'I'll try to take it slowly this time, give you some pleasure.'

Litsa was surprised. No one had ever suggested to her before that she would have any pleasure. He began to toy with her body and she found herself experiencing sensations that were new to her. He smiled at her as he lifted his mouth from her breast.

'Ready?'

'Yes.' Litsa's throat felt dry. Was this how it was supposed to be? Did the other girls reach a fever pitch where they actually wanted the man to be able to release their body from an agony of anticipation? She moaned with genuine pleasure, grinding her hips into his, wanting more and more of him until she felt faint with suppressed longing. Then it happened, they climaxed together, clawing at each other frenziedly, panting with the exertion, and Litsa had the ecstasy of relief, totally oblivious of the alarm clock ringing stridently.

'I guess that means my time is up?'

Litsa looked at him, uncomprehendingly for a moment. She stretched out her hand and silenced the clock. 'I could make an exception,' she murmured.

'I'm not sure I could manage to satisfy you again. You're incredible when roused.' He sat on the side of the bed and looked around.

'There's a bowl of water over there and a clean towel.'

'Will you be here tomorrow?' he asked.

'I'm usually around.'

'Save yourself for me. Who should I ask for if I can't see you?'

'My name is Litsa.'

'A beautiful name for a beautiful young lady.' He pulled on his trousers and uniform top. 'Until tomorrow, Litsa.' He kissed her moist lips and Litsa had an almost overwhelming desire to ask him to stay.

She lay for some time unmoving on the bed. She hoped he would come the following day. Earning money had suddenly become far less important to her than seeing the sailor again.

For the following three weeks he would arrive, a broad smile on his face when he saw Litsa was waiting for him and had not agreed to entertain anyone else. He paid for half an hour each time, but Litsa no longer set the alarm clock. He could stay as long as he wished, preferably forever.

Her heart sank when he announced that the overhaul of his ship had been completed and they would be sailing the following day.

'When will you be back?' she asked tremulously.

'We're scheduled to sail down the coast of Turkey, then sail around Cyprus, just to make our presence felt. We'll return for supplies and twenty four hours shore leave before we go to Piraeus and then home to Crete. It's a regular round trip.'

'Don't you get bored doing the same thing all the time?'

He shook his head. 'There's always plenty of work to be done on board. I should be back in about four weeks.'

'I'll be looking out for you,' promised Litsa.

'I'll think of you constantly whilst I'm at sea.'

Litsa smiled happily. He was the man of her dreams. She was sure that when he returned he would have missed her so much that he would want to marry her. She would spend the time whilst he was away looking for work in a shop or taverna so she could give up renting a room from Lakkis Pavlides. They would be able to afford a small apartment where they could live whenever he was back in Rhodes.

Her head full of dreams, Litsa kissed him a passionate goodbye and walked back to Anna's house where she was working that week. A customer was waiting impatiently for her and she felt reluctant and annoyed that she would have to pretend that she was enjoying his attentions so soon after saying goodbye to the man she loved.

The weeks seemed to take an age to pass and she did not have to take time off during the month and then realisation dawned on her. She was pregnant. She kept the knowledge to herself, longing to tell someone, but feeling that the child's father should be the first to know the good news.

His reaction was not as she had expected. 'I thought you girls knew how to look after yourselves and prevent accidents happening,' he said angrily.

Litsa hung her head. 'You were coming back and we could be married so it wouldn't matter that an accident had occurred.'

'Marry you? I can't marry you. You're a street girl.'

'I thought you loved me,' said Litsa miserably.

'You don't fall in love with the girls you make use of when you have shore leave.'

'I've been looking for a position in a shop or taverna. I wouldn't have to be a street girl any longer.'

'What you do makes no difference to me. I already have a wife waiting for me in Piraeus.'

Litsa cringed as if she had been hit. 'Married? I didn't know you were married.'

'You didn't ask. Just because I preferred to visit you rather than any of the other girls didn't mean I wasn't married.' He picked up his hat from the chair. 'I'll be off now. The next time we're here I'll look out for you if you're still working.'

Litsa lay on the bed and sobbed. What was she going to do? Even if she was able to obtain a respectable job her employer would probably dismiss her as soon as her pregnancy became obvious. If only he had told her he was married she would have taken her usual precautions against pregnancy. The knocking on her door told her that she had a customer waiting. Reluctantly she rose.

'Give me five minutes,' she said, 'then I'll be with you.'

Eleni was not sympathetic when Litsa finally disclosed her predicament to her.

'I thought he loved me and would come back and marry me,' she said miserably.

'You got carried away. We warned you not to take a liking to any of your customers. Just because he favoured you it didn't mean he gave you a second thought once his ship left the harbour. He was no different from any other sailor.'

'I didn't know he was already married.'

Eleni shrugged. 'It's better to assume they all have a wife around somewhere. Even if they are single they're not going to marry one of us just because we say we're carrying their child.'

'What am I going to do?'

'Have you told your mother?'

Litsa shook her head. 'Not yet. I keep hoping something will happen and I'll find it was just a mistake; that I had my dates wrong.'

Eleni pursed her lips. 'You can be out by a day or two, but not by over two months. You'd best tell her before it becomes obvious and neighbours begin to talk.'

Rhodes 1981 - 1992

Litsa had thought long and hard about telling her mother that she was pregnant. She knew her mother would be disgusted and disappointed with her, but she also hoped she would be willing to help and not throw her out on the street to take her chance.

She began by extolling the virtues of the absent sailor, how handsome, kind and considerate he was until Monique was expecting her daughter to ask if she could get married. Then Litsa confessed.

'I honestly thought he loved me and would be returning to marry me. He gave every indication that that was his intention.'

'So why didn't you bring him to the shop so I could meet him?' asked Monique.

'We just wanted to spend every minute of his shore leave together.'

'Have you seen him since? Does he know you're carrying his child?'

Litsa hung her head. 'Yes.'

'So when are you getting married?'

'I can't. He says he's already married.'

'What! You foolish child! Just because a man flatters you it doesn't mean he's in love with you. You see what happens when you believe everything you're told. Is his ship still here? I'll go and give him a piece of my mind.'

Litsa shook her head. 'No, he left a couple of weeks ago. I don't know when he'll return.'

'So what are you going to do about your problem? It won't go away, you know.'

'I hoped you'd be willing to help me, Mamma. To let me stay here and help in the shop when I became too large to go to work.'

'There's no reason why you shouldn't work until at least the last month. I'll explain to the bar owner that your husband is at sea.'

'No, Mamma, you can't do that. I haven't been working in a bar.'

'Where have you been working then? You've been earning good money, paying for your keep and buying new clothes.'

'I've been renting a room from one of the girls.'

'You've been what?' Monique was horrified. 'No wonder you've ended up pregnant; you could be diseased as well. You can't even guarantee that this sailor is the father. Even if he wasn't already married I doubt he'd be prepared to marry you. What proof does he have that the child is his?'

'I'm not sick in any way. I went to the clinic and asked to be checked. I know he's the father. I was far more careful and followed the other girls' instructions when it was anyone else.'

'How long have you been doing this, Litsa?'

'Since I left school. I talked to the girls and they said they made plenty of money, even after paying their rent to Mr Pavlides they had more left than if they worked in a taverna or bar.'

'You're only just sixteen! You're no more than a child yourself. Did you even look for another job or just take these girls' word that it was easy money?'

'I needed some money to buy some decent clothes so I could wear them when I went to ask around for work. I only planned to work for a few weeks, just to get enough for the clothes and to give you some extra money,' Litsa defended herself. 'You needed new shoes for the winter. Yours were split at the sides and had holes in the sole.'

'That was my problem to deal with. The shop doesn't take enough to more than feed us and pay the essential overheads. Now the season is finished there won't even be the occasional passing visitor who wants a drink or piece of fruit. How do you think we're going to have enough money to look after a baby if you're not working?'

'I have some money saved. I didn't spend it all on clothes. When I thought I was going to be married I started to put money aside for my wedding. I can go back to work for a few weeks yet, before I get too big.'

'Go back to selling yourself? Is that what you want?'

'I can't see any other solution,' replied Litsa miserably.

Monique shook her head in despair. 'We'll have to tell the neighbours you are married and your husband is at sea.'

Litsa looked at her mother scornfully. 'They'll never believe that. Even if I claimed to have been married in the New Town they'll wonder why we didn't tell them earlier and would guess the reason for a quiet and hasty marriage. I am sorry, Mamma. I didn't intend this to happen.'

'That's what every girl in your predicament always says,' Monique sighed.

Litsa sat in the window of Stasia's house crocheting a blanket. Each evening when she left the shop her mother would compress her lips and shake her head, but made no attempt to dissuade her. They both knew that whatever money she made now would be needed to see them through the months when she was unable to work. Now almost five months into her pregnancy she was keeping well and was only just becoming large enough to make her customers suspicious about her condition. The only noticeable difference was the enlargement of her breasts and her customers did not complain about that.

She had let out the tucks her mother had made in the old blouses and enlarged the waist of her skirts by sewing in a piece of elastic. There was no money for new clothes now. She looked longingly at the shops in the New Town where they sold a beautiful selection of baby clothes. They would have to wait until she had given birth and was able to work again. The money she earned now was spent on knitting wool to make blankets and tiny cardigans. Provided she did not suddenly balloon out she should be able to work for another couple of weeks, maybe longer.

Litsa waved at the man who passed by. He waved back, but continued to Eleni's house. Litsa shrugged. There was bound to be another who was looking for a girl who was not already occupied. As she recognised the jaunty walk of the sailor her heart missed a beat and she hurried to the door.

'I heard your ship was in and I hoped you'd pay me a visit,' she smiled.

He looked her up and down. 'I wasn't expecting to see you. I thought you said you were pregnant. Was that a ploy to try to get me to marry you?'

'I am.'

'Then why are you working?'

'I need the money.'

'So go and find a respectable job.'

Litsa caught her breath at his cruel words. 'You considered me respectable enough when you were patronising me.'

He shook his head. 'I chose you because you were young and naive enough to let me overstay my time without charging me extra.'

'I thought you liked me.' Litsa's lip trembled.

'I did, you're the most attractive girl in the street, but that doesn't make you any better than the others. What do you plan to do with this child when it's born? Send it to an orphanage like the other girls do when they get caught?'

Litsa looked him in surprise. She had never considered that option. 'Is that how you would want your child to grow up; not knowing its father or mother?'

'It's no concern of mine. You can't prove I'm the father. It's your child so you can do as you please.'

'You are the father. I swear this child is yours,' Litsa spoke vehemently.

'You can swear as much as you like. I told you, I'm already married and I have no intention of accepting responsibility for the child of a street girl. You should have been more careful.' He began to walk on down the road.

'Where are you going? Aren't you going to stop here with me for a while?'

He shook his head. 'I see Anna has her light on,' he called back.

Litsa gazed after him, hardly able to believe that the man she had thought she was in love with and who had appeared to be so kind and considerate, could be so heartless.

Litsa gave birth easily and as she held the tiny, red-faced bundle in her arms she felt an overwhelming love for the innocent little girl.

'Have you decided on a name for her?' asked her mother, relieved that her daughter's ordeal was over without incident and the child appeared healthy.

'I'm going to call her Monika, after you, Mamma.'

Monika was a good baby. She would lie happily in a cardboard box, wrapped snugly in a blanket, whilst her grandmother attended to customers. Litsa washed the baby's soiled clothing between the constant feeding that was demanded of her. Having had an easy pregnancy and birth she had not expected to feel so drained of energy now. If only Monika would allow her to have an unbroken night's rest she would feel better.

She carried the baby girl up to show her friends in the street and they duly admired her, each thankful that the responsibility was not theirs.

'Are you planning to come back to work?' asked Eleni.

'I'll have to. I want Monika to have the very best of everything.

At the moment she's sleeping in a cardboard box, but I'll have to buy her a proper cot in a month or so.'

'Let her sleep in with you.'

'I suppose she could, at least whilst I still have to feed her in the night.'

'You'll have to wean her off you and onto a bottle before you can come back here. You can't keep running home to feed her.'

Litsa sighed. Already Monika was growing out of her first clothes, and within a few more months she would be too heavy to carry around and need a pushchair. She had never envisaged that a baby could be so expensive. The sooner she was able to return to work the better.

Tentatively she approached her mother. 'If I'm able to get Monika to accept a bottle would you be willing to look after her for one night a week?'

'Why?' asked Monique warily, although she was sure she knew the answer to her question.

'I'd be able to go back to work. It would only be one night, but it would bring in some money.'

'We're managing,' replied Monique.

'I don't want to be just managing. Monika needs things bought for her and I've hardly any of my savings left.'

'One night?' Monique did not relish being woken during the night by the demands of the baby.

'Just one night each week,' promised Litsa. 'Once I've bought Monika some new clothes and a pushchair I can stop working. It would only be for a few weeks.'

Grudgingly Monique agreed, 'But only one night a week, remember.' She had an idea that when her daughter returned to her lucrative profession she would be loath to restrict herself to one night.

Litsa kept her word until Monika was eight months old and sleeping regularly throughout the night. She then approached her mother again.

'Once I've given Monika her late night feed she never stirs until six. I could leave the door to my room open and you'd hear her if she did wake for any reason. I'll make sure I'm home in time to wash and feed her in the morning.'

Monique raised her eyebrows. 'And when are you going to get any sleep? As she gets older she'll need attention and not be prepared to go back to bed each morning.'

'I thought, maybe, you could keep an eye on her.'

'You did, did you? And who is going to serve the customers whilst I am looking after a small child?'

'I'll make sure I'm home about three so I can get some sleep before she's awake. She could sit in the living room with a box of toys for a couple of hours whilst I go back to bed. In the afternoon I'll play with her or take her out for a walk. I don't expect you to have her all day; it will only be for a little while in the morning.'

'And if I refuse?'

'I'd have to take her with me and ask one of the girls to watch her.'

Monique looked at Litsa in horror. 'You can't do that. The child should not be allowed anywhere near those girls.'

'There's nothing wrong with them, Mamma. They were good to you when Pappa died. Every day one would call on you and ask how you were managing or bring you a cake they had baked or a bunch of flowers.'

'That was different.'

'No it isn't different,' Litsa shook her head. 'It just shows that they are good, kind hearted girls. They dote on Monika and love it when I visit them. You didn't refuse to let them visit me when they heard that she was born and they all brought little gifts.'

Monique sniffed. She loved Monika and the thought of allowing her to be cared for by the street girls, even for a few hours, was abhorrent to her. Who knew what the child would see and hear?

'I'll give it a trial,' Monique agreed reluctantly. 'If I find I can't manage you'll have to return to working only one night or find someone to look after her during the morning. What about your friend Rebekah?'

Litsa shook her head. 'Her mother forbade her to see me when they found out I was pregnant. They said I could be a bad influence. We still meet each other occasionally, but I know her parents wouldn't let her look after Monika.'

It became routine for Litsa to spend the afternoon amusing Monika, placing her in her mother's large bed for the night and leaving the house as soon as her daughter fell asleep. She found it difficult to manage when she returned in the morning, often only having had two or three hours sleep before her mother would wake her and say Monika needed attention. Often when she returned to her bed sleep would not come. On occasions she was tempted to stay home, but the need for a new pair of shoes for her daughter or a pretty dress she had seen that would fit Monika, made her brush her hair, wriggle into the short, tight skirt accompanied by a low necked blouse, and apply her lipstick. When she left the house she looked little different from the girls who were employed as waitresses at the tavernas.

During the summer Litsa would take Monika to the beach and sit on the edge of the sea whilst Monika tipped water over her legs from her bucket, laughing with delight as her mother squealed in pretended fear. Other days Litsa would walk to the playground in the New Town with her daughter. There she would place Monika in a swing and push her backwards and forwards until her arms ached. When Monika became bored Litsa would take her to the sand pit and sit beside her whilst Monika dug holes in the sand and Litsa showed her how to build a sand castle.

There were many other mothers around and Litsa was looking forward to being able to sit and chat with them once Monika was old enough to play without her close supervision. It would make a change to be able to discuss other topics. Most of the conversation that she had with her friends in the street was comparing notes about the previous night's customers or the new dress or skirt they had bought that day. She no longer looked for work elsewhere when she found out the pittance she would receive each week for spending long hours cleaning or washing up.

As Monika grew older she mixed happily with the other children and Litsa was able to spend some time exchanging gossip. She was extremely reticent about her circumstances, not mentioning that they lived with her mother in a general store in the Old Town; nor did she admit that she was working.

'I'm fortunate that my husband earns enough to enable me to stay at home and look after our child.'

As soon as she had spoken Litsa realised she had made a mistake. The two girls she was sitting with immediately clamoured to know his profession.

'He's in the navy.'

'So is mine. What does yours do?'

Litsa improvised rapidly. 'He's in charge of buying the supplies for the ships that are stationed out at sea doing research.'

'What ship is he on?'

'Prometheus.' Litsa remembered seeing a sailor wearing a hat emblazoned with the name earlier in the day.

'So he's in the harbour now; you must be pleased.'

Litsa nodded. 'I'm always happy when he's home.' She felt a pang of loneliness, wishing the handsome sailor she had fallen in love with would come home to her. 'He's had to stay on board today to supervise the delivery of the provisions.'

'It's hard on the children,' continued her companion. 'They become used to having their mother to themselves and suddenly she's more interested in their father. Just as they start to accept him he goes away again.'

'I'm sure Monika will understand when she's older.'

'I hope my Poppi will. She screams for attention from me as

soon as her father appears. I wish we could afford to send her to nursery school for a couple of hours each morning.'

Litsa nodded. She had not considered sending Monika to nursery school, but it could be the solution to a problem that she was now encountering. Monika was no longer content to sit and play with her toys in the morning and would go into the shop, where her grandmother had to be vigilant that she did not slip out through the open door. Monique had grumbled and said that she could not be forever running after the child and Litsa would have to return home earlier and be responsible for her child throughout the whole day.

'How old do they have to be before they can go to nursery school?'

'Three, usually, unless you go to one of the private nurseries where they'll take them at any age. They cost a good deal more than the government ones, though.'

Litsa smiled. 'We'll have to see what her Pappa thinks and if we can afford it.' She knew of two establishments in the New Town and would call in on her way home and ask for their rates. It would solve the morning supervision problems and Monika enjoyed the company of other children.

'I'd best be going,' she said. 'I like to have Monika bathed and fed by the time my husband comes home. That means we have the evening to ourselves.'

Monika looked bewildered when her mother left her at the nursery. She had always been in the company of her mother or grandmother, never left with strangers before. Her lip trembled and Litsa hurriedly left the room, waiting outside until she was sure that Monika was not going to cry for her. Much to Litsa's relief she settled well and seemed to look forward to going each morning. Monique was happy that she no longer had to look after her granddaughter and the shop at the same time, but Litsa was getting even less sleep.

'I cannot cope, Mamma. I'm getting really short tempered and impatient with Monika. By the time I arrive back from the New Town I only have about an hour before I have to return and collect her. I have been arriving home earlier, but even so I need more than four or five hours sleep each night. If you were willing to close the shop for a while in the morning and take Monika to the nursery I could sleep then.'

'What are people going to think if the mother cannot be bothered to take her child to the nursery?'

'I'm sure no one will think twice. Many grandmothers take the children to school as their daughter has gone off to work. I'd obviously meet her each day and keep her amused during the afternoon.'

Monique considered the proposal. For the first hour or so trade was quiet each morning. It would certainly be easier than trying to cope with the lively little girl in the shop. Once her regular customers knew of her closure they would adapt their habits rather than have to walk into the New Town or down into another area of the Old Town in the morning to purchase whatever they needed that day.

Litsa was relieved, knowing that she would not have to be up and dealing with Monika whilst she was still half asleep. She closed her bedroom door quietly when she returned ensuring that she did not disturb her mother or wake Monika who now slept permanently in the bed with Monique. When Litsa met her daughter from the nursery school Monika was always pleased to see her and would greet her with open arms and then show her the picture she had drawn or recite the numbers she had learned that morning.

'She's an intelligent little girl,' remarked one of the helpers. 'She's quicker than most of them and should progress well when she attends the infant school. If you have the time you could start teaching her how to write her letters and recognise some simple words.'

'If you think it would be beneficial to her I'll make sure I have the time, particularly when the weather is not good enough to go out for very long.'

'Do you have some suitable books at home?'

Litsa nodded. 'She has some books that I read to her and I ask her to point to things in the pictures, but maybe you can suggest some others.'

'Become a member of the library. Ask for advice about books that are suitable for her age group. You could also encourage her to write her numbers.'

Litsa agreed eagerly. She wanted to do whatever was best for her daughter.

By the time Monika commenced infant school she could write her name and read a simple book. She was proficient with her numbers up to ten, but after that she would become confused, saying "two lots of ten" rather than twenty. Her general understanding and vocabulary was advanced for her age and Litsa reasoned this was because she spent most of her time with adults. The library was helpful and Monika quickly progressed from picture books with one line of text to those with a smaller picture and a simple story. As Litsa read to her she would follow the words with her finger. The second time the book was produced Monika would read to her mother, stumbling over some of the words at first until they became familiar.

It was now a recognised part of their routine to visit the library each week and Monika was allowed to choose three books to take home. To Litsa's surprise Monika began to choose books that were suitable for older children declaring that the others on the shelf were for babies. Whilst Litsa prepared a meal she would sit happily with a book, reading to herself and then describe the story to her mother and grandmother whilst they ate.

Only once had Monika mentioned her father, asking why he did not live with them. Litsa had shaken her head sadly.

'Your Pappa was in the navy. There was an accident and he did not return.' It was a variation on the truth and Litsa could certainly not tell Monika how she had been conceived and that her father had disowned her.

'What kind of accident?'

'You are too young to understand. Just be happy that you have a grandmother who loves you just as much as I do. Not every child is so fortunate.'

When Litsa paid her rent to Lakkis Pavlides he told her that Anna was leaving.

'Leaving? Where is she going? She hasn't said anything to me.'

'She claims that she isn't well and needs some time off. There have been complaints. Just because she has been working here for a number of years she thinks she can refuse customers whenever she pleases. I've warned her before. If she isn't willing to work she has to go elsewhere. If you want to rent her house let me know next week otherwise I'll look out for another girl.'

'What's the rent?' asked Litsa warily, knowing that Anna's house was hardly more than a room.

'A hundred and twenty a week; and before you complain that the others are only paying a hundred their rent is also going up. I should have put it up before.'

'I'll let you know if I can afford it,' promised Litsa. It was a good opportunity. No longer would she have to rely on one of the girls not working so she could use their room. Provided her mother agreed to be responsible for Monika each day until she met her from school she would certainly accept Lakkis's offer.

There was no way she should be paying a hundred and twenty drachmas a week for such limited accommodation and lack of amenities, but she knew if she dared to complain Lakkis would turn her out.

The other girls grumbled about the increase in their rents.

'We ought to get together and buy a big house, one of the

"Knights of St John's" houses, and each have a room there. That way we wouldn't have to pay any rent to Mr Pavlides.'

Eleni eyed Stasia sceptically. 'Have you any idea how much a house of that size would cost? I don't know what you earn in a week, but I know that when I've paid the rent, bought my food and any other essentials I've not much left over.'

'We could ask the bank for a loan.'

Eleni laughed. 'The bank wouldn't lend money to girls like us. You have to prove you have a regular income.'

'We have,' protested Stasia.

'I don't think they'd consider us as a sound financial proposition. Look what's happened to Anna. She didn't take proper care of herself and now she's too sick to work.'

'Is she very ill?' asked Litsa.

'I understand it's a new disease that has developed and there's no cure.'

'How did she get it?'

'I don't know. One of her customers must have had it and infected her. The trouble is, she may have passed it on to others without realising. Apparently there are no signs at first so you don't realise you're sick.'

'How did she find out?'

'The clinic picked it up when she went for her check up.'

Litsa nodded soberly. She would be very careful and take every precaution when she had a customer. She would also ask about this new disease when she went to the clinic for her own monthly check up.

Monique looked at her daughter sadly. 'You mean you want to move out with Monika?'

Litsa shook her head. 'I can't take Monika, you know that. It won't be any different for you or her. I'll meet her from school each day and spend time with her as I do now. It will mean she can have her own room and not have to share your bed any longer.'

'I just wish you'd find yourself a respectable job.'

Litsa sighed. 'I have looked, Mamma. I have no qualifications for anything.'

'Whose fault is that?'

'I know,' admitted Litsa. 'I should have stayed on longer at school. I would have done had Pappa still been alive, but we needed some money.'

'Don't try to blame your occupation on me,' snapped back Monique.

'I'm not. I wanted some new clothes to wear so I could look smart when I applied for work. I knew you couldn't afford to buy them for me, so I turned to a quick and easy way. If that sailor hadn't turned up just when he did I wouldn't be working there now.'

Monique raised her eyebrows. She did not believe Litsa's protestations. Now Monika was at school Litsa could easily look for work in the town, however meagre the pay.

'And what are you going to tell Monika when she's older and asks where you are working?'

'I'll say that I work in a late night bar.'

'She'll have to know the truth one day.'

'I'll tell her when she's old enough to understand.'

Monika was puzzled when her mother said she was moving to a house nearer to the San Francisco Gate.

'Are Grandma and I coming with you?' she asked.

'It's far too small for more than one person; hardly any bigger than your new bedroom is.'

'I don't mind sleeping with Grandma, although she snores.'

'That was fine when you were a little girl, but as you get older you'll need a room of your own. You'll be able to have my mirror so you can look in that when you brush your hair and see if it is tidy. I'll put up a shelf for you so you can keep your books in there and you'll be able to lie in bed and read them until Grandma says you must put out the light and go to sleep.' Litsa could not think of any further inducements.

'Can I come and visit you in your house?'

'There'll be no need for you to visit me. I'll see you every day. I'll be meeting you from school and spending the afternoon and early evening with you just the same as I do now before I go off to work.'

'So I'll go to your house after school.'

'No,' Litsa shook her head. 'It's better that I come here. If your Grandma needs any help in the shop I'm around and whilst she's busy I can get our meals ready. I couldn't do that if we were in my house.'

'Do you have to go to work in the evening? The other children say their mothers stay at home or only go to work in the morning.'

'I have to go to work. How do you expect me to buy you nice clothes and give you good food if I don't go out to work?'

Monika could not complain. She had never been hungry; she had new boots each winter and a warm coat. When she said her shoes were tight or her jumper no longer fitted new ones were provided immediately. She was far better dressed than many of the other children.

'I'd like to see your house.'

'I'll take you there when I've cleaned it and I'm organised.'

'When?'

'Probably next Saturday, in the morning, when you're not at school.'

'Promise?'

Litsa sighed. 'I promise.'

Litsa looked around Anna's tiny house. It was no more than one room with a kitchenette in an alcove and a toilet out in the yard. There was no hot water and she would have to heat whatever she needed for her ablutions and those of her customers. As she waited for the saucepan and kettle of water to boil so she could commence cleaning she came to a decision. She was sure her mother would resist, but she had sufficient money saved and would insist that a proper shower was installed at the shop.

The first thing Litsa did on reaching her mother's shop was to go through to the toilet and examine the small room carefully. She was sure her idea would work. All she had to do now was convince her mother that it would be money well spent.

'There is something I want to do for you, Mamma. A way of saying thank you for all the care you have given to me and also Monika over the years. I'm going to pay for a shower to be fitted in the toilet.'

'A shower?'

Monika nodded firmly. 'I know we've always managed with some hot water in a bowl and a bath once a week, but it would be far easier and more pleasant if we could just have a shower each morning. You wouldn't need to heat the water; sometimes in the winter it's hardly warm.'

Monique looked at her daughter puzzled. 'But where would we put it?'

'I've looked and I'm sure there's enough space in the toilet. We only need a little shower tray to stop the water running all over the floor and a curtain to stop it from splashing out.'

'Where would the water go?'

'A drain would have to be made and an electric cable run through and connected to the shower unit. It can't be terribly expensive.'

Monique bit at her lip in consternation. They should have had a shower installed years; but she never seemed to have sufficient money saved and she was loath to ask Litsa

'I appreciate your offer, Litsa, but I can't take your money.'

'Mamma, you looked after me when I was expecting Monika and you are caring for her now so I can rent the house in the street. Please let me do something for you.'

Monique considered. 'How long would it take to install and how much mess would it make?'

'It shouldn't make any mess at all. There will just have to be a small hole in the floor for a pipe to run into the drain. Please, Mamma, agree to me speaking to a plumber and asking him to come and have a look. If he says it isn't possible or it is going to be ridiculously expensive we'll have to give up the idea.'

'It would certainly make life easier and more pleasant for everyone,' agreed Monique. She placed her arm around her daughter's shoulder. 'You're a good girl, Litsa. I would be so proud of you if you did not work in the street.'

'If I didn't work in the street I wouldn't be able to afford to install a shower for you,' replied Litsa flippantly.

Litsa enjoyed being in her own small apartment. She could not bring herself to call it a house. Having cleaned it thoroughly, discovering that Anna had not been particularly house proud, bought some new bedding and a rug for the floor she decided there was definitely an improvement in the premises and that it was respectable enough for Monika to visit.

'Why have you got a light over your door, Mamma?' asked Monika.

'There are no street lights down here. We need to see our way home.'

Monika looked at the closed shutters. 'Does everyone down here work in a bar like you?'

'We all do the same sort of work. That's why it's much better that I should live here rather than disturb you and Grandma when I come home.'

'You never disturbed me,' Monika assured her mother. 'I do like having my own room, though. If I shut the door I can't hear Grandma snore.'

'Just make sure you keep it tidy. Grandma won't be pleased if she sees your toys all over the floor.'

Monika shrugged. 'I don't play with toys any more. I'd rather

42

sit and read. Can we go to the library this afternoon? I finished my book last night.'

'They're closed on a Saturday. I'll take you on Monday.'

Monika's face fell. 'That means I'll have nothing to read in bed tonight or all day tomorrow.'

'We could walk into the New Town and buy a book.'

'Could we? Could we really? Can I choose?'

'Let's see what they have before we make any decisions. You always want to buy a book that you can enjoy reading.'

Monika looked at the shelf displaying the books suitable for children of her age group. 'I've read most of those.' She moved further along where there was a notice that declared the books were suitable for young teenagers. The picture of a ballerina on the front cover drew her attention. 'I think I'd like that one.'

Litsa looked at the book in surprise. 'It isn't an adventure story. It's the true story of a Russian ballerina and how she had to work hard to gain a place at the ballet school and become a star. I think it could be too advanced for you.'

Monika looked at her mother sceptically. Her comprehension was growing rapidly and she was growing out of story books designed for children of her age.

'I'm sure I will enjoy it.'

Litsa sighed and purchased the book. On their next visit to the library she would ask for some guidance about the books Monika should read.

Mrs Ethanides was helpful. 'I don't think you need to worry. She obviously has a reading and comprehension level at least two years above average for her age. You should be proud to have such an intelligent daughter. She is choosing well written, informative books. There are no books stocked in this section of the library that are unsuitable for a child under sixteen if that is part of your concern.'

Litsa nodded thankfully. 'You cannot always tell what is written inside by the title and picture on the cover. I certainly would not want her reading adult love stories.'

'See how she progresses. She may well become bored after a while and then would be the time to introduce her to some of the young adult novels. They are mostly about the lives of famous people. We have to read them before we agree to place them on the shelves and I have to admit I have found them quite interesting.'

'Could you suggest them to her?'

'I will. I have refused her books on previous occasions that I felt were too advanced for her and asked her to choose some others. Sometimes she has selected one of the historical or political books that are meant for the older students.'

Monika was completely happy. During the school holidays she was content to sit in the living room reading until her mother arrived and asked where she would like to go that afternoon. Provided her mother took her to the library each time she had finished her latest selection of books she did not clamour to be taken to the park or the beach every day to meet up with school friends. As soon as her mother left each evening she would open a book and sit engrossed, ignoring the television programme her grandmother would be watching. As soon as her grandmother said it was time she went to bed. Monika would take the book into her bedroom, undress as swiftly as possible and continue to read until her grandmother insisted it was time her light was out and she should go to sleep. She had read the complete collection of the Greek myths and was working her way steadily through Greek history, interspersed with the travel and historical books relating to other parts of the world.

Rhodes 1992 - 1997

Monika was happy to move to the junior school, although she often found the conversation and games that her peers played somewhat childish, and was delighted when she was moved to a higher grade.

'I realise it may be rather difficult for her at first,' explained Mrs Stamanides. 'She will be mixing with children who are a little older, but I am convinced she will flourish. If she was kept in her current year group she would very soon become bored with the work expected of her. A bored child is a disruptive and unhappy pupil. Monika's general knowledge is outstanding for a child of her age and she excels in spelling, grammar and reading.'

Litsa listened to the comments about her daughter's ability with pride. 'I know she is a clever little girl. I don't know where she gets her brains from; certainly not me.'

'In the higher grade she will also have basic English lessons. I think she would enjoy learning a new language. It will demonstrate a totally different grammar structure to her. It can be a difficult language as the same word can have two or more different meanings or be spelled differently but pronounced the same way. If she does show signs of struggling she can always join the less able pupils until she has grasped the basic principles.'

Litsa frowned. 'She appears to enjoy anything that involves words but will learning English benefit her?'

'She has a thirst for knowledge. English has become a very international language and some books are only printed in that medium. It would give her access to other information and could be useful to her later in her chosen career.'

'I wouldn't be able to help her. I only know one or two words that I have picked up from tourists.'

'She would probably enjoy helping you to expand your vocabulary,' smiled Mrs Stamanides.

'There is something else that worries me. Monika does not seem to have any close friends.'

Mrs Stamanides nodded. 'I agree; she does seem to be a loner. I've never seen her in a huddle with the other girls but nor have I noticed any animosity towards her. Maybe you could ask her if she would like one of the girls to visit your home after school for a while.'

'I could, I suppose.'

'You sound very hesitant, Mrs Kokanides.'

'I don't mix very often with the other mothers now Monika is older. Her grandmother sees her across the main road in the morning and I meet her there in the afternoon.'

'Maybe there is a family who attends the same church as you on a Sunday? Even if their daughter did not attend this school she could be a suitable companion for Monika occasionally.'

Litsa shook her head. 'I don't really know anyone who attends very well.' She could not admit that when they attended the services they usually sat alone, shunned by the other members of the congregation.

'I'll have a word with some of the girls. They could feel intimidated by her knowledge. She should enjoy relaxing with her peers rather than spending all her time studying.'

'I don't make her spend all her time reading,' Litsa hastened to assure the teacher.

Monika had told her companions at school that she lived with her mother and grandmother at the shop. When they asked about her father she said he had been in the navy and met with an accident. They appeared to accept her explanation and probed no further, but she often saw them looking at her with a sly expression whilst they muttered together. She was never invited back to go to their house after school or to meet at the weekend to wander around the shops. Each time she thought she had made a special friend within a few days the girl would look askance at her and avoid her. It became obvious after a while that their mothers were telling them that she was not a suitable companion for them and she was hurt and puzzled.

Each morning her grandmother insisted she took a shower and wash herself properly all over before she dressed in clean clothes. Her hair was washed regularly and she brushed it until it shone each day before being tying it back from her face, wishing it was as dark and wavy as her mother's. The girls could not be rejecting her because she was dirty or smelt bad.

No one ever spoke to them when they left the church on a Sunday or Saints Day, moving away into small groups, ignoring Monika and her mother and only acknowledging her grandmother cursorily.

'Why don't you talk to the other people?' asked Monika.

Litsa had shrugged. 'I've no time for gossiping with them.'

'I heard one of them say there had been a nasty accident. The man who runs the warehouse near the shop fell over the town wall.'

'When did that happen?'

'I don't know.'

'I'll ask some of my friends. They're bound to know.' Litsa knew the warehouse was a source of supply for the drugs that some of the girls used to help them cope with their profession. She had always resisted experimenting whenever they had tempted her, telling them she had no spare money to purchase drugs if she became addicted.

Monika loved her English lessons. She no longer spent all her evening reading, but practised writing the letters of the English alphabet and learning the spelling of the words. She would suck the end of her pencil as she concentrated on selecting the correct meaning of the words that were spelled the same but used in different contexts.

'I don't know why they decided to make their language so difficult,' she sighed. 'Do you know, Mamma, you can catch a fish, catch a cold or use the same word to mean the lock on a window?'

Litsa shook her head. 'I only know the simple words you teach me. I don't understand the grammar or how to write the words. If you're finding it too difficult I can ask Mrs Stamanides to let you go into the lower language group.'

Monika looked at her mother derisively. 'It's not too difficult for me to learn. I just wish I knew why they don't use different words to mean different things as we do. I find it puzzling.'

'Have you asked Mrs Stamanides to explain?'

'She said it was because the people there had to learn other languages when they were invaded by foreigners and they kept some of the words after their conquerors had left. When the Germans and Italians were in Crete did we have to learn their language?'

Litsa frowned. 'I don't think so. You could ask your grandmother. She might remember, although she was only a baby when the war ended.'

'I'll ask Mrs Stamanides. I expect she will know.'

'Mrs Stamanides is not as old as your Grandmother.'

'She's older than you, Mamma. She could have parents or relatives who remember.'

Litsa shrugged and turned away. She felt totally inadequate when her daughter asked her such questions.

Monika was considered old enough now to cross the roads safely and make her own way to school and back by way of the San

Francisco Gate. In the morning she would pass three old men sitting on a bench and they would point at her and make remarks that she did not understand as she walked by. They would still be sitting there when she returned and she had a fear that one of them would reach out and grab her arm. As soon as they came into sight she would take to her heels and run across the cobbles until she was safely inside the Old Town walls.

Sometimes she would take a deliberate detour, walking down to the harbour and entering the Old Town by a different gate to avoid seeing them. The first few times she had lost her way and wandered around until she finally found a landmark that she recognised, but now she knew every turning and shortcut through the maze of narrow streets.

She was allowed to go to the library on her own now and visited almost every other day. She knew about apartheid in South Africa and that now Mandela had been released from prison the black people were being given equal rights with the white population. The construction of the pyramids and temples in Egypt fascinated her and when she discovered there were also pyramids in South America she was intrigued and commenced to read about the expeditions the Spaniards made to take the gold and their efforts to convert the natives to Christianity.

It was often difficult for her to explain the sense of outrage she experienced when she read of the exploitation that had been practised on nations unable to defend themselves from marauders.

'You have to remember that a good deal of your reading has been either geographical or historical.' said the librarian patiently. 'When you are a little older you will be able to read and understand how the politics of the world has shaped events.'

'Why can't I read those books now?' asked Monika impatiently.

'Some of them do contain graphic descriptions of the atrocities that were carried out. They are in the adult section of the library and I would certainly not allow you to borrow one of those books without your mother's permission.'

'I have been told about Oxi Day, when the government refused the Italians permission to march through Greece. I know that the Germans took no notice and invaded anyway. I want to know why they were refused and why they ignored the decision.'

The librarian sighed. 'I'll have a look and see if we have something factual for you to read.'

'I don't want just bare facts. I can find those out from our history books at school. I want to know the reasons why people made certain decisions.'

'Monika, you are only fourteen. At your age you cannot be expected to understand the reasoning behind political decisions and make an impartial judgement.'

Monika tossed her head. 'I cannot make any judgement until I am informed of the reasons.' Frustrated by the lack of help from the librarian, whom she considered her friend, she placed a simple book written in English on the counter.

'If I can't be allowed to read anything more advanced I may as well revert to a child's book.'

'This is in English, not Greek.'

'I learn English at school. I want to know if my English is good enough to read a book written in the language. If I understand the story I can move on to something more advanced. My teacher has said that many books written in English have not been translated into Greek. I want to be able to read those.'

Mrs Ethanides smiled in amusement at the determination of the young girl.

Monika sat hunched up in a corner of the ruined church down by the Jewish quarter. Now she knew why she was considered an outcast and no one wanted to know her. Hot tears stung her eyes as she recalled the words Poppi had spoken.

'Good morning, prossy,' said Poppi as she walked into the classroom.

'Good morning, Poppi,' replied Monika, pleased that someone

had spoken to her and wondered why the other girls sniggered.

'Did you have a good night?'

'Yes, thank you.'

'Make lots of money?'

Monika frowned. 'I'm not old enough to go out to work.'

'Really? I didn't think there was an age limit. The younger the better, I've heard.' Poppi licked her lips. 'Fresh meat.'

'I really don't know what you're talking about. My grandmother has a general store; not a butchers.'

The girls who had been listening hooted with laughter and Poppi winked at them, pleased to be the centre of attention.

'Hasn't your mother taken you into the business? After all, she's getting a bit past it now; must be pushing thirty.'

'My mother doesn't have her own business and what does her age have to do with it?' Monika felt thoroughly confused.

Poppi thrust her face closer. 'I know where your mother lives. I walked past the other day with my mother and she was sitting in the window.'

'Why shouldn't she sit in the window?'

'Her light was on showing she was at home and ready for customers,' announced Poppi triumphantly.

'What do you mean?'

'Don't play the innocent,' said Poppi scornfully. 'You know your mother is a prostitute. That's why she lives in that road. That's where they all live.'

The colour drained from Monika's face. 'You're a liar,' she whispered.

The teacher entered. 'Good morning, girls,' she said briskly. 'No more chattering now. Save that for when you have your break.'

Monika sat at her desk, totally unable to concentrate. Twice she was asked the answer to a simple question and had been unable to answer.

'Are you not well, Monika? Would you like a toilet break?' The teacher was prepared to be sympathetic towards the pubescent girls. They were often too embarrassed to ask for permission to go to the toilet.

Monika nodded, not trusting herself to speak. She hurried out of the classroom and across the playground to the main road. She needed to get away and sit and think about Poppi's cruel words.

Sitting in the niche of the ruined church she tried to calm her racing mind. Until this moment she had not given any thought to the fact that only women lived in the houses along the short road and each had a red light outside and a name painted above the doorway. Her own mother had the name 'Litsa' above her doorway. She sighed deeply. Dare she speak to her mother or ask her grandmother? When she had asked about her father she had been told that he was in the navy but had met with an accident. His name was never mentioned.

Monika looked at her watch, a treasured gift from her mother on her last name day. This year she had planned to ask if she could have a Thesaurus, but she had no pleasure from the thought now; she just felt sick.

'Monika? It is Monika, isn't it?'

Monika looked up. Her mother's old friend Rebekah stood there, holding the hands of her two young children.

'Is something wrong? You don't look well. Would you like to come back to my house for a while until you feel better?'

Monika tried to smile. 'I'm alright, really.'

'Your mother and grandmother are not ill?'

Monika shook her head.

'Shouldn't you be in school or is it a Saint's Day? We don't keep them so I'm not always sure when they occur.'

Monika shook her head again.

'Something's troubling you. Would you like me to walk home with you?'

'No, I don't want my mother to know I'm not in school.'

Rebekah frowned. 'What are you up to, Monika? Are you deliberately missing school?'

Monika's eyes filled with tears. 'I wouldn't do that. I love school. It's just - just - one of the girls was saying very nasty things to me about my Mamma.'

'Did you tell your teacher?'

'I couldn't.'

'Well, I don't think sitting here and feeling miserable is going to help. You need to speak to your teacher or ask your mother to speak to her.'

'It isn't true,' muttered Monika.

'What is not true?'

'The things Poppi said. They can't be true. My Mamma is such a lovely, kind person.'

Rebekah nodded. She had an idea that Monika had just found out where her mother worked. She sighed. Litsa should have told her daughter long ago, rather than let her find out from a girl at school. Her own parents had forbidden her to see Litsa when it became evident that she was pregnant at the age of sixteen and she had dared not disobey them. Although they had met up on various occasions by chance she had not tried to rekindle their close friendship.

Now Monika genuinely needed the toilet. 'Could I just walk to your house with you and use your bathroom, please?'

'Of course. The last time I saw your mother she told me you were learning English at school. How are you getting on with the language?'

'I'm beginning to understand it.'

'I think it is probably easier than the Hebrew that my two will have to learn. I found it incredibly difficult; all the letters are written in such strange ways.'

'I'd be interested to see the writing,' said Monika. She could not go home yet or her grandmother would want to know why she was home so early and showing an interest in the Hebrew writing would give her an excuse to stay longer in Rebekah's house.

She looked at the script curiously. 'I've never seen anything like that. How do you learn the words?'

'The same way you learn any other words. You remember how the letters look and after a while you begin to recognise whole words. After that it becomes easier,' explained Rebekah. 'I'm taking the children up to the playground in the New Town. I could walk home with you and go through the San Francisco Gate.'

Monika hesitated; she thought Poppi might be waiting for her close to her home to taunt her further and she did not want to encounter the girl until she had spoken to her mother.

'If it's no trouble. It is out of your way.'

Rebekah shrugged. 'It won't hurt the children to walk a little further.'

'Could you tell me some more about the Hebrew language as we walk, please?'

'That depends upon your questions. I'll tell you what I know. I can follow the readings in the Old Testament but I've never tried to read anything else in the language.'

'Why not?' asked Monika curiously.

Rebekah shrugged. 'I've never felt the need. I attend the Synagogue in the same way as you attend your Church but I am not planning to go to Israel so I don't really need a full knowledge of the language.'

'Does everyone in Israel speak Hebrew?'

'To some degree, I expect. Many of the Israelites have arrived in the country from other parts of the world. They probably had no more knowledge of the language than I have and have had to learn how to cope with a new language in their daily life.'

'Do they teach it in the schools?'

'I'm sure they do, along with another language, probably English.'

Monika nodded thoughtfully. 'So if I went to Israel speaking English I would be able to make myself understood?'

'I'm sure you wouldn't have a problem in the town. Are you thinking of going travelling when you're older?'

'Maybe. I haven't decided what I would like to do yet.'

'You have plenty of time to make up your mind. I want my two to go to University so they can obtain really good jobs. You should consider doing the same.'

Monika smiled. 'I'm not clever enough to go to University.'

'You can always think about it when the time comes. Here we are at the end of your road. I'll leave you now and take the children to the play area. You're always welcome to come in and see me if you want to talk, Monika.'

Monika checked the time on her watch and walked slowly down the road to her grandmother's shop. Rebekah waited until the girl was out of sight before turning into the road where Monika's mother plied her trade. She knocked on the door, hoping she would find Litsa at home.

Litsa walked down to her mother's shop full of foreboding after Rebekah's visit. What was she going to say to her daughter and what would Monika's reaction be?

'I wish you had told me earlier,' sighed Monika. 'I just couldn't believe it when the girls were so nasty to me.'

'I didn't think you were old enough to understand.'

'Mamma, why do you do it? Surely you don't enjoy having so many different men visiting you?'

Litsa shrugged. 'It's not a question of enjoyment. If I don't work we don't have sufficient money to live the way we do now. We all have new clothes whenever we need them and I'm able to save money.'

'Couldn't you work in Grandma's shop,' asked Monika.

'The shop would certainly not bring in enough income for three of us to live the way we have become used to.'

'Is that why you started to – to – do other work?'

Litsa reached for her daughter's hand. 'I was young and

foolish. I was wearing old clothes and I was ashamed. I did not think anyone would employ me; I looked like a beggar. I knew the girls who lived along the road and they had always been kind to me. I needed money for some new clothes and it seemed like an easy and quick way to earn it. I thought once I had made sufficient for my immediate needs I would apply for a job in a shop or taverna.'

'Didn't Grandma know what you were doing?'

Litsa shook her head. 'I told her I had a job in a taverna in the evenings. I was able to give her some money each week and she thought it was from my wages. I truly intended to give up the work but then I met your father. I fell in love with him and thought he loved me. Whilst his ship was being refitted he was here for six weeks and we saw each other every day. The week after he sailed I found I was pregnant. I hoped I was mistaken but eventually I had to tell your grandmother.'

'What did she say?'

'A lot of very nasty things, threatened to turn me out, then she cried and asked how she could help.'

'Didn't my father come back? Surely if he had known about me he would have married you?'

Litsa nodded grimly. 'He returned some weeks later and I told him I was pregnant. It was then that he told me that he was already married. He said you could be any man's child, but I knew he was your father.'

Monika sucked in her breath. 'That was wicked of him.'

'I was also to blame. The girls had warned me not to get fond of anyone who visited me. I thought I knew better and because he had flattered me and told me how beautiful I was I thought he loved me. I took no precautions against becoming pregnant, but he was not to know I had been careless.'

'Do I look like him?'

'You look much as I remember him when we first met.'

'Enough like him that he would recognise me if he saw me?'

'I doubt it.'

'Didn't he ever come back again?'

'Yes, but he did not want to know me. I looked for some respectable work, but no one wanted a single woman with a child. I realised there was only one occupation open to me. Your grandmother agreed to look after you some of the time and I asked if I could rent a room regularly from whichever girl was not working that week. Lakkis Pavlides was more than willing to have another working girl and offered me Anna's house when she left.'

'And I lived here and Grandma looked after me,' added Monika bitterly.

'She was ashamed of me, but she loved you. I insisted I wanted to spend each afternoon and Sunday with you, so we worked out an arrangement that suited both of us.'

'Mamma, once I leave school and have some work you will no longer have me to feed and clothe. Couldn't you find some other work, like in a taverna or bar?'

'I want you to have the opportunity of a good education, going on to University if that is what you want. Until you have completed your education I can make enough money to support you.'

'I could work at weekends and in the holidays,' offered Monika.

Litsa smiled. 'I don't want you joining me, although it pays more than most jobs for less hours.'

Monika shuddered. 'I couldn't do as you do. I could find a cleaning job or wash up in a taverna. That would help, wouldn't it?'

Litsa squeezed her daughter's hand. 'You're a good girl, Monika. If you do go on to higher education you'll need to spend your time studying, not working all hours.'

Litsa walked back to her house that evening relieved that her daughter had behaved with such maturity; she could have shouted and raged at her; declaring she never wished to see her again. Even worse to contemplate would have been Monika insisting that she wished to make money in the same way.

Monika lay in bed deep in thought. She must ask Mrs Stamanides how long she would have to be in higher education until she could expect to find a suitable occupation. Once she was earning a decent wage she would insist that her mother stopped working in the red light district. It might even be possible for her to rent a small house where her grandmother and mother could live with her. Her grandmother could open up the shop each day and during the summer season there was always work available in the tavernas or bars that her mother could do, even stocking shelves in a supermarket was preferable to her current employment. Between them they should have enough money to live on.

With this comforting thought Monika finally fell asleep, but when she awoke reality returned to her. If she wished to continue with her education, and she was not yet old enough to leave school, she must go into school and explain to Mrs Stamanides why she had left the class the previous day and that would mean seeing Poppi.

Monika hurried past the three old men and then dawdled the remainder of the way to school. She did not want to arrive in the class before her teacher and have Poppi taunting her again in front of her classmates. She mistimed her arrival and as she walked to the main door she heard one of the boys calling out.

'Mon – nicker. Mon – nicker. No knicker. Have you any on today? We'll find out at break.'

Monika paled and hurried through to her classroom arriving at the same time as Mrs Stamanides.

'I'll have a word with you at break time, Monika.'

Embarrassed Monika slid into her seat. She had seen the sly smile Poppi had given, but at least the boys would not be able to carry out their threat to molest her if she was still in class at break. She did not raise her hand to answer any questions, hardly listening to them or their answers, and Mrs Stamanides did not press her. There was something troubling the girl.

'Why didn't you return to class yesterday?' asked Mrs Stamanides when her other pupils had left the room. 'Had you fallen out with your friends?'

'I haven't any friends. Everyone hates me.'

'I'm sure that isn't true.'

'It is. They said my mother is a prostitute. I thought she worked in a taverna or bar in the evenings,' said Monika miserably. 'If they were my friends they would not say nasty things about my mother whatever she did.'

Mrs Stamanides bit her lip. She knew Monika's mother worked as a prostitute, but it was not fair to taunt the child. It was not her fault. No doubt Poppi had been the ring leader. She was such a spiteful little girl.

'Have you spoken to your mother?'

Monika nodded, her eyes filling with tears. 'It's true,' she whispered. 'I'm the daughter of a prostitute and all I know about my father is that he was a sailor.'

Mrs Stamanides sighed with relief. At least the girl knew how her mother earned her money. 'I am sure your mother loves you very much or she would have given you up for adoption when you were born, Monika. Take comfort in that thought and don't think badly of your mother. She was obviously foolish when she was young.'

'That's what she said. She thought my father really loved her and would come back to marry her. When he came back he said he was already married and didn't want to know about me. My Mamma didn't deserve that. She's such a kind and loving person.'

'I'm sure she is and you should not be blamed for her mistake. Very often, Monika, girls say nasty things about each other. You must not take anything they say to you to heart. Ignore whatever they say and pretend you do not care. If you just shrug and walk away they will soon stop taunting you. They enjoy seeing you upset.'

'They're horrid.'

'They probably don't realise how cruel they are being. It is a part of growing up.'

'I wish I was all grown up and then I could go out to work,' replied Monika mutinously.

'The time when you have to work will come all too soon. Have you any idea what you would like to do?'

Monika shook her head.

'You are a clever girl. You should be able to go on to higher education. That way you can gain some qualifications. Maybe you would like to become a teacher?'

'I don't know.'

'Well, you think about it. There could be any number of careers open to you.' Mrs Stamanides patted Monika's shoulder. 'No more leaving the class and not returning to your lessons. If you have a problem you can come and talk to me.'

Over the next years the kind words Mrs Stamanides had spoken stayed with Monika. She ignored Poppi and the crude and spiteful remarks she made when out of the hearing of the teacher, and eventually the taunting had ceased, along with the rude remarks from the boys. She continued to work hard and disciplined herself to complete her homework before she immersed herself in the latest book she had borrowed from the library. She also knew that she must decide if she wished to go on to higher education or leave school at the end of the year and find some work.

Monika sought out Mrs Stamanides. 'So what can I do for you? No more problems with your peers I hope.' Mrs Stamanides did not say that she had spoken to the class and threatened to tell their parents about their cruel behaviour.

Monika smiled. 'I took your advice and ignored anything that was said either about me or my mother. I remembered you mentioned going on to higher education and obtaining some qualifications. I'd like to find some work that pays well enough for my mother to stay and work in the shop with my grandmother.'

Mrs Stamanides nodded. 'The only way you will find remunerative work is if you go on to University. You don't want to spend all your life in a mundane job that you hate. You have a brain that needs to be kept active.'

'If I went on to any form of higher education it has to be paid for. I don't know if my mother could afford it. She only continued working in the street to provide for me. I shouldn't be a burden to her any longer than necessary.'

'There are scholarships. If you sat for an entrance exam and gained high enough marks you could have some of the fees paid for you. Talk to your mother. If she agrees then I can put your name forward with some of the others.'

'Has Poppi asked to have her name put on the list?' Monika did not want to have to spend a further three years in close proximity with the girl.

'Not as yet. Forget Poppi. You speak to your mother and see what she says. She should be pleased that you are intelligent and want to better yourself.'

Monika hesitated. 'Wouldn't they want to have my mother's address?'

'We have you registered as living with your grandmother. That should be sufficient.'

'You wouldn't have to declare my mother's occupation?' asked Monika anxiously.

'We would put nothing detrimental on your application form. If a place is applied for it is for you, not your mother.' Mrs Stamanides always chose her words carefully when talking with Monika. If the girl was allowed to opt for higher education her mother's occupation could be mentioned in confidence to the Principal if she was accepted.

Monika nodded slowly. 'I'll speak to my Mamma after church on Sunday and see what she says.'

'If she agrees ask her to come and see me after school one

day. I can explain the procedure fully to her then.' Monika's mother had never visited the school and asked after the progress of her daughter as the other mothers did frequently and Mrs Stamanides would be quite interested in meeting the lady. She had preconceived ideas about how a prostitute would look and to the best of her knowledge she had never met one.

When Litsa Kokanides entered Mrs Stamanides's room with Monika the teacher looked at the woman in surprise. She was clean and tidy, wearing fashionable but not ostentatious clothes and with a minimum of makeup. She looked far more respectable than many of the other mothers who came to discuss their daughters' future with her and Mrs Stamanides hoped the surprise had not shown on her face.

'I'm very pleased to meet you, Mrs Kokanides.' Mrs Stamanides extended her hand and Litsa shook it firmly.

'Monika tells me that you have suggested she goes on to higher education. She was rather vague about the details and said I should come and talk to you.'

Mrs Stamanides nodded. 'Monika is a very intelligent girl and I feel she could benefit from further education once she has to leave this school. I have suggested a few careers that would then be open to her at a later date but Monika has not shown any particular interest in any of them.'

'I don't want to be a teacher or a nurse.'

'I'm sure you will find there are many opportunities for work in other fields. During the first term you will study a number of different subjects. Once you have completed the term these will be discussed with you and you will have to make a decision. You will then be given a list of appropriate courses where you would study selected subjects in depth for the remainder of the year. You would then take an examination to confirm that your knowledge and ability is adequate to progress further.'

Litsa frowned. 'How many years is this higher education going to take and what is it going to cost?'

'The minimum amount of time would be a year to qualify for basic office work. That would mean taking telephone calls and messages, photo copying, filing,' Mrs Stamanides spread her hands. 'Not exactly exciting work for a girl of Monika's capabilities. If she decided to study a second language the course would be three years. I would recommend that whatever course she took she incorporated computer studies. Computers are becoming widely used now and knowledge of programming should qualify her for work in a bank or some of the large commercial companies. Alternatively with her language skills she should be able to find a position in one of the hotels as a receptionist or with a travel company.'

'What happens at the end of the three years if she decides she doesn't want to work in any of those occupations? Do I get the money back?'

Mrs Stamanides shook her head. 'I'm afraid not. It is a purchase like anything else. The authorities do not treat education lightly. They expect the pupil to be committed, not decide at the end of the course that they have made an incorrect choice. They have the opportunity at the end of their first term to select the subjects that interest them or if they do not feel that there is anything suitable being offered to them they can leave.'

Litsa looked sternly at her daughter. 'If I pay for you to continue your education I expect you to complete the course and find a decent job at the end. We can't afford to throw money away.'

'I will work hard, Mamma, I promise.'

'If you are satisfied, Mrs Kokanides, I'll add Monika's name to the list of pupils applying. That does not guarantee her a place. The school has to send a reference regarding her work and behaviour.'

For the first timer Litsa Kokanides looked disconcerted. 'Could I have a few words in private with you, Mrs Stamanides?'

'Of course. Monika, would you go and wait outside please.'

Mrs Stamanides waited until Monika had closed the door behind her. 'Is there a problem, Mrs Kokanides?'

Litsa licked her lips nervously. 'If you have to send a reference do you disclose family circumstances?'

Mrs Stamanides understood the question Mrs Kokanides was asking. 'According to the records we hold Monika lives at her grandmother's address. The University would only be interested in Monika's scholastic ability and her general conduct over the years.'

'Wouldn't they want to know why she lived with her grandmother rather than with me?'

'Who is to say that you do not live there also?' Mrs Stamanides leaned forward. 'I realise that you do not want to jeopardise Monika's opportunities for a career. She is an intelligent girl and deserves the opportunity to go to University. When I first spoke to her she said she wished to have a job where she earned sufficient for you to work in her grandmother's shop. She is reluctant to be a financial burden to you any longer.'

Litsa felt tears coming into her eyes and she shook her head. 'Monika is no burden to me. If she wants to go to University I'll work day and night to ensure her fees are paid.'

'I'm sure that will not be necessary. I did tell Monika that she could apply for a scholarship. If it was granted that would mean you had assistance with the fees. I need your permission to add her name to the list of applicants.'

Monika looked at her mother anxiously. 'Will I be able to go on to higher education? I'd really like to learn another language.'

'Mrs Stamanides seemed to think there would be no problem.'

'Will you be able to afford it?'

'Mrs Stamanides said she would add your name to the list of applicants for a scholarship. Even if you do not obtain an assisted place there will be enough money.'

'I don't want you doing any extra – work, Mamma. I want to have a good job with plenty of money so you can give up working altogether.'

Litsa gave her daughter a watery smile, fighting to hold back her tears. 'I just want you to be happy. Money is not the most important thing in the world.'

Rhodes 1998 - 2002

Monika considered the various occupations Mrs Stamanides had mentioned to her. She wondered which would be the most lucrative, although none of them appealed to her. She was interested in learning another language and also how to use a computer; when she had mastered both would be the time to think about putting them to a practical use and choosing her career. She needed to earn enough money to enable her mother to give up working at night and be able to help her grandmother in the shop instead.

Once she had accomplished that objective she would think about her own dream; she wanted to learn to drive and have a small car. She had never been further than a bus ride outside the Old and New Town of Rhodes and longed to visit the other places she had heard about on the island. There was a valley that was full of butterflies, a beach that was nothing but sand and another beach at the very end of the island where the Aegean and Mediterranean Seas met. The one time she had visited Lindos she had been enthralled by the spectacular view and the narrow winding streets, so like the Old Town, but so much smaller.

However much she daydreamed about her future Monika still had no idea which subjects would be of most use to her. How could she decide when she did not know her eventual occupation? She almost wished Mrs Stamanides had not suggested the idea of

University, then she could go around the local shops and tavernas and apply for work.

Poppi looked at her smugly. 'When I leave school my Mamma says I can work in her dress shop. Are you going to work with your Mamma?'

Monika shook her head. 'I shall continue with my education.'

'You don't need any education to lie on your back for a man. I'm sure your mother could teach you all you need to know.'

Monika turned away. She had learnt never to answer Poppi back when she made a snide and nasty remark to her or veiled comments about her mother.

When Monika's name was read out to the class as having gained a scholarship to attend the University the surprised look on Poppi's face gave her a certain amount of pleasure.

'How did you get a scholarship? Who did your mother sleep with as a bribe, or did you do the bribing?' asked Poppi maliciously.

'I worked hard at school,' replied Monika and turned away. She was not prepared to let Poppi upset her.

That weekend she visited numerous tavernas and shops asking if there was any opportunity for her to work during the holidays before she took up her place at the University. Each establishment turned her away. It was too late in the tourist season now to find casual work. Monika was perplexed. She could not apply for work during a scholastic term so how was she supposed to work in her holidays? Undaunted she spent the following week visiting shops and tavernas in the New Town, but was met with the same refusal.

She treated herself to a frappe and watched the children in the play area of the park as she considered where else she could look for employment. Next weekend she would approach some of the larger hotels and ask if they needed an extra chambermaid. The thought of spending her day cleaning rooms did not appeal to her, but it was better than asking for work at the airport where she would probably spend the day sweeping the floors.

The kiosk was busy, serving hot snacks, ice cream and drinks, the queue continually growing longer and the children fractious as they were forced to wait. There was only one man serving and he was doing his best to keep up with the demand, red faced and sweating profusely, as he dealt with the orders and gave the customers their change. Monika waited, making her frappe last, until the queue lessened and she took her place at the end of it.

'Yes?' he asked abruptly.

'I don't actually want to buy anything; I bought a frappe earlier.'

'What was wrong with it?'

'Nothing, but I couldn't help noticing how busy you were. Could you do with an assistant?'

'What are you suggesting?'

'I'm looking for some temporary work until I commence University in October.'

'Move aside and let me serve,' he ordered and Monika dutifully stood and waited.

'Have you any experience?' he asked when he had sold an ice cream and a drink.

'My grandmother has a shop.'

'So why don't you work there?'

'It's only a small general store. She doesn't need any extra help.'

The man mopped his face. 'I can't afford to pay much and it would only be for a few hours each day.'

Monika nodded eagerly. 'I'm willing to work hard.'

'You certainly will if you work for me. Be here at ten tomorrow. You can make up the sandwiches and then cook the beef burgers and sausages whilst I make up the rolls. You'll not get a break so be prepared to work until two or later every day.'

Monika felt elated. 'Thank you. I'll be here. How much will I earn each day?'

'I can't afford to pay you more than forty drachmas. If you're not satisfactory I'll tell you to leave at the end of a week.'

Monika nodded. It was less than she would have earned in a shop or taverna, but at least it was work and she would be able to start saving. Until she had sufficient savings her driving lessons would have to wait.

'I'll take it. I'll be here tomorrow.'

It was hard work. Monika spent all day on her feet cooking over the hot plate, cleaning the fat that splattered onto the work surfaces whenever she had an opportunity, or making up a further supply of sandwiches, whilst her employer continually urged her to work faster.

Litsa regarded her daughter with concern. 'You are working so hard for so little money,' she remarked.

'At least I'm working,' replied Monika cheerfully. 'At the end of each week I'm paid nearly two hundred and fifty drachmas. I'm saving it all and by the time I start University I should have earned almost three thousand.'

Litsa sniffed. It was a paltry sum compared with her earnings. She was used to earning far more than that each month.

'I'll be relieved when you're no longer working at that kiosk.'

'I thought I would stay on at the kiosk, working just on a Saturday and Sunday afternoon. Mr Dimitris is pleased with me and that way I will have some work during the holidays. The money I earn should cover any books I need.'

'Surely you should be spending your time studying. Have you thought any more about the courses you want to take?

'I've looked at the brochure, but I think I should complete the first term before I make a decision. I certainly want to learn another language and continue to study English. I'm not sure about the computer and I'm certainly not interested in any of the mathematical courses offered.' Monika smiled happily.

Monika was surprised when she saw Rebekah at the park with her two children on a cold and miserably damp day.

'Fancy coming here on such a horrid day. I would have thought you would have wanted to stay indoors in the warmth.'

Rebekah smiled. 'I'd be quite happy to stay in, but the weather has been so wet that the children have hardly been outside all week. It's too cold to stay long, but I thought it would be good for them to get some fresh air and run around for a while.'

Monika rubbed her cold hands together. 'Would you like some hot soup? We have chicken or tomato.'

Rebekah considered. 'I'll have two tomatoes. Whatever the boys don't drink I can finish. Are you working here all the time? Your mother said you had gained a scholarship and were going on to University.'

'I've just completed my first term. I only do this at the weekends to make some pocket money.'

'Have you decided what you want to do when you have completed your course?'

Monika shook her head. 'I'm not sure. I certainly don't want to be a teacher; that could be boring. A travel company might be more interesting.'

'Are you still an avid reader?'

'Oh, yes. I still go to the library each week.'

'So why don't you apply to work in the library? You'd have access to more books than you could ever read in a lifetime and it would be warmer than working here.'

'The library?' Monica frowned. 'I hadn't thought of that. I might be able to get a job there during the holidays. I'd be willing to put the books back on the shelves in the proper order. I find it so frustrating when they're all muddled up.'

Rebekah took a mouthful of soup from each carton then called her boys over and handed them one each. 'You don't have to drink it all,' she advised them. 'Give the carton back to me when you've had enough.'

For the remainder of the afternoon Monika thought over Rebekah's suggestion. She was sure she would enjoy working in the library and it would at least be warm in there during the winter months. She would speak to Mrs Ethanides, whom she considered to be a friend, the next time she visited. She should have thought of asking the librarian when she was first looking for work.

Monika approached Mrs Ethanides tentatively. 'I've just completed my first term at University and I wanted to ask if there was any work available here in the library.'

'What subjects are you taking?'

'Advanced English and computer studies. I think I'll also choose another language, probably German.'

'Are you planning to become an interpreter or tour guide?'

'I haven't decided on a career yet. I just enjoy language, the construction of the sentences and grammar.'

'Have you considered classical Greek?'

'I've read all the Greek classics. I don't think I would want to read them again.'

'You would gain an understanding of the way the language has changed over the years.'

'I'm sure I would find it interesting, but I'm not sure it would help me in the future unless I wanted to decipher the ancient Greek writings that are stored in the museum. I'd probably need to become a professor to be capable of the work. I don't think I'm clever enough to specialise in a subject like that.'

'So why do you want to work here? Are you considering becoming a librarian?'

'Would I be able to work here now; just putting the books in order on the shelves?'

'You could, but the work would be voluntary. I would not be able to pay you.'

Monika's face fell. 'I really need to earn some money. At the moment I'm working in the kiosk in the park at weekends but I don't really want to work there throughout the winter; it's becoming cold.'

'Do you need the money for your University fees?' Mrs Ethanides could hardly imagine a more unpleasant place to work during the winter months.

'No, I obtained a scholarship so my fees are paid. My mother pays for any books or extras that I need, but I can't expect her to give me pocket money as well; besides I'm saving up. I want to give her a surprise.'

Mrs Ethanides raised her eyebrows and Monika continued.

'I want to have some driving lessons and when I've passed my test I want to buy a car. That would mean I could take my mother and grandmother out at the weekends and we could visit some of the places in Rhodes that we cannot reach by bus.'

'Is it necessary to buy a car? A car is expensive to maintain. You live in the Old Town so would have to purchase a permit to bring it inside the walls to park. If you are only planning to use it at the weekends it could be more practical to hire one. There may be some weekends when you would not want to go out and then the car is sitting there for no good reason.'

'I thought the hire cars were only for the tourists.'

Mrs Ethanides smiled at Monika's ignorance. 'Not at all. If you owned a car and needed it for your work what would you do if it broke down? You would have to hire one. I'm sure your mother and grandmother would love you to take them out at the weekends, but using a hire care would probably work out cheaper than actually buying one.'

'I still need to earn money for the driving lessons.' Monika frowned. 'What exactly do you have to do to be a librarian? I only see you here recording the books that are borrowed and returned.'

'You have to fully understand the cataloguing system and that has now been computerised. There is also the ordering process for new books. Each year we have to check our stock and replace those books that have become damaged or worn out. We also store old maps and historical documents that are not available to the general public. Academics apply for access to them for their research and you have to be familiar with the cataloguing system so you are able to find and produce the items they ask for. Of course, you also have to deal with any queries a reader may have and know the correct section in the library for the books they want.'

'It doesn't sound very difficult.'

Mrs Ethanides smiled. 'If a particular book is requested you need to be able to communicate with other libraries and see if they have one they would be willing to send us rather than spend money on a purchase. We have to keep within our budget which means investigating which book sellers will give us the best price. They often offer a bargain price the more copies of a title that you buy, but if the books are not taken off the shelves by readers they are simply taking up valuable space.'

'How do you decide which books will be popular?'

'Partly from experience and also researching the current trends in literature. If you decided you wanted to become a librarian you would have to complete a year's training course when you have completed University.'

'A year!'

Mrs Ethanides nodded. 'If you were accepted as a trainee you would have to learn how to use the computer programme that has been specifically designed for libraries. It deals with the classification of the subject matter as well as the ordering process. You would be given exercises to complete that would demonstrate how well you understood the financial process. Our allocation differs each year. You cannot assume that you will have an increase in funds next year; the amount could be reduced. If that is so you have to re-evaluate your purchase plans.'

'I'm not very good at figures.'

'Provided you type in the correct amounts the computer does the calculation for you.'

'I had no idea that library work was so complicated.'

'I think you would be an ideal candidate to become a librarian.

I have seen you mature over the years and you obviously love reading for both pleasure and knowledge.' Mrs Ethanides spread her hands. 'I wish I could help you. You're welcome to come in at any time to replace the books on the shelves, but I'm not able to pay you.'

Disappointed not to have gained any paid work Monika still felt that her visit had been worthwhile. The work Mrs Ethanides had described sounded interesting. She would certainly ask to take German and classical Greek when she returned to University and concentrate harder in the computer lessons.

Monika rarely visited her mother in the house she rented in the red light area, but decided today she wanted to tell her of her visit to the library. She was sure her mother would be pleased that she had finally made a decision on a future career.

Once she had mastered typing Monika began to enjoy the computer lessons. She was now fluent in English and had also expanded her subjects to include German along with the classical Greek language and literature. When Mr Dimitris said he no longer needed her assistance at the kiosk as he was only opening for a couple of hours each day she was relieved, despite losing her pocket money. She had not expected to find German and classical Greek to be so difficult and would be able to use her time giving them extra attention and also taking up Mrs Ethanides offer of voluntary work in the library.

'May I come back when the weather is warmer?' she asked. 'When the children are on holiday at Easter you will probably be busy again.'

'You can come and ask. No promises.' Mr Dimitris knew his niece would be looking for work when she left school after Christmas.

Monika found replacing the library books back into order on the shelves frustrating. Just as she thought she had finished placing a shelf of books in the correct alphabetical sequence she would find a reader had placed a book out of order. She would remove it and having found the correct place she would not have room on the shelf and have to move a quantity of books to make sufficient space.

'If people are capable of reading they should also know their alphabet,' she complained to Mrs Ethanides.

'It's laziness more than anything. They select a book; then see another they think they would prefer and place the original in the space they've created.'

'A shame there isn't some sort of mechanism that shouts "wrong place" to them.'

Mrs Ethanides smiled. 'I think such a device would cause some of our readers to have a heart attack. It's something you get used to after a while, although I do admit it can be annoying. You're very conscientious, Monika, but there's no need to be a perfectionist. Provided the books are in the correct section and the authors' surnames start with the same letter no one will complain.'

Monika loaded her arms with another pile of books. 'I'll try to take your advice, Mrs Ethanides,' knowing that with her orderly mind she would have to place each book in strict alphabetical order, however much inconvenience it caused her. At least it was warm and dry working in the library and occasionally someone would ask her where they could find a particular book.

At the end of her first year at University Monika was given a certificate to say she had completed her English course and graduated with honours.

The Principle congratulated her. 'It isn't many of our pupils who manage that in their first year. I hope you will be as successful in your German and classical Greek studies.'

Monika blushed. 'I had the advantage of being taught English whilst I was at school. As I no longer have to attend English classes I wanted to ask if I would be allowed to learn another language, maybe French or Italian.'

The Principle shook his head. 'I don't think that is advisable yet. Concentrate on your current subjects and depending upon your examination results at the end of next year it could be a possibility. Trying to cope with too many languages at once might only confuse you. Better to become proficient gradually.'

With that Monika had to be content. The books she had needed to purchase had made inroads into her savings and when she approached Mr Dimitris he told her that his niece would be working in the kiosk in future and there was no place for her. She had given up the idea of having driving lessons during the winter months in favour of purchasing a computer, but now she would have to wait until she had found some part time work that enabled her to have some savings. If she was allowed to take another language the following year at University she would need to buy books again to cover the course work and a computer of her own would be more useful than knowing how to drive a car.

Monika was on her knees assiduously placing the books into order on the shelf when she heard a voice behind her.

'Are you able to help me, please?'

Monika looked up and saw a young man standing there with an annoyed expression on his face. She rose to her feet, brushing down her skirt and smiled at him.

'I'll try,' she smiled.

'I'm looking for books that deal with real crime, not fictitious murder stories. Everything is so badly arranged I can never find the books where they should be.'

Monika frowned. 'Are you talking about the criminal atrocities that were carried out during the war?

'No, I'm talking about crime that the police have to deal with in other parts of the world. We have very little serious crime on Rhodes and I would like to know how other nations deal with their problems. On the rare occasions when something drastic does occur the police in Athens are drafted in. That should not be necessary.' The man spoke forcefully. 'We should be capable of dealing with our own problems. We should be in control.'

Monika hesitated. She had read murder mystery stories whilst a teenager and considered most of them out of touch with reality. No one could be murdered and buried in their garden without people realising they were missing.

'Do you read English?'

'Not very well.'

'That's a shame because I believe most of the books you are looking for cover crimes that took place in America. Only a few have been translated into Greek.'

The young man shrugged. 'Well I can at least start with those, I suppose.'

'Why are you so interested?' asked Monika curiously.

'I'm a policeman and I want to progress up the ranks. I am aiming to become the chief of police.'

Monika smiled. 'Don't you have to take examinations to gain promotion?'

'I'm studying for those. I thought some books on crime might give me a useful insight into procedures that other countries use. If I approve of their system I will adopt them in Rhodes when I am in control.'

'I think the section you want would be at the end of the room. Follow me and I'll show you the appropriate shelves.'

'You're new here, aren't you?'

'I'm only here occasionally to help out. I'm at University.'

He whistled through his teeth. 'What subjects are you taking?'

'German, classical Greek language and computers, of course.'

'Why German?' he asked with a frown.

Monika shrugged. She felt as if she was being interrogated for a crime. 'It seemed like a good idea.'

'Why not English? That's a more universal language I understand.'

'I already speak English.'

'Do you? Really speak it?'

Monika laughed. 'I can read, write and speak.'

'So if I borrowed one of the books I want in English you'd be able to help me out if I was really stuck?'

'Possibly, but I'm not prepared to sit and read to you.'

'Now that's an attractive thought.' He smiled suddenly and held out his hand. 'I'm Emmanuel, Manu to my friends.'

Monika returned his handshake. 'I'm Monika. Here you are. I'll leave you to browse. If you have any more problems you know where I am.'

Monika thought no more about the policeman. As soon as the tavernas and bars began to open up in readiness for the Easter tourists she began a systematic tour of those that were situated in the Old Town. She declared that she was willing to work at the weekends and some evenings and finally a busy taverna in the centre of the town agreed she could work taking orders from the customers.

At first it was somewhat of a novelty to her, but as the weather improved and the taverna became busier she found the work quite exhausting and she was expected to increase her hours. However hot it was she had to rush from table to table, deliver the orders back to the kitchen, where it was even hotter, and then take out the drinks that had been requested. She would no sooner have placed the drinks on the table than she would see another table waiting for her attention or the kitchen would call to say that the food was ready.

She had no spare time to visit the library either to collect books for herself or to help voluntarily. By the time she returned to her grandmother's shop she was thankful to remove her shoes, have a quick wash and fall into bed. When she did have time to herself she would occupy her time by studying, not wishing to find herself behind the other students when she returned to University.

'I will be so pleased when this summer is over,' she declared to her grandmother. 'It was busy when I worked at the kiosk, but at least I wasn't running all over the place and having to remember the food each table had ordered.'

'It sounds as though they are working you too hard,' observed Monique.

'I'm not working harder than anyone else. We're allowed a fifteen minute break at the end of every two hours, but it isn't always possible to take it. You can't tell a customer you are on your break and their food will have to sit and wait.'

'I hope they tip you well.'

Monika shrugged. 'Some do. Others just pay the total that is on the bill and walk away without even saying thank you. I can't wait to return to University. At least my feet won't be sore at the end of the day and I'll be able to sit and read again. I'm far too tired when I arrive home at night. I can't keep my eyes open. Even when I have a day off I'm too tired to concentrate properly and lie on the beach in the sun and go to sleep.'

'Too much sun is not good for you. You would do better to stay here in the house where it's cool.'

'I like to be out in the fresh air. At least on the beach I am away from all the cooking smells from the tavernas and can go into the sea when I become too hot.'

'There are no cooking smells here,' said Monique starchily.

'I know, Grandma, but there's nowhere to sit except outside of the shop. I enjoy going to the beach, particularly if Mamma joins me. I loved it when she used to take me there nearly every day in the school holidays.'

Monique sniffed derisively. She had never ventured into the sea. 'You need to be careful down there. A wave could take you out to where you cannot stand.'

'I can swim, Grandma,' Monika assured her, 'besides, we don't get big, strong waves during the summer and I certainly wouldn't go in the sea in the winter.'

'I should hope not. You'd be asking for pneumonia.' Monique continued to unpack a box and place cartons of tea onto a shelf. The beverage appeared to be popular with the English tourists.

Monika accepted her last weeks' wages from the taverna gratefully. She could add that to the considerable amount she had saved over the previous weeks. Until she knew if she would have to buy books on French or Italian grammar she did not think it advisable to spend money on a computer. She also needed a new pair of shoes, the ones she had worn whilst she was working had a hole in the sole and no amount of polishing disguised their scuffed appearance. She could not wear those to University and did not want to start wearing her boots until the weather became really cold and wet.

Mrs Ethanides welcomed her back to the library. 'I hoped you'd come back and not be tempted to leave University for some paid work.'

Monika shook her head. 'I'm very glad to have the money, but even if they had offered me double pay each week to stay on I would have refused. I didn't enjoy the work at all. I would far rather be here or at the University.'

'Did you keep up with your studies over the summer?'

'As best I could. Even on my days off I was so tired. Working here will be like a holiday to me.'

'I'm not sure I would describe it in such glowing terms,' smiled Mrs Ethanides. 'Once you start on your training course you'll probably find the work here as exacting as your University studies have been.'

'If I do well in my German and classical Greek exams I'm hoping I will be allowed to take French or Italian.'

Mrs Ethanides raised her eyebrows. 'You seem to be fascinated by other languages.'

'I just enjoy learning, besides, if I can read in other languages I'm sure there will be many books that have not been translated into Greek that I will be able to enjoy. I certainly don't want to have to tackle them with a dictionary by my side. There would be no pleasure in continually having to look up words that I didn't understand.'

Mrs Ethanides looked at Monika speculatively. 'There are opportunities for librarians to attend conferences in the European countries. If you are fluent in the language I would be able to put your name forward when the invitations are sent out.'

'Really? I hadn't realised I would be able to visit other countries if I was a librarian. I thought I would just stay here.'

'You might. Don't get your hopes up. It wouldn't happen until you were fully trained and had some years' experience.'

Monika smiled happily. 'I would love to travel. I'm going to buy a computer so I will have to put off driving lessons for a while. When I finally gain my licence there's all of Rhodes to see before I go anywhere else.'

Manu entered the library and walked over to where Monika was placing books on a shelf. 'Hello, I didn't think I would see you again. I was told you were working in a taverna.'

'That was only a holiday job. I'm back at Uni now. How is your reading going?'

Manu shook his head. 'I admit I'm finding it difficult. There are some words I just do not understand and a dictionary doesn't help.'

'Have you looked on the internet?'

'I haven't got a computer at home and I'm not allowed to use the one at the police station for private work.'

Monika hesitated. 'If you made a list of the words you don't understand I could try to help you.'

'Oh, I suppose that is part of being a librarian, explaining words people don't understand.' Monika was not sure if he was making fun of her.

'Some of them I would probably be able to explain to you quite easily,' she replied calmly. 'If I'm not familiar with them it will be good for me to investigate.'

'When will you be in the library next?' asked Manu.

'Tomorrow.'

'I'm on duty tomorrow. How about this time next week?'

'I should be here. If I'm not Mrs Ethanides will be able to tell you when she expects me to be in next.'

'It's a date. I'll see you next week.'

Monika smiled in amusement. It was not a "date". It was an arrangement to meet on an intellectual level, not for pleasure.

'Who is your friend?' asked Mrs Ethanides. 'He was a frequent visitor during your absence and seemed quite upset when I said you were not working here for a few weeks.'

'He's not really a friend. He asked me where he could find the books he wanted and has asked me to explain some of the American words he doesn't understand.'

'So you are a teacher now?'

'No,' Monika shook her head. 'The Americans use some words that are different in the English language but mean virtually the same thing. It can be confusing.'

'Don't let him take advantage of you.'

'I'm sure he won't. He's a policeman.'

'That's not what I meant. If he wants you to give him English lessons he should pay you.'

'Oh,' Monika blushed. 'I thought you meant – you know.'

'I think you are far too sensible to be taken advantage of in that way.'

Monika was expecting to see Manu the following week during the afternoon and had begun to think that he had forgotten or been asked to stay on duty as he did not arrive. Five minutes before the library closed he walked in and beckoned Monika towards him.

The imperious action was not lost on Mrs Ethanides and she took an instant dislike to the man as he stood by the desk and waited until Monika came over.

'We're just about to close. If you know which book you want I'll have a quick look for you.'

'I'm not after a book. I've come to meet you, remember? You said if I made a list of the words I'm struggling with you'd explain some of them to me. I didn't think it appropriate for me to take up your library time so I'm inviting you for coffee or a glass of wine.'

'Oh!' Monika blushed. So it was a date after all. 'I won't be able to stay too long. My grandmother will be expecting me home. I'll just say goodbye to Mrs Ethanides.'

'Remember what I said,' Mrs Ethanides cautioned Monika.

'I promise I will take good care of her. I'm a policeman.'

Monika giggled. 'That is not what Mrs Ethanides meant. She said I should be charging you for lessons.'

Manu raised his eyebrows. 'I was not expecting to pay. If I buy you a drink today I think that should cover expenses?'

'We'll see. It depends how long I have to spend explaining words to you.' Monika felt unsure of herself. At University she had joined in sessions at the coffee shop with her peers. She listened to their conversation, but rarely offered an opinion of her own and had never been invited to accompany a lone male student anywhere. She was not sure if this was because rumours of her mother's occupation had reached them or she was so unattractive that she did not excite their interest.

Manu steered Monika into the taverna a few doors from the library. He aimed a kick at a cat that was sitting in the shade beneath a chair and held it back for Monika. 'Vermin' he muttered. 'What would you like? Coffee or a glass of wine?'

'Just coffee for me, thank you.'

Manu ordered a beer for himself and waited until the drinks had been placed on the table. He raised his glass. 'Cheers. Here's to us.'

'Us?' repeated Monika.

'Why not? I hope you consider me a friend, so why not drink to that friendship?'

Monika lifted her cup. 'To us.' She placed the cup down. 'Now how can I help you?'

Manu took a piece of paper from his pocket and leaned forward. 'I made a long list of the words that I didn't understand

83

and as I read more I began to realise their meaning, but I'm still confused about the different terms they use.'

Monika nodded. 'Once you see a word in context the meaning usually becomes clear.'

Manu frowned. 'Why do they talk about lawyers, solicitors, barristers and attorneys? They all seem to be doing the same work. It's ridiculous to keep using a different word.'

'Basically they are, but some are more qualified than others to carry out their obligations. It is a question of seniority depending upon the examinations they have taken and their results. I don't think you need to understand the qualification differences between them.'

'And a sheriff?'

'Another term for being a policeman in America.'

Manu drank the remainder of his beer and signalled that he would like another. 'They seem to use different words, depending upon whether the book was written in America or England. Why do the Americans talk about "homicide" and the English call it "murder"?'

'That is just a language difference that you have to accept.'

'What is the difference between a post mortem and an inquest?' He fired the question at her as if it was an interrogation.

'They both mean an enquiry. A post mortem is a procedure carried out after someone has died unexpectedly to ascertain the cause of death. An inquest is where the cause of death is suspicious. If a man in his nineties fell and banged his head subsequently dying from his injury the post mortem would confirm either the blow had killed him or he had died from the shock of falling. If a man in his twenties was found on the ground it is unlikely he would have died from shock. A Coroner would be asked to hold an inquest to examine the head wound in detail and decide if someone had hit him or was it unfortunate that he had landed on something that had penetrated his skull. I don't think you need to worry unduly about the difference.'

Manu scowled. 'So you think I'm stupid?'

Monika shook her head. 'Not at all. I just don't think you have read enough books yet to have a complete grasp of the different legal words they employ. You should borrow some of the well written books by the writers who specialise in crime. They are not factual like the ones you have read, but you would become familiar with the different terms that are used. I think the authors often gain their ideas from true events and weave a story around them. You could start with those that have been translated into Greek and have some easy reading matter.'

'I'm not sure if they will be of any use to me.'

'Give them a try. If they're not to your liking you can return to the factual books.' Monika finished her coffee and looked at her watch. 'I really ought to go home now. Thank you for my coffee.'

'When will I see you again?'

'I'll be in the library next week. I can show you the books I've mentioned and you can have a look for yourself. Goodbye Manu.'

Monika picked up her handbag and began to walk swiftly away. She did not want Manu offering to see her home and she knew he would have to pay for their refreshment before he could leave; by then she would have taken some side turnings and unless he was as familiar with the Old Town as she was it was unlikely he would find her. Monika thought about their conversation as she hurried home. Manu should have been able to work out the answers to his queries without her help. Maybe the police were not as intelligent as she had assumed.

'You're late,' commented her grandmother.

Monika blushed. She was not going to admit to her grandmother that she had spent time having coffee with a young man. 'I was explaining something to one of our readers. It took longer than I had expected.'

Manu arrived at the library a little earlier the following week and made his way to Monika's side. 'I'm willing to try these other books that you recommend, but I still have some questions for you. Are you able to come for a drink when the library closes?'

'Provided I am not too late home.'

'Doesn't your mother allow you to meet friends?'

'Of course, but she worries if I have not told her I am going to be out. Now, if you follow me down to the section I'll point out a selection of books that I think you might find easier reading, and help you gain familiarity with the terms that are used.'

'Can you recommend some?'

Monika shook her head. 'I'm not qualified to give an opinion on any particular author. I've not received any training yet. I'll meet you outside when we close.'

Monika did not see the scowl Manu gave as she returned to the shelves where she had been working. She could feel Mrs Ethanides's eyes on her and hoped she would not be rebuked for having a few moments private conversation.

Manu led her to the same taverna as before and Monika requested a lime and soda.

'You wouldn't prefer a glass of wine?'

Monika shook her head. 'I enjoy a glass with a meal, but at this time of day I prefer a soft drink. Which books did you choose?'

Manu placed them on the table and Monika looked at the titles. 'I see you've chosen three different authors. That's good. It will give you a chance to compare their different writing styles.'

'I've a couple of questions for you arising from the books I read last week.'

Monika smiled. 'Go ahead. I'll do my best to answer them.'

'What is this "pro bona" that they mention?'

'Someone who will represent you for free. They consider you to be innocent of the charge and you cannot afford to pay the legal fees to clear your name. I believe it happens mostly in America. The large legal firms there make a good deal of money and will take a few cases where they do not charge for their expertise.'

'So who is more qualified? A Judge or a Magistrate?'

'The Judge, always the Judge. A Magistrate can hand out a sentence to a petty criminal who has committed a robbery, but if murder is involved the case would have to go before a Judge and jury. The Judge would have to abide by the decision of the jury when passing the sentence or dismissing the case.'

'Suppose he thinks the jury has made the wrong decision?'

Monika shook her head. 'I don't know the answer to that. I can only imagine that the case could be investigated further and if new evidence was uncovered the case would be tried again.'

'Wrong!' Manu smiled triumphantly. 'Once someone has been cleared of an offence they cannot be charged with it a second time.'

Monika shrugged. 'You obviously know more about the law than I do, but the Double Jeopardy ruling does not apply everywhere and exceptions are made.'

Manu looked annoyed at being corrected and called for another beer. 'Will you have another?' he asked and Monika shook her head.

'If I fill myself up with liquid I'll not be able to eat my meal.' She drained her glass. 'I must be off now. Enjoy your books.'

Manu put his hand firmly on hers. 'Can I see you next week?'

'I'll be in the library.'

'No, I mean will you join me for a drink when you finish work?'

Monika withdrew her hand. 'No promises. I may have other things to do.'

As Monika walked away she could feel Manu watching her. She had an idea that Manu knew the answers to his questions and they had simply been an excuse to see her. The thought gave her a warm glow inside.

Rhodes 2003 - 2004

The end of the University term seemed to arrive quickly and Monika waited with baited breath whilst the results for each pupil were read out. She gave a deep sigh of relief when she heard her name called and she received her certificate to say she was fluent in German and had a working knowledge of French and was thoroughly conversant with classical Greek.

Mrs Ethanides read Monika's University report and congratulated her on doing so well. 'I was so sure you would receive high marks and a good recommendation that I put your name forward as a candidate six months ago. Do you still wish to train as a librarian?'

'Oh, yes. I can't think of anything I would enjoy more. I will be surrounded by books and I shall be able to read as many as I wish.'

'I'm pleased to hear it. You can have a couple of weeks' holiday and then you will be expected to be at the library each morning at eight until three in the afternoon.'

Monika's face lit up. 'So I'll still be able to work voluntarily when the course finishes each day.'

Mrs Ethanides shook her head. 'I would have thought you had had enough of putting books in order and would welcome the break.'

'I enjoy doing it. I suppose I have an orderly mind.'

'Just make sure you take advantage of the good weather and

go to the beach. I don't want to hear that you have taken a part time job at a taverna or back at that kiosk.'

Monika frowned. How had Mrs Ethanides known that she had intended to look for some part time work during the summer?

Monika enjoyed her training. Once she understood how the computer programme worked she became more confident in completing the exercises set for her. She fully understood the cataloguing system and was becoming more familiar with the spread sheets that kept track of the books in the library and out on loan. She still had to tackle the financial problems of the budget that was allocated for the renewal of worn out books and the purchase of new publications, but felt confident that she would be proficient by the end of the course.

Mrs Ethanides called Monika to her desk. 'Your training has been coming on very well. I think you'll be quite capable of converting the prices into Euros on the computer now. We are all going to have to become proficient in dealing with the new currency. When the time comes to re-order books it should be easier than when we dealt in drachmas.'

'If everyone is using Euros what will happen to the old drachmas?' asked Monika.

'For some time you will be able to use the drachmas when you shop and receive your change in Euros. Anyone who has savings at home in drachmas should ask the bank to change them into Euros. There will be no point in holding on to them as eventually they will be valueless.'

Monika considered Mrs Ethanides's words. She must speak to her mother and advise her to change her savings into Euros. None of them had a bank account. Litsa would not have wanted anyone to see the amount she made each week, feeling that her money was safer in the old shoe box she kept hidden beneath her bed. Monique had always dealt in cash when buying goods for her shop and Monika kept her own savings in a box amongst her clothes.

The change over from drachmas to Euros went relatively smoothly, although Monika was sure that some shops had used the transition as an excuse to raise their prices. Her mother had brought home a role of blank sticky labels and spent a considerable amount of time writing new prices on them and sticking them on the items in the shop. Monique had grumbled that it was a waste of time, but her daughter insisted.

'When someone pays you in Euros how will you know how much change to give them if you don't know the price? We'll soon get used to using Euros.'

Litsa had taken Monika's advice and each day she had taken some drachmas from her savings to a different bank and asked for them to be exchanged for Euros.

'Don't take more than about a five hundred a time or they may want to know where you got it from and make sure you use different banks,' warned Monika.

'I've seen people changing far more than that,' observed Litsa. 'No one seems to ask any questions.'

Monika shook her head. 'I don't want you to take any chances.'

It became a regular occurrence for Manu to arrive at the library each Wednesday and ask Monika to join him for a drink and she began to look forward to his company. It made a change from talking to her grandmother about the shop or the latest television programme that had taken her fancy. He flexed his well developed arm muscles as he talked and explained that he was visiting the local gymnasium regularly.

'I need to be fit. The force put us through a rigorous training when we first apply. They can ask us to go for a re-assessment at any time and expect us to still be as fit. I don't want to be demoted because I cannot run fast enough to catch a criminal. I am determined not to fail.' His mouth set in a determined line. 'I should be promoted to the rank of an Inspector soon and I won't stand any nonsense from anyone. They have sessions for ladies,' added Manu. 'Why don't you consider coming along?'

Monika smiled and shook her head, never having had any desire to take part in any physical exercise herself. 'I don't think it would be something I would enjoy.'

'Rather have your head stuck in a book, no doubt.'

Monika did not pick up on his sneering tone. 'Knowledge of books is more valuable to me in the library than being able to run around the shelves more quickly.'

Manu scowled. 'You're making fun of me.'

'Not at all. I appreciate you need to be extremely fit and I admire you for having the discipline to go and train regularly.'

'Discipline,' replied Manu, 'that's a priority in life.'

'Of course. Self discipline comes naturally with growing up. I arrive at work on time and I do not leave early with a lame excuse.'

Manu banged his hand on the table. 'That's not the kind of discipline I'm talking about.'

Monika looked at him in surprise. 'Then what are you talking about?'

'Being in control. Ensuring you are obeyed. Making people do as you tell them.'

Monika shrugged and for the first time felt uneasy in Manu's company. 'I'm sure that is necessary in the police force, but I don't think it is relevant for library work. I really ought to go, Manu. My mother worries if I am too late home from work.'

'You are obviously an obedient daughter. I'll see you next week.'

Manu told her that his father was a chemist and his mother did not go out to work, but Monika was reticent about her own family. She had no qualms about telling Manu that her grandmother had a general store, but she was not prepared to tell him the truth about her mother's occupation saying her mother worked in a bar and her father had met with an accident.

'My mother still finds it difficult to speak about him. Please don't mention him if you meet her.'

'Is that an invitation?'

'I haven't told my mother that I'm meeting you.'

'Wouldn't she approve?'

'I'm sure she would have no objection to us meeting.' She would need to approach her mother carefully before she dared to ask Manu to visit the shop.

'Maybe you should come and meet my parents first. You can assure your mother that they are decent, respectable people. I will arrange a convenient time.'

Her late arrival home from the library each Wednesday did not go unnoticed by her mother.

'What is keeping you late each week at the library?'

Monika blushed. 'I'm meeting someone. I helped him find some books and we became friendly. He comes on a Wednesday and asks me to join him when the library closes. We usually discuss the books he has chosen. I've been seeing him for some time and now he has asked me to visit his parents.'

'You're not .....'

'No, we've only met at the library and had a drink together at the local taverna. I didn't even think he was seriously interested in me until he mentioned meeting his parents.'

'If he's interested enough in you to want to introduce you to his parents I'd like to meet him also.'

'I'll be happy to bring him up to Grandma's shop, but I don't want him to know where you work.'

'Are you so ashamed of me?' asked Litsa sadly.

'No, but he's a policeman.'

'I work legally. I don't tout for custom on the streets.'

'I've told him you work in a bar. Please don't tell him differently.'

'Suppose he asks which one?'

Monika shrugged. 'Tell him you work for one of the companies and go wherever they send you.' Monika took her mother's hands. 'I've been thinking, Mamma, and please listen to me. You're approaching forty. How much longer will you be able to work? You've been fortunate so far and no customer has made you ill, but it could happen.'

'I'm very careful,' Litsa assured her daughter.

'I'm sure you are. I'm terribly grateful to you for paying my Uni expenses, but now I have a salary from the library you could stop working and return here to live.'

Litsa shook her head. 'There's not enough room for me to live here.'

'I don't mind sleeping with Grandma again. You could have my bedroom.'

'Well we don't have to make any decisions immediately.' Litsa knew her time as a prostitute was drawing to an end. She already looked older than her years. Eleni had left, her place having been taken by Natasha and even Litsa's regular customers had begun to visit the new girl. If this young man that Monika was seeing was seriously interested in her daughter they could be married and have their own home. No longer having to support her daughter in any way she would be able to return to the shop and be available to look after her mother in her declining years.

Monika gave a sigh of relief. She had been dreading confronting her mother about returning to live at the shop. There was no reason for her mother to continue to support her now she was working at the library. The remuneration during her training had not been very much and although she was saving a small amount regularly she would have to wait a little longer before she seriously considered having driving lessons.

'Tell me more about this young man,' ordered Litsa. 'He may be a policeman. But that doesn't mean he is suitable for you.'

Monika smiled. She had been expecting an interrogation. 'Well, he's older than me....'

'How much older?'

'About six years.'

Litsa frowned. 'Has he been married before?'

'No.'

'So where does he live?'

'With his parents in the New Town. His father is a chemist and his mother does not go out to work.'

'What have you told him about your father?' Litsa interjected sharply.

'I told him my father was in the navy and there was an accident. I've asked him not to question you about him as it still upsets you to speak about him. I didn't tell him I was the accident!'

Litsa nodded. 'It's best left that way. So why did he choose the police as a career?'

'He did not consider he was clever enough to go to University, but I'm sure he could have done. He's working on examinations in the police force so that he will earn promotion to the rank of an Inspector and he keeps himself very fit by going to the gym. I find him interesting to talk to and he's very good looking.'

'There's more to a man than his looks.' Litsa warned her.

'I hope his parent's apartment will not be too grand. I don't want them to consider I'm a pauper just because I live in the Old Town.'

'Most of the people who live in the Old Town have inherited the property. It's expensive to buy anything here.'

Monika raised her eyebrows. 'I always thought that because the buildings were old they wouldn't be worth very much; not like the new buildings outside the walls.'

'Most of them are worth considerable more.'

'So why does Grandma keep her shop? Why doesn't she sell it?'

Litsa shook her head. 'It's family property. You don't sell family property. One day it will belong to you.'

Monika looked at her mother dubiously. She was not at all sure that she would want the shop premises. There were only two proper rooms, if you discounted the room that was used as a general store, with a kitchen and bathroom built on at the back.

'I'm sure that won't happen for a long time yet,' she said cheerfully. 'I'll tell you about Manu's parents' apartment when I've seen it and arrange a time when he can come and meet you and Grandma.'

Monika found Manu's parents welcoming and his father was interested in her University studies. 'I was such a dunce at languages,' he admitted. 'I could learn chemical formulas like reciting my alphabet but a foreign language was quite beyond me. How do you plan to use your language ability? You should become a teacher,' he said firmly. 'They earn a good salary.'

'I don't think I would be a very good teacher,' smiled Monika. 'I don't think I would have the patience.'

'Like Manu,' smiled Mr Graphides, giving his wife a dig in the ribs with his elbow. 'He doesn't suffer fools gladly. If he was a teacher and you handed in your homework late you would regret it. He says you work in the library. What made you do that? I wouldn't have thought there was a lot of scope there for a University graduate.'

'I love books and reading.'

'So do I,' agreed Manu's mother with a sideways glance at her husband. 'Those sad love stories have me in tears.'

Monika smiled politely. She had never read love stories. 'I have been told that conferences take place in different parts of the world and if I speak the language I may be selected to attend.'

Manu looked at her sharply. 'Who would pay for you to go off travelling?'

'The library service. According to Mrs Ethanides I will need to have more experience and take a higher examination before I could be considered as a candidate.'

Manu's visit to Monika's mother and grandmother was equally successful and when Manu called on them a month later and asked if they would agree to Monika marrying him they agreed without any reservations.

Monika could hardly believe it. The handsome policeman actually wanted to marry her.

Monika shared her news with Mrs Ethanides who frowned. 'Are you quite sure? How well do you know this man? You've met him for a drink after work regularly, but how much time have you actually spent in his company? Don't you think you should wait a while and get to know him better. He's quite a bit older than you and seems quite aggressive at times.'

'He's a policeman. I think appearing aggressive is just to intimidate whoever he is arresting,' Monika defended Manu.

'He doesn't need to have that attitude towards you.'

'I'm sure it's just because he uses his authority as a policeman and it has become a habit. Our parents are happy with the arrangement.'

'Then I can only wish you happiness. I hope this won't mean you give up being a librarian?'

'Definitely not. I would hate to spend all my day cleaning and cooking; besides we will need my salary. We have to find an apartment to rent in the New Town and make our wedding arrangements. We don't plan to get married until next Easter but I'll have to start saving for my wedding now. My driving lessons will have to wait again'

'Can't your fiancé help you with driving?'

Monika looked at Mrs Ethanides in surprise. 'I hadn't thought to ask him. I don't think it would be allowed, though, he drives a police car.'

'If he hired a car he could take you somewhere quiet in the country and show you the basic principles. That would save you from having to pay for so many lessons.'

'I couldn't ask him to do anything against the law.'

'I'm not suggesting that he lets you drive around the town. He could probably give you some useful hints to enable you to pass your test the first time you tried.'

'I'll think about it,' promised Monika. She was not at all sure how Manu would receive such a request.

Manu announced that he had found an apartment that would be suitable for them once they were married. 'The current tenants are leaving in four months and we will be able to move in as soon as they have gone.'

Monika frowned. She wished she had been consulted. 'Suppose I don't like it?'

Manu continued as if she had not spoken. 'It's in the New Town, not far from my parents. The rent is reasonable and only a short distance from where I work. Most of the basic furniture will be there, tables and chairs, cooker, fridge and,' Manu squeezed her hand hard, making her wince, 'most importantly the bed. We'll only need some bed linen and towels.'

Monika felt her heart flutter, her earlier annoyance dissipated. 'It sounds like a bargain.'

'It is. You can share the cost of the rent with me and buy our food. I'll be responsible for the remainder of the rent and the utility bills. We should be able to manage provided we are careful.'

Monika was about to say that she had money saved, then thought better of it. Manu might insist that she handed it all over to him once they were married. If they were to share the costs between them it would take her a long time to save up again for the longed for driving lessons.

'I'll be able to do some of the shopping at my grandmother's. I know she won't overcharge us.'

'I should hope not. She should let you have everything at cost price.'

'She has to make a living,' Monika reminded him.

'Just bring me back the bills to look at. If I think she's too expensive you'll have to shop elsewhere.'

Monika opened her mouth to say that her grandmother did

not give bills. She added the amount for the goods up on a piece of scrap paper and charged the customer accordingly; then she changed her mind. She could always present some scraps of paper herself with the amounts written on them and ensure they showed she had paid less than at any of the other shops.

'That's settled, then,' declared Manu. He jabbed Monika in the ribs with his elbow making her gasp for breath. 'All we have to do now is arrange a final date for the ceremony. We don't want anything expensive afterwards. A few drinks at a taverna will be sufficient, after all, there's only your mother and grandmother along with my parents and some of my friends.'

'I'd like to invite Mrs Ethanides.'

'She's not family.'

'Nor are your friends, but she has been very good to me.'

Manu scowled and shrugged. 'If you insist.'

Monika relayed the news of the apartment to her mother and the arrangements for the cost.

'Will you be able to afford it? I can always give you a helping hand.'

Monika shook her head. 'I appreciate your offer, Mamma, but I would far rather you kept your savings and returned to live here with Grandma.'

'I suppose I could look for some work in one of the shops.'

Monika nodded eagerly. 'If I see an advert asking for staff I'll let you know.'

'Suppose they ask where I've worked before?'

'You tell them in Grandma's shop, but trade is bad so two of you are no longer needed every day. I doubt if they will make any enquiries and if they do I'm sure Grandma will confirm that you have worked here. Just do it, please, Mamma.' Monika looked at her mother hopefully. She would be so relieved if her mother left the street.

'If I don't find work what are we going to live on once I've used my savings? I won't be able to get my house back in the street. That Alecos is even worse than Lakkis as a landlord. He puts the rent up every year. He'll soon find someone to take my place.'

'I'll leave my savings here with you. You can use those if necessary.'

'I wouldn't want to take your hard earned money.'

'I accepted yours for years. It would be my turn to help you,'

'What would Manu say? He would expect you to use it to help with the expenses at the apartment.'

Monika shook her head. 'He doesn't have to know. He's never asked if I had any savings and I've never told him. He assumes that my earnings from the taverna last year were spent on my University course.'

Litsa looked at her daughter doubtfully. 'Married people should not have secrets.'

'We already have a secret. I've never told him about your profession. He still thinks you work in a bar at night. What he does not know does not hurt him.'

Monika invited Mrs Ethanides to their wedding reception, explaining that it was just for a few celebratory drinks at a local taverna, and added that her husband was welcome to accompany her.

'Why did you ask him?' queried Manu. 'I'm not made of money.'

'It's only one more person and it was a matter of courtesy. You would expect to come with me if I was invited to a wedding.'

'Well I hope he's not a heavy drinker.'

'If I gave you some money maybe we could ask them to provide a few snacks?'

'Where are you going to get the money from? You said you had spent your last month's wages on bedding and towels. It's a good job my parents were able to help me with the initial deposit on the apartment.'

'I'm very grateful to them,' Monika answered humbly.

She was still loath to open a bank account, feeling that her money was safer in the old shoe box she had hidden beneath her mother's bed. If she had a bank book, however carefully she hid it, Manu was sure to discover it and demand that she contributed more to their expenses.

Three months into their marriage Monika found she had little left from her salary each month after paying her share of the rent and completing the food shopping. Manu had asked her twice to give him some money to help pay a utility bill. He made her feel guilty when she had to refuse him, showing him only a few coins, as she had bought herself a new pair of shoes.

'Why didn't you go to the cheap shop and buy a pair from there?'

'By the time I had spent the bus fare to get there and back they would have cost the same and not been of such good quality. These will last.'

'I certainly hope so. We don't have money to throw away on frippery.'

'They were essential and I bought them from my salary. You know I've not had anything new since we were married.'

'You don't need anything. You work in the library. Hardly anyone sees you. When the laundry has finished ruining my uniform shirts I need new ones as I am on view to the public and have a duty to look smart.'

'I'm not complaining, Manu.'

'I should hope not. I have provided you with a home. What more do you expect of me?' He pinched her upper arm, making her squeal and squirm away from him.

'That hurt, Manu.'

'Don't be silly. It s what is called a "love nip."'

Monika rubbed her arm. 'I'll have a bruise in the morning.'

'Then you must bruise very easily.'

Monika turned away. The first few months of their marriage had been idyllic, but she was seeing a different side of Manu now. He was rough with her and if she protested he insisted she was making a fuss. He continued to go to the gym three evenings each week and she excused him by telling herself that he was a strong man who did not know his own strength. Manu had never disclosed his wages to her, but she knew they would be considerably more than she was earning, yet he always claimed he was short of money. She knew the amount they were paying for their apartment and also the utility bills when they came in. Manu was earning enough to cover them and also to put money aside all the time she paid half of the rent and bought their food.

'Have you any savings, Manu?'

'Why? What do you want now?' asked Manu warily. He was not going to disclose that despite earning twice as much as Monika a good deal of it was used to purchase alcohol.

'Nothing. I have been told that now the Euro is in full circulation the drachmas will be gradually withdrawn. Anyone who has savings in drachmas that are not in a bank account should change them over or they will eventually lose them.'

'Savings! How am I likely to have any savings when I have a wife that spends money on new shoes whenever she feels like it?'

'I needed them, Manu.'

'Needed! Needed! I need my supper so where is it? Not on the table as it should be.'

'Five minutes,' Monika promised and took down a tin of tomato and olive paste from the cupboard.

'What's that?' Manu took the tin from her hand. 'No wonder we have no money if you buy readymade rubbish in tins.' He threw it at Monika hitting her in the eye.

For a moment Monika looked at him in surprise; then collapsed in a sobbing heap on the ground. Manu immediately knelt down beside her.

'Stop making a fuss. You're not really hurt.'

Monika looked up at her husband. There was a red mist before her eye and she tried to blink it away. 'I can't see properly and it hurts.'

Manu placed his arms around her. Now he was so close to her Monika could smell the alcohol on his breath. 'Have you been drinking, Manu?'

'I had a few beers with one of the boys, celebrating his name day, nothing more. Here let me help you up. Come and sit down for a while. I can wait for my supper for once.'

Monika sat on the kitchen chair with her head in her hands. Her grandmother had slapped her leg on occasions when she was a child, but no one had ever thrown anything at her. Was Manu drunk? Had he had more than a few beers with his colleagues?

After a few minutes Monika rose unsteadily to her feet. 'I'd like to go and lie down for a short while.'

'Of course. You'll soon feel better after you've had a rest.'

Monika lay on the bed. Her head and eye throbbed until she felt she could not bear it any longer. She went into their small bathroom and wadded up some tissue that she ran beneath the cold tap. A compress would help with the pain and bring out the bruising. She looked at her face in the mirror and was horrified. There was a small cut just below her eyebrow, but her eye was completely bloodshot and the surrounding area already turning black.

'Feeling better now?' asked Manu from the doorway. 'I'm still waiting for my supper, remember. I need to get to the gym.'

Monika turned to face him. 'How could you? Look what you've done to me.'

'That tin certainly hit you hard when it fell from the cupboard.'

'It didn't fall, Manu, you threw it at me.'

'Don't be silly. I saw it fall. I tried to stop it; then it hit you.'

Monika stood there speechless. Did he genuinely think the tin had fallen from the cupboard? She was sure he had thrown it at her, but she dared not challenge him. He might decide to throw another at her.

'I'll finish getting our supper,' she said quietly.

Mrs Ethanides raised her eyebrows when Monika arrived for work the following day. 'My goodness, what happened to you?'

'A tin fell from the cupboard in the kitchen.'

'Have you visited the medical centre?'

'There's no need,' Monika assured her. 'It looks worse than it is.' She was not going to admit that she still had a throbbing headache and felt nauseous.

'You certainly need to go and get it checked before I allow you to work on the computer. Maybe you should take the whole day off.'

Monika shook her head. 'I'm sure I will be able to return to work.'

Monika was pleased when the day finished. Her eye had been thoroughly examined and the oculist had assured her there was no permanent damage. She did not offer to stay on and replace books on the shelves when she had completed her computer work, excusing herself by saying that she had developed a headache. She was longing to see her mother, yet she knew she could not confide in her. If Litsa thought Manu had laid a finger on her daughter in anger she would very quickly have a word with Alecos. Being a policeman would not prevent Alecos's thugs from giving him a severe beating.

Litsa looked at her daughter suspiciously. 'A tin? Fell from the cupboard? A tin has fallen off a shelf in the shop onto me before now and never done so much damage.'

'It obviously hit me just wrong. I was looking up at the time.'

'You should have been standing on something so you could reach it properly,' chided Litsa. 'Did you go and have your eye checked to makes sure there isn't any permanent damage.'

'I did, Mamma. They want to see me again next week when the bruising has gone down, but they're confident there is no real damage to my eye. It's just painful at the moment.'

'You could speak to Manu's father. He could probably give you something to help soothe it.'

'I really don't need to bother him. Have you looked around anywhere for some work?'

'I haven't seen anyone advertising for help in the Old Town.'

'Have you been into any shops and asked?'

'Not yet. I'll have a look in the New Agora tomorrow.'

Monika sighed. Her mother was unlikely to find work in either of those places. The New Town offered far more opportunity.

Manu was more solicitous towards Monika and as the bruising around her eye faded she began to relax and believe his version of her injury. She was delighted when he returned home and she could announce that having completed her library probation she was now permanently employed.

'That's really good news. Cause for a celebration. I knew you were getting the result today so I bought a bottle of wine so we could celebrate.'

'How very thoughtful. Thank you, Manu.'

'Will it mean your salary is increased?'

'Yes, thank goodness. I won't earn anywhere near as much as Mrs Ethanides. She's been there so long that she is on the top of the scale, but at least I will receive a decent wage and it will be increased each year.'

'We'll be able to afford a few more bottles of wine, then,' smiled Manu as he filled Monika's glass.

'I'd rather spend the money on something else.'

Manu raised his eyebrows. 'What's that?'

'Some driving lessons.'

'Driving lessons?'

Monika nodded eagerly. 'I've wanted to learn for ages. Mrs Ethanides suggested you might be able to help me.'

'Don't be stupid. I can't let you drive a police car.'

'I wouldn't expect that. Mrs Ethanides said if you hired one we could drive somewhere quiet and you could show me the gears and explain the road signs.'

'Mrs Ethanides is an interfering old woman. She needs to keep her nose out of our affairs.' Manu raised his voice angrily.

'I would pay for them myself, from my salary increase,' offered Monika hopefully.

'I don't know why you need to know how to drive anyway. We live close enough to the library for you to walk in to work. The next thing is you'll be bothering me for is a car of your own.'

'I wouldn't want to own one. I'd just like to be able to take my mother and grandmother out occasionally. They never have the opportunity to go for more than a bus ride.' Monika tried to placate him.

'My parents don't go out joy riding in their car. What's so special about your precious mother and grandmother? You call in on her every day after work and now you want to spend the weekends with her.'

'I only call in to shop there and I like to check that she and my grandmother are alright. They have no one else to care for them.'

'Whose fault is that? Your mother should have found herself a new husband by now.'

Monika ignored the jibe. 'It's on my way home.'

'So are my parents, but you don't call in on them every day.'

'You call on them regularly.'

'That's a son's duty.'

'And I have a duty to call on my mother.'

Manu replaced the cap on the bottle of wine. 'If you are in such an argumentative mood we'll save this for another day. You'd better get the supper before you drink all of that glass.'

Monika rose to her feet. She should have known better than to argue with her husband. He had a stressful job, being a policeman. It was no wonder he often had little patience at the end of the day.

Having had an increase in her salary Manu demanded that Monika now contributed regularly towards the utility bills.

'I thought we might be able to start saving some money,' she suggested tentatively.

'If you're still thinking about those driving lessons you can forget it.'

'I just thought it could be a good idea to have some money put aside for emergencies.'

'What kind of emergency?'

Monika shrugged. 'I don't know. I just thought we ought to try to have some savings. Suppose our tenancy was not renewed and we had to move somewhere else? That could be expensive.'

'So you want to move to a larger apartment? This one is quite sufficient for our needs. When you think back to that pokey little place you used to live in this must seem like a palace to you. You're getting ideas above your station. Give me a beer.' He threw an empty can towards the kitchen door where it landed on the floor.

Monika picked it up and placed it in the rubbish bin to join the other two that were already in there. 'Haven't you had enough for one evening?'

'I'm the judge of when I've had enough to drink, not you. You're enough to drive a man to drink continually wanting things.'

Monika placed a fresh can on the low table in front of him, making sure she was far enough away from her husband so that he could not pinch her arm or jab her in the ribs. Manu frequently came home from work smelling of drink now and she wondered just how much money he was squandering on alcohol. He placed his feet up on the table and turned on the television, going from channel to channel and finally switching it off.

'There's nothing but rubbish on there. I'm thinking of joining a card school with some of the men from the gym. At least it will give me something to do in the evenings. You're no company. Your head is always stuck in a book.'

'I enjoy reading.'

'I would have thought you would have seen enough books each day without wanting to read all evening.'

'We could go out for a walk.'

'I've not spent my time sitting down at a computer. I've had a busy day on my feet. I want to relax now, not go out walking.' He drank some more from the can. 'I'm going to bed.'

Monika did not offer to join him. It could be a good idea if Manu joined a group and played cards some evenings. He did not seem to have any hobbies that he wished to pursue other than visiting the gymnasium. One evening each week they did go out together but it was always to a bar where he would meet up with his friends from the police force. She would be excluded from their conversation and feel isolated and bored, making a glass of wine last whilst the men continually ordered more beer and became louder. She sighed and picked up her book. Married life was not as she had envisaged.

To Monika's delight her mother had found some work in the New Town.

'It's only temporary, I think,' explained Litsa. 'I have a little machine that spits out labels with the Euro price. I have to stick them on all the tins and packets.'

'If you work hard they may ask you to stay on, or at least give you a good reference when you apply somewhere else.'

'It brings in enough to cover our expenses. Now you're fully qualified it's a weight off my mind. I'm sure Manu must be proud of you.'

Monika shrugged. 'The way he talks about me to his friends he makes it sound as if I run the library single handed.'

'I'm sure you could. When Mrs Ethanides retires you'll be bound to be given her job.'

'That's years away. She's hardly any older than you, Mamma.'

'But you're happy?'

Monika hesitated. 'I love my work. Mrs Ethanides has

suggested that I start to work towards another examination to gain even higher qualifications. If I pass them I will be entitled to have letters after my name.'

'I meant generally, happy with Manu as well as your work.'

'Most of the time we get along very well. We have our disagreements, of course, like any other married couple.' Monika could not tell her mother that now Manu was out most evenings playing cards and returning home the worse for drink that she was always fearful of saying the wrong thing, giving him an excuse to quarrel with her. On some occasions he had hit her hard in her chest or on the base of her spine where the bruising would not show, saying it was her fault he had become angry with her.

'You'll both have to come up for a meal one evening.'

Monika frowned. 'I'm not sure if Manu will be able to do that at the moment. Some evenings he arrives home quite late and wouldn't want to go out again.'

'Well at least you could join us.'

'I have to be at home when he arrives to give him a meal.'

'Why don't you leave something ready for him? Surely he could manage to feed himself one evening?'

'I don't think he would be very happy about that. Leave it for the time being, Mamma. When Manu manages to arrive home earlier we could think about it again then.' Monika knew her husband would not give up an evening with his companions to spend time with her family.

Manu was not happy when Monika told him she was studying for another library examination.

'So you're going to have your nose stuck in a book again the whole time and neglecting me.'

'Of course I won't neglect you. I can study in the evening whilst you're out. I thought you'd be pleased,' she said miserably.

'Just because you've been to University and can pass a few examinations you think you're more intelligent than me. You're not.' Manu spoke roughly to her and pushed her back against the wall. Monika cringed expecting a blow to land on her.

'Having been to University does not make me more intelligent than you. You've worked hard so you can progress and gain promotion.' Monika tried to placate her husband. 'I could not be in the police force and pass those examinations.'

'But you're happy to take examinations for your precious library. You need to remember you are my wife and should have asked my permission before you agreed to take on any extra work '

'I enjoy studying.'

'Well I don't!' Manu slammed the door back as he left the apartment trapping Monika's arm against the wall as she tried to stop the handle from making another dent in the plaster.

Monika held her arm against her side and took a shaky breath. No doubt that would be another bruise she thought ruefully as she closed the door to their apartment quietly.

By the time she undressed her arm was throbbing painfully and was turning black around her elbow. 'At least it's my left arm,' she thought as she looked at it. 'I can manage most things with my right.'

During the night the pain she had in her arm increased, continually waking her and she lay in the darkness gritting her teeth, trying hard not to disturb Manu.

'What's wrong?' he asked when he saw her struggling to get dressed.

'My arm hurts.'

'What have you done to it?'

'The door hit it when you left yesterday.'

'Stupid to stand close to a door when someone is going out. You should have moved out of the way. You never know how far it will swing back.'

Manu gave her his customary peck on her cheek as he left and Monika picked up their cups from the table. She turned on the tap to rinse them and realised she could not lift even an empty cup with her left hand. It must be more badly bruised than she had realised.

Mrs Ethanides looked at Monika in concern as she sat at the computer using only her right hand on the keyboard.

'What's wrong with your arm?'

'The door swung back on me.'

'Let me see.'

Monika pulled up her sleeve and Mrs Ethanides sucked in her breath. 'You can't work with an arm like that. You're to go to the medical centre immediately.'

'I'm sure there's no need. It's only bruised. It will be better by tomorrow.'

Mrs Ethanides shook her head. She touched Monika's arm gently and noticed how she flinched. 'I am insisting you go to the medical centre. I am going to phone them when they have had a chance to examine you and ask if you are fit for work.'

'I'd rather be here than sitting at home on my own.'

'You'll be welcome to come here and read, but I think it unlikely they'll say you can use the computer. Your arm is badly swollen and will need to be rested. Be sensible. Go to the medical centre otherwise I have no option but to send you home and report you as absent due to sickness. If I do that you'll need a certificate from the medical centre so you might just as well go there now.' Mrs Ethanides glared at Monika. 'Go along, girl. They will at least be able to give you something to ease the pain you are in.'

Reluctantly Monika picked up her handbag. If she went to the medical centre she would have to pay to be examined. 'I'm not sure if I have enough money with me.'

'Stop making excuses.' Mrs Ethanides opened her own purse and took out two one hundred Euro notes. 'That should be sufficient. You can pay me back later.'

Monika's eyes filled with tears. 'You're very good to me.'

'Nonsense. Off you go.'

It was four hours later that Monika left the medical centre, her arm encased in plaster and wearing a sling. On her way back to the library Monika called in at her grandmother's shop.

'It's nothing to worry about,' she smiled as her grandmother regarded her arm in horror. 'I just banged my elbow and I've chipped the bone. I don't suppose Mamma is at home?'

'She'll be at work for a few hours yet, sticking her little labels on. I hope no one will expect me to do that.'

'I'm sure Mamma would do it for you, Grandma,' smiled Monika. 'I'll just go through and collect something Mamma has left for me. I'll only be a minute.'

Monika knelt down and withdrew the shoe box from beneath her mother's bed, lifting the lid and peering inside at the notes that were stored in there. She counted out three hundred Euros and placed them in her purse, leaving a scrap of paper in their place - "Three hundred Euros taken by Monika for the medical centre".

'Come and collect this on your way home. You can't be expected to cook with your arm in a sling.' Monique wrapped a polythene bag around a dish holding a large helping of moussaka and placed it on the counter.

'Surely that's your supper, Grandma. I can't take that.'

'Of course you can. I can easily make something else. When you call in tomorrow and I'll have another dish ready for you that can just be heated up.'

Monika kissed her grandmother's cheek. 'Thank you. I was wondering how I would manage to cook.'

Mrs Ethanides raised her eyebrows. 'So it was more than a bruise?'

'I've chipped my elbow. It must have happened when my arm hit the wall.'

'I thought you said a door had slammed on you?'

'It did. I put my hand out to stop it banging into the wall, but it was too heavy. They're fire doors.' Monika fumbled in her purse. 'I have your money here. I called on my mother on the way back and she said to repay you immediately and thank you for your kindness to me.'

Monika did not explain that she would not dare to ask Manu for the money and nor could she take that amount home with her. He was sure to find it and want to know how she had obtained the sum when her wages were not due for another two days.

'Were you told to stay home from work?' asked Mrs Ethanides suspiciously as she replaced the notes into her purse.

Monika shook her head. 'I can work with one hand for a few days. It's nowhere near as painful now it's in plaster and I've taken some tablets.'

Mrs Ethanides shrugged. 'It's up to you, but don't stay to put books back on the shelf.'

'I'll leave when I've caught up with my work,' promised Monika.

Manu pointed to Monika's arm. 'Is that an excuse not to give me any supper tonight?' he asked.

'I have your supper ready.'

'So why are you wearing a sling?'

'My arm is in plaster. I've chipped my elbow.'

'No doubt you did that when you stood too close to the door. You know you should be careful. Those doors are heavy. They have to be to stop a fire spreading.' Manu removed his jacket and sat down at the table waiting for Monika to bring his meal over to him. 'And a beer,' he reminded her.

'I can only carry one thing at a time,' she said as she placed a can in front of him.

'I thought you said it was your elbow that was damaged, not your hand.'

'My elbow affects my hand. It's very painful.'

Manu pointed his fork at her. 'Does that mean you're going to disturb me all night long with moaning and groaning like you did last night?'

'I'm sorry. I tried not to disturb you.'

'You'd better sleep out here on the sofa tonight. I need a good night's rest after being kept awake half of last night.'

'Yes, Manu.' Monika was sure she had not disturbed him unduly the previous night but she certainly did not have the energy to argue with him. She would bring a blanket and pillow out from the bedroom as soon as she had washed their dishes and be happy to lie down on the sofa and sleep.

For some weeks after the plaster cast was removed from Monika's arm it still felt sore and was tender when she touched it. She tried to disguise her discomfort from Manu but when he gripped it firmly she could not avoid crying out in pain.

'What are you making a fuss about?' asked Manu. 'I only held your arm.'

'The doctor said it would take some considerable time before it stopped hurting completely. It's bruised internally.'

'You're making a fuss about nothing as usual. It couldn't have been as bad as you made out. You managed to prepare an adequate meal each night.'

'My grandmother did the preparation. I just cooked it.'

'You're a lazy slut.'

Monika looked at Manu in disbelief. 'Lazy? I go out to work and when I return I cook and clean the apartment. I don't think I should be called lazy.'

'Are you saying I don't work hard?' Manu's face darkened.

'I know you work extremely hard and I don't expect you to help me in the house.'

'I should hope not. That's a woman's work.' Manu looked around their living room. 'If you took your nose out of those books for a while you could take the curtains down and take them to the laundry. They're dusty.'

'They're too heavy for me to manage on my own. If you helped me get them down I could take one at a time into the laundry.'

113

'I've no time to do that. Once I've had my meal I'm going to the gym and meeting my friends.'

Monika said no more. She knew the curtains that ran from floor to ceiling were too heavy for her to remove without help. She would give them a good brushing tomorrow when she returned from work to get rid of any dust and hope Manu did not mention them again. She sighed. His moods were so unpredictable. Most of the time he was affable and appeared considerate and loving towards her, then he would return home and find fault with her and every word she said, usually culminating in him hurting her in some way and leaving the apartment to go drinking with his friends in the force.

At first, when she realised that he was in one of his "moods", as she called them, she had stayed silent and accepted whatever criticism he had made of her. He would then accuse her of sulking and hit her anyway. She was relieved that the bruising rarely showed and she did not have to make excuses to her mother or Mrs Ethanides.

Monika would have liked to ask Mrs Ethanides if her husband ever treated her roughly, but felt it would be disloyal to Manu to imply that sometimes he had hurt her deliberately. He always made it clear that she had been the cause of his angry outburst. Had it not been for those occurrences she was sure she would be completely happy with him as she had been during the first few months of their marriage; instead she awaited his return from work each day with trepidation.

Rhodes 2004 - 2005

Monika had worked out a reading routine. She would borrow two books written in English and when she had read those she would take home two books written in German. That way she felt she would be able to remain conversant with both languages and it was gratifying to her to be able to understand the snatches of conversation she overheard when tourists thronged the streets in the summer months. Just occasionally a tourist would visit the library and Mrs Ethanides would call Monika over.

'He's German,' she would say in an undertone. 'Can you deal with him, please?'

Monika was only too delighted to speak to the visitor in his own language, but the first time she had mentioned this to Manu she decided she had made a mistake. Manu had glared at her.

'So if you can have a conversation with a foreigner why can't you have a decent conversation with me in the evening?' Manu seized the fleshy part of her arm above her elbow and pinched her hard.

'I try, Manu, but you're not really interested in my library work and you're not allowed to discuss police business.'

'If I did you wouldn't understand what I was talking about.'

'I'm sure I wouldn't.'

'It's time you had something else to occupy your mind,' he said, pinching her arm a second time.

'I'm not eligible to take another library examination for two years.'

'I'm not talking about the library and your precious examinations.' Manu's voice had risen and Monika steeled herself for a physical onslaught. 'It's time we had a child or my parents will think there is something wrong with our marriage.'

Monika frowned. There was something wrong with their marriage due to the unpredictability of Manu's moods which could change within minutes from being pleasant and affectionate to impatient and sometimes violent.

'I'm not sure I'm ready to be a mother yet.'

'Why not? I should have ensured you were pregnant as soon as we were married. That would have knocked all that stupid library stuff out of your head.'

'We couldn't afford to have a child when we were first married,' Monika reminded him.

'We're in a more secure financial position now.'

'That's due to you being promoted to an Inspector.' Monika knew that was the answer that Manu would want. Despite his salary increase that had come with the promotion she was still expected to buy all their food and contribute to the rent and utility bills, adding extra whenever he declared he was short of money.

'We should think about it carefully. It would mean I had to give up work if we started a family.'

'Not for long. Once the child was a few months old my mother would look after him. Give her something to do each day.'

Inwardly Monika recoiled in horror. If she had a child she would want to be the person spending her time looking after him. Although her grandmother had looked after her well when she was young her mother had always spent each afternoon taking her out or playing with her.

'Give me a little while to get used to the idea.'

'Why do you need time?' This time he pinched her thigh. 'It's natural for women to have children.'

'Of course,' agreed Monika. 'You've just taken me by surprise. I hadn't thought of starting a family yet.'

'Well you should have done. In fact we'll start thinking about it right now.' Manu pulled Monika to her feet. 'I'm ready to do far more than think about it.'

Monika lay docilely in Manu's arms, her body aching after his vigorous and prolonged attack. Manu smiled complacently.

'That should certainly have done the trick How long before you'll know for certain?'

'About three weeks.'

'Get one of those test kits from the chemist. We'll keep trying until it shows positive.'

'I'm not sure how quickly you can get a result. I may have to wait a week or so. I'll ask your father tomorrow.'

'No you won't,' Manu rounded on her angrily. 'You go to a chemist where you're not known. If you go to my father he'll be asking me the result every day.'

Monika determined that she would get a kit the following day, but she would also ask her mother if there were any precautions she could take to delay the inevitable until she became more enthusiastic about the idea of becoming a mother.

Litsa was sympathetic. 'If you don't feel ready Manu should not insist. You have plenty of time; you're only in your early twenties.'

Monika bit her lip. 'I thought you might know of some way that would stop me from becoming pregnant, without Manu knowing, of course.'

'I used to get a pill from the clinic every five months. Why don't you go and ask if you can have a supply?'

Monika shook her head. 'Manu might find out and he would be furious. He seems set on having a baby now the thought has entered his mind.'

'I can give you the ones I have left. I certainly don't need them now,' smiled Litsa.

'How often do I have to take them?' asked Monika anxiously.

'Only once a day. You could take it when you call in on your way home from the library.'

'What about at the weekends?'

'I could give you a couple to take home. I haven't that many left. They won't last you for more than three months.'

Monika sighed. 'Maybe Manu will have changed his mind during that time.'

Litsa looked after her daughter anxiously as she left. The girl had been married for over a year. Most young women in that position would have been overjoyed to think they were finally able to start a family.

Each month Monika was relieved when she could tell Manu that she was not pregnant.

'What's wrong with you?' he asked.

'Maybe we have been trying too hard,' suggested Monika tentatively.

'Rubbish. The more we try the more success we are likely to have. Make an appointment at the clinic for an examination. You may have an obstruction that needs to be removed.'

'That could be expensive. An examination without any treatment would be fifty Euros.'

'Well you get paid at the end of the week. Make an appointment for next Monday or Tuesday.'

'Yes, Manu.' Monika thought it would be a waste of money going to the clinic. She had taken the last of the tablets her mother had given her and now she had no choice but to submit to Manu's advances and await the result.

According to the pregnancy testing kit Monika was pregnant. She felt nervous about telling Manu, sure he would be delighted, but she also felt he should wait a little longer before celebrating.

'These kits have been known to make a mistake,' she warned

him. 'It's very early days and anything can go wrong. Please don't go telling all your friends until we are really positive.'

He took her in his arms. 'You see, that examination at the clinic was all you needed. You'll need to rest. When are you giving up work?'

'I won't need to give up until I'm at least seven months, maybe eight or even later. I don't need to do any heavy lifting. I'll be sitting at the computer most of the time.'

'Your time would be better spent at home making baby clothes.'

'I can knit some jackets in the evenings and I'm sure both our mothers will start to make clothes as soon as we tell them.'

Manu frowned. 'Well, I suppose whilst you work we at least have the money coming in to buy the essentials we'll need.'

Monika looked at him perplexed. 'You said we could afford to have a baby now.'

'That doesn't mean you can spend as you please on all sorts of nonsense.'

'We'll need a crib for when he's tiny and then a cot later on. I'll also need a pushchair when he's too heavy for me to carry around.'

'At least we can look on those items as an investment for the next one.'

'Manu, we haven't had this one yet,' smiled Monika. 'Give me a chance.'

'They tell me that after the first one the next is much easier to conceive. That should mean I won't have to work so hard.'

'I thought you had enjoyed working hard.'

'I hadn't expected it to take so long for you to become pregnant. The novelty began to wear off. At least I can go out straight after we've eaten tonight and not have to hang around to do my duty. I had to make all sorts of excuses for arriving late at the gym.'

Monika sighed. She had expected Manu to want to stay in and have a glass of wine with her to celebrate the news this evening. Obviously the gym took priority.

The pregnancy testing kit appeared correct and when she visited the clinic two months later her pregnancy was confirmed.

'Before you leave make sure you go to reception and book a date for a scan and also an appointment for your next visit.'

Monika nodded happily. Since becoming pregnant Manu had been more considerate towards her, although he was still confrontational about anything that displeased him. His moods when he had been out for the evening drinking were unpredictable but the only physical abuse she had suffered was being pushed roughly to one side or her arm being pinched or twisted. The only real problem she was having was a craving for apples and would eat three or four each day.

Mrs Ethanides was pleased for her. The girl looked happier than she had for some months; she had obviously been concerned that it was taking them so long to start a family. Manu's parents were delighted at the idea of becoming grandparents and Manu would sit beside her in their apartment stroking her enlarged stomach gently.

'He'll make such a good father,' his mother assured her and Monika nodded uncertainly. She hoped that once they had the baby Manu would stay home in the evenings and not return having had too much to drink.

Litsa and Monique were equally delighted. 'You don't realise just how precious a baby is until you hold her in your arms for the first time,' remarked her grandmother.

Monika laughed. 'You talk about the baby as "she" and Manu and his parents always say "he". You can't both be right.'

'I expect Manu is hoping for a boy; most men like to have a boy first. Once the baby is born he won't mind whether it is a boy or a girl. Just be careful as you get larger. Your balance will not be as good and you must certainly not carry heavy shopping. Are you resting each day?'

'I can usually lie down for half an hour once I've prepared our meal. I'm going to bed early and most of the time I get a good night's sleep.'

'Make the most of it. You'll be up half the night feeding at first.'

'I can always catch up during the day as I won't be working for a few months.'

Once Monika had accepted that she was pregnant she began to look forward to being a mother. She was still not happy at the thought of relinquishing her child to the care of Manu's mother each day, but it was no different for her than for many other mothers. Going out to work for most women had become essential as prices had risen far more quickly than wages.

Walking from their apartment in the New Town to where the library was situated in the Old Town was becoming tiring as she grew larger. Whichever route she took she had to climb a hill. She was loath to take a short cut through the grounds of the Music School as Manu had warned her that some unsavoury characters often hung around in the grounds waiting to buy drugs and she did not want to be accosted by them.

Returning each evening was easier as she knew a route that was almost flat that brought her to the end of the road where her mother had once worked. It was only a short distance from there to her grandmother's shop where she could sit down and rest before walking along to the main gate and tackling the short, steep hill before she turned down and was able to walk on level ground again.

As soon as she reached home she would climb the steps to their front door and kick off her shoes in relief before preparing an evening meal. That particular evening she was feeling particularly tired and uncomfortable. She had been warned by her gynaecologist that when the baby turned she could well feel discomfort for some hours and that it could happen on a number of occasions before the child settled into the optimum birth position.

Monika sat down on the sofa. She would have a few minutes rest before she began the supper preparations. The next she knew

Manu was opening the front door and she struggled to get to her feet.

'What's wrong with you?' he asked roughly.

'I'm sorry. I must have fallen asleep.'

'Is supper ready?'

Monika shook her head. 'I wasn't feeling well when I reached home. I had to sit down for a while. I'll get it immediately.'

'You're always full of excuses.' He slapped her face hard leaving the imprint of his fingers.

'Manu, the baby, mind the baby,' said Monika frantically, expecting a blow to her chest or stomach to follow.

'That's your excuse now, is it? The baby. I've told you before, you're lazy. You spend all day sitting down and then expect to sit down when you get home and don't bother about preparing a meal for your husband.'

'I am sorry, Manu. It won't happen again.'

'I should hope not. I'll expect my meal to be on the table by the time I've showered and changed.'

Monika walked unsteadily into the kitchen. There was no time to check her face and place a cold compress on it to bring out the bruising.

'What's wrong with your face,' asked Manu as she placed a dish in front of him.

'You hit me, Manu.'

'Rubbish. You must have walked into the cupboard door. You were half asleep when I arrived home.'

Monika did not argue. She sat as close to the table as she could to avoid spilling any food onto her blouse. Her mother had made her three loose tops that she could wear, one was waiting to be washed and she did not want to add another.

They ate their meal in silence. Finally Manu pushed his chair away, pushing the table towards Monika as he did so and it hit her arm as she was raising her fork to her mouth, spilling the contents down her blouse.

'Not only are you lazy, you're becoming dirty as well. You'll need to wash that blouse before you wear it again and when you've done that I have a shirt that needs to be ironed.'

'Yes, Manu.' Monika sighed wearily. Manu had plenty of clean shirts hanging in the wardrobe, but now she would have to wash out both her blouses and iron his shirt before she could think about going to bed or even sitting down again for a rest.

As she rubbed at the marks on her blouse she could feel her face throbbing. Once again Manu had said she had caused the injury herself through carelessness. She knew that was not true and a worrying thought occurred to her – would he chastise their child violently? Had he been chastised so severely by his parents that he thought such violence was acceptable and normal? If that was the case Monika certainly did not want them looking after their child.

Manu's finger marks were still visible on her face when she arose the next morning and she hoped that once she went outside into the fresh air they would fade rapidly. A bruise she could excuse away, but finger marks could only have been inflicted by a hand.

Mrs Ethanides spotted them immediately. 'What has happened to your face?'

Monika tried to smile. 'I fell asleep on the sofa and my hand was against my face. It left the imprint of my fingers.'

Mrs Ethanides raised her eyebrows. She did not believe that falling asleep on your hand would leave finger marks that showed the following day.

Reluctantly Monika walked up towards her grandmother's shop. The finger marks still showed and she knew both her mother and grandmother would want to know how she had come by them. As she reached her short cut through the street where her mother had worked she could see the girls were huddled together, talking avidly and casting wary glances around them.

'What's wrong?' she asked of Nadia.

'We've had the police up here all day. They've been talking to Suzi, but wanted to know if we had seen or heard anything. That Joseph who lived with her was found dead this morning.'

'Oh, how awful.' Monika disliked the man intensely. He had never spoken to her when he had lived in the warehouse at the end of the road. Now he was crippled he spent most of the day sitting in the small courtyard of the house where he lived and Suzi looked after him. If she used the street as a short cut he would shout after her and she was frightened that one day he would leave his wheelchair and catch her. 'Poor Suzi. Fancy waking up and finding him dead.'

'It wasn't like that,' Nadia looked over her shoulder. 'He was found strapped into his wheelchair at the bottom of the Street of the Knights.'

'Why would Suzi take him up there? If he wanted to go to the bottom of the Street she would take him down through the Jewish quarter. It would be far easier than pushing him up the hill.'

'Suzi says she didn't take him there. She took him down to the "The Grapevine" and then went to meet someone. When she returned Joseph was still out and she expected Alecos to push him back home when "The Grapevine" closed as usual. She said she had no idea he wasn't at home in bed until the police came knocking on her door. Woke us all up at some unearthly hour and have been a perfect nuisance to us all day.' Nadia yawned. 'I don't know how I'll manage to work tonight without having had a decent sleep.'

'They took Suzi off to the police station. First she had to go and identify Joseph. That can't have been very nice for her,' added Natasha.

'They've been talking to everyone in the area,' continued Nadia. 'They wanted the names of any customers who came last night. As if we ask for their names! We're only interested in their money.'

'I'm on my way to visit my grandmother. I hope the police treated her gently if they questioned her.'

'They seemed polite enough when they questioned your mother.'

'My mother?'

'She came up to see what the commotion was about. One of the policemen wanted to know if she worked up here, but we told him she gave up a few years ago. Maybe he took a fancy to her and wanted to visit.' Natasha laughed. 'It takes all sorts.'

'Come back and tell us if she knows anything that we don't,' urged Nadia.

Monika returned home full of foreboding. Litsa had told her that she had gone up to the street and was talking to the girls when a policeman had asked to have a few words with her. She had told him that she lived at the shop nearby and confirmed that she had heard nothing untoward the previous evening. Having written down the details of her name and address she had seen him approach an Inspector and realised he was relaying her information to Manu.

'What did you do, Mamma?' asked Monika her eyes wide with fear. She wished she knew exactly what the policeman had told Manu.

'I came back and told your grandmother and then I went off to work. I'm allowed to serve now if we're busy, but the owner is the only one who deals with the money. It's a bad business. I didn't like either Suzi or Joseph but I certainly didn't wish them any harm.'

Monika prepared their meal, but was quite unable to relax. She sat in the corner of the sofa waiting for Manu to return from work. She heard him come running up the stairs and he flung the door wide open.

'You slut. You whore. You're the daughter of a prostitute. You lied to me.'

Monika was about to deny lying to him when she remembered that she had told him when they first met that her mother worked in a taverna.

'Manu, please, come in, let me explain.'

'Explain! What is there to explain? Your mother was a prostitute. You're no better than a prostitute's bastard. You don't know who your father is and nor does your mother.'

'She does know, Manu.' Monika went towards him. 'I have your supper ready. 'Please come in and let us talk sensibly.'

'I'm not interested in any more lies from you. I'm going out.'

'We need to talk. I have to make you understand that I loved you and thought you would leave me if you knew the truth about my mother. I am sorry, Manu.' Monika looked at him imploringly from the doorway.

'Sorry! So you should be. I'll make you sorry. You're not fit to be the mother of my child. I'd be within my rights to throw you out.' He grabbed a handful of her hair and threw her with as much force as he could muster towards the wall in the hallway.

Monika screamed as her back hit the end of the hand rail; she stumbled forwards, lost her footing and fell down the stone stairs.

The door of the apartment below them opened and the owner looked out. 'What's going on now? You two are always making a racket.'

Manu immediately rushed down the flight of steps and dropped to his knees beside Monika's crumpled body. 'My wife. Call an ambulance please. She's fallen down the stairs.'

Manu accompanied Monika to the hospital in the ambulance, urging them to hurry, although the lights were flashing and the siren screaming clearing the traffic from their path.

'She fell down the stairs,' he kept repeating. 'Will she be alright?'

The paramedics did their best to calm him, assuring him that his wife would receive the best of treatment once they arrived.

Manu gave Monika's details at reception whilst she was rushed to the operating theatre.

The receptionist smiled at him sympathetically. 'I understand how you must be feeling. I suggest you go home, try to get some sleep and return tomorrow. Your wife will be in the operating theatre for some considerable time and will then need to recover from the anaesthetic. Maybe you could advise her mother of the situation and she could come and help you look after her?'

Manu realised he would have to tell Litsa that her daughter had been injured. It would certainly be necessary for her to look after Monika whilst she was in hospital. He was not prepared to take time off work. The enquiry he was involved with looked like becoming a murder investigation, not an accident. It was the first time he had been involved in such a major incident and he was not prepared to miss contributing to the proceedings.

Litsa was shocked when Manu told her that Monika had fallen down the stone stairs leading to their apartment.

'Is she alright? What about the baby?'

'I don't know. They had just taken her to the operating theatre when I left to come here.'

Litsa picked up her cardigan and handbag. 'There's bound to be a taxi by the main gate. It will be quicker than going up by bus.'

'They told me she will be in the operating theatre for hours. There's no point in rushing back up there now.'

'I need to be with my daughter,' replied Litsa firmly.

'I'm not sure if I have enough change on me for a taxi. I just left the apartment with the ambulance. I wasn't thinking of anything except Monika.'

'How did you get here from the hospital?' asked Litsa.

'I walked until I saw a police car and asked them for a ride.' Manu did not mention that he had stopped in the first taverna he had reached and fortified himself with a double whisky before using the telephone outside to call a friend who was on duty nearby and asking for a lift.

'How did it happen?' asked Litsa,

'She was going to the corner shop for some apples. She's been eating them the whole time she's been pregnant and said she only had one left. I offered to go for her, but she said she would only be

127

a few minutes and I should come in to get washed and changed. She seemed to trip on the top step. She's one of those naturally clumsy people, always bumping into things and bruising herself.'

Litsa frowned. She had never considered Monika to be unduly clumsy.

Monika lay with her eyes closed. Her whole body ached and her face was throbbing. Was this what it was like to give birth? Slowly she moved her hand down to her stomach – it was flat and covered in a bandage. Where was her baby? She wanted to cry out and ask the nurse, but she could not form the words properly.

Manu's voice seemed to come to her from a distance. 'Well, you gave everyone a fright. I thought you might have broken your neck when I saw you lying at the bottom of the stairs. The doctor says you must rest. Get plenty of sleep. Your mother is going to stay with you.'

Monika did not answer. Maybe she was asleep and when she awoke she would find she had had a nightmare.

Manu turned to Litsa. 'I'll leave you with her. She's obviously still recovering from the anaesthetic. There's no point in us both sitting here looking at her. I'll call in later when I finish work.'

Litsa looked at Manu in surprise. She would have expected her son-in-law to want to stay with his wife until she became fully conscious and comfort her.

Litsa held her daughter's limp hand. She wished a doctor or nurse would appear and she could ask about the extent of her daughter's injuries. She seemed to have been sitting there for hours before Monika opened her eyes and blinked.

'Mamma.'

'Don't try to talk. You've had an accident and you are in hospital. I'm going to stay with you. Get some rest. I'll still be here when you wake up.'

Monika closed her eyes then opened them again. 'My baby?'

'Nothing to worry about at the moment.' Litsa hoped she was

speaking truly and the child had not suffered due to Monika's accident.

Monika could hear an unknown voice speaking to her gently. 'Monika, Monika, open your eyes.'

Slowly she blinked and tried to focus on the face in front of her. 'That's better. I'll come and talk to you properly in an hour or so when you're fully awake. You're mother's here beside you.'

Monika tried to turn her head to check on her mother's presence and groaned.

'Just lie still. Your mother will give you a wash and that will make you feel considerably better.' The doctor patted her hand gently and began to walk away.

'Doctor,' Litsa hurried after him. 'Can I speak to you for a moment? What's happened to my daughter?'

'She had a fall down the stone stairs outside her apartment. Fortunately her husband was there at the time and called for an ambulance immediately. She bruised her spine very badly and we have placed a collar on her to prevent her from moving and causing any further damage. She has broken her left leg and wrist, along with dislocating her shoulder on that side. She has multiple lacerations and bruises to her arms and legs. Some of the bruises look quite old.' The doctor raised his eyebrows quizzically. 'Has she suffered any other falls recently?'

Litsa was not concerned about bruises. 'The baby?'

The doctor shook his head. 'I'm sorry. We gave her a Caesarean, but we were unable to save the child. It had been too badly injured due to her fall.'

Litsa's lip trembled. 'Does she know?'

'Not yet. I'll explain to her when I return.'

Monika listened to the doctor in silence and a tear crept down her cheek. 'My husband – does he know?'

'I'll speak to him when he comes in to see you. I'm sure he will be as distressed as you. Once you have fully recovered from your injuries there's no reason why you should not have another.'

'What's wrong with me? Why do I hurt so much?'

'You can't expect to bounce down a flight of steps without becoming severely bruised. I'll ask the nurse to give you something so you will be more comfortable.'

'I can't move my head.'

'We have placed a collar around your neck as a safety precaution. Once movement is not so uncomfortable for you we'll take you back down to X-ray and check your spinal column and give you another brain scan. Provided there's no actual damage we'll remove the collar.'

'Brain scan?' asked Monika.

'You were unconscious when you were brought in. It's normal practice when a patient has suffered concussion.'

'Thank you,' whispered Monika and closed her eyes again.

'Do you remember how your accident happened?'

'Not really. I just remember falling.' Monika knew exactly how she had ended up falling down the steps, but blaming Manu would not help her recovery.

Manu arrived at the hospital still wearing his uniform and Litsa walked out of the room to leave them together. 'Are you feeling better?' he asked abruptly.

'A little.'

'Soon be up and about again, then?'

'I'm sorry about the baby,' whispered Monika.

'My parents are most upset. They had been looking forward to a grandchild. You should have been more careful.'

'Yes, Manu.' Monika did not have the strength to remind him that he had thrown her into the wall causing her to lose her balance. She closed her eyes again.

'Well, if you're going back to sleep there's no point in me being here with you. I'm staying with my parents and my mother will be expecting me home in time for a meal. She understands the shock I'm in and realises I could not possibly cope on my own at the moment. She said they would come in and see you if you are still here next week.'

'Thank you, Manu,' murmured Monika without opening her eyes. She did not want her husband keeping her company. She wanted to lie and think.

Monika's neck collar was removed at the end of the week after further X-rays showed that no bones in her spine were chipped or broken.

The doctor held her hand. 'I sympathise with you over the loss of your child, but you really have been very fortunate. You could easily have ended up paralysed from such a nasty fall. We'll allow you to sit up tomorrow for a short while and by next week you should be able to get out of bed. I've arranged for someone to come and talk to you. They're very experienced with bereavement and will be able to help you to overcome the trauma.'

Monika smiled shakily. 'Once I can get up and see to myself again it will be a relief. My mother has been so good to stay and look after me each day.'

'She wouldn't entertain the idea of leaving you.'

'What about her work? I hope she hasn't lost her job.'

'I'm sure that's the last thing on her mind at the moment. Don't you worry about anything, just concentrate on recovering.' The doctor gave her hand a final pat and left to visit his next patient.

Litsa regarded her daughter anxiously. 'What did the doctor say?'

'Never mind me for a moment. How is Grandma and are you still working at the shop? I seem to have lost track of the days since I have been in here.'

'Your grandmother is fine and we'll both be visiting you on Sunday afternoon. I still have my job. They have been very understanding. As soon as Manu arrives to spend the evening with you I leave and go along and replenish the stock and change any labels as necessary before coming back here to be with you overnight.'

'Oh, Mamma, I don't like to think of you having to work in the evening so you can be with me.'

'It's only right that I spend my time with you. Manu cannot be here during the day and overnight. He has to work and needs his sleep.'

Monika nearly said that Manu did not spend the evening with her and stopped herself in time. If her mother knew that she was alone for some hours each evening she would very likely tell the shop owner that she was unable to go in to work at all.

Manu arrived for his usual brief evening visit. He was furious. The murder investigation had been taken out of the hands of the local police and handed over to detectives from Athens. He had heard some wild story about a boy taking a video of the incident. He eyed Monika dispassionately.

'You're sitting up I see.'

'Yes, fortunately my spine was not damaged, just bruised. I've been told I can get up next week. Could you bring me in some clothes, please?'

'I suppose so. I'll ask my mother to sort some things out for you. She can bring them in and visit you at the same time.'

'Thank you. That will be kind of her. Just some underwear and a blouse and skirt.'

'You can apologise to her at the same time for causing so much trouble. It's not easy for her to have me living back at home again, having to cook and look after me.'

'I didn't mean to cause any trouble, Manu.'

'You're always full of excuses for your behaviour. Just think how much this is costing me to have you lying here doing nothing. I'm off. I'm having a meeting with some of my men to discuss the latest developments in the case we've been working on.'

'Thank you for coming, Manu. Please remember to ask your mother about some clothes for me.'

Manu glared at Monika. 'I don't forget things.'

Manu's mother arrived three days later with some clothes for Monika in a carrier bag. 'I hope these will be suitable. Manu only told me at the last minute when he was leaving this morning.'

'I'm sure they'll be fine.' Monika had a suspicion that Manu had either forgotten or deliberately not passed on her request. 'I'm very grateful that you are looking after him whilst I'm in here.'

'He's no trouble. We hardly see him. Off to work each day and then he leaves as soon as he's eaten his meal to visit you all evening. He often returns quite late. He's so concerned about you. He says that when he saw you lying at the bottom of the stairs he thought you were dead.'

'He wished,' thought Monika bitterly.

'I had concussion. It's no wonder he thought I was dead.'

'Such a shame about the baby. Manu was looking forward so much to becoming a father,' Mrs Graphides sighed. 'Never mind, no point in dwelling on that. You'll just have to be more careful next time.'

Monika felt irritated. It was unfair that Manu and his mother should place the blame on her. Manu did not arrive at the hospital each evening smelling of drink, but Monika was sure that as soon as he left he was spending his evenings in the gym moving on to a bar to play cards with his friends, although telling his parents he had been visiting his wife until late.

'How much longer are you expecting to be kept in? Manu is beginning to be concerned about covering your expenses, what with the operation and everything.'

'I'm not sure. When they have assessed how well I am managing once I'm out of bed they'll probably be pleased to be rid of me. I'll only have to come back then to have the plaster removed from my leg and wrist.'

Mrs Graphides patted Monika's hand. 'You're a brave girl. When you first go home I'll ask Elias if I can cook a meal for you both each evening. You can either walk around to us or Manu can collect it. It would save you from having to go out shopping and spending time on your feet doing the preparation.'

'I'm sure I will appreciate that, at least for the first week.'

'You'll probably find you are more tired than you expected. At least you won't be going in to work.'

'Not at first,' replied Monika. There was nothing she wanted more than to be back amongst her beloved books.

'You give yourself plenty of time to recuperate,' ordered Mrs Graphides. 'There's no need to go rushing back. I'm sure they've managed perfectly well without you.'

'I expect so.'

Mrs Graphides rose. 'Well, I must be off. Elias is waiting outside in the car for me. He insisted on driving me here so I wouldn't have to carry this heavy bag on the bus.'

'Thank him for his trouble.'

'It was no trouble. Ask Manu if you need anything else and I'll bring it up to you.'

'Thank you. I'm sure whatever you have brought will be sufficient. My mother will do any necessary washing.'

'I should hope so!' She placed the bag in the locker beside Monika's bed. For a moment Mrs Graphides hesitated as if she was going to say something more, then she hurried from the ward.

Once Monika was allowed out of bed she realised just how weak she felt and after an hour asked her mother to call a nurse and help her lie down.

'I feel so stupid,' she complained to her mother. 'I kept thinking I should get dressed, but I don't have the energy.'

'It's not surprising,' Litsa consoled her. 'You had a very nasty accident, ended up concussed and with broken bones, then having an operation. You're probably still bruised internally.'

'I need to be able to get myself to the bathroom unaided, have a wash and get dressed. They'll not let me home until they know I can manage those simple chores.'

'I think you should come back and stay with us for a week or so when you're first discharged. It won't hurt Manu to rely on his mother for a bit longer.'

'I'll see what he says,' promised Monika. She expected her husband to agree to the proposal immediately and was surprised at his reaction.

'You will not,' stated Manu angrily. 'You are my wife and you will do your duty and look after me.'

'I thought you would be pleased to be rid of me.'

'I shall expect my meals ready for me each day. The only difference will be that you sleep on the sofa. I won't want you anywhere near me. It will be no good you going whining to your mother. If you hadn't lied to me about her being a prostitute this situation would never have arisen. I would not have married you.'

'We could have a divorce,' suggested Monika tentatively.

'Unfortunately I don't have any grounds to divorce you – yet.' Manu turned and left her room leaving Monika to ruminate on his veiled threat. What was he planning to do that would give him grounds for divorce?

October & November 2005

Monika lay there thinking about their marriage. At first it had seemed happy enough, although Manu had a bad habit of digging her in the ribs with his elbow or pinching her upper arm. However much she had remonstrated with him he persisted. She felt sure now that he had thrown the tin at her; it had not been an accident, any more than slamming the door back on her and chipping her elbow. The pinching of her arms and legs she had learned to endure in silence and he always made sure the marks he left would not be seen below the sleeve of her blouse or the hemline of her skirt.

Mrs Ethanides arrived with some books for Monika. 'I thought you might like these to keep you occupied.'

Monika smiled at her gratefully. 'I'll appreciate having something new to read. I've finished those you sent up with my mother. I just feel miserable if all I have to do is lie here and think.'

'You're no doubt grieving for your baby. That's natural. You'll find it easier when you are well enough to return to work. Work will give you something else to think about.'

Monika hesitated. 'Can I ask you something? It's rather personal.'

'Of course. I can always refuse to answer.'

'You and your husband are happily married?'

Mrs Ethanides nodded. 'We've had our difficult times, but no real problems.'

'Does he spend the evenings with you or go out to meet his friends?'

'Occasionally he goes out, but usually we spend our time together.'

Monika frowned. 'If he goes out with his friends and has a drink does he return in a bad temper?'

Mrs Ethanides smiled. 'I've never known him bad tempered. Cross sometimes, like when our son broke a window or a neighbour scraped the side of his car. Why are you asking, Monika?'

'He never hurts you?'

'Never. A man should always treat his wife gently and with respect. Has Manu hurt you?'

Monika nodded, her eyes filling with tears. 'I thought it was the way all men behaved towards their wives,' she said miserably.

Mrs Ethanides took Monika's hand. 'The bruises on your arms? I've seen them just above the level of your sleeves. I thought you'd carried the books awkwardly and caused them.'

'Those and others.'

'You don't have to put up with it, Monika. You should report him to the police before he really hurts you.'

Monika shook her head. 'I can't do that. They'd believe him rather than me. He always says I caused my injuries through carelessness.'

'Was he responsible for your arm?'

'My arm, my eye and the baby.'

Mrs Ethanides looked at Monika in horror. 'You mean he caused ....?'

'He was angry and threw me against the wall. I lost my balance and fell down the stairs, so it was my fault.'

'Monika, you cannot be expected to tolerate such treatment. You need to speak to someone. Does your mother know?'

'I couldn't tell her. She knows people who would hurt Manu and then it could be worse for me.'

Mrs Ethanides shook her head in despair. 'You should leave him, Monika.'

'Where would I go? He would soon find me in the Old or New town.'

'Then go to a different area; somewhere he cannot find you.'

'It would mean giving up my work in the library if I went away.'

'You could find some other work. I'll help you if I can. Give it some serious thought; discuss it with your mother, but I don't think you should return to live with Manu if that is the kind of treatment you receive from him.'

Monika looked at Mrs Ethanides doubtfully. 'I'll think about it.'

When Litsa arrived later to spent the night at the hospital tending to any needs her daughter might have Monika smiled at her brightly.

'Well, you look better. Did you tell Manu that you are coming to stay with us for a while?'

Monika nodded. 'He wouldn't hear of it.'

'I hope he won't expect you to do too much at first. He'll have to make allowances for you.'

Monika gave a short, bitter laugh. 'He'll not do that. I've been thinking, Mamma, and I'll need you to help me.'

'Of course.'

Monika smiled grimly. 'You don't know what I want yet. I'm pleased I lost the baby.'

'Monika! You don't know what you're saying. How can you be pleased?'

'Yes I do know. I could never have trusted Manu with a baby.'

'What do you mean?'

'He drinks too much and has violent, unpredictable moods. He caused me to fall down those steps.'

'Surely not.' Litsa frowned. 'You've had a bang on the head. You could be imagining things.'

'I'm not imagining anything, Mamma. Remember my eye, my arm and the marks on my face.'

Litsa nodded. 'Why didn't you tell me before?'

'I thought that was the way all men treated their wives. Mrs Ethanides visited me earlier today and I asked her if her husband ever hurt her.' Monika gave a deep sigh. 'Remember that crippled man who lived in the street and was found dead? A policeman asked for your details and passed them on to Manu. One of the girls told him you used to work up there.'

Litsa's hand flew to her mouth.

'He came home furious because I had lied to him and had told him you worked in a taverna. He didn't even shut the door of our apartment. I tried to reason with him and he grabbed hold of me and flung me against the outside wall. I just lost my balance and fell down the steps.'

'He must be blaming himself terribly now.'

Monika shook her head. 'No, he considers it was my fault. It was always my fault when he ended up hurting me. He threw that tin at me; it didn't fall when I opened the cupboard door. My elbow was chipped when he slammed the door into me. They were the worst injuries. Sometimes he hit me and he pinched my arms or legs regularly. Mrs Ethanides said I should leave him.'

'So what are you planning to do?'

'Manu insists that I have to go back and live in the apartment with him, but that I will be sleeping on the sofa. I don't mind that. As soon as my wrist and leg is out of plaster I will go away and he won't be able to find me.'

'Where will you go? Faliraki?'

Monika shook her head. 'I'll go to Kos. If I stay here and move to a different area he's bound to find me sooner or later. I have to go right away. It's not that long on the hydrofoil. You and Grandma would be able to visit me.'

'What about your work?'

Monika shook her head sadly. 'I'll be sorry to leave that, but I expect I can find some work on Kos. Will you help me, Mamma?'

'Of course. Lakkis Pavlides knew exactly how to solve any

problems that arose. Pity he's not around still. There – I never thought I would say that! I'll speak to Alecos, he's sure to have some contacts.'

'No, Mamma, not that way. Once I'm back at the apartment I will return to work at the library. On my way each morning I will bring a few of my clothes and leave them with you. I want you to take some money from my shoe box and buy me a suitcase and two mobile 'phones with pre-paid cards.'

'Why do you want two 'phones?'

'One is for you to keep hidden and the other is for me. I'll call you every Sunday evening, I promise. That way I can tell you exactly where I am. Please don't contact me unless it is a real emergency. The call area could probably be traced the same as it can on our current mobiles. Whatever you do, don't let Manu know where I am. I'll tell you when I'm leaving and collect my case and the money from the shoe box. There should be enough in there to keep me for a while until I find some work.'

Litsa shook her head sadly. 'I don't like this, Monika.'

'I don't like it either, but I asked Manu if he wanted to divorce me. He said he didn't have enough grounds for a divorce at the moment.' Monika looked at her mother with distressed eyes. 'I'm scared of him, Mamma. I'm scared he will hurt me so badly that I'll end up as a helpless invalid or else he'll injure himself deliberately and accuse me. I could end up in prison and then he would have grounds for a divorce.'

'He seemed such a nice man.'

Monika sighed. 'I thought so too.'

Mr Graphides collected Monika from the hospital in his car.

'This is very kind of you,' said Monika as she struggled to get into the back seat, her leg still immobilised in the plaster cast.

'Manu insisted. He doesn't want you to overdo things.'

'He's so considerate,' added Mrs Graphides from the front seat. 'I asked you both to come over for a meal this evening and he refused. He thought it would be too tiring for you. I've called in and left you some dolmades that you can heat up for this evening or eat cold and there's some salad items and bread, so you won't have to think about going out for shopping tomorrow.'

'Thank you. I am very grateful to both of you.'

Mr Graphides carried her carrier bag up the stairs for her and deposited it beside the front door. 'You sit and rest. You've spent nearly a month in bed and you still have those heavy plasters to carry around. How much longer before they will be removed?'

'Ten days and then they have said I will probably need physiotherapy to get the muscle tone back.'

'Yes, well, as I say, you sit and rest until Manu comes home. If there's anything you need tell Manu and he'll ask his mother to bring it along.'

'Thank you,' said Monika again. She thought it very unlikely that Manu would ask his mother to bring her anything she might need. Once Mr and Mrs Graphides had left she was determined to walk up and down the stone steps. Both her legs felt weak and she needed to get the strength back in them.

Manu arrived home and opened the door with a frown on his face. 'So you've been discharged?'

'Yes, Manu. I could still go and stay with my grandmother if you would prefer to have the apartment to yourself.'

'I told you that was out of the question. Is there a meal ready for me?'

'Yes, Manu. Your mother has made some dolmades and I've made up a salad.'

'That must have really tested your strength! I'll expect a more substantial meal than that tomorrow.'

'Yes, Manu.'

'Well, get it on the table whilst I shower and change.'

Dutifully Monika rose to her feet and limped across the room to the kitchen.

'How much longer are you expecting to wear those?' asked Manu pointing to the plaster casts on her arm and leg.

'I have to return to the hospital in ten days for an examination'

'What is there to examine?'

'An examination to ensure that I am healing well from my operation,' explained Monika. 'Then they'll X-ray my leg and wrist to ensure the bones have mended and remove the casts.'

'Just as well you are sleeping out on the sofa or you'd be kicking or hitting me every time you moved.' Manu eyed her speculatively.

Monika did not answer. She was relieved that Manu did not want her to share his bed. She hoped she would not have any new bruises she would have to explain away to the doctor when she visited the hospital. Apart from some scars on her arms and legs there were no bruises she could attribute to her fall down the steps.

Manu also appeared to realise that she would have to expose her body when she was examined and any further injuries would be queried. He contented himself with kicking the plaster cast on her leg whenever he walked past her. The action did not hurt Monika at all, but each time he kicked her she uttered a groan. If he thought he was hurting her leg it could keep him from attacking any other parts of her body.

Monika was so used to having the plaster cast on her leg that it no longer impeded her and she walked to the shop where her mother was working.

'Can you take a break for five minutes?' she asked.

'Manu?' asked Litsa immediately.

'No, he's not given me any problems so far. I just wanted to talk to you and I wasn't sure if I could walk all the way to the Old Town and back. Have you managed to purchase the items I asked you for?'

Litsa nodded. 'You're still set on the idea, then?'

'I have to go, Mamma. I'm sure that once I have been discharged completely from the hospital he'll feel free to treat me as he pleases. I'm going to tell him that I have to return for another check up two weeks' later and also go for physiotherapy.

I hope that will keep him away from me. By then I should be fit enough to travel to Kos.'

'You can take my savings with you.'

Monika shook her head. 'Thank you, Mamma, but no. I would rather you kept your money. If you lost your job you would need the money to live on until you found another. I'm also hoping you and Grandma will visit me next summer. You'll need some money for the hydrofoil and probably for somewhere to stay overnight. I'm sure I'll soon be able to find some work and earn enough to pay for a room and my meals.'

Litsa saw the owner looking in her direction. 'I must get on,' she said. 'When your leg is a bit stronger come up and visit me.'

'I will,' promised Monika, wishing it was Manu who was leaving Rhodes.

The gynaecologist was pleased when he examined Monika. 'You're healing well, no infection thank goodness, and all those other bruises have disappeared. I understand your casts are being removed today. You may be a bit off balance at first so make sure you don't have another fall.'

Monika shrugged. 'I'll do my best to stay on my feet.'

He nodded. 'Take care of yourself and please don't consider having another child for at least six months. You need to be completely healed internally.'

'We don't have any plans for starting another baby so soon'

'That's good to hear; so many of you young people think that everything is back to normal after just a week or two.'

'I did wonder if you would be willing to give me a prescription for the birth control pill; just as a precaution?' Monika dreaded Manu going back on his word and she would become pregnant before she had managed to accomplish her plan to leave him.

'No reason why not. They don't suit everyone, read the leaflet that describes the side effects and if you have any problems go to the clinic.' He scribbled a prescription and handed it to her.

'Thank you. Thank you for everything.'

'Just part of the job, my dear. Go along and get those plasters cut off now. You must be longing to get rid of them.'

Whilst Manu was out Monika worked on the exercises the physiotherapist had given her to strengthen her arm and leg and by the end of the week she decided she could certainly walk up to the Old Town and see her mother. She placed some underwear, a pair of old shoes and a nightdress in a carrier bag. Tomorrow she would take some blouses and skirts and then continue down to the library to visit Mrs Ethanides.

The walk was more tiring than she had anticipated and by the time she reached her grandmother's shop her leg was aching and she was pleased to be able to sit down in the living room whilst she waited for her mother to return from work.

'You look so much better than when you were in the hospital,' her grandmother fussed over her. 'I just couldn't believe it when your mother told me you had fallen and caused yourself so much damage – and the poor baby.'

Monika shrugged. 'It would have been far worse if the baby had been born and I was carrying him in my arms when it happened. At least this way I never knew him.'

'You'll have to be far more careful next time. Maybe you could move to a different apartment and be on the ground floor?'

'Manu could look for one,' agreed Monika. Obviously her mother had not told her grandmother the circumstances that had caused her accident. Monika felt resentful. Why was everything always her fault?

During the next two weeks Monika surreptitiously loaded a carrier bag with some of her belongings and deposited them with her mother. She hoped Manu would not have an excuse to look in her drawers and see how much of her clothing was missing. Each day she continued on to the library and tried to catch up on some of the outstanding computer work.

'You're not to stay late or work too hard,' said Mrs Ethanides solicitously. 'Do just a few hours each day and return full time next week.'

'I would rather be down here than sitting in the apartment on my own. I've enjoyed being able to read so much, but I'm used to being with people during the day. It becomes lonely having no one to speak to for hours.'

Mrs Ethanides regarded the young woman anxiously. She looked tense and strained. 'Have you made any decisions about your future?'

Monika smiled. 'I'm considering my options.' She was not prepared to confide her plans to Mrs Ethanides. Manu would be bound to question the librarian and it was better that she knew nothing of her intentions.

'I'm leaving tomorrow,' she finally announced to her mother. 'I'll take the hydrofoil and call you on the new mobile 'phone when I arrive. Make sure you keep it hidden from Manu. He's bound to come and ask if you know where I am. I'll pack my case now so all I'll need to add to it tomorrow are my toiletries and a towel.'

'Are you sure the hydrofoil is running?' asked Litsa. 'They usually finish at the end of September.'

Monika frowned and shrugged. She had not considered that possibility. 'If they're not I'll take a ferry. I haven't dared to go near the travel companies to enquire in case anyone saw me and told Manu. He'd want to know what I was doing.'

'Are you going to tell Mrs Ethanides you are leaving the library? I thought you said she was expecting you back at work full time this week?'

'If I hadn't planned to go to Kos I would be. I'm going down to see her now. I know she will understand.' Monika's eyes filled with tears. 'I'm so sorry, Mamma. I don't want to leave you and Grandma.'

Litsa hugged her daughter. 'I'd far rather you were safe. Had I known how Manu was treating you I would have urged you to leave him sooner. Make sure you 'phone me often.'

'I will; at least once a week. Don't worry, Mamma. I will be looking forward to seeing you and Grandma on Kos next summer.'

Monika continued on to the library, pleased she could spend the day on the computer dealing with details of her beloved books, but sad that it would be the last time she was able to do so. She would speak to Mrs Ethanides when she finished for the day and explain that she was not returning; confident that Mrs Ethanides would understand.

Mrs Ethanides greeted her with a smile. 'I'm pleased to see you and know you'll be here today. I have to go to a funeral and I'm not sure that I'll be back before closing time. If you find staying all day too much for you just leave when you're ready and tell the caretaker. He'll lock up after you if I'm not around.'

'Oh,' Monika sucked in her breath. This was obviously not the time to explain her proposed actions. 'I hope the funeral is not too depressing.'

Mrs Ethanides shrugged. 'It's a man my husband used to work with. I knew him, but not well. It's more to support my husband and a courtesy to the family. It's unfortunate that it's being held in Gennardi; it's such a long drive. After his wife died he retired down there to be with his married daughter and her family.' Mrs Ethanides picked up her bag and patted Monika gently on her arm. 'Remember what I said. If you find you're becoming tired you are to leave. I'll see you tomorrow.'

Monika nodded. She did not plan to see Mrs Ethanides the following day.

Monika found it difficult to concentrate on her work. She was continually interrupted by readers with a request to order a book, find a book or just chat for a while. They all asked where Mrs Ethanides was that day and some of them remarked that they had not seen Monika for a number of weeks and asked for news of her baby. She accepted their sympathy stoically when she said she had suffered a miscarriage, but did not explain how it had occurred.

It became obvious that Mrs Ethanides was not going to return to the library that day and Monika decided she would leave her a letter. She could not tell her she was going to Kos and ask if she would be willing to give her a reference for the library on the island as she had planned. It was better that she had no knowledge of Monika's whereabouts should Manu ask. She drew a sheet of paper towards her and began to write:

Dear Mrs Ethanides,

Thank you for your kindness to me over the years.

Unfortunately I have to tender my notice with immediate effect due to personal circumstances.

I hope you will understand.

Monika signed the letter and placed it in an envelope on Mrs Ethanides's desk before advising the caretaker that she was leaving. One more night at the apartment with Manu and then she would be free. She was dreading that he might hurt her that evening so that she would be unable to put her plan into action the following day.

Monika buttoned her coat up to her neck. The weather had changed dramatically and the wind was blowing hard, buffeting the carrier bag of toiletries she was carrying. She entered her grandmother's shop and was surprised when she found the door was locked behind her.

'What's this I hear about you going away?' demanded her grandmother.

'I have to leave Rhodes, Grandma. Mamma understands; she'll explain to you.' Monika unbuttoned her coat. Once inside out of the wind it was not cold.

'Where are you going?'

Monika bit her lip in indecision. 'I'm not going to tell you, Grandma. Manu may come here to ask you where I am and it's better for you to be able to say you don't know. I've promised to telephone Mamma regularly and she will tell you that I'm safe and well.'

'What good will running away from your problems do?'

'I'm planning to give Manu a reason to divorce me. He can say I deserted him.'

'You could come back here and live.'

Monika shook her head. 'If he knew I was here he would make me go back to him.'

'He couldn't make you return.'

'Grandma, Manu would make it impossible for me to stay here with you. Talk to Mamma when she comes home, then you'll understand. I'm just going to get my case and then I'll ask you to unlock the door for me.'

Monika went into her mother's bedroom and took the shoebox with her money from beneath the bed, transferring some of the notes to her purse and placing the remainder in a paper bag in her case. She took a last look around, a lump coming into her throat.

Monika walked into the travel office to purchase a ticket for the hydrofoil to take her to Kos.

The cashier shook his head. 'Hydrofoils finished at the end of September.'

'Then I'll take the ferry.'

'When do you plan to travel?'

'Today.'

'You should have checked earlier. Ferries to Kos are cancelled today due to the wind. The forecast is better for tomorrow. You could go then.'

Monika felt a surge of panic. 'Are there any ferries running?'

'Only to Piraeus. They're large enough to cope with bad weather.'

'I'd like a ticket, please.'

'I thought you wanted to go to Kos?' The cashier frowned.

'I can change my itinerary and go to Kos later. What time does the ferry leave?'

'You've missed the early one,' said the cashier as he took her money and handed her a ticket. 'The overnight one goes at five.'

'Is there nothing earlier?'

The cashier shook his head. 'Only two a day; early morning and late afternoon. You can go on board at four.'

Monika nodded and took the ticket, stowing it carefully into her purse. She did not want to return to her grandmother's shop, she could not go to the library after leaving the letter for Mrs Ethanides and nor could she spend all day sitting in a taverna. What other option did she have apart from sitting on the quayside in the wind?

'Is there anywhere I can wait?' she asked.

'There's a taverna up the road, but you'd have plenty of time to walk into the Old Town and have a look around. The museums are still open.'

'I'll probably do that then.' Monika lifted her case and walked out. If she went to the museum no one would query the amount of time she spent in there and she would be out of the wind. There was no reason for Manu to visit the museum and she would be able to get something to eat and drink in the snack bar before she left.

Once in the shelter of the Old Town walls the wind was less noticeable and she moved slowly trying to mingle with the groups of tourists and stopping to look at the goods on display in the various shops. She constantly looked around, dreading that Manu would suddenly appear. As soon as the ferry sailed she would telephone her mother and tell her of her change of destination.

The time dragged for Monika as she wandered around the museum, making herself read the notice on every exhibit four times before she moved on. As she toured the rooms and galleries for a fourth time she noticed that the guardians sitting at each door

149

were regarding her suspiciously. It was time to leave and make her way to the snack bar.

She studied the items on offer, continually letting others go ahead of her. Finally she could delay making a purchase no longer. She carried a sandwich and a frappe to an empty table and sat there eating as slowly as possible. When she had finished she returned to the counter and bought a Danish pastry, again making it last as long as possible before she looked at her watch. It would take her no longer than ten minutes to walk from the museum to the ferry and it was still only half past three.

She did not want to draw attention to herself by waiting to be allowed aboard. She must somehow force herself to stay in the Old Town until four or even a little later. She browsed in the gift shop, looking at her watch every few minutes, finally deciding that if she walked slowly she could leave the museum and arrive at the ferry terminal shortly after four. The wind was blowing more strongly now and Monika hoped they would not declare the sea too rough for the ferry to sail. She felt incredibly nervous. She had never been on the sea before and had not considered that she might have a rough crossing and be ill; or even worse, that the ferry might capsize.

Monika produced her ticket and was waved aboard where she made her way to the lounge. To her surprise there were already a number of men in there, sitting in the easy chairs with a drink in their hand. They all appeared to know one another and she selected a seat as far away from them as possible and placed her case at her feet. More men joined the group, moving the chairs to form a semi circle.

Just before the ferry sailed a steward walked around, checking the tickets were valid for travel on that day. Monika held hers out to him.

'Have you booked a cabin?' he asked.

Monika shook her head. It had not occurred to her that she would need to sleep on the journey.

'Would you like me to see if there is a free bunk in one of them? It will be an extra fifteen Euros. You're not likely to get much rest up here with the lorry drivers. They get pretty noisy after a while.'

Monika hesitated. If the men became noisy they could also be a nuisance to her; thinking that a woman travelling alone was "available".

'I wouldn't want to share with any men.'

'You stay here whilst I finish checking the tickets, then I'll have a look at the cabin list and see what's available. I'll be back in about half an hour.'

As soon as the ferry left the shelter of the harbour it began to pitch and roll and Monika held onto the arms of her chair tightly. She had been foolish. She should have stayed at a cheap hotel for the night and travelled when the weather had improved. She hoped the steward would return and tell her there was a bunk available. At least she would be able to lie down.

It was more than half an hour when the steward returned to say there was a mother travelling with her two children so the fourth bunk in the cabin would be free. Monika gave him fifteen Euros and received a pink ticket in exchange.

'Do you want me to show you where it is?'

'Yes, please,' answered Monika weakly. 'Is there a toilet in there?'

'You not feeling too good?' he grinned. 'This is nothing to worry about. Here, I'll take your case.'

Monika was thankful that she had both hands free to grab hold of the handrails on both sides of the walkway and down the stairs to the lower level as the ferry rolled from side to side. The steward appeared to have no problem keeping his balance and finally stopped outside a cabin door.

'If you hear the fire alarm going off you're to grab your life jacket and come up on deck.'

Monika looked at him in alarm. 'Are we in danger of sinking?'

'I don't think so for a minute, but we have to make sure all the passengers know what to do if there is an emergency. Read the instructions on the back of the door; make sure you know where your life jacket is and how to fit it on. There are arrows showing you the way to the exits.'

Monika nodded and crossed herself. She would certainly make sure she knew how to fit her life jacket and the way to the nearest exit.

She looked around the small cabin. Which bed should she have? If the children were young it would be safer for them to have the lower bunks. She placed her suitcase on the higher one and inspected the bathroom. It was adequate provided all four occupants were not taken ill at the same time.

Now she was lower down in the ferry it did not seem to be rolling so vigorously and she drew a deep breath. Her stomach was settling. She opened her suitcase and pulled out her mobile 'phone, checked that she had a signal and pressed in the numbers for her mother's 'phone.

'I was beginning to become concerned as you hadn't 'phoned from Kos. I expected you to do so during the afternoon, then I thought you might wait until you knew I was home from work.'

'I'm sorry, Mamma. I should have called earlier, but I wanted to wait until I was sure we had sailed. I'm on the ferry to Piraeus.'

'Piraeus? You said you were going to Kos.'

'The ferries weren't running there today. They said it was too rough, so I took the one to Piraeus. I didn't dare stay in Rhodes. It's very rough but the steward has found me a cabin so I can lie down.'

'Are you feeling ill?'

'Well, my stomach can't decide whether to go round and round or up and down. Now I've called you I'm going to try to get some sleep. I'll 'phone again tomorrow to let you know I've arrived safely in Piraeus. If Manu visits you please tell him you don't know where I am.'

Monika pushed her suitcase to the bottom of the bunk and lay down. The motion of the ferry that she was experiencing now was more a gentle rocking than the lurching it had been doing earlier. She closed her eyes, realising that she was in fact very tired. She had spent most of the day walking around in the museum and now her leg ached. It seemed no more than a few minutes later than the light in the cabin came on and she sat up abruptly.

A woman pushed two young boys into the cabin, telling them to be quiet.

'It is no problem,' Monika spoke to the woman in English. 'I was not yet asleep.'

'We'll get ready for bed as quickly as we can. Dominic, go and wash and clean your teeth whilst Samuel undresses.'

'Can I have the top bunk, Mum?'

'No you'll both use the lower bunks. If the ferry rolls you could fall out from the top one.'

'You could fall out from there.'

'I'm twice as heavy as you. It would be more difficult. Hurry up, now. The lady is trying to go to sleep.'

Monika turned her back on the cabin whilst they all undressed and used the bathroom before they climbed into the bunks and their mother turned out the light. For a while Monika lay there, listening to the two boys wriggling around in their bunks until they were comfortable, then her eyes closed and she fell into a deep sleep.

She was awoken by a banging on the cabin door and sat up in alarm. Was the ship sinking? Did she need to put on her life jacket?

'Come on, boys. Get dressed and use the bathroom quickly then I'll take you up on deck to watch us dock.'

Monika relaxed back on the bunk. She realised she had slept better than she had done for some months. As soon as the family left the cabin she climbed down from the bunk, used the tiny bathroom and picked up her case. The ferry was no longer rolling and pitching and she guessed they must be inside the harbour.

She made her way to the deck where the passengers would disembark, feeling both nervous and excited. Someone touched her shoulder and she turned to remind them there was a queue. Standing behind her was a friend and colleague of Manu's. She gasped in horror. Surely her husband had not found her so quickly?

'Hi, Monika. It is Monika, isn't it? What are you doing over here?'

Monika swallowed nervously. 'A - a library conference,' she stuttered.

'Manu didn't mention it.'

'He's not very pleased. He thinks it's too soon after my accident to be going away.'

Stenos raised his eyebrows. 'Manu didn't tell me you'd been hurt. What happened?'

'I had a fall and broke my leg.' Monika was not prepared to tell Stenos the details.

'Here, let me take your case.'

Monika had no choice but to relinquish her suitcase to Stenos.

'You've some weight in there! Books I imagine.' Monika nodded and Stenos continued. 'Where are you headed?'

'The taxi rank.'

'I'll walk you there; then I must be off. I'll tell Manu I saw you. He'll be pleased to know you've arrived safely.'

'There's no need. I will be phoning him soon to say I have arrived.'

Stenos opened the door of the taxi as it drew in and helped Monika inside, placing her case on the seat beside her.

'Hope you get some time for sight-seeing whilst you're here,' he said as he closed the cab door.

Monika nodded. 'Thank you, Stenos.'

'Where to?' asked the driver.

Monika hesitated. 'Anywhere for ten minutes; then bring me back here, please.'

The taxi driver shrugged. The young woman obviously wished

to rid herself of her companion. Monika looked out of the cab window and saw Stenos being greeted and ushered into a police car.

'Where's the police station?' she asked.

The driver braked. 'You want the police station?'

'No,' Monika shook her head. 'I just want to know where it is.'

'Up in the centre. Do you want me to take you there?'

'No, just drive around a little longer and then take me back to the port, please.'

'If you wanted the port why didn't you stay where you were? Would you like me to drive you up to Athens? You could see the Acropolis.'

Much as she would have liked to visit the Parthenon Monika felt she did not dare to stay in the vicinity. If Stenos did telephone Manu and say he had seen her at the port of Piraeus he would know where she was.

'Another day, maybe. Just back to the port, please.'

Grumbling, the driver took a side road and began the short drive back to the harbour. The girl had probably spotted the metro station and realised she could reach Athens quickly and cheaply by using it. He stopped at the taxi rank at the end of the road and waited whilst she alighted and paid him.

'Where will I find the ticket office for the ferries, please?' she asked.

'Across the road. There are a number of different companies.' The girl was obviously deranged. Who arrived at the port, took a short taxi ride and then asked to be returned to the ticket office?

Manu had spent the evening drinking, first at home, expecting Monika to return at any moment. He would give her a real beating when she finally decided to put in an appearance. There was no meal waiting for him and no message from her. Having consumed the six cans of beer from the fridge and with still no sign of his wife Manu decided to go out. She was obviously spending time with her mother and neglecting him. He would spend the evening with his friends as usual and deal with Monika the next day.

He rose the next morning with his head pounding. He stumbled out of the bedroom, still half asleep, and made his way to the sofa, grabbing the blanket expecting to feel Monika beneath it. She'd be sorry once he got hold of her. The blanket came away in his hand and there was no sign of his wife. He walked into the kitchen and it was exactly as he had left it the night before; the empty beer cans lying on the side.

Slowly it dawned on him that Monika had not returned to their apartment. He went into the bathroom and realised her toiletries were no longer on the shelf above the basin or beside the shower. Returning to the bedroom he pulled open the door of Monika's wardrobe; it was virtually empty. A quick look in the drawers where she kept her underwear produced the same result. Where was she? If she had decided to leave him the only place she could go would be to her grandmother's; unless, he ran a hand across his head, wishing he could think more clearly, unless she was with that interfering woman at the library.

He would visit the shop; it was possible she had turned up there later in the evening and if her mother and grandmother did not know where she was he would go to the library and confront Mrs Ethanides.

Manu strode into the general store. 'Where is she?' he demanded of Monique.

Monika's grandmother looked at the angry man in front of her. 'If you are asking for Monika I would expect her to be leaving the apartment about now to go in to work.'

Manu glared at her. 'Is your daughter here?'

'I'll call her.' Monique raised her voice. 'Litsa, Manu is here. He wants to know where Monika is.'

Litsa shrugged. 'I have no idea where she is.'

'She didn't come home last night.'

'Well, she certainly didn't stay here and she isn't here now. You can come in and look.'

Manu pushed his way through to the living room. The large bed that Monique used was neatly made, likewise Litsa's. Nowhere could he see anything that might belong to Monika, despite looking into the chests where the two women kept their clothes and inspecting the kitchen and bathroom area.

He rounded on Litsa angrily. 'Where is she? She's my wife. I have a right to know.'

'I have no idea where she is at the moment,' replied Litsa steadily and honestly.

Manu glared at Litsa. 'If you know where she's hiding it will be the worse for you when I find her,' he threatened.

'I've told you I don't know her whereabouts. Please leave. You are frightening my mother.' Monique did not look in the least frightened. She was standing behind the counter with an open packet of pepper in her hand.

Manu took a last look around the shop and went out, slamming the door behind him. Monique sneezed violently before closing the packet of pepper and placing it back on the shelf.

'What are you doing with that?' asked Litsa.

'I was going to throw it into his face if he threatened you physically.' Monique sneezed again. 'Then I was going to go outside and shout that we were being attacked and robbed.'

Litsa shook her head. 'He's a policeman, Mamma. He's hardly likely to rob a shop.'

'It would have stopped him from hurting you,' replied Monique truculently. 'Thank goodness Monika has left him if that is the way he behaves. Have you heard from her?'

'Not this morning. She said she would call me later today when she was in Kos.'

Manu walked down into the Old Town to the library. Mrs Ethanides was sitting behind her desk and smiled at him when he arrived.

'Good morning, Manu.'

'Where's my wife?'

'Monika? I have no idea.'

'She's staying with you. I know she is.'

Mrs Ethanides shook her head. 'Monika is certainly not staying with me.'

Manu banged on Mrs Ethanides desk. 'Tell me where she is.'

'Stop that. You may be a policeman, but you have no right to behave like that in here. If you persist I will have to ask security to remove you from the premises.'

'Where is my wife?' asked Manu a little more calmly. 'You must know where she is. She works here.'

Mrs Ethanides shook her head. 'She no longer works for the library service. There was a letter of resignation from her waiting for me this morning.' Mrs Ethanides opened the drawer and took out the letter Monika had left for her.

Manu opened it and read the page in disbelief. 'She has left?'

Mrs Ethanides nodded. 'That's what it says.'

'Where has she gone?'

'I have no idea. She did not confide her movements to me.'

Manu threw the letter back on the desk and walked out. When the stupid girl had used up her money she would come crawling back to him, begging for forgiveness. He would make quite sure she regretted her foolish action once he had his hands on her again.

Monika walked into the travel office and studied the information displayed on the walls. The only ferry that was scheduled to go to Kos went via Rhodes. She dared not go back there. Finally she approached the counter; she would go to Crete. The island was large enough for her to become lost amongst the inhabitants and tourists and she should be able to find some work.

'What time does the ferry to Crete leave?' she asked.

'Nine this evening.'

'Not until then?'

The cashier shook his head. 'No. Do you want a ticket?'

'What time does it arrive?'

'Six in the morning.'

'I'll need a bunk for the night. Is there any way you can ensure that I share with other women or families that are travelling?'

'You'll have to speak to the steward when you board.'

'Is there anywhere I can leave my luggage for the day?' Monika did not want to carry her suitcase around whilst she filled in the time until she could go on board.

'Over there. Two Euros.' He pointed to a row of wire cages, some already containing suitcases or holdalls, others empty with the doors open and a key in the lock. 'Leave the key in the lock when you collect your belongings.'

Monika nodded and handed over her money. She calculated that she should have enough Euros in her purse for the day. She certainly did not want to be seen removing money from the paper bag in her case.

'Can I get to the centre of Athens from here without taking a taxi?' There was bound to be a museum there where she could spend the day, but she did not feel she could spend any more money on taxi fares.

'Along the road.' The cashier indicated the direction with his pen. 'You can't miss it.'

Monika deposited her suitcase into the locker and attached the key safely to the zip on her purse. At least if she was seen by Stenos she could say she was taking advantage of some free time before the conference to visit some of the sights.

Once at the metro station she studied the tourist information and finally decided that a return ticket to and from Monastiraki Square would at least place her in the centre of the city and there was certain to be a museum there where she could pass the day.

Each side of the concourse there were coffee bars and tavernas. The smell wafting out from them reminded her that she had not eaten anything since the previous afternoon and she walked from one to the other studying the prices. The cheapest place appeared to be "Wendys" selling a variety of burgers and wraps.

Monika collected her food and took a seat as far back in the eating area as possible and ate slowly. She must find out how frequently the trains ran in the evening and also how late "Wendys" stayed open. She could not afford to miss the ferry.

She took her mobile from her bag and pressed in the numbers to call her mother, relieved when she answered swiftly.

'Mamma, I'm in Piraeus, but I'm not stopping here. I was seen by one of Manu's friends and he said he would let him know I had arrived.'

'What are you going to do? Manu came this morning. He was sure you were staying here.'

'I'm catching the ferry to Crete this evening. I won't be there until tomorrow morning and I'll call you again then.'

'Crete? I thought you intended to go to Kos.'

'I can only get to Kos by travelling back to Rhodes. Was Manu very angry?'

Monika heard her mother chuckle. 'Grandma thought he might hit me so she had an open packet of pepper ready to throw in his face. He looked everywhere, but when there was no sign of you he left and just slammed the shop door. Just take care, Monika and let me know you are safe.'

Monika would have enjoyed her day in Athens had she not been continually looked around warily in case Stenos should suddenly appear. She walked from Monastiraki Square to the Parthenon and wandered slowly around the columns, admiring the view from each side of the structure until she shivered in the keen wind. Once inside the museum where the marbles were displayed she soon became warm again and decided to walk down through the Agora and back into the centre to find the museum where she could spend the afternoon.

It took her well over an hour to walk from the Acropolis to

where the museum was situated. There had been so much that she stopped to look at on the way. She had detoured to watch the Guards outside the Parliament building as they did their slow march, stifling a smile when one lifted his leg showing there was a large hole in his stocking.

Finally arriving at the museum she checked the closing time. She must not become so involved in looking at the exhibits that she missed the ferry. One gallery led to another and she was amazed at the size of the building and the quantity of beautiful items they had on display. It was far larger than the museum in Rhodes, containing important artefacts from all the other islands as well as the mainland. The bell, when it rang, denoting that the museum was closing took her by surprise. She had spent far longer than she realised going from case to case and reading the notices, and there was still another floor that she had not visited. She wished she had been sent to Athens for a library conference so that she would have been able to see more of the fascinating city.

Finding her way back to Monastiraki Square was not as easy as she had expected. There was no view of the Parthenon to guide her and she hoped she was walking in the right direction for the metro station. Feeling uncertain she entered a shop and asked the assistant how far away she was from the metro station that would take her to Piraeus.

'I just need to check that I am walking in the right direction.'

The assistant smiled. 'Keep going until you reach Syntagma Square. There will be a sign there directing you to the metro.'

Feeling more confident Monika walked on. It seemed considerably further than she had walked earlier in the day and decided that was because her leg was tiring and she was anxious about the time, although it was three hours before the ferry was due to sail. If she did not find the metro station in the next hour she would have to wave down a taxi and ask to be taken to Piraeus.

Monika sighed with relief when she saw the sign saying she had reached Syntagma Square and looked around for a sign post for the direction of the metro. She waited for the lights to become red and stop the traffic. Looking cautiously from left to right she made her way across the road and along to where the road sign said "Ermou Street". Once she saw the Cathedral in Monastiraki Square she knew where she was again and her confidence returned. Once she reached Piraeus she would have time to return to "Wendys" for another burger and chips before she retrieved her suitcase and went aboard.

Her journey from Piraeus to Heraklion was uneventful and once again she slept well, pleased that she had been able to share a cabin with two young women from New Zealand who had been travelling across the country. They were impressed by her knowledge of English and delighted in describing the places they had visited to her. When she was asked the purpose of her journey she once again used the excuse that she was attending a library conference.

As Monika carried her suitcase off the ferry she looked around warily and was relieved when no one touched her shoulder. It was only just light and she shivered, despite her warm coat. She needed to find some lodgings and also visit the employment centre to see what jobs they had available. It would be too early for either place to be open and she entered the comforting warmth of a coffee house that was advertising breakfast.

She made her meal last as long as possible and when she paid she asked directions to the centre and enquired if the employment exchange was there also.

'Go up the hill and follow the road to the museum. The tourist information office is opposite. You can't miss it.'

Monika was about to say that she did not want the tourist information office and then thought better of it. She could probably obtain a map of the area from them and they should know where the employment offices were situated and also where she would find the cheapest rooms to rent. She sighed heavily as she toiled up the hill. It had all seemed so easy when she had planned to go to Kos. She was sure Mrs Ethanides would have provided her with a reference for the main library on the island and they would have been able to recommend a cheap room that she could rent.

She saw the large museum at the side of the square and gave a wry smile, hoping she was not destined to spend a third day wandering around inside looking at the exhibits; at a later date she would be interested to return.

Already there were people sitting in the chairs at the employment office waiting for attention. She took a ticket from the machine and waited patiently for her number to be called.

'Have you completed your application form?' asked the man behind the desk.

'I didn't know I had to.'

'Everyone has to fill in a form.' He handed her one from beneath the desk. 'Take another number and fill this in whilst you're waiting.'

Monika felt annoyed. If she was expected to complete an application form surely there should have been a notice advising her and a supply of forms to hand. She took another ticket and stood at the side of the room and studied the questions.

She would use her maiden name as that was the one that was on her identity card. She could not enter an address and when it asked for previous occupation she debated whether to insert library assistant or say catering, relying on the few weeks she had spent working at the kiosk in the park. She read through the remaining questions – how much did she expect to earn – was she willing to contemplate a different occupation – did she want to undertake training for a profession – what qualifications did she already have – when would she be available for work? She chewed at her finger and finally entered "immediately" regarding her availability and left the answers to the other questions blank.

When her number was called a second time it was to a man at the other end of the counter. He scrutinized her form and handed it back.

'You have not completed the questions.'

'I'm not able to complete them. I only arrived on Crete today so I do not have an address. I was hoping that you might be able to advise me where I should go to find some cheap lodgings.'

He frowned at her. 'What kind of work are you looking for?'

'I have a thorough knowledge of computers and I speak English and German.'

He shook his head. 'There's no call for linguists at this time of year. The travel centres are closed for the season. Those that stay open all year round have their permanent staff. Have you worked in an office?'

Monika hesitated. 'Not exactly. I worked as a librarian.'

'So why have you left?'

'Personal reasons.'

'Were you given the sack?'

'Oh, no.'

'References?'

Monika shook her head.

'So I only have your word for it that you worked in a library and were not dismissed.'

Monika sighed. 'I worked in the library on Rhodes from when I left University until last week, well, this week. I am sure Mrs Ethanides would give me a reference.'

'I doubt there's any call for library work. What else are you willing to do?'

'Anything. I'd rather work anywhere than be unemployed.'

'Well the hotels always want cleaners.' He shuffled through his papers and drew out a typewritten list. 'They always do a certain amount of redecorating during the winter months and the mess that's left behind needs to be cleaned up.' He ran his finger down the list, leaned back in his chair and called out to his four colleagues. 'Anyone taken the job at "The Central"?'

The men shook their heads and he turned back to Monika. 'I'll call them and check.'

Monika waited impatiently whilst he spoke to someone. 'Go over now and the housekeeper will see you. Do you want me to keep your details on file?'

'Yes, please. Where is "The Central"?'

'Across the road from the museum. If they turn you down I have one or two other smaller hotels you could try.'

'Thank you.' Monika lifted her suitcase and walked away. She had not envisaged becoming a cleaner; but at least it would provide her with some money to live on. If she had the security of a job she could afford to spend the night in a cheap hotel if she had not found anywhere else suitable to stay before it grew dark.

Mrs Planatakis eyed the girl up and down. She looked clean and respectable. 'Come into my office.' She led the way across the large vestibule and opened a door on the far side. 'Have a seat and tell me about yourself.'

Monika placed her suitcase on the ground beside her. 'There isn't very much to tell. My name is Monika Kokanides.'

'So, Monika Kokanides, where have you come from?'

'Rhodes.'

Mrs Planatakis raised her eyebrows. 'So why have you left Rhodes to become a cleaner on Crete.'

Monika dropped her eyes. 'I had to leave for personal reasons.'

'Are you in trouble with the police?'

'I assure you I am not a criminal.'

'That did not answer my question. I asked if you were in trouble with the police.' Mrs Planatakis sat back and folded her arms. 'I see you are wearing a wedding ring.'

Monika flushed. She should have thought and removed it. 'I am married,' she admitted. 'That was why I had to leave Rhodes.'

'So where is your husband?'

'On Rhodes. I wanted to go to Kos, but it was too rough for the ferry so I went to Piraeus. A friend of my husband saw me there so I caught the ferry to Crete.' The words came out in a rush from Monika.

'Are you saying that you have left your husband?'

Monika nodded miserably. 'I had to,' she whispered. 'He was so violent.'

'Was it necessary to travel so far away? Why didn't you go to a different town on Rhodes or home to your mother?'

'I couldn't. Wherever I went on Rhodes he would find me.'

'Why didn't you speak to the police and ask for protection?'

'He is a policeman.' Monika stood up. 'Thank you for your time, but you obviously do not want to employ me.'

'Sit down, girl. I haven't refused you employment. I have to enquire into your background. This is a very respectable hotel. Mr Iliopolakis would not contemplate employing anyone who had a criminal record, even as a cleaner. Is there anyone on Rhodes who could vouch for your character? Where did you work there?'

'I was a librarian. I'm sure Mrs Ethanides would give me a reference but I don't want her to know where I am in case my husband goes to the library. If she doesn't know I'm on Crete she cannot tell him where I am.'

'Would you object to me telephoning her?'

Monika hesitated. 'She could check your number and know you 'phoned from Crete. If Manu found out it would be easy for him to trace me here.'

'I can withhold my 'phone number. Do you have any other objections to me speaking with her?'

Monika shook her head.

'Very well. Go and sit in the vestibule. I'll ask one of the attendants to bring you a drink.'

Monika sat nervously, watching the visitors going in and out, and it seemed an interminable time before Mrs Planatakis opened her door and beckoned to her.

'I've spoken to Mrs Ethanides. She's very relieved to know that you are safe.'

'You didn't tell her I was on Crete, did you?' asked Monika anxiously.

Mrs Planatakis shook her head. 'She did not ask where you were and I did not tell her. We had quite a long and informative chat. Apparently your husband called thinking you could be staying with her. She showed him the letter you had left for her and she has not seen him since. I understand you were in hospital recently. Are you fully recovered now?'

'Yes, thank you.'

'Fit enough to do cleaning? It can be quite a strenuous job.'

'I'm sure I can manage.'

'Mrs Ethanides also told me that you are a trained librarian and fluent in English and German. Are you sure a cleaning job is suitable for you?'

'I'll take any work that is available. I only need enough money to pay my rent and buy some food.'

'How much is your rent?'

'I have no idea. If you gave me the job I was going to ask if you could recommend some lodgings to me.'

'So where were you planning to spend the night? Sleeping on the street?'

'Oh, no.' For the first time Monika smiled. 'I was going to look for a cheap hotel if I hadn't found anywhere satisfactory by this evening.'

'Be here at seven tomorrow morning and you'll be shown your duties. I'll have a word with some of the other members of staff and see if they know of any decent lodgings.'

'I'm very grateful.' Monika rose to go.

'You haven't asked about wages. How will you know how much rent you can afford if you don't know how much you are being paid each week? Cleaners are paid five Euros an hour and you will be expected to work from seven until five, including every other weekend. On Sundays and Public Holidays you are given double pay. You will be entitled to two breaks; fifteen minutes at

167

ten and an hour at one thirty. You are not paid for your break time. During your lunch break you are allowed a meal provided by the kitchen that you can eat in the communal rest room.'

'I'm sure I can manage to live on those wages.'

Mrs Planatakis nodded. If the girl proved her worth she could be promoted to being a chambermaid where the hours would be less but she would earn six Euros an hour and probably receive tips from some of the guests.

'I'll put someone experienced with you for the first couple of weeks to ensure you know exactly what is expected of you and where the supplies are kept.'

Manu waited impatiently over the weekend for Monika to return. When there was still no sign of her returning to him he decided he would declare her to be a missing person. Once the police on Rhodes were looking for her she would soon be flushed out from wherever she was hiding.

Stenos looked at the notice that appeared on the screen of his computer. 'Is this from you, Manu?'

Manu nodded. 'My wife has gone missing. I'm hoping if I circularise her description and photograph someone will find her.'

'That's a worry. If she's gone missing in Athens she may not be found for months.'

'What makes you think she's in Athens?'

'I saw her. When the ferry docked at Piraeus I carried her case and saw her into a taxi. She said she was attending a library conference.'

Manu looked at Stenos angrily. 'Why didn't you tell me before?'

'I thought you would know. She said she would 'phone you to let you know she had arrived safely. Maybe she didn't have any credit or had forgotten her charger.'

Manu glanced at his colleague sourly. If Monika had gone to Athens for a library conference why hadn't Mrs Ethanides told him and why had Monika left her a letter of resignation?

'Have you tried calling the library in Athens? They must know where she is,' continued Stenos. 'Would you like me to look up the number for you?'

Manu shook his head. Monika had removed all her possessions from their apartment. She would not have done that if she had only been attending a conference for a few days. He felt his anger against her mounting. She had obviously gone to Athens thinking he would be unable to find her there. He would speak to the Athenian police and explain that his wife had been ill and he was very concerned about her mental state. It was essential she was found as quickly as possible and returned to Rhodes to be looked after.

Manu was about to contact the Athenian police when he decided it would be prudent to speak to Mrs Ethanides again. If Monika had genuinely gone to Athens to attend a conference the librarian must know where she was and when she was due back. He would look foolish if she returned the following weekend and he had declared that she was missing simply because she hadn't contacted him.

'I'm going out. I'll contact Athens when I return.'

Manu walked into the Old Town and went straight to the library. Mrs Ethanides saw him arriving and she spoke quietly to the security guard.

'I know this man is a policeman, but he has a very nasty temper. Please step in immediately if you see him raise his fist at me.' Mrs Ethanides forced herself to smile at Manu as he reached her desk. 'Good morning, Manu, how can I help you?'

'Where is my wife?'

'I have told you; I do not know where your wife is. I showed you her letter of resignation. I have not heard from her.'

'Did you send her to Athens for a library conference?'

Mrs Ethanides shook her head. 'The conference is in January. I would hardly send her there now.'

'She was seen in Piraeus and said she was going to a conference.'

Mrs Ethanides shrugged. 'If she was it was certainly not arranged by me. Your information could be incorrect.'

Manu leaned across the desk. 'I am registering her as a missing person. If you do know where she is I suggest you tell me now. Once she is found you could be arrested for withholding information.'

'I have no information about her to withhold so it would be a waste of time to arrest me. All I can tell you is that I did not send her to a library conference anywhere and I do not know where she is.' Mrs Ethanides glared at Manu. If Monika did contact her she would advise her that the police were looking for her and suggest she did something to change her appearance.

Crete 2006 - 2008

With the help of Eirini who had been assigned to work with her, Monika had found a small furnished apartment at a reasonable price not too far from the hotel. A good deal of her initial savings had now been used up due to her travelling and having to pay a month's rent in advance. The meal she received at lunch time, although usually the excess left from the previous evenings' diners, was sufficient for her to only need a snack in the evening and she often took home the cake or fruit that had accompanied the dish.

'Damage and breakages have to be paid for,' she had been told by the owner of her apartment. 'I know accidents happen, but I can't afford to keep buying new furniture where it has been mistreated or you have dropped the china on the floor. If such a thing happens I expect you to tell me immediately. I don't want to find anything broken or damaged when you leave.'

Monika found the cleaning work tiring, particularly at first, but she was thankful that she had a job that brought her in enough money to pay her rent and buy her food. She was responsible for the rooms on the third floor where the decorators had worked and been told they must be spotless when she had finished so that a guest could be accommodated immediately if necessary. The windows leading to the small balcony were to be cleaned, the balcony, along with the floor in the bedroom was to be scrubbed by hand. Once that had been done the curtains would be re-hung and the room declared ready for the chambermaid to make up the bed and hang the towels as required.

She telephoned her mother each week and assured her that she was safe and well, but refused to divulge any details about her work or address. 'When I feel confident that Manu is no longer looking for me I'll tell you. In the meantime it's better that you don't know where I am and then you cannot tell him.'

'When am I going to see you again?' asked Litsa.

'I don't know, Mamma. I cannot come back to Rhodes. Maybe you and Grandma could come over to Crete to visit me?'

Litsa considered the idea. 'I think it could be too soon for us to do that. Manu has had your details and photograph displayed in the shops and tavernas saying you're a missing person. There's even one in the window of the shop where I work. I'm sure he would know if we left Rhodes and find out where we had gone.'

Monika was disconcerted to know that her photograph and description was on display in Rhodes. She walked to the nearest internet cafe and paid to use a computer. She requested a list of missing persons in Greece, trawling down until she came to the name "Graphides, Monika". Thank goodness she had used her identity card in Crete as it was still in the name of Kokanides. She read her physical description and that she was believed to be in Piraeus or Athens. She was pleased now that she had met Stenos that day. He had obviously told Manu that he had spoken to her and Manu believed that she was on the mainland.

She studied her photograph that Manu had inserted. It was an excellent likeness. If a visitor, or even someone on business, came from Rhodes to Crete they just might recognise her. Hurriedly she closed the computer and left the cafe. Monika looked at the prices displayed in the various hairdressers as she walked back to her apartment, but found it impossible to calculate the amount it would cost her to have her hair cut and lightened; she would have to walk in and ask them for a price. If she took such a drastic move she would have to ensure that she could afford the lightening treatment each month.

When she finally looked in the mirror she could hardly recognise herself. Her long dark hair had been cut to a bob and bleached two shades lighter than her natural colour. Due to her hard work over the previous months she had lost weight and now the loss showed in her face, making her cheek bones more prominent. She certainly looked different from the photograph Manu had placed on the internet.

Pleased with her altered appearance she waited for comments from her work colleagues.

'You look like a film star,' remarked Eirini. 'What made you have your hair cut and coloured? A new man in your life?'

Monika shook her head. 'I just fancied a change. If I become tired of it I can let it grow out and go back to my natural colour.'

Eirini looked at her enviously. She would love to have sufficient money to be able to go to the hairdresser, but with her husband forced to accept any low paid unskilled work he was offered and two children such a luxury was denied to her. 'Don't you go out in the evenings? You'd probably meet a man you liked.'

'I'm not really interested in finding anyone. I'm quite happy spending my evenings reading.' Monika had joined the library and revelled having a selection of books to choose from each week, indulging in her love of learning about other countries and ensuring that she borrowed books in English, French and German to keep herself fluent in the languages.

Eirini shrugged. Reading in the evening was another luxury she could not afford. By the time she had prepared a meal for her family and coped with the washing each evening after finishing work she was too tired to think of anything except going to bed. 'We've been moved to the top floor this week. Have you been up there?'

Monika shook her head. 'I've not had any reason.'

'That's where the Conference rooms are situated. There's one taking place next week and the big room has to be ready. That means all the furniture has to be polished, along with checking that none of the china is stained or damaged.'

'Well that will make a change from cleaning windows and scrubbing floors.'

'Don't be so sure. They have a counter at the side where they can make their own coffee and the mess they leave behind has to be seen to be believed. Once the conference starts our first job each morning will be to wash all their dirty cups, empty the ash trays and clean the counter. They have toilets adjoining the room and they have to be cleaned each day. The table has to be polished to get rid of their grubby finger marks and then the carpet hoovered.'

'What time do they start arriving?'

'Officially at ten, but there are always some who come early, so we are expected to be finished by nine thirty.'

'Suppose we haven't finished by then?'

'There's no "suppose", we have to be; otherwise a complaint will be made to Mr Iliopolakis. He would probably overlook it once, but if it happened a second time or on a regular basis we'd probably get the sack.'

'Who is Mr Iliopolakis?'

'He owns the hotel. You'll probably see him around when the conferences start. He comes in to ensure all the arrangements are in place. I'll point him out to you. He's always very polite and says hello to any of the staff he sees.'

Monika nodded. She hoped Eirini would be with her when he arrived and she did not mistake him for a guest at the hotel. That could be embarrassing.

Monika was surprised at the size of the conference room and the enormous table that stood in the centre, surrounded by heavy wooden chairs. 'It will take hours to clean up here every day,' she observed.

'Not as long as you think. You can do the counter and cups, then ensure the toilets are clean and stocked up with toilet rolls, tissues, soap and paper towels. Whilst you do that I'll do the polishing and hoovering. I'll swap with you each day. If they need to use two rooms they'll fold back the partition doors and Maria and Eleni will be sent up to help us.'

Monika nodded; maybe the task was not as daunting as she had envisaged.

Despite working hard, Monika felt well. She was no longer stressed about Manu returning home in a bad temper, walking to work and up and down the stairs at the hotel seemed to have strengthened her leg and her arm no longer ached when she had finished polishing or scrubbing. It was mundane work and she missed the library, but once the weather began to improve she spent her free time walking around Heraklion. The buildings, despite the Venetian influence, were very different from those on Rhodes.

There were none of the large "Knights of St John" houses here. The island had been used more as a trading outpost than as a centre for their association. The fortress, that was down by the harbour, had been used to defend the island from invaders, not as a palatial residence. She had visited the museum across the road from the hotel on a number of occasions and enjoyed being able to wander around at her leisure, not having to worry about being seen.

During her telephone conversations with her mother she had described how she had had her hair cut and lightened and the difference it had made to her appearance. 'I don't think Manu would recognise me if he walked past me in the street, but I dare not take the chance and return to visit you.'

'He still calls at the shop regularly to see if there is any sign that you have returned here. I keep telling him that I don't know where you are, but I'm sure he doesn't believe me.'

'I'm hoping that when he can't find me he realises I have actually left him and he starts divorce proceedings against me for desertion. When I came out of hospital I asked him if he wanted a divorce but he said he had no reason to divorce me at that time. Now I'm giving him a good reason.'

'You should be divorcing him,' said Litsa indignantly. 'He should be the one made to suffer, not you.'

'Mamma, I'm not suffering, except by being apart from you and Grandma. I have some regular work and a small apartment. I'm in a more fortunate position than many others.'

'Suppose you met someone else and wanted to get married again?'

'I'll think about that if the situation ever arises. At the moment I'm quite happy being alone.'

The day before the first conference was due to commence Vasilis Iliopolakis entered the room unannounced accompanied by Vasi. He looked around and nodded his approval to Eirini.

'Make sure it looks like this every day. Satisfied visitors to the conferences mean the hotel is able to stay open during the winter months and ensures you have a job.'

Eirini inclined her head. 'Yes, sir. Thank you, sir.'

Both men smiled at Monika as they left and she turned to Eirini. 'Was that Mr Iliopolakis?'

'Yes, the younger man is his son. He was the manager when I first started working here. He certainly made some changes.'

'Is he still the manager? I've not seen him around before.'

'I understand they have other hotels further down the island. He's probably working at one of the others.'

Monika made no attempt to look for a higher paid or more congenial job. She accepted the mundane work and had made friends amongst the staff, although she rarely socialised with them. Mrs Planatakis had offered her a position as a chamber maid rather than a cleaner and she had thanked her and refused.

'I'm quite happy working the hours, but I know someone who would appreciate becoming a chamber maid.'

Mrs Planatakis looked at her, expecting her to ask for a position for her mother or another relative.

'Eirini, the lady who partnered me with the cleaning of the conference rooms, she would appreciate working less hours and maybe earning a little more. Her husband is often out of work and I know they are struggling. She continually tells me that she has had to buy new shoes or trousers for her boys where they are growing so rapidly.'

Mrs Planatakis frowned. 'She hasn't mentioned anything to me.'

Monika smiled. 'She is under the impression that you have to be better educated than she is to be a chamber maid. She is doing cleaning now and the only extra duty of a chamber maid is making up the beds each day.'

'Are you sure you wouldn't like to progress or have you applied for work elsewhere more fitting to your qualifications and abilities?' Mrs Planatakis had expected Monika to accept with alacrity and she was surprised that she had asked for the job to be given to another

Monika shook her head. 'I'm not looking anywhere for another job. If you offer the position to Eirini and she turns it down then I will accept it, but I think she deserves it more than me. She has worked here far longer and has a family. I earn enough to live on.' Monika hesitated. 'There is one thing I would like to ask you, though, well, two, actually.'

Mrs Planatakis raised her eyebrows and Monika continued. 'Down in the vestibule there is a shelf with books that the visitors borrow or they place a finished book there when they leave. Could I have permission to borrow them? I'd return a book as soon as I'd finished it.'

'Most of the books down there are in English.'

'I know; that is why I would like to read them. I'm only allowed to take three books at a time from the library and I've often finished them before I can go again. I would appreciate

177

being able to borrow some of the paperbacks that are down there.'

Mrs Planatakis nodded. 'There's no reason why you shouldn't make use of them.'

Monika's face lit up with a smile. 'Thank you. I didn't like to borrow any without permission. I wouldn't want you to think I was stealing them.'

'What was the other thing you wanted to ask?' Mrs Planatakis hoped the next request would be as easy to deal with as the first.

'Please don't tell Eirini you offered me the work as a chamber maid and I asked you to give it to her.'

Eirini could hardly believe it when Mrs Planatakis asked if she would like to become a chamber maid. She would still be expected to start work at seven but she would finish at four and earn an extra three Euros a week, along with any tips the visitors left for her. The extra money would be useful, but finishing at four would mean she would be home shortly after her boys returned from school.

Now the conferences had finished the rooms where they had been held were closed and Monika spent most of her time alone cleaning the stairs and hallways. Her most hated job was cleaning the glass doors at the entrance to the hotel. No sooner had she removed all the finger marks and smudges than a visitor would arrive and push the glass rather than the handle to open them. It was her first job each morning to clean them, then again after her morning break, when she returned from her lunch and before she left each afternoon.

As she worked she occasionally saw Vasilis Iliopolakis arriving, she would immediately open the door and stand aside respectfully for him whilst he entered, being rewarded with a smile of thanks. She watched as she saw him help an attractive woman from his car and escort her into the vestibule as she leaned heavily on his arm.

'I'll not be long, Cathy.' To Monika's surprise he spoke in

English. 'You sit here whilst I take the car around to the back. I only need to check some dates with the manager.'

'I have a magazine with me,' replied the woman as she lowered herself carefully into the armchair. She removed two magazines from the bag she had carried over her arm, placed the bag and one magazine on the table beside her and began to flick through the pages.

Monika craned her neck to see if it was an English magazine the woman was reading. She hoped she would leave it behind when she left so she would be able to pick it up and read it for herself. Having access to the books in the vestibule and no longer having to rely on visiting the library was a great advantage, but she could not justify the purchase of a magazine. Her dream of learning to drive was even more unattainable now; any money she was able to save would eventually be used to take a flight back to Rhodes, rather than having to spend two days travelling by ferry.

Cathy frowned at the magazine she was looking through and sighed. She had inadvertently picked up the one she had read before. As she placed it on the table beside her and reached for the other one her arm brushed her bag and the magazine fell to the floor. Cathy leaned over the side of her chair to try to retrieve it.

'I will get it,' said Monika as she hurried over and picked up the magazine from the floor.

'Thank you. I stupidly picked up one I had already read.'

'It is an easy mistake to make. Is there anything else you would like me to get you?'

Cathy looked at Monika in surprise. 'You speak English?'

Monika nodded. 'I learnt some years ago.'

'At school or did you pick it up from the tourists? '

'School and then University.'

'So why are you working here as a cleaner?'

Monika flushed; she could not tell a perfect stranger that she had left her husband and was virtually in hiding from him. 'It gives me time to study.'

Before Cathy could question her further Vasilis arrived. 'I told you I would not be long. I've brought the car back to the entrance.'

Monika stepped away, but she heard Cathy say 'Did you know that your cleaner speaks excellent English and has been to University?'

From the corner of her eye Monika could see Vasilis look in her direction. 'I didn't employ her. The cleaning staff are the responsibility of Mrs Planatakis.'

'I would have thought she would have been more useful to you doing something other than cleaning.' Cathy placed a magazine in her bag and allowed Vasilis to help her up. 'Would you like this?' she called to Monika and held up the magazine she had already read.

'Yes, please,' answered Monika immediately. 'Thank you very much. I borrow books from the library, but I can't afford magazines.'

'Do you read the books in English or only those that have been translated?'

'I prefer to read them in their mother tongue. Very often the meaning has been lost or distorted where it was translated.'

'I'll send some magazines in for you when Vasilis visits next. Tell me your name and if you are not around he can leave them with reception.'

Monika beamed. 'That would be very kind.' She hugged the magazine to her. 'It will help me to keep up with the colloquial. My name is Monika.'

Vasilis looked thoroughly bemused. 'What are these colly things she wants?' he asked as he took Cathy's arm and helped her towards the door.

Cathy laughed. 'Colloquial. It means the modern conversational or slang words. She picked up my magazine for me and I spoke to her automatically in English. I was so surprised when she answered me. If I see her again I must ask her if she read my father's books when she was a child.'

'If she learnt her English at University it is unlikely she was given children's books to read.'

Cathy shrugged. 'I'll save my old magazines for her. You could take them in the next time you visit.'

Monika hugged the magazine to herself in delight, then pushed it into her apron pocket. She would resist even opening it until she was back in her apartment that evening. Still smiling she bent and plumped up the cushion in the chair where Cathy had been sitting. As she did so something caught her eye at the side and she slipped her fingers around it and drew out a gold bracelet. She closed her fingers around it quickly and turned away before dropping it into her pocket along with the magazine. It must belong to Mrs Iliopolakis and she should give it in at reception so it could be collected; she certainly did not want Mr Iliopolakis to think she was going to keep it for herself.

She hesitated. In all probability Mrs Iliopolakis would have no idea where she had lost it and reception could deny all knowledge of it being handed in. She would speak to Mrs Planatakis and ask if there was a telephone number where Mr Iliopolakis could be contacted. She would be much happier leaving it at reception once he knew it was there.

Mrs Planatakis shook her head. 'I cannot give you Mr Iliopolakis's private telephone number. It is confidential between just a few members of staff.'

'You don't have to give it to me,' Monika assured her. 'It is very important that I speak to him. If you were to telephone him I am quite happy for you to hear the conversation.'

'I understand he was here only a short while ago. Why didn't you speak to him then?'

'This is about something that happened after he left.'

Mrs Planatakis shrugged. 'I suppose I can try. You realise you are wasting your break time?'

'That is no problem. I'd be terribly grateful if you could contact him and allow me to speak to him briefly.'

Vasilis answered tersely. He hated using the mobile 'phone that was in the car whilst he was actually driving.

'Mr Iliopolakis, it is Monika, the cleaning lady.'

'Yes?'

'I found a gold bracelet caught on the cushion in the chair where your wife was sitting. I will leave it at reception for you to collect.'

'Just a minute.'

Monika heard him speak to Cathy and a few seconds later he spoke on the telephone again.

'Thank you very much for telling me that you found it. My wife had not realised she had lost it and would have been most distressed. It has great sentimental value for her. Ask reception to place it in the safe and I will collect it tomorrow.'

'Thank you, sir.' Monika handed the telephone back to Mrs Planatakis. 'Thank you very much.' She took the gold bracelet from her apron pocket and held it up. 'It is so pretty. It would have been a shame for her to lose it. Mr Iliopolakis has asked me to leave it at reception so they can put it in the safe.'

'Why didn't you hand it in to reception immediately?'

'I was concerned that Mrs Iliopolakis would be upset that she had lost it and not think to ask at the hotel. If Mr Iliopolakis came when a different receptionist was working they might not know it was in the safe. Now Mr Iliopolakis will know it is there whenever it is convenient for him to call.'

Mrs Planatakis nodded. It was a wonder the girl had not kept it. She could have denied finding it and sold it for a considerable sum. 'Take your break time, Monika. You deserve it.'

Cathy made a pile of her old magazines and added a book she had finished with the intention of asking Vasilis to take them to "The Central". He had been visiting the hotel daily, Vasi driving up from Elounda to join him twice each week and Cathy understood there was a problem.

'It's to do with the computers,' he explained when Cathy questioned him. 'I didn't understand how they worked, but Vasi convinced me they would be a good idea for keeping the accounts at "The Central". He employed Dimitra to teach him and also to transfer the accounts over. The system seemed to be working well until Vasi contemplated buying the "Imperia". He pulled out of the deal after the structural survey and it was then that we found out that money had been transferred from our business accounts into another.'

'Couldn't you prove that and reclaim it?'

'Of course, the bank manager was very helpful and we thought the problem had been rectified.'

Cathy frowned. 'But surely Vasi has bought the "Imperia"?'

'He had no choice. Alecos, who had been mainly responsible for siphoning off the money from our accounts with the help of Dimitra, had bought the hotel. He insisted Vasi purchased it back from him or he would accuse Vasi of forcing him off the road and causing his car accident.'

'Oh, Vasilis, why didn't you tell me? You must have been so worried.'

'I didn't see any need to bother you with the details. You were equally distraught when Vasi was accused. Thankfully he was cleared of the charges.'

'I thought Dimitra was still working at "The Central"?'

'She is. We both felt sorry for her after her experience with the rapist and decided to give her a second chance. She's still in a bad way mentally.'

'So all is well now?'

'Not really. I am going in every day to check the accounts, but I need Vasi with me to explain exactly how the system works.'

'Can't Dimitra do that?'

'I'm sure she can, but I don't trust her fully. She could tell me anything. Vasi knows what he is doing and she is no longer allowed access to the finance account as before.

All the outgoings have to be sanctioned by me or by Vasi. It means we have to check that no fictitious name has been added to the staff and the hours they have worked are correct. It's time consuming. I need to know exactly what I am doing before Vasi goes to England.'

'I wish there was something I could do to help.'

Vasilis smiled at his wife. 'Just be patient with me for a short while longer. I feel I am neglecting you badly at the moment.'

'Don't concern yourself with me. Just get everything finalised so Vasi can go off to visit Saffron. I would like you to take that pile in with you tomorrow, though.' Cathy indicated the magazines. 'It's likely to fall over any minute.'

'I'm sorry it took me so long to remember to bring them,' said Vasilis as he handed her a heavy carrier bag. 'I've had one or two other things to deal with.'

Monika smiled at him gratefully. 'It is very kind of your wife. I do appreciate it. Thank you for bringing them.'

'It was no problem. I was coming in to the hotel. Has my son arrived yet?'

'I haven't seen him, but he may have entered when I was having my break.'

'I'm pleased to hear you take one. You always seem to be polishing the doors whenever I arrive.'

'I try to keep them clean, but it is difficult.'

'You're doing a good job. I hope you have other duties, otherwise polishing glass all day would be very monotonous.'

'I am responsible for ensuring that the whole of the vestibule is clean.'

Vasilis gazed around. 'Well, it all looks very satisfactory.'

'Thank you, sir.'

Vasilis left Monika to continue with her work. She was longing to look inside the carrier to see which magazines Cathy had sent her, but she knew if she did she would be unable to resist taking them out. She hugged the bag to her. She would have to wait until her lunch break to satisfy her curiosity.

'Did you give the girl the bag?' asked Cathy when Vasilis returned home.

'I certainly did and she was very grateful. I also told the manager I had given them to her. I didn't want her to be accused of walking off with something that did not belong to her.'

'That was thoughtful of you. I suppose when you have a low paid job you are always suspected of pilfering.'

'Do you think she is planning to sell them?'

Cathy shook her head. 'She could easily have sold my bracelet if she wanted extra money. She wouldn't get very much for second hand magazines. I imagine when she's finished with them she'll pass them to a friend who reads English or throw them away. I feel it's wrong that someone who is well educated should be working as a cleaner. Could you help her to find a decent job?'

'What are you suggesting?'

'I don't know, but maybe one of the other hotels would like a member of staff who speaks English.'

'They all have their receptionists who speak a variety of languages. She'd need to be able to communicate in various other languages before they would consider employing her; besides she may be familiar with the English language but you don't really know how fluent she is.'

'She appeared very capable when she spoke to me.'

Vasilis sighed. 'Alright, I'll have a word with Mrs Planatakis and see what she knows about her background.'

Mrs Planatakis was surprised when Vasilis asked her about Monika. 'Has she displeased you? I have no complaint with her work, but if she has been rude to you or a guest that is unacceptable.'

'Not at all. She appears to be a very pleasant young woman and undoubtedly honest. I also understand that she is well educated.

According to my wife she speaks excellent English and attended University. Why is she working as a cleaner?'

Mrs Planatakis hesitated. The owner of the hotel had every right to know the personal history of his staff, but provided they had no criminal record and were given a good reference from a previous employer she did not familiarise him with details of the cleaners and chamber maids whose employment was her responsibility.

'Maybe if we went into my office we could talk privately.'

Vasilis followed her into the small room and sat down on the chair opposite her desk. 'I feel as if I am being interviewed for a job,' he smiled.

Mrs Planatakis immediately offered him her chair, but he declined. 'I was joking. I am certainly not looking for any extra work. Tell me what you know about this girl.'

'This is completely confidential, Mr Iliopolakis. I have not divulged her references or circumstances to anyone. If I have done wrong I apologise.'

Vasilis raised his eyebrows. 'You are beginning to intrigue me. What has the girl done?'

'To the best of my knowledge she has done nothing wrong at all. She has been the victim of circumstances. She agreed that I could speak to her previous employer provided I did not let the lady know where I was calling from. Mrs Eth - Ethanides – I think that was her name – confirmed that Monika had worked for her as a library assistant after leaving University on Rhodes. She has excellent qualifications in English, German, classical Greek and a knowledge of French. She had taken some of the library examinations and was conversant with the computer programme that is used universally.'

'So why would the girl want to leave?'

'An unfortunate marriage, various injuries due to her husband's rough treatment that finally resulted in a miscarriage.'

'Better to have left the husband than a lucrative and satisfying job.'

Mrs Planatakis shook her head. 'She was convinced that if she tried to hide from him on Rhodes he would find her, so she came to Crete. She was willing to take any work that was available. I did offer to promote her to the position of a chamber maid recently, but she declined and asked me to offer it to her work colleague.'

'Why was that?'

'She said Eirini had worked here longer and she also had a family to care for.'

'She sounds like a very kind and considerate young woman.'

'I think she is. I cannot fault her. She even asked permission to borrow books from the shelf in the vestibule. No one would ever have noticed is she had helped herself.'

Vasilis nodded and rose. 'Thank you, Mrs Planatakis. I'll make sure the information remains confidential.' He would tell Cathy of his findings that evening, but she would have no reason to tell anyone. 'I will go and see if my son has arrived.'

Crete 2008 - 2009

Monika continued working as a cleaner at "The Central". Despite finding the work boring and monotonous she felt safe at the hotel. Her mother had told her that the notices Manu had placed around the town had gradually been taken down and he was no longer calling on them.

'I'm sure you could come home for a visit.'

'I can't risk him seeing me,' said Monika sadly. 'Until I know if he has divorced me I would be frightened to go out in case someone recognised me and told him I was there.'

'Monika, you will not know if he tries to divorce you. It is a legal requirement that the papers should be sent to you so you can defend the action if you wish.'

'I certainly wouldn't defend it. Can't they be lodged with a lawyer? They could then place an advertisement in the newspapers and ask me to contact them.'

Litsa sighed. 'I don't know how these legal things work. Why don't you consult a lawyer on Crete and ask him to explain the procedure?'

'I don't know any lawyers.'

'You don't have to know them. You just choose one and make an appointment.'

'Are they expensive?'

'I have no idea, but I could send you some money,' offered Litsa.

'No, Mamma, I still have some savings,' Monika sighed. Her dream of taking driving lessons would have to be postponed once again if she was going to spend money on a lawyer. 'I'll look around the town when I have my weekend off and see if there is one that specialises in divorce and find out how much he charges.'

Despite Monika's assurances to her mother that she would seek out a lawyer she hesitated. If she confided in one would he have to divulge her whereabouts to any lawyer Manu had employed? There was no certainty that Manu was planning to divorce her anyway. He may not have met anyone else since she had left him and could be content with a bachelor existence. He would probably prefer to be a widower than divorced and the thought chilled her; she was convinced that if he did find her he would treat her so brutally that she would not survive her injuries.

Monika wondered if she dared ask Mr Iliopolakis for his advice. He was a business man and would know people in the legal profession. She was so busy thinking about the problem whilst she hoovered the carpet in the conference room that she did not hear the door open and see Mr Iliopolaki until he stood in front of her. Immediately she switched off the hoover.

'I'm so sorry, sir. I didn't hear you enter.'

'No problem. You appeared very deep in thought.'

Monika blushed. 'I was trying to decide if I could ask your advice.'

Vasilis raised his eyebrows. 'You are welcome to ask, but I don't know if I will be the right person to advise you. What is your problem?'

'I would like to speak to a lawyer, but I would like the conversation to remain confidential. I don't know if that would be possible.'

Vasilis hesitated. 'That could depend upon the nature of your business. If it involved anything illegal he would be bound to pass the information on to the police to make enquiries.'

'Oh, no. It's purely personal.'

Vasilis leaned back against the conference table. 'I'm sure I could recommend someone, but I would need a little more information. Why would you want a lawyer? If you have a complaint about your working hours or conditions and Mrs Planatakis is unable to help you I would be willing to advise you of your rights.'

Monika blushed even more deeply. 'I have no complaints at all about working here. I just need some advice about a matrimonial problem – on behalf of my mother,' she added.

'Surely if it is your mother's problem she should be the one seeking advice? I don't think any lawyer would be willing to discuss the problem with you without her permission.'

'I just want to make sure that whatever details have to be given will remain confidential, even if the lawyer has to make enquiries.'

'Without wanting to pry into your affairs I still need a little more information so I can direct you to a law firm that would be conversant with your problem and be able to give you reliable advice. Does it concern land or property ownership, building regulations?'

'No,' Monika shook her head. 'I think I need someone who knows about divorcing a missing person.'

'I see. I have to admit I have never had to use a lawyer in that respect, but I am sure my legal adviser could give me the name of a reputable firm.'

'And it would be confidential?' persisted Monika.

'I can impress that fact upon them. Leave it with me. If I don't see you when I come next I will leave a name and address for you at reception. By the way, I've left some magazines there for you.'

'Thank you very much, Mr Iliopolakis, for the magazines and the advice.'

Vasilis shrugged. 'I have done nothing. The magazines are from my wife, I am just the errand boy and I have not helped you with your problem as yet.'

Monika smiled with relief as Vasilis left. At least when she telephoned her mother this week she would be able to say that she had made enquiries and was waiting to be given the name of a legal firm.

Vasilis considered Monika's request. Despite her reticence he was sure it was a personal matter relating to the information Mrs Planatakis had divulged about the girl. Maybe she had at last summoned up the courage to divorce her husband and now did not know where he was located.

Once back at his apartment he called his legal adviser. 'Yiorgo, can you recommend a reliable lawyer who deals with divorce?'

'Divorce Mr Iliopolakis? This is not for you, I hope.'

'No, I'm pleased to say that my marriage is happy and stable. One of my employees asked me if I could recommend a legal firm to her that dealt with divorce.'

'The lady wishes to have a divorce?'

'I don't know any details. She was very unwilling to tell me what kind of legal advice she needed. She is very insistent that whoever she speaks to should keep any information she gives them confidential.'

'Naturally. In the initial stages there should be no need to disclose any details to the other partner. If proceedings are initiated it becomes another matter. It then becomes essential that both parties are in possession of the full facts.'

'So who would you recommend?'

'Is the matter urgent?'

'I don't know.'

'Well, we will assume that it is not. Should it become so we can always escalate proceedings and if necessary use a different firm. I suggest you telephone Antipolakis. See if Yiannis can take it on. He's pretty reliable.'

Vasilis wrote down the details and sealed them inside an envelope which he addressed to Monika, adding "the cleaner" after her name. If he did not see her the next time he visited he would leave it at reception for her.

Three times Monika dialled the number Vasilis had given her, only to cut the call off as soon as it began to ring. Was she being foolish? Would it not be better to leave things as they were? They were bound to want her name and address and she was unwilling to disclose either. After two sleepless nights turning the problem over in her mind she decided she would give her name, but declare her address to be "The 'Central" hotel. If they thought she lived at a hotel it would probably increase their fees but that was a risk she must take.

The receptionist she spoke with accepted her name and address without question and Monika breathed a sigh of relief. If she was not happy with the man she met on Thursday after work she would thank him for his time, pay his bill and not return.

Yiannis looked at her critically as she entered his office. She was clean and smart, but her clothes were not of the quality he would have expected a woman who lived at "The Central" to wear. Monika sat in the chair he indicated and twisted her fingers together nervously.

Yiannis smiled at her. 'Please relax. There is nothing to worry about. I understand you would like some advice. Would it be more comfortable for you if you spoke with my female colleague?'

Monika shook her head. 'I don't mind who I speak to provided I am assured that whatever I say will be kept confidential.'

'Nothing that you tell me will be divulged without your express permission. In return I have to ask for complete honesty from you, however painful that might be. I would not contemplate taking a case if I thought the client had held back information or lied. The discrepancies would come to light and I would look foolish and inefficient. Now, with that out of the way, would you like to tell me your problem?'

'How can I find out if my husband has started divorce proceedings against me?'

Yiannis raised his eyebrows. 'When a party takes out divorce proceedings the other party has to be notified. That gives them the opportunity to contest the action if they think the grounds are unjustified or incorrect or to reply with their consent to proceed. Are you under the impression that your husband has started proceedings and you have not been notified?'

'He doesn't know my address.'

'In that case his lawyer should have placed an advertisement in the newspapers asking you to come forward. Have you seen any such thing?'

'No, but I haven't looked. Suppose it has been there and I've not seen it or replied?'

'Provided there is proof that the notice was in the newspapers for a reasonable amount of time and you had not replied the divorce would be finalised by default.'

'But how will I know?'

'If your husband is not aware of your current address how do you expect to know?'

'I thought it might be listed somewhere, like at the Town Hall, and I could go and look,' answered Monika miserably.

Yiannis sighed. 'I think we need to start at the beginning. What grounds does your husband have for divorcing you?'

'I left him.'

'Was that with mutual consent?'

Monika shook her head. 'I didn't dare tell him I was leaving.'

'Had you discussed the possibility of a divorce between you?'

'Not really. I asked him if he would like to divorce me and he said he had no grounds yet. I thought if I left him that would give him grounds.'

'That puts a slightly different complexion on things. How long ago did you leave him?'

'Almost three years.'

'Without the consent of both parties a two year separation is not sufficient for a divorce. You leaving him without his agreement would be classed as desertion and he would need to wait five years before he could commence proceedings.'

'Two more years!' Monika gasped. 'I can't wait that long.'

'Is there a new man in your life?'

'Oh, no. I want to see my mother and grandmother again.'

'Why should that be a problem?'

'If I visited them I would be sure to be seen and he would know I was in the area. He would force me to go back to him.'

Yiannis smiled at her dramatics. 'He could not force you to live with him.'

'He would find a way. He'd probably threaten to hurt my mother or grandmother if I didn't do as he said.'

'Are you saying you husband behaved abusively towards you?'

'Yes' whispered Monika.

'You realise you could divorce him for unreasonable behaviour. You would need proof, of course.'

Monika shook her head. 'You don't understand; whenever I was injured he claimed it was my own fault through being clumsy or careless.'

'Were these injuries serious enough for you to have to attend the hospital to have them treated?'

'I went to an oculist to have my eye checked, the hospital for a chipped elbow bone and I spent some weeks in hospital with multiple injuries and a miscarriage.'

'And how do you account for the injuries?'

'He threw a tin at me and hit my eye, he slammed the door back on my arm and that caused my elbow to be chipped. I didn't trip going down the steps, he threw me against the wall with such force that I lost my balance and fell.'

'And that resulted in a miscarriage?'

'I was given a Caesarean but they were unable to save the baby.'

Yiannis sat forwards. 'If these assaults were carried out on your person why didn't you report him to the police?'

'He is a policeman. I didn't think they would believe me.'

'Did you take any legal advice? You could have instigated a restraining order preventing him from coming near you.'

Monika shook her head. 'I was frightened he would hurt me so badly that I would end up crippled in some way. That's why I cannot risk visiting my mother. If he found out I had been there he would try to force information from her. I don't want her or my grandmother to be hurt.'

'Does your mother know where you are now?'

'Not really. All she knows is that I am working at a hotel in Heraklion.'

'Has he visited her to ask where you are?'

'He did at first, but she truly did not know where I was. He put posters around saying I was a missing person, but they have been taken down now.'

Yiannis frowned. 'To the best of my recollection I've not seen any posters around with your details.'

For the first time during their interview Monika smiled. 'You wouldn't. I came here from Rhodes.'

'To satisfy my curiosity what made you come here?'

'I intended to go to Kos, but the ferries weren't running so I went to Piraeus. I was seen by one of my husband's colleagues so I took the next ferry that was available and ended up here.'

'Now, Miss Kokanides, I do not disbelieve anything you have told me, but before I can decide on a plan of action I need more details from you, your husband's name, the address where you lived, dates of your injuries and whether there is anyone who can corroborate your accusations.'

'My mother.'

'She would not be considered an impartial witness,' smiled Yiannis. 'You understand I have to be certain that the facts you have given me are not a product of your imagination. No, hear me out,' Yiannis held up his hand as Monika was about to protest. 'Putting aside any other injuries you may have sustained, however caused, losing your baby was obviously a very traumatic event. You may have placed undue blame on your husband and the other incidents you mention have become magnified in your mind.'

Monika shook her head. 'I thought all men treated their wives roughly until I spoke to Mrs Ethanides.'

Yiannis wrote down the name. 'Who is this lady?'

'I worked for her at the library. She agreed to give me a reference for the hotel work.'

'You worked in a library? What work are you doing now at the hotel?'

'I'm a cleaner.'

'Is that what you did in the library?' asked Yiannis.

'I am a qualified librarian.'

'So why didn't you apply for a position in a library on Crete? If there was nothing available in Heraklion there are other towns with libraries.'

'I just wanted some work so I could afford my rent and food. I didn't declare that I was a trained librarian. That would have been the first place my husband would have looked for me. Being in the police he could have approached every library in Greece and asked for a list of their employees.'

Yiannis sat back and regarded Monika gravely. 'You have two options. You either wait a further two years and hope that your husband does divorce you for desertion or you can start divorce proceedings against him for unreasonable behaviour. It would have been better if you had taken out a restraining order against him when you had injuries to show and followed that up with divorce papers.'

'Is there no way you can find out if he is trying to divorce me? I won't contest it, whatever reasons he gives.'

Yiannis frowned. 'I can make some enquiries, but we don't usually disclose the name of our clients. I have promised you anonymity so I cannot say why I want to know if your husband has instigated any proceedings against you.'

Monika shook her head resignedly. 'It's better that I forget it. Thank you or your time and advice.'

'You're welcome to return when you've had more time to

consider the situation. Of course, your husband may wish to marry again and he would need to have a divorce finalised before he could do that.'

Monika smiled wanly. 'All I can ask is if you receive any enquiries about my whereabouts coming from Rhodes you let me know. I can be contacted at "The Central". The reception desk would give me a telephone message and I could call you.' She did not expect to hear again from the lawyer.

Monika looked for Mr Iliopolakis so she could thank him for giving her the telephone number but he did not appear at the hotel, although some magazines had been left at reception for her.

'I didn't see Mr Iliopolakis come in.' she said as she collected them.

'Mr Vasi brought them. Mr Iliopolakis is at home looking after his wife as she has had an accident.'

'Not a serious one, I hope?'

'She fell and has hurt her back. It will take some time for her to recover fully.'

'When will Mr Vasi be coming in again?'

'Tomorrow.'

Monika nodded. The least she could do was buy a bunch of flowers and leave them at reception to be given to him to take to Cathy. 'May I leave some flowers for Mrs Iliopolakis and a message?'

'Leave them here and I'll see he gets them.'

The following morning Monika took advantage of her morning break to go to the local flower stall. She felt embarrassed as she handed them to the receptionist. The Iliopolakis apartment was probably full of large, expensive bouquets and she had only been able to afford to purchase a bunch. When she returned to her duties after lunch she noticed that the flowers had gone. Once again she had missed seeing Mr Iliopolakis's son.

To Monika's surprise the receptionist called to her and indicated that she had a telephone call. Her heart jumped? Was it the lawyer she had consulted with some good news for her?

'Hello?' she said nervously.

'Monika? It's Cathy Iliopolakis here. I wanted to telephone and thank you for the flowers you sent me. That was a very kind thought.'

'It was nothing. I appreciate the magazines you have sent in to me.'

'I have some more here for you. I wondered if it would be possible for you to call in and collect them?'

'Certainly I can. When would be convenient?'

'Any afternoon when you have finished work. I'm not going anywhere for quite a while. Do you have a pen and paper available and I'll give you our address.'

Monika wrote the address down quickly on the pad at the receptionist's desk. He frowned at her; the pad was for visitors to write down any details they required to remember.

'I could come tomorrow,' answered Monika immediately. She would love to go to their apartment, although she did not expect to see more than the hallway.

Monika considered taking the clothes she thought of as her best to the hotel and changing into them before she visited the Iliopolakis's apartment. The she told herself not to be so foolish; she would be wearing her coat and Mr Iliopolakis would not know what she was wearing when he answered the door to her.

Before leaving the hotel Monika washed her face and hands and combed her hair carefully. She regularly applied a lightening shampoo, but her roots were looking dark and her hair needed a professional trim to restore its shape. She could call at the hairdresser on her way home and make an appointment for the following week.

She walked slowly down the road leading to the Iliopolakis's apartment. It was a very select area; everyone probably had a cleaner and it was likely that a maid would answer the door to her and she would not even see the interior of the hall. Feeling depressed at the thought she pressed the bell and heard it ring somewhere inside. She was totally unprepared when Vasilis Iliopolakis opened the door with a smile and invited her inside.

'Cathy is looking forward to your visit. As you know she has had an accident and is in considerable pain whenever she moves. Rest is the only cure until the bone has healed. Mind the chair; don't trip over it.' He pointed to the wheelchair that was folded up against the wall of the entrance hall. 'Let me take your coat. We keep the apartment quite warm in the winter. Cathy aches if she begins to feel cold.'

Feeling helpless, Monika unbuttoned her coat and handed it to him. She should have taken her best clothes to the hotel and changed there before she left.

'Come on in.' Vasilis opened the door to the lounge. 'Have a seat next to Cathy and I will fulfil my duties as instructed.'

Monika sat on the edge of a deep armchair, whilst Cathy reclined on the sofa, surrounded by pillows and cushions.

'I'm so pleased you could come,' smiled Cathy. 'I'm tired of reading, I don't understand the television programmes and Vasilis has to be allowed to get on with his work some of the time.'

'Thank you for inviting me.' Monika was not at all sure how long she would be expected to stay. Vasilis could reappear at any moment with a carrier bag of magazines and that would be her cue to leave; instead Vasilis entered pushing a small trolley.

'Cathy is English and she does like her cup of tea. She has tried to educate my taste buds, but without success. Would you care to have a cup of tea or would you prefer coffee?'

'I would like to try to drink a cup of tea.'

Vasilis nodded. 'If you dislike it I will fetch a clean cup and you can join me with coffee. Usually Cathy pours the tea – it is called being Mamma I understand – but she cannot manage even a simple job like that at the moment.' He poured two cups of tea and Cathy looked at him disapprovingly.

'Where is the milk? I have explained that you always put the milk into the cup before you pour in the tea.'

'Monika may prefer it without milk and suppose I put in too much? If I leave it for you to do it is at the strength you like.'

'That is just an excuse. You forgot. Would you like sugar, Monika?'

'I do not know. Is tea sweet?'

'Not unless Vasilis has added sugar to the teapot! Some people prefer it sweet. I like it without any sweetener.'

Monika did not add any milk and took a cautious sip. It was not unpleasant. 'I think this suits me,' she said.

Vasilis placed a small table between them with an assortment of pastries. 'I will ask you to pass the cakes to Cathy, Monika, and if she wants a second cup of tea I am sure you will make a better job of it that I do. I shall leave you ladies for a while to chat about whatever ladies chat about whilst I take the opportunity to do some work.'

Cathy smiled as her husband left the room. 'He is so considerate. He is usually only gone for a few minutes and then he returns to ask if there is anything I need.'

'I'm sure he is very concerned about you.'

'He is, but it is only a minor injury; painful none the less, but I have had worse. There were a few years when I thought I would never walk again.'

Monika looked at Cathy in horror. 'How awful. What happened?'

'I had a car accident. My spine was badly damaged and my pelvis broken. I had convinced myself that I would never be able to walk again so I made little effort.'

'Didn't you want to walk?'

'I think I was frightened that I would fall and do more damage. My brain said "don't walk" so I didn't even try.' Cathy smiled ruefully at the memory.

'But you overcame the problem?'

Cathy shrugged and gave a wince of pain. 'Vasi was drowning and there was no one else around. I had to do something.'

'Mr Vasi? Mr Iliopolakis's son?'

'He was only a little boy and he fell into the swimming pool.'

'And despite being unable to walk you saved him? That was very brave of you. You are a heroine.'

'Not at all. I could swim as the water supported me. I just held Vasi up until help arrived. Do have another pastry and I would like a second cup of tea, please.'

Nervously Monika lifted the milk jug. 'How much milk do I put in?'

'Not too much. I'll tell you when to stop. Now. Just pour the tea on top and it will all mix in well. No, I'll not have another pastry, thank you. I don't want to put on weight. It will take far too long to get rid of again.'

Monika sat back down and selected a small pastry, holding a serviette carefully beneath it so that no crumbs would fall on the chair.

'Now, tell me about yourself, Monika. I know you are working as a cleaner at "The Central". You told me you had learnt your English at school and University so why are you working as a cleaner?'

Monika flushed. 'I needed some work and there was nothing else available at the time.'

'But you have been there for ages now. Haven't you looked for something better?'

'I'm very happy working there.'

'It must be very boring. How do you keep your brain occupied when you are cleaning?'

'I think about the book I am currently reading and recite verbs and participles.'

Cathy looked puzzled. 'I was not a very good scholar. What is a participle?'

Monika smiled. 'It is the way a word changes its ending depending upon the sentence. I could say "I may fall off this chair" using the future tense or "I fell off this chair" if it happened in the past.'

Cathy nodded; she still did not fully understand. 'And you are taught this at University?'

'The rules of the grammar, but understanding the context correctly comes from reading.'

'Have you ever read any of Basil Hurst's books?'

Monika frowned, then smiled. 'I read all of them when I was a child, first in Greek then English.'

Cathy smiled also. 'I'm pleased to hear that. He was my father.'

'Your father!' Monika gasped. 'How wonderful.'

'I thought nothing of it at the time. His first books were the fairy stories he told me at bed time. As I grew older he had to think of more grown up stories to tell me. Vasi tried to teach me Greek using them. He would make me read to him in Greek and roar with laughter when I couldn't pronounce the word properly or didn't know what it meant. He finally gave in when he realised I was a useless pupil. I still cannot speak Greek, despite all the years I have lived over here. My father was fluent in the language and could not understand why he should have such a stupid daughter.'

'Your father was Greek?'

Cathy shook her head. 'No, he was English but lived on Crete until the end of the war. That was when he returned to England and met my mother.'

'And began to write?'

'No, that was much later. He had a small general store. When he began to make some money from his books he sold the shop and spent all his time writing.'

'My grandmother has a general store. It does not make very much money, but it gives her enough to live on.'

'Is that locally?' asked Cathy, knowing full well that the shop was on Rhodes.

'No, it is on a different island.'

'That's a shame. How often are you able to visit her?'

'I have not seen her or my mother for nearly three years now.'

Cathy frowned. 'Surely you could afford a flight or ferry fare?'

'It is not so easy.'

'If money is the problem I am sure Vasilis could arrange something and you could repay him each week from your wages.'

Monika shook her head. 'Thank you. That is a kind thought, but I cannot visit them yet.'

'Why don't they come here to visit you? Again, I'm sure Vasilis would be able to make an arrangement with you.'

Monika felt tears coming into her eyes. 'The time is not right.'

'I'm sorry; I didn't mean to upset you.'

Monika blinked rapidly. 'I am not used to such kindness.'

'I hope no one at the hotel is unkind to you.'

'Oh, no,' Monika hastened to assure her. 'Everyone there is very nice and kind to me. I am not ungrateful for your offer, but I cannot go to my home yet.'

'So you are planning to stay working as a cleaner at "The Central" forever?'

'I hope not. One day I would like to use the knowledge I gained at University.'

'Surely with your proficiency in English you could find work as a translator?'

'I was told there was no work available for people who knew other languages. I imagine the Cretan people fill the jobs as soon as they become vacant.'

'Do you speak another language, apart from Greek obviously?'

'I also speak German and a little French. I am trying to improve my French as my certificate said I had a knowledge of the language, not that I was fluent.'

'Where did you work before you came to Crete?'

Monika hesitated. There really was no reason why she should not tell Cathy where she had worked. 'I was a librarian.'

203

'So why haven't you applied to become a librarian here?'

'I do not want to draw attention to myself. It is better that no one knows I am working on Crete apart from my mother.'

'Did you do something wrong?'

Once again Monika's eyes filled with tears. 'I did nothing wrong. I was not asked to leave.'

'I'm sorry; I was becoming personal and prying into your life. Shall I tell you about mine?'

Monika nodded. She really did not want to talk about herself any more.

'I was a hairdresser and became a model. I then had a car accident and was unable to work any longer. I came to Crete on holiday and met Vasilis. I had been feeling very sorry for myself, and now I am so grateful that I had the accident. If I had not done so it is unlikely I would have come to Crete and Vasilis and I would not have met.'

'It sounds very romantic.'

Cathy shook her head. 'Not really. It is quite a long and involved story. Had I not met Vasilis my father would never have returned to Crete. One day when we have more time I will tell you the details.'

Monika looked at her watch. This was obviously a hint that she should leave. 'I must go. I have little chance to speak English and it has been a pleasure to talk with you. I had no idea it had become so late.'

'You do not have to leave, unless you have another engagement somewhere else.'

Monika thought wildly for a moment. 'I need to call in at the hairdresser before she closes. I need a trim and my colour renewed by an expert.'

Cathy looked at her critically. 'When I am back on my feet I can cut and colour your hair for you. I told you I used to be a hairdresser.'

'That would be very kind of you.' Monika stood up. 'Shall I see myself out? I don't want to disturb Mr Iliopolakis if he's working.'

'He would be very distressed if you left without saying goodbye to him. I will call him. This little contraption that runs off a battery is so useful.' Cathy pressed a buzzer on the side of the table and within seconds Vasilis appeared.

'Do you need me?' he asked Cathy, looking at her anxiously.

'I wanted to tell you that Monika is leaving.'

'No problem. I will just get my coat.'

'Vasilis will take you home in the car. I'm sure you can call in at your hairdresser's tomorrow and it will save you having to carry that heavy bag of magazines.'

'No; really, it isn't far; I can easily walk.'

Cathy shook her head. 'We wouldn't hear of it. It's dark and cold. It will take Vasilis no more than a few moments to drive you home. You'll have to excuse me not getting up to see you out. I hope the next time you visit I will be a little more mobile.'

'Thank you very much, Mrs Iliopolakis. I do hope you will recover very soon.'

'Please, call me Cathy. I thought it a very exotic surname to have when we first married. I then found out it was as common as "Smith" is in England. My friends just know me as Cathy.'

Monika smiled with her; there were at least six members of staff with the surname "Iliopolakis" working at the hotel and none of them claimed to be related either to each other or to the owner.

Vasilis returned to the apartment within twenty minutes. 'I'm pleased I ran her home. It really is cold out there now.'

'She's a nice young woman, Vasilis. We spent a very pleasant afternoon.'

'Did you find out anything about her that I had not told you?'

'Nothing. She was very careful and reticent whenever I tried to probe into her life. I wish you could provide her with a decent job that befits her education. She has read all of my father's books.'

'So have hundreds of other people,' remarked Vasilis dryly.

It became routine for Monika to visit Cathy every other week and Monika felt that she was accepted by Mr Iliopolakis, although she was only a cleaner at his hotel. She and Cathy had become friends, despite the disparity in their circumstances. Once the injury to Cathy's back had improved sufficiently she insisted on cutting and colouring Monika's hair.

'You can trust me,' she assured Monika. 'I cut Vasilis's hair regularly. Have you looked in any of the magazines and decided if you would like a change of style or will you stay with the bob?'

'Is there anything you think would suit me better?'

Cathy took the comb and swept Monika's hair back at the sides, holding it with her hands. 'What do you think of that? It takes some of the hair away from your face and would reduce the weight. You have lovely thick hair, but without thinning it becomes difficult to style.'

Monika looked at her appearance in the mirror she held. 'I like it, I think. It will always grow again if I change my mind.'

Whilst Cathy cut and coloured Monika's hair they chatted easily together. 'I'm so pleased you visit me. I have few friends in Heraklion. It was different when we lived in Elounda. In those days I was able to go down to the village and I would always meet someone I knew or I would call on the family.'

'You have a family down there?'

'No, they're just friends, but known by everyone as "the family". Different generations living and working together.'

'Why did you move to Heraklion?'

'Our house was up a steep hill. We had a beautiful view out over the bay and I loved it when I first lived there. Vasi decided to buy this apartment when he was managing "The Central" and when Vasilis and I visited we fell in love with it. There was the added benefit that it is on level ground. Vasi agreed to sell it to us and return to live in the house in Elounda. It was practical then for Vasilis to take over the running of "The Central" and leave Vasi in control of the other hotels lower down the island. I would love to return, but I would certainly need a house on level ground. I realise that my arthritis is going to prevent me from walking eventually and I could not expect poor Vasilis to push me back up the hill in a wheelchair.'

'You have a car. Surely he could take you up and down the hill.'

Cathy shook her head. 'There is the added complication of the hotels. I would be unable to leave the house once Vasilis had left for Heraklion each day and Vasi would have to drive down to Elounda. We go back to visit friends, of course, but it would not be practical to return down there to live. When you have your holiday you should go down to Elounda. I am sure Vasilis could arrange somewhere for you to stay.'

Monika smiled politely. 'I don't usually take holidays.'

'So what do you do in your free time?'

'I've been to the museum on a number of occasions, but never ventured outside the town further than Knossos.'

'There are many interesting places to see. Some you can reach by bus, others you really need a car unless you're prepared for a long walk.'

'I don't mind walking, but some of the bus journeys seem to take so long that you would no sooner be there than it would be time to catch a bus back.'

'I've been spoilt. I've always been taken everywhere by car. Now, what do you think of that?' Cathy held up the mirror for Monika to look in again.

Monika smiled. 'I like it. When I went to the hairdressers the first time I just asked them to cut my hair and colour it. They didn't offer me any alternative styles.'

'What made you have it cut?'

Monika hesitated. 'I was making a new start so I thought a new hairstyle would be a good idea.'

'Quite right. I had no choice when they cut mine when I was in hospital. I couldn't wait for it to grow again. We'll ask Vasilis's opinion when he arrives home. I've asked him to bring a Chinese takeaway with him. You do like Chinese, don't you?'

'I can't expect to stay for a meal when you have been good enough to save me a visit to the hairdresser.'

'Rubbish. I told Vasilis I did not know how long it would take so it seemed practical to order a takeaway for three of us. If you leave now there will be far too much for us to eat.'

Monika had never seen so many different dishes when Vasilis placed the cartons on the table. 'Just take a little of each and come back for more of the ones you like best. I asked for a wide selection as I know the ones that Cathy and I prefer, but I didn't know your taste.'

Monika blushed. 'I appreciate your thoughtfulness, but I'm sure I would have been happy with anything you chose.'

'Thank goodness you're easy to feed,' smiled Vasilis.' Vasi used to be a nightmare. He turned his nose up at anything that was new and poor Cathy did not know how to cook Greek food.'

'I'm sure he used to do it to annoy me. He would eat chocolate cake and lemonade and when I produced a meal he would say he had no appetite or spit the food out. Thank goodness my father made him see sense.'

'How did he do that?' asked Monika.

'He talked to him and said he understood how difficult it was for him to have a stepmother whom he could not communicate with, but that he must be patient with me. He laid no blame on Vasi and encouraged him to learn English so he could tell me why he didn't like something. Once we were able to talk together life became much easier. Within a couple of years we were actually friends and I enjoyed having a child to look after.'

'My mother said she always enjoyed the time she spent with me, although a good deal of it was in the library. All I wanted to do was read.'

'That reminds me; did you contact that lawyer and solve your mother's problem?'

Monika blushed deeply. 'It was more complicated than I had realised. He said he would call me if he had any news.'

'Hmm, sounds as though he decided to put your problem to one side thinking you would go away. He should at least have advised you that he could not help.'

'I haven't paid his bill yet so I am expecting him to contact me.'

Vasilis nodded. He would call Antipolakis and see who had spoken with Monika and remind him that the girl was waiting for an answer.

Monika did not hear from Yiannis apart from receiving a small bill for his services that she paid immediately. When she telephoned her mother she said the lawyer had really been unable to help her. If Manu planned to divorce her for desertion he would have to wait for at least five years after she had left and then advertise widely to see if anyone knew of her whereabouts.

Litsa sympathised at first and then she laughed. 'I hope he does advertise. Think how sick he'll feel after spending the money and I step forward and give him your address having known it all the time.'

'No, Mamma,' replied Monika in alarm. 'You must do no such thing. If you receive an official enquiry from a lawyer continue to say you do not know where I am. Tell me and I will then get in touch and disclose my address. If Manu found out that you had known where I was all the time he would be so angry.'

Yiannis sounded quite aggrieved when Vasilis spoke to him. He had made enquiries and when nothing was forthcoming he had placed the matter to one side and thought no more about it. Had he known Mr Iliopolakis was involved he would have made a more vigorous effort.

'I told the woman that it would be difficult to find out the information she wanted. If I could pick up the 'phone and ask outright if Mr Graphides had started divorce proceedings against her it would be quite simple, a straight forward yes or no. I had to be very circumspect in the way I asked any questions as she was most insistent that she did not want anyone to know where she was enquiring from, particularly her husband. None of the lawyers I spoke to have any knowledge of the man.'

'What about the police? Do they have their own legal representatives that he could be using?'

Yiannis nodded. 'If I make any enquiries of them the information is very likely to be passed on. I sent the girl a bill and she has paid me so I feel that has to be the end of the matter.'

Vasilis felt helpless. He had no right to interfere on behalf of Monika, but he had become fond of the girl and could sympathise with her longing to visit her mother and grandmother. He also had a problem of his own.

Although Vasilis had been worried about Cathy when she had fallen and been incapacitated for weeks he had enjoyed spending the time at home with her and relying on Vasi to arrange the winter conferences. Vasi had been efficient and was quite capable of running the hotel without any help from his father, but he no longer wished to make the journey up from Elounda every other day.

Cathy's fall had affected her mobility and she was now using a stick when she walked around their apartment. Vasilis was using this as an excuse to stay at the apartment with her rather than go to "The Central". The embarrassing accidents he had suffered so far had happened whilst he was at home, but the thought of such an event happening whilst he was at the hotel was mortifying. What would the staff think if they saw the owner with wet trousers?

He had finally agreed to visit his doctor after Vasi had confronted him. His frequent disappearances to the bathroom had been noticed by Saffron when she visited. She had mentioned her concerns to Vasi who had spoken to his father, assuring him that his complaint could easily be rectified with a small operation. Vasilis felt embarrassed that Saffron should have noticed and was even more reluctant to go to "The Central" each day. The staff would soon realise that he had a problem.

'She's a doctor,' Vasi had assured him. 'Nothing medical would embarrass her. At least visit your doctor and ask his advice.'

The doctor had sent a sample of urine for analysis and prescribed a diet for Vasilis that could help, with a second appointment for a consultation in three months to see if there had been any improvement.

After examining the results from the second urine sample the doctor shook his head. 'Unfortunately the diet does not appear to have been effective. I will send you for an X-ray and when we have the result we can discuss further treatment.'

'You mean I need an operation?'

'It is quite a simple procedure and provided it is carried out early enough there is no reason why you should have any problems in the future.'

'Suppose when they operated they found there was already an abnormality?' asked Vasilis nervously.

'It would be removed and you would be sent for further treatment to stop the disease from spreading. Ignore the condition now and it could be too late for effective treatment in a year or so. I cannot force you to have the operation, Mr Iliopolakis, but if it was me I would want to have it done as quickly as possible. Come back tomorrow and collect a letter from me to take to the hospital and they will give you an admission date.'

Vasilis had been alarmed at the doctor's warning, but did not see how he could leave Cathy and go into hospital. She could certainly not accompany him and look after him as a wife generally did. Vasi was needed at the hotels and there was no one else he felt he could ask to attend to his personal needs whilst he made his recovery.

Before speaking to Cathy, Vasilis telephoned his son. 'The diet hasn't made any noticeable difference. The doctor wants me to go in as soon as possible to have the operation, but I can't.'

'Why not?' asked Vasi.

'Well, there's no one who can come to look after me whilst I'm in there. You need to be at the hotels and Cathy can't be expected to spend all her time sitting on a hard chair and sleeping in a makeshift bed each night.'

'So you employ someone,' answered Vasi impatiently. 'You have plenty of money and the hospital will have a list of competent people who are willing to come in and attend to you. Many of them are retired doctors or nurses.'

'I can't leave Cathy on her own. Suppose she had another fall? She could be lying there for hours, even days, before anyone found her.'

'Pappa, you are making excuses. You need that operation. Why don't you ask that girl, Monika, from the hotel that Cathy is friendly with to come and stay? I'm sure she'd be happy to accept double wages for a week or so.'

Vasilis sighed. 'That might be possible, I suppose. I'll consider it.'

'Pappa,' Vasi spoke sternly, 'You need that operation and the longer it is left the more serious the condition could become. Ask Cathy if she would be happy with the girl staying for a few days. If she is you must speak to Monika tomorrow and then you can arrange a date for your admission.'

Vasilis sat and considered his son's advice. Provided Cathy had no objection to Monika staying in the apartment it could be the answer to his dilemma. If Cathy rejected the idea out of hand then his operation would have to wait, whatever the consequences.

'Of course she can stay,' said Cathy immediately when he made the suggestion. 'I'm quite capable of looking after myself, but it will be reassuring to know there is someone on hand if I do need any help.'

Monika followed Vasilis into his office nervously when he asked to have a private word with her. She hoped no one had complained about her and she was not about to lose her job. She also hoped that Cathy still wished her to visit. She would miss sitting there, talking about the trivia of fashion, hair styles and cosmetics.

'Sit down, Monika.' Vasilis waved his hand towards the seat opposite his desk. 'I have a favour to ask of you.'

Monika sat obediently and nodded. What favour could Mr Iliopolakis possibly want from her?

'I have to go into hospital for a short while for a minor operation and I hope you will be able to help solve a problem that I have.'

A look of horror crossed Monika's face. 'I am not a nurse, Mr Iliopolakis. I have had no training. Please do not ask me to look after you.'

'I wouldn't dream of it,' smiled Vasilis, equally horrified at the thought of the young woman having to deal with his body intimately. 'What I would like you to do is be at the apartment with Cathy. She is perfectly able to see to her personal needs, but I would be happier if I knew there was someone reliable around in case she should have another fall or an accident of any kind.'

'After I have finished work here, you mean? Call in each evening and check that she doesn't need anything.'

Vasilis shook his head. 'I would like you to be there with her day and night. Five minutes after you left she could have a fall and would then be lying there until you arrived the following day.' Vasilis did not add that Cathy was more likely to be found by the cleaner when she arrived each morning.

Monika frowned. 'But my work here, Mr Iliopolakis. What will happen about that?'

'I will speak to Mrs Planatakis. I am sure you have not taken any holiday leave since you arrived here. You are obviously entitled to some time off.'

'I saw no reason to have leave and spend it wandering around on my own.'

'You could have gone to a different town and stayed there for a week; discovered a new area; seen new things.'

Monika shrugged. 'I have been used to working every day, except when I was in hospital.' She did not admit that she did not want to spend any of her hard earned savings that she was accumulating to pay for her driving lessons.

'You would not be expected to work whilst you were staying with Cathy, just to keep her company. I have spoken to her and she is more than happy to have you coming to stay.'

'I would be happy to go shopping and do the cooking. I have to do that for myself.'

'I'm sure she would appreciate that.' Vasilis smiled with relief. 'That's agreed then? I'll make the appointment for my hospital admission and then I will speak to Mrs Planatakis and tell her you are taking two weeks' leave. You will remain employed at the hotel and receive the usual retainers' wage. In addition I will pay you for the time you spend at the apartment.'

Monika frowned. 'That would mean I was being paid twice.'

'Whilst you are on your holiday you will be working for me so it is only right that I pay you. If Cathy asks you to go shopping you bring back the bills and I will see that you are reimbursed; expenses are separate from your wages.'

'Thank you, Mr Iliopolakis. I hope you will recover speedily from your operation, but I will enjoy spending time with Cathy whilst you are in hospital.'

November 2009

Monika enjoyed staying with Cathy. Her room was larger than the bedroom she had shared with Manu, and at least four times the size of the room she had slept in at her grandmother's shop. Her current apartment was only a little larger.

She was pleased that she had her own bathroom and did not have to share Cathy's. Every day she made sure her shower and basin were spotless, although Cathy had assured her it was not her job and the cleaner would do whatever was necessary. When she placed clean towels in Cathy's bathroom she looked at the array of bottles that stood on the shelf. She could not imagine that it was necessary to have so many different lotions, although she had to admit that Cathy's skin glowed radiantly without a blemish.

Each morning Monika would sit with Cathy and they would discuss the meal they would have later in the day. Monika would open the cupboards and fridge to check on the contents and Cathy would make a list for Monika to take to the local shops. Once Monika was assured that Cathy was settled in the lounge, with her magazines and a book beside her, the television remote control, her mobile 'phone and a glass of fruit juice at hand along with her stick, she would accept some Euros from Cathy and depart. This also meant she was out whilst the cleaner was in attendance in the event of Cathy having a fall.

Upon her return she would place her purchases on the

counter top in the kitchen and Cathy would join her. Under Cathy's direction Monika would place the grocery items into the cupboards and between them they would begin preparations for their evening meal. Usually Cathy would sit and chop the salad ingredients whilst Monika prepared the pastry, meat or fish that she would cook later.

One afternoon she was surprised when Vasilis's son arrived accompanied by an English woman. 'Saffie,' cried Cathy in delight. 'I knew you were coming over, but I didn't know you were coming to see me.'

'Of course I would come to see you. I could not come to Crete and not visit you. Have you recovered completely from that nasty fall you had? How have you managed on your own without Vasilis?'

Cathy indicated Monika. 'This young lady has been absolutely marvellous. Nothing has been too much trouble for her.'

Monika blushed. 'Would you like me to prepare a tray of tea?' She wanted an excuse to escape to the kitchen.

'Yes, please. Coffee for Vasi, of course, and some of the pastries you bought this morning.'

Monika nodded. 'I will bring it in as soon as it is ready.'

'And a cup and plate for yourself,' called Cathy after her. 'You must meet Saffie. Have you visited your father?' asked Cathy turning to Vasi.

'We've just come from the hospital. The doctor says he is recovering well and they confirmed nothing alarming was found when they operated. He'll telephone you this evening with some other good news.'

Cathy breathed a sigh of relief. 'I know he told me all was well when he 'phoned, but the doctors often delay telling you the truth. It was no good me asking them for information. They would have told me in Greek or used long and complicated medical words that I didn't understand. Thank you, Vasi.'

When Vasilis telephoned that evening Monika discreetly retired to her room to ensure their conversation could be conducted privately. She felt disheartened when Cathy announced that Vasilis was being discharged from the hospital the next day. She would obviously be expected to return to her own apartment and the cleaning job at "The 'Central".

'I'll get my case packed,' she said quietly, trying to smile. 'It's good news that Mr Iliopolakis has recovered so well.'

'You can't leave yet.' Cathy spoke firmly. 'Vasilis will have to recuperate. He won't be able to run around doing the shopping or helping me with the cooking for a while. Please stay, for at least another week.'

Monika agreed readily to stay, although she expected to spend most of her time sitting in her bedroom; Cathy would not want her company now her husband was home.

Vasilis opened the front door to his apartment and the taxi driver placed his case inside the hallway for him. Monika hurried forward.

'Welcome home, Mr Iliopolakis. I'll take your case to your room. Cathy is waiting for you in the lounge and I will be in the kitchen if there is anything you want.' Monika was not sure if she should unpack Vasilis's case or leave it for him. She placed it on a chair and decided she would offer to do so when Cathy asked for some drinks to be taken in to them.

Vasilis smiled at his wife. 'I'm sure Vasi told you that there was no evidence of a growth. The doctor says I should make a satisfactory recovery and will just need to go for a check up each year. If I notice the symptoms have returned then I must go back at once.'

'I was so pleased to see Vasi and that Saffie was with him. I understand she has given her notice in at the hospital and is planning to stay over here with him.'

'So she told me. I have a lot to thank her for. I thought my condition was due to getting older. Now I will be able to return to work without having to worry about embarrassing myself and the staff.'

'Not yet, Vasilis. I'm sure the doctor didn't say you could go back to work immediately. I've asked Monika to stay on for at least another week. She has been amazing. Nothing was ever too much trouble for her and she was always willing to sit with me; sometimes we both read and sometimes we talked. I told her about life in England and she told me about growing up in Rhodes. Eventually she even confided in me how she had suffered at the hands of her husband. He sounds like a brute.'

'She is a very nice young woman. I wish I could do something for her. If I had a vacancy for a receptionist I would promote her. She says she's happy with her cleaning job and has no desire to be a chambermaid or waitress.'

'I'm sure you can do something. I've an idea that I'll discuss with you later.'

'Why can't you tell me now?'

Cathy shook her head. 'You might refuse and I would hate to raise Monika's hopes.'

'So what is this idea you have for Monika?' asked Vasi as he lay beside Cathy in their bed. 'Do you want her to live here permanently as your companion?'

'No, I'm more than happy to have you as my permanent companion.' Cathy snuggled closer to her husband. 'You have a great deal of money, Vasilis. Every year you complain about the amount of tax you have to pay. You should spend it. Speak to your accountant and ask if charitable donations would decrease your bill.'

'I already donate to charities and I gave the staff a pay rise last year.'

'And no doubt you increased the prices for the visitors to cover it. I have something different in mind. Why don't you arrange for Monika to go to Rhodes to visit her mother?'

'She can have time off for a visit whenever she likes.'

'That's not the answer, Vasilis. She is frightened of her

husband. She's convinced that if he sees her he'll insist she returns to him and probably injure her in some way. If you sent her over there with Vasi she should be safe enough.'

'Vasi? Why should Vasi have to go to Rhodes?'

'I'm sure you can think up some excuse. He has to attend a business meeting and needs someone who can speak the language.'

'Vasi speaks perfect English.'

Cathy sighed in exasperation. 'Think, Vasilis, suppose the meeting was with German or French speakers? He would need an interpreter.'

'But I don't know any Germans or Frenchmen to do business with.'

'You don't have to. You tell Monika you need an interpreter and will only be there for three days. Once they have arrived Vasi finds the meeting has been cancelled. He can escort her to and from her mother and no one will take any notice of them. They will just be a couple on holiday.'

'I'm not sure. You're serious that I should spend money on Monika?'

'Not on her exactly, she could repay you gradually. She needs help to extricate herself from her unhappy situation. Vasi could speak to a lawyer whilst he was there. Monika would be very relieved if she could obtain a divorce from her husband. At least she would know then that he could not make her return to live with him and she would be able to see her mother and grandmother again. Tell your accountant you are investigating a business opportunity and need Vasi to go to Rhodes with an interpreter. You could put it down to business expenses.'

Vasilis looked thoughtful. 'I could 'phone Giovanni and ask for the name of that American at the Embassy who dealt with the fire at his self catering apartments. He might be able to recommend a local lawyer who would be more helpful than the one she saw here.'

'Call Vasi tomorrow, tell him you're home and discuss it with him. If he refuses there's nothing more to be said. If he agrees then you can speak to Monika. They need only be gone for three days,' Cathy insisted. 'They fly in and arrive in the afternoon, Monika can spend the following day with her mother and they fly back the next day. Hardly long enough for anyone to find her.'

Monika could hardly contain her excitement. Vasilis had asked her if she would be willing to visit Rhodes and act as an interpreter between Vasi and some German business men. At first she had refused, saying she could not visit the island as she was sure her husband would find out she was there.

'I am so frightened that my husband will force me to return to him.'

'He cannot make you live with him. You are an adult.'

'If he threatened to hurt my mother or grandmother I would have no choice. I was worried that some harm would come to them when I first left Rhodes.'

Vasilis had brushed aside her fears. 'You and Vasi will be booked in at a hotel; separate rooms, of course. If anyone asks you are his secretary and interpreter. You will arrive in the afternoon, spend the day at the meeting and leave the following day. Hardly time for anyone to know you are there and Vasi will be with you.'

'Would I be able to make a quick visit my mother?' asked Monika timidly.

'I'm sure Vasi could arrange to fit in a visit to her. Let Vasi do any talking that is necessary at the airport or hotel, you just stay in the background so no one will take any notice of you.'

'What about my clothes? I'm not sure I have anything to wear that would be suitable. Should I buy a suit?'

Vasilis smiled at her. 'There is no need for you to buy anything. Your ordinary clothes are perfectly adequate. It is quite an informal meeting.'

Despite her excitement Monika was nervous about the impending visit. Would her knowledge of German be sufficient to act as an interpreter? She had borrowed a book on German grammar from the library to take with her. She hoped Vasi would tell her the nature of the discussion that was to take place as that would help her. She was also nervous about spending the time in Vasi's company. She did not know him as well as she knew his father and hoped he would be as easy to talk with.

Monika had misgivings about flying from Crete to Rhodes as she had never flown before, but Vasi appeared delighted.

'I love flying,' he said. 'I wanted to be an airline pilot.'

'Why did you change your mind?'

'It was changed for me. I went for my medical and they found I had high tone deafness. It is no inconvenience to me but you need perfect hearing to be a pilot. I had been looking forward to flying to England to spend time with Saffron, but Cathy's accident meant a change of plans.'

'Why are you meeting these Germans?'

Vasi looked nonplussed by her question and hesitated before answering. 'Something to do with opening another hotel, I think. I will telephone my father this evening to find out the details.'

Monika frowned. Surely Vasi should know what the meeting was to be about.

Monika looked out of the small window of the aeroplane; she could see they were approaching Rhodes and she suddenly felt quite sick with apprehension. Suppose she was recognised by airport security and Manu was informed that she had returned to the island?

She closed her eyes and tried to keep the thought at bay. Vasi glanced at her anxiously. 'Are you feeling alright? We'll be landing in a few minutes.'

Monika nodded. 'I haven't flown before.' She could no longer hear the sound of the engines and Vasi's voice seemed to be coming from far away. 'I have only travelled by ferry.'

'That was brave of you. I do not like travelling on the water. I feel far safer when I am in the air. Keep swallowing to clear your ears and you'll be fine,' advised Vasi, thinking that was the cause of her discomfort. He had his own problems to consider. Would Monika believe him when he told her the meeting was cancelled and would she agree to meet her mother? If she refused it would have been a wasted journey and the elaborate subterfuge unnecessary.

They walked through the passport control area with only a cursory glance being given to Monika's identity card and Vasi led her to where a taxi driver was holding up a placard with his name. They followed him to the taxi and Monika gave a sigh of relief as she sank into the seat.

The road was familiar to her after a while and she wished she was returning to her home. The taxi finally drew up outside a large, modern hotel facing the sea and Vasi led the way into the foyer and strode over to the reception desk. Monika hung back behind him whilst he completed the formalities to check in and accepted the swipe card to her room silently. How was she supposed to behave in such opulent surroundings? Her room, when she entered was larger than any at "The Central". The window looked out onto a balcony with a view of the busy main road and across to the sea; in front of the window stood a table and two armchairs. Monika placed her case on the table and felt the tears dribbling down her cheeks. This was luxury beyond her wildest dreams, but she would rather be at her grandmother's shop in the cramped rooms and knowing that she would be sharing a bed with her that night.

The telephone that stood beside the bed rang and she stiffened in horror. Was it Manu? Had he already found out that she was on Rhodes? The ringing was insistent and finally she lifted the receiver.

'Hello,' she whispered.

'Monika, it's me, Vasi. May I come along to your room?'

Monika drew a sigh of relief. 'Certainly.' She replaced the receiver and swiftly entered the bathroom area where she wetted a tissue and rubbed it over her face. She did not want Vasi to see she had been crying.

Vasi swept his gaze over her room as he entered. 'Are you comfortable? You haven't unpacked. Is anything wrong?'

'Everything is fine. I was just looking at the sea.'

Vasi sat down in one of the armchairs and indicated that Monika take the chair opposite. 'We have to make some arrangements,' he smiled and Monika was expecting him to tell her the time she needed to be ready the following day.

'You realise why we are here, don't you?'

'A business meeting with some Germans. I have been brushing up on the language. I have continued to read in German but I have rarely spoken the language since I left University. I hope I will not disappoint you.'

Vasi shook his head. 'We are not meeting any Germans so you do not have to worry about the language.'

Monika looked at him in surprise. 'Has the meeting been cancelled?'

Vasi ran a hand through his hair. 'I telephoned my father and he agreed with me that I should tell you now rather than wait until tomorrow.'

Monika looked alarmed. 'Am I involved in something illegal?'

Vasi shook his head. 'Not at all. Cathy has become very fond of you and it upsets her to think you cannot visit your mother. She persuaded my father, and myself, I might add, that if you were told you were needed as an interpreter at a business meeting you would agree to return to Rhodes for a few days. I was supposed to tell you tomorrow that my father had called, said the meeting had been cancelled and we were unable to change our return flight. It was to look like a fortuitous change of plans at the last minute. You will have arrangements to make and I would hate you to have a sleepless night worrying about a non-existent meeting.'

'What do you mean?'

'I would like you to telephone your mother and arrange to meet her tomorrow. You can spend the day together.'

Monika gasped. 'Do you mean that?' Her face fell. 'I can't. I dare not go into the Old Town. A neighbour is bound to see me, besides my mother will be at work.'

'You don't have to go into the town. Call your mother and ask her to meet you at the hospital. We will meet her there.'

'The hospital? We cannot spend all day sitting at the hospital.'

'We will have a taxi back to this hotel. No one will question a hospital visit and our return here with grieving relatives.'

Monika looked at Vasi in disbelief. 'A whole day?'

'Unless you want to spend it wandering around with me.'

Monika smiled shakily. 'A whole day! Could I see my grandmother as well?'

'I don't see why not.'

'Mamma could put a notice on the shop to say it was closed as my grandmother had a medical appointment. That way they could both meet us at the hospital. A whole day,' Monika said again and she made no attempt to stop her tears from flowing.

Vasi patted her shoulder. 'Make your phone call. Say you will be at the hospital at ten waiting for them. I will return shortly and we will then go for a quick stroll along the promenade before it gets too dark and cold.'

Monika looked at him dubiously. 'Suppose I am seen?'

'There is little danger of you being seen and recognised in this area. If by any unfortunate chance we are approached we speak only in English and are tourists. Trust me, Monika. My father and Cathy would be disappointed if you did not take this opportunity. It is not something we can repeat regularly.'

Monika nodded. 'I am truly grateful to them and also to you. I just would not like you to get into trouble here because of me.'

'Keep your call brief and do not tell your mother where you are staying. You can talk all you want tomorrow.'

Monika stood with Vasi just inside the hospital doorway. The receptionist asked if she could direct them to a department or ward and Monika shook her head. 'We're waiting for someone to join us.'

An ambulance arrived, followed by a private car and finally a taxi. 'That's my mother,' said Monika excitedly and clutched at Vasi's arm.

'Wait until the taxi has left and they have entered the building. It will not matter how emotional your meeting is, provided it is done quietly. You will be considered to be grieving relatives. I will then call a taxi and we will depart.'

Monika nodded, unable to speak as her mother helped her grandmother from the cab and they walked into the hospital, both looking bemused and apprehensive.

Her mother and grandmother had clutched her as if she was going to disappear before their eyes and all three had sobbed. Anyone seeing them would have been certain they were grieving over the sudden death of a much loved relative.

Finally Vasi had separated them and called for a taxi. 'Please, you do not talk whilst we are driving to the hotel. Taxi drivers have big ears and even bigger mouths.'

'Who is he?' asked Litsa quietly of Monika.

'I'll explain later. Just do whatever he says or I will be in trouble.'

Litsa rolled her eyes. Surely her daughter was not in a relationship with another violent man?

'Take our relatives up, whilst I settle the taxi fare. I will follow you shortly.'

Monika nodded and checked that she had her swipe card in her pocket. As they entered the lift she placed her finger to her lips and shook her head. 'I'll explain in a few minutes.'

Litsa and Monique looked in awe at the large room as Monika took their coats and asked them to sit down.

'Your friend must have plenty of money,' remarked Monique. 'I would have thought he would have insisted on buying you a new winter coat. That one begins to look very shabby.'

Monika shook her head. 'He is the son of my employer and his wife. I have become friendly with them and they arranged this visit. I am sure he will explain better than I can. Tell me, how are both of you? You look well.'

For the first few minutes the talk between them was strained and stilted. Monika felt like a stranger, meeting people for the first time, although she had telephoned her mother every week whilst she had been away. The questions she wanted to ask most would have to wait until she had satisfied their curiosity about the way she was living and working in Crete.

Vasi arrived, knocking decorously on the door until Monika ushered him in. 'I can introduce you properly, now. This is my mother and my grandmother.' Monika indicated with her hand. 'This is Mr Vasi, my employer's son.'

Litsa regarded him critically. Despite his casual dress he was obviously a wealthy young man.

Vasi drew up a chair and joined them at the table. 'I have arranged for some refreshments to be brought up to the room along with a menu. When you have chosen a meal I will telephone the order through. I hope you will find that agreeable. It relieves us of the necessity to go out to eat or visit the dining room.'

Once the refreshments had arrived and Vasi had telephoned the orders for their meal he rose. 'I am sure you have much to talk about. I will join you again later. I do have some business to attend to on behalf of my father.'

Monika looked at him gratefully. It would be far easier for her to ask about Manu if Vasi was not in attendance.

Litsa told her again how Manu had arrived at the shop at various different times during the day or early evening to see if there was any sign of his wife. He had continually questioned Litsa about the whereabouts of Monika in Piraeus and also demanded to examine her mobile 'phone to see the numbers she had contacted.

'That was a good idea on your part, Monika, to buy the new 'phones. He called the numbers I had stored and the only one I had for you was your original number. When he tried that he was told it was no longer in use. He actually threw the 'phone back at me.' Litsa laughed at the memory.

'I thought he was going to hit me,' she confided. 'I just stood there and looked him in the eye, daring him to lay a finger on me. I was pleased that a customer had entered the shop. I would have had an independent witness had he done so. I would have reported him to the police and told them exactly why you had left him and why he had assaulted me. Once he arranged for the posters to be displayed saying you were a missing person, last seen in Piraeus, he came less frequently. I haven't seen him now for at least six months.'

'I suppose I ought to let the police know I'm not missing. I could be arrested for wasting their time.'

'I'm more likely to be arrested than you are,' replied Litsa cheerfully. 'Did you ever see any posters on Crete?' Monika shook her head. 'So how were you to know you were supposed to be missing? I doubt the police are looking very hard for you. You are an adult and at liberty to go where you please. I have not confirmed that you are missing. I said you had told me you were going away for a holiday to recuperate after your spell in hospital.'

'I'm surprised they haven't returned and asked if you have heard from me.'

'After the first visit from a policeman it has only been Manu who has come asking after you. He doesn't want his colleagues to know you left him due to his mistreatment. He would prefer you to remain listed as a missing person.'

'The lawyer I spoke to said Manu would have to know my address if I wanted to divorce him. He would have to be given an opportunity to reply.'

'And are you planning to divorce him? Have you formed a relationship with that nice man who is here with you?'

'Oh, no, Mamma. I don't really know Mr Vasi very well. There's nothing at all between us, he lives with an English lady, but I would like to divorce Manu if I could.' Monika shook her head sadly. 'I wish I had reported him when I was in the hospital. They had said some of my bruises looked quite old. I didn't think I would be believed, whatever I said. No one actually saw Manu do anything to me.'

'So what are you going to do, Monika? You cannot spend the rest of your life hiding away.'

Vasi walked from the hotel up towards the main area of the New Town, examining the signs he saw closely. His father had spoken to Giovanni and asked if Adam Kowalski would be able to help with the situation. Adam had declined, explaining that as the problem did not involve an American citizen he had no right to become involved. He had given Vasilis a telephone number and address for a reliable lawyer in Rhodes and Vasi hastened towards his appointment.

The elderly man greeted Vasi cordially and asked him to explain the nature of the services he required. Vasi looked concerned.

'I'm not at all sure. It does not actually involve me. The person I am representing does not even know I am visiting you for advice.'

'Then I do not see how I can be of any assistance.'

'May I explain the situation before you make a final decision?'

'You may.' Angelos Spanides did not think any amount of explanation would make him change his mind, but the man would be paying him for his time and could take as long as he wished.

Vasi outlined Monika's situation as best he could. 'The young woman has tried to find out if her husband has taken out divorce proceedings against her. She will not contest them.'

'If her husband has tried to bring proceedings against her it would be impossible for him to proceed without an address to send the papers.'

'She is reluctant to disclose her whereabouts. Her husband is of a violent nature and she is frightened he would harm her physically once he knew where she was living.'

Angelos tapped his fingers together. 'He has injured her before, you say? Have you any proof of this?'

Vasi shook his head. 'Not personally; I only have her word that she was admitted to the hospital for some weeks due to injuries that resulted in a miscarriage.'

'So why did she not start divorce proceedings then?'

'She was frightened he would hurt her further or possibly attack her mother or grandmother.'

Angelos sighed. 'She should have taken professional advice at the time. Provided the hospital was willing to confirm that she had been injured through no fault of her own she could have claimed brutality or unreasonable behaviour. At the very least she could have obtained a restraining order against him. It is rather late in the day to start proceedings on those grounds now. Is there any likelihood that her husband will want to marry again?'

'I have no idea.'

'He may, of course, be having a relationship with someone with the promise of marriage at a later date. After five years he could divorce her for desertion; after seven years he could ask for her to be declared legally dead. He would have to prove that every effort to find her had been made and if she did not come forward during that time she would be committing a criminal offence.'

'My father was wondering if it would be possible to investigate the behaviour of her husband over the past three years. He may have injured another woman and she did report him. If so it should be on his record and would lend weight to my friend's claim.'

Angelos looked at Vasi impatiently. 'Is that what you are asking me to do?'

Vasi nodded, hoping he had made the right decision.

'So why didn't you say so? It would have saved both of us time.'

'I thought I ought to explain the circumstances and reason behind the request.'

'I am not interested in the reasons or circumstances. You tell me what you want me to do and I either agree or disagree.'

'Then I would like you to look into the conduct of Mr Emmanuel Graphides over the past three years and see if there is any record of violence, either against a person or in the course of his work,' answered Vasi firmly.

'And what is the nature of his work?'

'He is in the police force.'

'The police are known to be heavy handed when they make an arrest.'

'I understand he is a detective so he should not be arresting people, only conducting interviews.'

'You think he may have used undue pressure to extract confessions?'

Vasi shrugged. 'I don't know. I've been told he has an unpredictable temper and can become violent. He may, of course, keep it well in check whilst he is at work.'

Angelos shook his head. 'I think it most unlikely that I will be able to find out anything detrimental about the man. I will make some discreet enquiries, but I think you could be disappointed with the outcome.'

Vasi extended his hand. 'I appreciate your time. My father would be grateful if you would contact him with any news.' Vasi handed his father's business card to the lawyer. 'Mr Kowalski recommended you so I am sure any information you give him will be accurate.'

Angelos looked at the card. The name Iliopolakis meant nothing to him but if Adam Kowalski was involved he would not be able to ignore the request as he had intended.

Vasi returned to the hotel late in the afternoon and knocked gently on Monika's door. A look of alarm crossed her face and she held her finger to her lips to stop her mother talking.

'Who is it?'

'It's me, Vasi. May I come in?'

Monika opened the door a crack and once she had ascertained that it was Vasi standing there she smiled and opened the door wider so he could enter.

'I trust you have had an enjoyable time?'

Monika nodded. 'We haven't stopped talking. Did you complete your business?'

'Yes, but it was not entirely satisfactory. My father had arranged for me to visit a lawyer and request that he made enquiries about your husband,'

'Oh!'

'I know, he should probably have consulted you first and gained your permission but my father is used to making his own decisions and having his own way. The lawyer has agreed to make some enquiries to see if Manu Graphides has any record of violence, either in his personal life or in the line of his duties. He said you should have started proceedings against him as soon as you left the hospital so your medical records could be used as evidence.'

'I'm sure some other girls could provide him with plenty of information.'

'Mamma,' said Monika warningly.

'Why shouldn't I ask the girls? They don't keep written records of visits and they only go for medical treatment if the injury is serious. They rarely report it to the police.'

Vasi looked at Monika's mother. 'Who exactly are these "girls" you say you could ask?'

Monika flushed with embarrassment as her mother continued. 'They live in the street just up from us. They've known Monika since she was a child, most of the original girls have retired now, but I know the ones who have taken their place. They don't cause any trouble for us; they just provide a service for those who need it.'

Vasi frowned. 'I'm not sure if a lawyer would be willing to accept their evidence.'

'Why not? They have the right to practise their profession without being molested. If they were shown a photograph of Manu they could at least confirm if he had visited them and how he had behaved. It's a shame Lakkis Pavlides is no longer around. He would have sorted Manu out quickly enough with the help of a couple of his thugs. That Alecos is useless.'

Monika looked at her mother in disbelief. Was she serious when saying that she would have asked Lakkis Pavlides to attack Manu? The man had a criminal record for drug dealing and rumour had it that he had engineered the "accident" that had resulted in Joseph being crippled. She shivered. He would have been a dangerous man to deal with.

'I don't think you should do anything at the moment, Mamma. If Mr Iliopolakis has employed a lawyer on my behalf we should wait and see if he finds out anything.' Monika was horrified at the amount of money she was going to have to repay Mr Iliopolakis. There was the cost of the flight, hotel, taxi fares and now a lawyer. She would never have enough money for driving lessons.

Vasi insisted on escorting Litsa and Monique back to the Old Town. Tactfully he instructed Monika to say her goodbyes whilst he was collecting his coat and ordering a taxi.

'I'll knock on your door when I return. I'll probably walk back as this hotel is not far from the Old Town.'

'Will you know your way?' asked Monika anxiously.

Vasi tapped his pocket. 'I have a map. I am sure I will have no problem.'

Vasi asked Litsa to give instructions to the taxi driver and was surprised when they stopped at the San Francisco Gate.

'We have to walk from here,' Monique informed him. 'The barrier is down for the night.'

'What happens if you live inside the town and have a car?'

'You need a permit to bring your car inside the walls and you would be given a key to unlock the barrier. Some of the taxis have been given a key for access, but you often have a long wait before one will arrive.'

'I'm sorry. I didn't realise,' apologised Vasi. 'I thought a taxi would deposit you at your door.'

'It will take us no more than a few minutes to walk.'

'I would be happier if I escorted you to your house. These cobbles are slippery and Monika would be most distressed if she heard later that you had fallen and been injured.'

Litsa smiled at his concern. 'You are more likely to fall that we are. We're used to them.'

'I still insist on coming with you.' Vasi did not add that he was curious to see the street where the girls lived. 'Do you always have to enter and leave by this way?'

'It depends where you are headed. There are other gates, but this is the nearest one to where we live.' Litsa led the way, whilst Monique held Vasi's arm to steady herself.

They turned into a narrow street and Vasi noticed there was a red light above each doorway. One girl was lounging in the doorway, well wrapped up against the cold.

'Hi, Litsa, Mrs Monique. You're out late. I see you have a handsome young man with you. I'm sure he'd like to enjoy himself once he has seen you home.'

She extended her hand towards Vasi and he shook his head, blushing furiously. 'I imagine that is the street you mentioned.'

'That's right. Marina won't take it personally that you refused her. She'll ask you again as you make your way back.'

'Is there another way I could go out; one of the other gates?'

'If you want to walk along the top road you'll reach the main entrance or you could go down through the Jewish quarter and out onto the waterfront.'

'I think the top road would be preferable.'

'We're home.' Litsa stopped outside the door of the shop where there was a notice saying it was closed that day. 'Thank you, Mr Vasi, and please thank your father. It was a great relief to see that Monika was well and to be able to spend the day with her was, well, amazing.' Litsa's voice broke. 'I miss her so much.'

Angelos considered the difficult request Vasi had outlined to him. He was not a private detective and therefore unused to unearthing details of a person's private life. The only avenue of enquiry that presented itself to him was to approach the chief of police who was a neighbour and see if he could find out any details about Emmanuel Graphides. He would have to be discreet with his questioning as Vasi had impressed upon him the need for confidentiality.

His opportunity arose four days later. As he walked home he saw Kostas Yianides sitting inside the local taverna with a drink before him. Angelos decided that if he joined him he might be able to engage him in conversation and glean a little information.

Angelos ordered a drink and carried it over to the table where Kostas was sitting. 'Mind if I join you?'

Kostas waved his hand towards the empty chair. 'Just thought I'd have a quick one before returning home; help me wind down after the day.'

Angelos raised his eyebrows. 'Bad day?'

'No worse than usual. Too much paper work. Filling in the forms takes more time than anything else.'

Angelos nodded sympathetically. 'Mothers complaining that their little boys were clipped around the ear when they were arrested? They should have meted out some of that treatment to them when they were younger.'

Kostas sighed. 'There's always one who insists their boy is innocent, even when the youth has confessed.'

'No doubt claiming the confession was beaten out of him. Do you actually have much physical coercion to deal with?'

Kostas shook his head. 'My men know their limits.'

'What about Emmanuel Graphides? Some of my clients have told me he has a short fuse and a heavy hand when making an arrest.'

'I've had to discipline him a few times. A bit too enthusiastic sometimes when arresting a suspect and the other officers were a bit uneasy about working with him. Promoting him to the role of a detective took him off the streets.' Kostas was thankful he had made that decision. Becoming a detective meant Manu no longer carried a gun. He had never used it, except as a threat, but the other officers had not been happy at the way he produced it without any provocation. 'There've been no complaints about him since. I understand he drinks a bit more than he should when he's off duty, but that's understandable with his wife missing.'

'Missing? What do you mean?'

'She disappeared about three years ago. Was seen arriving at Piraeus and she hasn't been seen since.'

'Has he looked for her?'

'Of course, but there's been no news of her. She'll no doubt turn up one day and they'll have a murder investigation on their hands.'

Angelos nodded. 'That's hard on him. Until she is found, one way or the other, he can't really move on with his life. Suppose he wanted to marry again?'

'I've not heard that he's seeing anyone on a regular basis. Are you busy?'

Angelos spread his hands. 'Pretty quiet at the moment. You know what it's like. During the winter it's mostly representing your young criminals in court and insisting they're innocent. Nothing to work on with any enthusiasm.'

'Yes,' Kostas sighed. 'I suppose I should be grateful that we have very little real crime. Since putting a stop to the drug cartel Lakkis Pavlides was running our crime rate is definitely lower.' He drained his glass. 'Are you up for another?'

Angelos shook his head. 'I ought to get home. I've promised my wife I'd take her to the cinema tonight.'

Monika returned to work feeling happier than she had for a considerable amount of time. Both her mother and grandmother had appeared well and she also felt relieved that she had not had to attend a business meeting conducted in German. She would not have wanted to let Vasilis Iliopolakis down by having difficulty with the language.

'Enjoy your time away?' asked Ariadne.

'Very much.'

'Where did you go?'

'I visited my mother and grandmother.'

'Where do they live?'

'A long way from Heraklion.' Monika did not want to have to go into the details of her visit with Ariadne.

'I'm sure they were pleased to see you.'

'They were.' Monika smiled at the memory.

'When are you visiting them again?'

'I haven't any plans for another visit at the moment. It takes all day to get to them and another day to return, so it is expensive and I can't visit as often as I would like.'

The next time Vasilis Iliopolakis visited "The Central" she asked if she could speak to him privately and he ushered her into his office.

'What can I do for you? I understand from Vasi that your visit was most successful.'

'It was amazing. I cannot thank you and Cathy enough.' Monika smiled happily at the memory.

'So what is the problem? I cannot arrange another visit for some considerable time unfortunately.'

Monika shook her head. 'I wouldn't dream of asking you and it is going to take me a long time to repay you. I have some savings and I thought you could deduct some Euros from my wages each week until the debt was cleared.'

Vasilis shook his head. 'I am not asking you to repay anything for your visit to Rhodes. My accountant will accept that it was a business appointment that failed. I am hoping that Angelos, the lawyer Vasi visited, will be able to find some evidence against your husband. If that was forthcoming you could sue for divorce and also ask for reparation and then you will be liable for the lawyer's fees.'

'Reparation?'

'Compensation for having to leave your home, your relatives and your job.'

'Would that be possible?'

'We will have to wait and see. I think it unlikely that your husband has spent the years since you left him without any female companionship. Vasi tells me your mother had some ideas.'

Monika blushed. 'I'm not sure we should take any notice of her suggestions. It would mean asking the street girls.'

Vasilis smiled. 'There is no reason why they shouldn't be questioned. Your husband may never have been anywhere near them, but on the other hand, having paid for their services, he may have thought he could do as he pleased to them. If his behaviour against any of them was unreasonable it is possible they have filed a complaint against him. In that case we could ask for their injuries to be taken into account along with yours. I will speak to Angelos and suggest it to him. In the meantime, you save your money. You'll be visiting us again this week I hope. Cathy is longing to know all about your trip to Rhodes.'

Monika shook her head. 'I can't take any proceedings against Manu unless I know my mother and grandmother are safe.'

Angelos was not happy when Vasilis telephoned and asked him to visit the red light area in the Old Town. 'If you are able to speak to the girls one of them may recall a man who mistreated them. If so, see if you can get a description.'

'Does he patronise them?'

'I have no idea, but it's possible.'

'I just hope no one who knows me sees me visiting them,' grumbled Angelos. 'It's certainly not an area I'm familiar with.'

Litsa thought carefully about her idea of the street girls. During her time working there she had been bruised and threatened by customers if she refused to meet their demands, so why shouldn't the same have happened to the other girls? She removed the photograph of Monika and Manu taken on their wedding day from the frame and placed it inside a book. On her way to work she would have a photocopy made and enlarged. She would cut Monika off the photocopy and show Manu's picture to the girls. If one of them had suffered at his hands she would be sure to recognise his face.

Most of the girls she had worked with had moved on, retiring when they lost their looks and were no longer popular or their health had deteriorated. The girls were a close knit community, supporting and helpful to each other. New girls had taken their place, but the camaraderie for a girl they considered to have been one of them continued. Litsa remained friendly with them all and often stopped to chat. Although she saw Rebekah regularly she still thought of the street girls as her real friends now.

When Litsa finished work that evening she walked up to the street. It was the most likely time to find a girl waiting for customers and able to speak to her. She stopped at Marina's window and beckoned to her. Marina drew her shawl around her shoulders before opening the door and inviting Litsa inside.

'Too cold to stand out there tonight.'

'Not as bad as it has been some days. The wind has dropped.'

'You had an attractive young man with you the other night. Surely he could keep you warm?'

'He is a business acquaintance.'

Marina raised her eyebrows. 'Still in business then, are you? Alecos won't take kindly to knowing that you're free lancing. He would expect a cut.'

'Not that kind of business. He's making some enquiries on behalf of a client and asked if I might be able to help him as I know all of you.'

'What's he after? A special price or has he got strange ideas?'

Litsa drew the photocopied picture of Manu from her bag. 'He just wanted to know if you had had any dealings with this man.'

Marina looked at it and shook her head. 'I don't recognise him. They all look the same to me.'

'Do you think any of the other girls would know him?'

'It's possible. You'll have to ask them.'

Litsa sighed. That would mean she had to go from house to house and even then there was no guarantee one of the girls would know him, even if he had visited her at some time.

December 2009 – February 2010

Angelos Spanides drove up to the Old Town and parked his car in one of the permitted spaces outside the San Francisco Gate. Vasilis had told him that was the area where the girls lived and he hoped he would be able to find it without having to ask directions. He followed the contours of the old city walls and walked along the road, looking for any sign that it was an area where the girls offered their bodies.

Nowhere seemed likely; there was a warehouse on one side, flanked by a couple of houses and some waste ground before the road curved up to one of the main thoroughfares. Opposite there was a high wall with a gate. Inset into the wall was a bell push and an English name neatly painted on a wooden plaque. Angelos stood and considered whether he should ring the bell and ascertain if the occupants were locals and running a brothel under the guise of being foreigners.

'You're in the wrong place, dearie, if you're looking for entertainment. You need the road down there. Follow me and you'll not regret it.'

Angelos shook his head. 'I have business with these people.'

'You won't find them at home until later. Why don't you come and pass the time with me?'

Angelos considered the woman's words. 'I hope I have not misinterpreted your invitation but you may be able to help me over another matter.'

Natasha raised her eyebrows archly. 'If you're looking for a man you're in the wrong area.'

Angelos shook his head vehemently. 'No, nothing like that. I was hoping to ask a few questions of the ladies who work up here.'

'What kind of questions?' Natasha was suddenly on her guard.

'I just wanted to know if any of your clients had ever molested you in any way.'

'Why would that be a concern of yours?'

'I've been asked to make some enquiries by a client. I'm a lawyer, by the way.' Angelos took his business card from his pocket and held it out to her.

Natasha shrugged without glancing at it. 'It happens occasionally.'

'Has it always been the same person who has caused you trouble?'

'Not to me. If he calls again I say I'm already busy. Some of the other girls have complained amongst themselves, but you can't always be too choosy. The rent has to be paid.'

'Would I be able to speak to those girls? They might be able to give me a description and I would know if this is the man I am enquiring about.'

'So what's your interest?' Natasha had stopped walking and stood in front of Angelos challengingly.

'A young lady was injured a while ago. She believes the man she was friendly with caused her injuries deliberately and is claiming compensation. He, of course, insists it was accidental. I have been asked to make enquiries and see whether he has a reputation for injuring female companions who are not in a position to complain about him.'

'Who can we complain to? If we tell the police they laugh at us and tell us to go away. If we tell Alecos he does nothing. He's too concerned with avoiding any trouble with the police now he's in charge; not like Mr Lakkis was. Anyone who crossed him regretted it.'

'Could you introduce me to any of these young ladies?'

'I might be able to. I'll speak to them this evening. Come back tomorrow and I'll let you know. They'll charge you the current rate for their time, even if they only talk to you, so make sure you have your money with you.'

'Where can I meet you?' asked Angelos. He had not expected to have to pay to ask the prostitutes a few questions.

Natasha waved her hand towards the turning a short distance away. 'Walk down the street. My name's above the door. Don't come before two; not all of us rise early.'

'Thank you; you've been very helpful.'

'Good; you can pay me tomorrow. We're not allowed to accept money outside of our houses.' Natasha turned away and Angelos watched as she turned into a narrow street. He would have to speak to Mr Iliopolakis and see if he was willing to pay for any information he was able to obtain.

Angelos advised Vasilis that he had questioned the prostitutes. They all claimed to have suffered at the hands of their customers at some time, but never seriously and could not name any of them. He also enclosed his bill to date, adding an extra one hundred Euros to cover his time and rounded the figure up to five hundred Euros.

Vasilis paid promptly with a bank transfer and asked Angelos to keep the information to hand until he contacted him next. He did not feel he could proceed until he had spoken to Monika and gained her permission.

'Would you like me to instruct Angelos to proceed with divorce proceedings for you? The evidence from your medical records should ensure that it goes through smoothly.'

'Wouldn't I have to disclose my address or go to Court?'

'No, it can all be done through the lawyer. Your address can be kept confidential due to his previous record of abuse.'

Monika shook her head. 'It isn't possible. He knows where my mother and grandmother live.'

'I understand the Court can place a restraining order on him. He would be forbidden to go anywhere near them. Speak to your mother, I would instruct Angelos to ask for back dated compensation for you and for a custodial sentence as well.

Monika shook her head again. 'Even if he was sent to prison he would certainly hurt my mother and grandmother when he was released or ask someone else to act on his behalf. I can't take that risk.'

Vasilis looked at her gravely. 'I understand your concerns and I have given it some considerable thought. I also discussed it with Cathy. Suppose your mother and grandmother left Rhodes?'

'Left Rhodes?' Monika looked at Vasilis in amazement. 'My grandmother has her shop there.'

'Surely she could close the shop?'

'It is her living and also their home. Where would they go?'

Vasilis nodded. 'I understand that it would be a big decision for them to make. If you are in agreement I would happily speak to your mother and assure her that if she came to Crete I would guarantee her some work and also a place to live.'

Monika looked at Vasilis in disbelief. 'You would do that?'

Vasilis shrugged. 'It is the obvious solution. You want to ensure the safety of your relatives and you cannot do this whilst they are on Rhodes. You disappeared very successfully from the island, why shouldn't they?'

'I don't know. I suppose, maybe, it might be possible.'

'It is certainly possible, provided they agree. Think about it, Monika, and talk to your mother. Find out her opinion and let me know when you have made a decision.'

Monika spent a considerable amount of time on the mobile 'phone to her mother that evening. She explained that the lawyer would be able to use her medical records from the Medical Centre and the hospital provided she signed a permission form for them to be released.

'There is just one problem; you and Grandma.'

'We'll both back up anything you say,' Litsa assured her daughter.

'Once Manu hears from the lawyer he'll no doubt come looking for both of you at the shop. I hope he thinks I am still in Piraeus or Athens. I want you and Grandma to catch the ferry to Piraeus and then another one to come to Crete. There is nothing direct from Rhodes. Mr Iliopolakis said he would arrange somewhere for you to live in Heraklion.'

Litsa was hesitant. 'How long would we be away?'

'I don't know, Mamma. That would depend upon Manu being given a custodial sentence.'

'Your grandmother couldn't just close up the shop. What would people think?'

'Say you are taking a holiday or Grandma has to go into hospital and you will be staying there with her. Any excuse, but don't tell anyone the truth. Please, Mamma, speak to Grandma. If you are willing to come to Crete please insist she comes with you. She cannot stay in the Old Town on her own. If you refuse to come then I'll ask the lawyer to halt the proceedings. Think about it and talk to Grandma. I'll 'phone you again tomorrow evening.'

Litsa placed the mobile 'phone she and Monika used back into the drawer amongst her underwear. She had expected Monika to return to Rhodes once the lawyer had negotiated her divorce from Manu, not be asked to join her daughter in Crete. This was something she would have to think about very seriously.

Monika telephoned her mother each evening trying to persuade her to leave Rhodes. Litsa kept raising objections until Monika finally broke down in tears.

'Very well, Mamma. I'll tell Mr Iliopolakis that he must instruct the lawyer to stop any legal proceedings that involve me. I'll obviously have to stay married to Manu and spend the rest of my life as a cleaner.' She could no longer control her emotions and began to sob, terminating the call. She had not realised how hopeful she had become that her mother and grandmother would join her in Crete.

Two hours later, Monika was lying restlessly in her bed, trying to think of a final persuasive argument she could put to her mother, when the mobile 'phone rang again. Although she only ever used the cheap mobile for calls to her mother she checked the number that was calling, finally satisfied that it was her mother Monika answered.

'Monika, we are coming.'

'Mamma,' gasped Monika. 'Do you mean that?'

'I'm sorry, Monika, I was being selfish. I didn't like the thought of leaving my home and Grandma closing the shop. I should have been thinking of you.'

Monika's heart was beating quickly with suppressed excitement. 'I'll tell Mr Iliopolakis tomorrow. When will you come?'

'I don't know. We will have to think about our arrangements and closing the shop. We can't do that over night.'

'You would have to if Grandma was ill.' Monika crossed herself hurriedly to ward off the evil of illness. 'I will have to give Mr Iliopolakis a date, Mamma. Make it definite for three weeks from today.'

'I suppose we might be able to manage that.' Litsa sounded dubious.

'I'm sure you can. Tell Grandma not to order or buy any more perishable stock. If she has any left when you leave she can give it to the girls. They'd probably be grateful. You could tell them you are going to Piraeus to visit me.'

'But you're not in Piraeus.'

'I know, but if Manu saw the shop was closed he might well ask one of the girls if she knew where you had gone. You have to travel to Piraeus in the first place so it isn't entirely untrue.'

'You don't think we'll be stopped?'

'Why should you be? You have your identity cards and

245

provided you have a valid ticket there is no reason for anyone to stop you leaving Rhodes, travelling to Piraeus and buying a ferry ticket to Crete. You agreed you could be here in three weeks and that is what I will tell Mr Iliopolakis. You call me when you leave Rhodes and again when you are on the ferry to Crete. I'll make sure I'm at the port to meet you.'

'What should we bring with us?'

'Just your clothes. As much as you can manage in one suitcase each. You only have to carry it to the San Francisco Gate and then call a taxi to take you to the port. Buy your tickets the day before and make sure you book a cabin. The booking office will give you the information you need about the time to be there to go aboard.'

'What about the stock in your grandmother's shop?'

'Just leave it. Provided you have removed anything that will go bad and smell the rest of it can stay there until you return. Put a notice on the door that says "closed" and turn the key.'

Monika heard her mother sigh. 'You make it sound so easy.'

'It is, Mamma. Now you have made up your mind you will find it far easier than I did. You and Grandma are together and you know that once you are here you will be looked after. When I left I thought I was going to Kos. I wasn't expecting to end up on Crete with nowhere to live and no work available.'

'We can't stay on Crete indefinitely without any work.'

'Mr Iliopolakis said he would be able to find employment for you both, however temporary.' Monika hoped some work for her mother and grandmother would be possible as there was no way she would be able to support her relatives financially indefinitely on the wages she was earning.

'Your grandmother can't be expected to do cleaning at her age.'

'I'm sure Mr Iliopolakis would not expect her to be a cleaner. I'll talk to him and I'm sure he will arrange something suitable. Trust me, Mamma, just get your bags packed, close the shop, buy your tickets and be in Heraklion harbour in three weeks' time.'

It was hardly light when the ferry berthed and Monika watched her mother and grandmother struggle down the gangplank and onto dry land. She waved wildly at them as they stopped and looked around, evidently bewildered by the bustle that was taking place. Officials directed the motorised traffic to the right, whilst the foot passengers were made to alight on the left and expected to make their way to the kiosk where their identity cards or passports would be checked.

Once she was certain her mother and grandmother were headed in the right direction Monika hurried over to wait for them to emerge. She could hardly contain her excitement. The previous day Vasilis Iliopolakis had given her the keys to the apartment where they would live and requested that she telephoned him when they arrived to confirm a meeting with him at "The Central" for later the same afternoon.

Now Monika suddenly felt sick with apprehension. Suppose the apartment was totally unsuitable, in a bad area and in need of essential maintenance and repair? If Mr Iliopolakis expected both her mother and grandmother to work as cleaners as she was she could well imagine they would both refuse. It would leave her in a very difficult position and she berated herself for not insisting that she visited the apartment and also ascertained the nature of the work that was expected of them.

'Mamma! Grandma! I can hardly believe it. You are actually here.'

Monique sighed deeply. 'It was a terrible journey. The ferries didn't stop moving all night. How were we supposed to sleep?'

'I told you to book a cabin,' frowned Monika.

'We did,' smiled Litsa. 'Your grandmother slept well, far better than me. I kept hearing strange noises and then I was worried that we may have caught the wrong ferry and would end up back in Rhodes.'

'You had to show your tickets. They would have told you if you were trying to board the wrong ferry. Let me take your case, Grandma.'

Monique relinquished her case to her granddaughter gratefully. 'Where are we going?'

'To the taxi rank, then to the apartment Mr Iliopolakis has arranged.'

'Where is it?'

'Not far from his hotel and quite close to my apartment.'

'I thought we would be staying with you.'

'My apartment is far too small to accommodate two more people. I only have a pull down bed and once it is down there is nowhere to sit comfortably.'

'I thought you said you had a nice apartment,' said Litsa accusingly.

'I have. I'm quite happy with it, but it is small. At least I have a balcony where I can hang my wet washing.'

'Why don't you take it to the laundry?'

'There aren't laundries here like we have in Rhodes. Here they only deal with the laundry from the hotels and tavernas, not personal washing. Most people have their own washing machine.'

'Have you?'

Monika shook her head. 'I manage to do all my washing by hand. Here, leave your case with me, Mamma and you and Grandma get settled into the taxi. I'll sit in the front.'

Monika was relieved when the taxi finally drew up. The property looked clean and well cared for and she hoped fervently that her mother and grandmother would approve.

The front door opened easily and Monika looked at the names displayed against the numbers of the apartments. "Kokanides" was displayed opposite a bell push for apartment three.

'I think that must be yours,' she smiled, 'unless there are other people living here with the same name. It should be up on the next floor and there doesn't appear to be a lift. Wait here whilst I take Grandma's case up and check that we're in the right place; then I'll carry yours up, Mamma.'

'I'm sure I can manage.'

'I'd rather you waited. If there is a mistake you'll only have to carry it back down again.'

Litsa shrugged; she felt tired and dirty. Neither of them had showered whilst aboard either of the ferries concerned that the motion from the waves would throw them off balance; nor had they changed their clothes. All she wanted was a shower and some clean clothes, followed by a cup of decent coffee.

Monika opened the door to apartment three, pushed her grandmother's case inside and looked around cautiously. Everywhere was clean and the furnishings looked new. She drew a breath of relief. The lounge was a reasonable size, with a sofa and two rocking chairs; at the far end was a small table and chairs that folded up to fit beneath it. Two doors stood partly open on the far wall and she peered behind both of them; one had a small cooking area and the other led into a bedroom with two single beds and through the door that was fully open she could see a small bathroom.

Compared with her tiny apartment it was luxurious and she hoped her mother and grandmother would be satisfied. She closed the door carefully behind her and ran back down the flight of stairs.

'Well?' said Litsa. 'Is it our apartment?'

Monika nodded. 'I'm sure it is and I think you will be pleased.' She lifted her mother's case and led the way back up the stairs.

Monique was out of breath when she reached the door. 'I wish there was a lift,' she muttered.

'It is only one flight, Grandma, you'll soon get used to the stairs.' Monika opened the door with a flourish and stood back to allow them to enter.

Monika stood and waited whilst her mother and grandmother inspected each room and then took their cases through to the bedroom. 'Whilst you unpack I'll have a look in the cupboards. Provided there are some cups I'll make some coffee. I brought some with me.'

Litsa shook her head. 'There's no point in us unpacking. We can't possibly stay here.'

'Why not?' Monika was both surprised and disappointed by her mother's reaction.

'We won't be able to afford the rent on an apartment as grand as this.'

'I'm sure you can, Mamma. Mr Iliopolakis says he has arranged some work for you and you have your savings.'

Litsa snorted. 'There's not much left of my savings now. I've had a good deal of expenditure recently. I paid the utility bills for the shop for six months, then buying suitcases and ferry tickets.'

Monika shook her head. Her mother was obviously expecting to be back in Rhodes within a few months. Legal proceedings took a considerable amount of time and they were more likely to be away for a year. She would have to speak to Mr Iliopolakis and ask how the utility bills could be paid when they were next due.

'Alright, Mamma, I'll not expect you stay here if you cannot afford it. At least meet Mr Iliopolakis this afternoon and stay here tonight. If you think it is too expensive then we will have to explain to him and look for somewhere else.'

Slightly mollified Litsa nodded. 'I'll just get out my washing kit and some clean clothes.'

Monika looked at her grandmother, hoping for support.

'Your mother's right, Monika. We can't afford to live anywhere like this.'

Monika telephoned Vasilis Iliopolakis, confirmed that her relatives had arrived and agreed to meet him at two that afternoon at the hotel. She assured her mother and grandmother that it would take them no more than fifteen minutes to walk to the hotel and provided they allowed sufficient time they could stop at Wendy's for a snack on the way.

Litsa shook her head. 'I can't eat anything until we've sorted out what is happening with the apartment. We ought to look for a cheap hotel for the night.'

Monika looked at her mother in despair. 'Please, Mamma, don't worry. I'm sure Mr Iliopolakis understands that the rent has to be reasonable. Mr Vasi saw where you lived on Rhodes and he is bound to have told his father that you only had a small house.'

'At least I owned it,' commented Monique. 'I didn't have to pay rent to anyone.'

'I still have some savings. I can always work some extra hours and earn a little more if it's necessary,' offered Monika. She felt cold at the thought of handing over any of her savings. She was going to have a large bill to pay to the lawyer eventually and if Manu did not pay her any compensation she would probably be in debt for the rest of her life.

Litsa sighed. 'You should have a decent job where you earn considerably more than you do as a cleaner. Maybe your friend Mr Iliopolakis could have a word and get you a job in the local library.'

'No, Mamma. If I can get a divorce from Manu then I'll apply for work in the library. Once the lawyer contacts him he is going to be looking for me again and the first place he would look would be a library.'

Vasilis greeted them cordially and took them into his office. 'Refreshment, ladies?'

Monika shook her head. 'No thank you. I insisted we stopped for a snack at Wendy's on our way here.'

'Then we will talk business. Firstly I would like to welcome you to Crete. I do not know Rhodes, but I believe it has a very interesting medieval town. Unfortunately we do not have the same here. There are old buildings around, but many have been demolished and the area modernised. I trust you found your apartment to your liking. It is in a relatively new building so there should not be any problems.'

Monika looked at her mother uncertainly. 'I'm not sure, Mr Iliopolakis.'

'There is something wrong?' Vasilis looked most concerned.

'It is a question of the rent, Mr Iliopolakis. I don't think my mother and grandmother could afford to live there.'

'How much is the rent?' asked Vasilis.

'I don't know,' answered Monika miserably. 'If they can stay there for a few days until we have found somewhere cheaper I would be very grateful.'

'If you do not know the rent you do not know if it can be afforded. I understand that you, Litsa – may I call you Litsa – have been working in a general store.'

Litsa nodded.

'And you would be happy to continue working in a shop?'

Litsa nodded again.

Vasilis smiled. 'Good. I have arranged that you will have a position in the local supermarket. At first you will refill the shelves and change any prices as increases occur. You will also be expected to advise the manager if certain items are running low and should be ordered. No doubt within a few months you will have worked your way up to a cashier's position which should be considerably more interesting.'

'Thank you.' Litsa did not like to ask how much she would be paid or the hours expected of her. She was relieved that she was not going to become a hotel cleaner.

'Mrs Kokanides, I would prefer to address you by that name so there is no confusion between you and Monika if you are agreeable.'

Monique shrugged. 'I was called Mrs Monique by my customers, but Mrs Kokanides is my name.'

'A lady of your mature years and experience is no doubt an excellent needlewoman,' continued Vasilis. 'Some years ago when my son was the manager at "The Central" he was horrified by the waste he saw here. He made a number of changes and had other ideas that I have not yet implemented. One of his suggestions was to have a room where a competent lady could make repairs to the furnishings.'

Monique frowned. 'I've never really made anything except clothes for myself and my daughter.'

Vasilis smiled. 'I am not asking you to make clothes. Each week a visitor will have caught the heel of their shoe in the bed cover and made a tear, pulled a curtain too vigorously and stitching has been damaged, or the seam of a pillowcase has become undone. At present there are three ladies working on the repairs. In most cases they only need a few stitches and we can continue to use the items in the hotel saving a considerable amount of money. Would you be willing to undertake the work?'

Monique nodded. It sounded simple enough.

Monika was still not happy. 'How much will they earn each week? Is it going to be sufficient to pay the rent, pay the utility bills and buy food?'

'Your mother will earn the current hourly rate for working in the supermarket. Your grandmother will earn four Euros an hour and can work whatever hours she pleases. She is eligible to draw her State pension so that gives her a modicum of independence over the number of hours she works.'

'Thank you, Mr Iliopolakis. I'm sure both my grandmother and my mother would like to accept the work you have offered, but we will need to find cheaper accommodation.'

Vasilis shook his head. 'I do not think you will find anywhere less expensive to live in Heraklion. I have explained to my accountant that I am giving you sanctuary for six months to allow you to re-build your lives. If my tenants are not paying rent I cannot be making a profit.' Vasilis spread his hands. 'You will be responsible for the utility bills, but nothing more.'

Monika gasped. 'Mr Iliopolakis, you mean they would not pay you any rent?'

Vasilis nodded. 'That is correct for six months. At the end of that time I will consult with my lawyer and see if sanctuary time can be extended. At present there will be no legal tenancy agreement signed so no one has to know you are living there.

You are now in a position to ask the lawyer to go ahead with divorce proceedings without having to worry that your mother or grandmother will be harassed by your husband.'

'Even if I am granted a divorce that doesn't mean he will stop looking for me.'

'There can be an injunction taken out against him due to his record of domestic violence so your address is not disclosed. If by any chance he did discover your location he would be forbidden to contact you in any way. You will be quite safe, Monika.' Vasilis smiled reassuringly at her. 'Now I will take your grandmother up to the room where she will spend her time sewing and introduce her to the ladies. Unfortunately it is on the top floor, but there is a lift,' he added when he saw the horrified look on Monique's face.

Litsa looked at her daughter when Vasilis had left the room. 'Do you think he means it when he says we don't have to pay any rent for six months?'

Monika nodded. 'If Mr Iliopolakis said that then he means it. It might only be a temporary arrangement for six months, but it will give you the opportunity to save some money.'

'And then we can all return to Rhodes.' Litsa smiled happily at the thought.

Rhodes March 2010

Manu was furious when the papers were delivered to him by hand from the lawyer advising him that Monika was petitioning for a divorce on the grounds of physical abuse during the time they had been married. The lawyer had his offices on Rhodes so the girl must be on the island somewhere. He would visit her grandmother at the shop and insist she told him where Monika could be found. By the time he had finished dealing with his wife she would be quite incapable of asking for a divorce.

Manu walked into the shop where his father was making up a prescription. He had terminated the agreement for the rented apartment he had shared with Monika and returned to his parents. It was far more convenient to have his mother cook his meals and not have to worry about rent or utility bills.

'I need a lawyer, Pappa.'

Mr Graphides raised his eyebrows. 'A lawyer? Whatever for? Have you done something wrong?'

'That stupid girl that I married is now asking for a divorce.'

Mr Graphides nodded. 'I would have thought you would be pleased.'

'Pleased! She ran off and left me. Goodness knows where she has been hiding all this time, but now she says she is divorcing me, claiming unreasonable behaviour and abuse. It was her behaviour that was unreasonable.'

'Why does she say your behaviour was unreasonable?'

'She claims I caused her miscarriage and injuries when she fell down the stairs.'

'Rubbish. No one will believe that.'

'According to the letter I have received the hospital has released her records. They say she had signs of old bruising along with her current injuries. She'd been to the medical centre and hospital before. I need a lawyer, a good one.'

Mr Graphides raised his eyebrows. He knew his son had an unpredictable temper. 'Did you ever touch her?'

'She should have done as she was told,' growled Manu.

'So you did hit her?'

'Not as often as I should have done. She was a lying little bitch and deserved all she got. A shame she didn't break her neck when she fell.'

'Manu!'

'She told me her mother worked in a shop and her father had been in the navy before he had an accident. A pack of lies. Her mother was a prostitute and she didn't know who her father was.' Manu pounded on the shop counter with his fists. 'I'll beat her to pulp when I get hold of her again.'

'Manu, control yourself.' Mr Graphides slapped his son on the side of his head.

'Don't you hit me, Pappa.' Manu leaned across the counter and grabbed his father's collar. 'If you do I'll hit you back. I'm not a little boy any longer who can be knocked around.'

Elias Graphides pulled his son's hand away. 'Threats and violence toward me will get you nowhere. Why don't you visit the shop to ask her mother or grandmother where she is? They must know. Once you have found her you could try to mediate, arrange an amicable divorce.'

'I tried to find her when Stenos said he had seen her in Piraeus,' replied Manu sulkily. 'She could be living up in Athens and that city has a tremendous population. She could be there or moved on to another town on the mainland.' Manu clenched his fists again. 'That mother of hers must have known where she was all along. When I get hold of her she'll regret it.'

'It's no good you getting yourself worked up, Manu. Reply to the lawyer and tell him you are agreeable to have a divorce, but she must drop all charges against you or you will claim desertion on her part.'

Manu leaned across the counter towards his father again and Elias took a step back. It was true, his son was no longer a small boy that he could chastise with impunity and Elias knew he would suffer badly if Manu began to use his fists on him.

'Don't you understand?' Manu shouted. 'She is claiming that she left because I was violent towards her.'

'Stop shouting at me and start to think clearly. Whatever happened between you both in the past has to be proved. It is her word against yours. Deny her claims of abuse. Act quietly and reasonably. Accuse her of being depressed or emotionally unstable after losing the baby and say that is why she left you. After all, you registered her as a missing person and put up notices on Rhodes to that effect. I don't know what you're making so much fuss about. Give the girl a divorce and be done with her.'

Manu gritted his teeth. 'You just do not understand, Pappa. If the lawyers found in her favour I could be asked to pay compensation to her along with all the legal fees. I don't have that kind of money.'

Mr Graphides looked at his son perplexed. 'You have a good job and pay your mother very little for living here. You should have plenty saved.'

'Well I haven't.' Manu stormed out of the chemist shop. He had expected his father to be sympathetic and helpful, probably offering to help him financially if necessary.

Manu strode up to the Old Town, inwardly seething and his mind reeling. He would go to the shop and beat the information from her mother or grandmother if they continued to deny knowing Monika's address. To his surprise the door to the shop was locked and there was a notice that simply said "closed". He banged on the door vigorously, attracting the attention of the immediate neighbours.

'What's the problem? They're not there. Can't you read?'

'Where are they?'

The man shrugged. 'How would I know? Went off one morning with their cases and I've not seen them since.'

'Where did they go?'

'No idea.' The man retreated behind his door and Manu stood there fuming. If he could get his hands on Monika now she would regret ever having left him.

He walked up to the street where the girls plied their trade and knocked on the first door he came to. It was not until he had knocked on the fourth door that it was opened and a girl stood there yawning.

'I'm not open for business. I'm having a few days off.'

Manu placed his foot inside the door. 'I want to ask you some questions.'

'I've done nothing wrong. Who are you, anyway?'

'I'm from the police. Where is the old woman who lives at the shop?'

'I don't know.'

'They are wanted criminals. Where have they gone?'

Natasha laughed. 'What have they done? Overcharged you for an apple? Criminals! Don't talk rubbish.'

'Where are they? You must know?'

Natasha shrugged. 'They told me they were going away on a holiday.'

'Where? Where were they going?'

'Down to the port to catch a ferry I think. Interpol might know. Why don't you contact them if these people are such important criminals? Now get your foot out of my door and let me get back to bed.'

Manu pushed Natasha roughly to one side and slammed the door behind him. 'I don't believe you. Tell me where they are now or you'll regret it.'

Natasha walked backwards into her tiny living room that also doubled as a bedroom. 'I told you all I knew. They were going to catch a ferry to Piraeus.'

Manu placed a stinging slap to her cheek. 'You know more than that.'

'That was all they told me.'

Natasha stepped further backwards until she could feel the side of her bed behind her legs.

'When are they coming back?'

'They didn't say.'

'Liar. All you girls are liars.' Manu lunged at her with his fist and Natasha ducked her head down, groping beneath the bed for her knife. She grasped it firmly and pointed it at Manu.

'If you touch me again I'll not hesitate to use this. I'll scream so loudly that all the girls will come to watch you being castrated.'

Manu looked at her calculatingly, then grabbed her wrist forcing her to drop the knife which he kicked away.

'By the time I've finished with you screaming will be out of the question.'

Natasha wrenched her arm free and ducked away from him again, this time towards her window. He caught her by the hair and wrenched her head back. As he held her he punched her in her ribs, the pain making her gasp for breath. She tried to grope her way forwards; if she could open the window she could call for help. Someone was sure to hear her.

Manu swung her round to face him and punched her full in the face, releasing her at the same time so she fell to the ground. Half blinded by tears and pain Natasha saw the knife was within her reach. Without a second thought she grabbed it and slashed at Manu's ankles. He gave a yelp and leapt backwards. Taking her chance Natasha regained her knees, steadying herself with one hand on the floor as she tried to clear her swimming head by taking deep breaths. If he came any nearer she was in the ideal position to do some serious damage to a very sensitive part of his body.

Manu appeared to realise that he was in a vulnerable position. He backed away and looked around the room, finally picking up the large china bowl that Natasha used to clean herself when a client had left. He hurled it at her and as he did so Natasha moved to one side; the bowl hit the window, breaking the glass and shattering as it hit the ground. Her hand pressed to her side Natasha rose to her feet and began to scream for help.

'No one is going to hear you,' sneered Manu and advanced on her menacingly. This time Natasha kept the hand that was holding the knife behind her back. As he pulled her around to relieve her of it for a second time she plunged it into his body with as much force as she could muster and ran to her door. She had no idea if she had been able to injure him severely through his clothes or just scratched his skin. Without waiting to find out she pulled open her door and found herself face to face with Marina.

'What's wrong, Natasha? It was you I heard screaming, wasn't it?'

Natasha pointed a shaky hand at Manu who was getting up from the floor. He pulled the knife from his jacket and threw it on the ground before pressing his hand against his side.

Marina pushed Natasha outside the door of the house and stood there with her arm around her as other girls began to look out of their doors and come down the road towards them. As they congregated Manu emerged from the house, still clutching his side.

'You'll pay for this,' he threatened. 'I'll have you all arrested.'

'In your dreams,' called Lola from her doorway. 'We've all seen what you've done to Nat and you smashed her window. You'll be the one that is arrested.'

Shivering with both shock and the cold Natasha allowed Marina to lead her into her own house where she was wrapped in a blanket. Marina knelt beside her, chaffing her hands, whilst Effie heated some water to wash the blood from Natasha's face.

'Wait,' said Natasha thickly. 'Take a photo first.'

'You're a mess. Let me clean you up. You don't want a photo of yourself looking like this.'

'Evidence.'

Effie looked at Natasha in surprise. 'You mean you're going to report him?'

Natasha tried to nod and groaned as the searing pain shot through her temples.

'I hope you hurt him as much as he has hurt you. Hold still. I'll take come photos, clean you up and then take some more.'

''Phone the police and ask them to come here. They can see for themselves what he has done.'

'Ask Nadia to call Alecos and tell him Natasha's window needs to be boarded up. It can't be left like that over night.'

Marina nodded. 'I'll call the police first.'

'Why did he attack you, Natasha?'

'He wanted to know where Monika's mother and grandmother had gone.' Natasha wished Effie would stop dabbing at her face.

'What's that to do with him?'

'I think he was the man in that photograph that Litsa showed us.'

'Good job she's away at the moment then,' said Lola as Natasha pushed her hand away.

'He told me he was a policeman.'

'I don't care if he is the Prime Minister of Greece he had no right to hurt you.'

'Do you think we should call that lawyer who was here and let him know? Your visitor might be the man he was enquiring about,' suggested Marina.

'That's a good idea,' agreed Effie. 'Ask him to come immediately. The police will listen to him, if they bother to arrive, that is.'

'I might need a lawyer.' The enormity of her actions against

Manu were realised by Natasha. 'I stabbed him. They'll probably arrest me.'

Angelos Spanides was not best pleased when he received a 'phone call from one of the street girls asking him to visit them immediately.

'What is so urgent?' he asked

'Natasha has been attacked and badly hurt. We think it could have been the man you were asking about. She can give you a description of him.'

'Have you telephoned the police?'

'Yes, but they'll take their time about arriving. If you were here they would take more notice of you as you're a lawyer. Natasha might need your professional services anyway. She fought back and stabbed him.'

'She did what?'

'She stabbed him with the knife she keeps under her bed.'

This was obviously a far more serious offence than an assault and it was quite likely the girl would be arrested and charged. Angelos sighed. 'Very well. I'm on my way.'

Manu hurried along the road past Monique's closed shop and then walked more slowly down towards the gate that was closest to the entrance of the New Agora where there were some public toilets. His side was hurting with every step he took and he needed to see how badly the girl had injured him.

Once in a cubicle he removed his jacket and sweater, pulling up his shirt to reveal the gash that was in his side. It was bleeding and there was a large stain on his shirt and another on his jumper. However hard he tried to see the extent of the damage it was impossible to turn his neck that far around and he explored the wound with his fingers, wincing as his fingers came into contact with his raw flesh.

The wash basins were outside the cubicles and he was loath to clean his injury in full view of the other men who were making use of the facilities. He wadded up some toilet tissue and placed it over the wound, pulling the flaps of skin together as best he could before tucking his shirt firmly back into his trousers, hoping the make-shift dressing would stay in place until he reached his father's shop. He did not want the stains to show on his jacket to arouse the curiosity of the people he would pass on his return to the chemist shop.

Mr Graphides was surprised when his son entered. 'Have you found out where she is?'

'Not yet,' growled Manu. 'I had a problem to deal with and have come back here for a shower and to change my shirt.'

Manu hastened up the stairs to the apartment, hoping his mother would not question him too closely. He entered his room and threw his jacket on the bed and his sweater and shirt onto the floor. They would need to be soaked to remove most of the staining before his mother sent them to the laundry.

Gingerly he removed the pad of toilet tissue; his blood had soaked through the make-shift dressing. He looked in the mirror and was horrified at the length of the gash he saw. The knife had not penetrated sufficiently to injure him internally, but it was at least six inches long and by the amount of blood he was losing it must be relatively deep.

For a short while he stood there transfixed; his heart racing. He would certainly go back later and give the girl a taste of her own medicine. Her face would never look the same again when he had finished with her. He removed the rest of his clothes, annoyed to find that he had a small cut on each ankle where she had slashed at him, but the blood had only risen to the surface; they were no more than scratches he decided, although his socks were ruined.

He stood beneath the shower and allowed the hot water to soothe him, although it also made the cut in his side bleed more profusely. He continually washed it away and then a horrific thought struck him. The girl was a prostitute. She could be carrying a number of diseases. He had examined his side in the toilets and treated it before he had washed her blood off his hands. He could be contaminated.

The thought brought him out in a cold sweat, despite the heat of the water. He would have to go to the medical centre and have tests taken and ensure it was properly dressed. He towelled himself dry, mopping up the blood he was losing with the towel, wondering how he could cover the wound and stop it from staining the clean clothes he intended to put on. He wrapped the towel firmly around himself and then donned his dressing gown. He would have to help himself from his father's shop.

Hoping his father would be busy with a customer Manu entered cautiously. His father stood at the counter, reading a pharmaceutical magazine.

'Feel better now you've had a shower?'

Manu nodded and helped himself to a large pack of plasters from the shelf along with a pack of gauze.

'What do you need those for?' asked Mr Graphides.

'None of your business,' replied Manu curtly and hastened back to his room. He removed his dressing gown and threw the soiled towel on the floor to join his clothing. He struggled to hold the gauze over the wound whilst fixing it with the plaster strips, finally satisfied that it was firmly in place. Hurriedly he dressed and donned his jacket.

As he left by the shop entrance his father looked at him. 'Where are you going now?'

Manu ignored his father's enquiry, slamming the shop door behind him and hurrying up the road to the medical centre, his hand pressed to his side.

Angelos walked into the street where the girls lived and saw Natasha's broken window. He hesitated. It was unlikely the girl would be inside her house before the window had been repaired. Marina came out and called to him.

'We're in here. I've been looking out for you.'

Angelos entered the house warily, not knowing exactly what to expect. Natasha sat there, still wrapped in a blanket and shivering intermittently.

'She's very shocked,' said Marina quietly. 'None of us has ever been hurt like this before.'

Angelos looked at Natasha's bruised and swollen face. 'You poor girl. Can you tell me exactly what happened?'

'He wanted to know where Mrs Monique and Litsa had gone. I told him I didn't know, but he wouldn't believe me.' Natasha spoke thickly through her swollen lips.

Angelos frowned. 'Who are these people and why would this man think you would know where they were?'

Natasha sighed and waved her hand at Marina. 'You tell him.'

'Mrs Monique has the shop just down from here. Litsa is her daughter. They suddenly closed the shop and have gone away. Litsa brought us up some fruit and eggs saying we might as well use them before they went bad.'

'How long have they gone away for?'

'We don't know. Litsa didn't say, just that they were going to catch the ferry to Piraeus that evening.'

Angelos looked back at Natasha. 'The lady who telephoned me said you thought you knew the name of your attacker?'

'I don't know his name.' Natasha tried to draw a deep breath, holding her side and wincing in pain as she did so. 'Litsa came up here one evening with a photograph of a man. She asked us all if he had visited at any time and hurt us.'

Angelos waited for her to continue, but it was Marina who answered. 'We none of us recognised him; then a week later you came up here asking if we had been hurt. After the attack on Natasha we wondered if you were looking for the same man. Natasha is sure he is the one in the photo that Litsa showed us.'

'But you don't know his name?'

Marina shook her head. 'Litsa must know.'

'Quite, but we do not know the whereabouts of Litsa.'

'You can ask her when she comes back.'

Angelos nodded. When he returned to his office he would telephone Mr Iliopolakis. It was just possible that he might be able to help. He returned his attention to Natasha.

'I understand that you actually stabbed your attacker.'

'Self defence,' said Marina immediately. 'You don't stand and do nothing when someone is beating you.'

'What kind of a knife did you use?'

'A carving knife.'

'So you were able to go into your kitchen and collect a carving knife?' Angelos raised his eyebrows in surprise.

'I keep it under my bed. I thought if anyone ever turned really nasty I could threaten them and they would leave me alone.'

'Have you ever used it before?'

'No.'

'How badly injured was the man?'

'I don't know. When Marina came he ran off down the road.'

Angelos drew a breath of relief. At least the girl had not killed him; there was not a body lying on the floor of her house.

'You say you have called the police?'

Marina nodded. 'This was a serious assault, not the usual odd punch or slap. They haven't arrived, of course.'

Angelos considered the situation. 'I think it would be advisable for me to telephone them and impress upon them that this is a serious situation. They will want a statement from you and you will have to admit to using a knife. Your injuries are evidence of the violence of his attack so they should accept that you acted in self defence. Although you cannot name the man you could probably give them a reasonable likeness by using their photo fit equipment if you wanted to press charges. Where is the knife now?'

'Lying on my floor.'

'Did you touch it?'

'She couldn't have used it without touching it!' interjected Marina.

'I meant have you touched it since you used it?'

'No,' Natasha shook her head and groaned again as the pains shot through her temples. 'He pulled it out of his coat and threw it on the floor.'

'Then that is where it must stay until the police arrive. I will go in with them and insist they take the knife away to be tested for fingerprints; they can be used as evidence if an arrest is made.'

'He'll say I attacked him. I'll go to prison."

'Very likely, and that could be the safest place for you at the moment. If the police do decide to arrest you I will insist they take you to the medical centre before going to the police station.' Natasha was taking shallow breaths and was still shivering. 'I am willing to act as your defence lawyer and no doubt these ladies will be prepared to act as witnesses.'

Marina nodded. 'I was first on the scene. I would recognise him again.'

Angelos took out his mobile 'phone and called the police, gave his credentials and impressed upon them the need to attend the area immediately.

The police drew up in their car outside the house, the barrier having been lifted immediately for them. One took out his notebook whilst the other looked at the three girls and Angelos.

'Can you tell me exactly what has taken place here?'

Angelos cleared his throat. 'As the lawyer acting on behalf of the injured lady I will explain the situation as I understand it. I appreciate that you will probably have to make an arrest, but I will insist that Natasha is taken to the medical centre for treatment before taking her to the station to make a full statement.'

The two policemen looked at each other. A suspect usually called their lawyer after they had been arrested, not before.

Angelos related the events that had taken place. 'I understand the knife is still lying on the floor of the house next door. I would like to come in with you when you retrieve it so I can confirm that it was taken away as evidence.'

'I'll come with you and get her some clothes and a coat,' added Marina. 'She can't go anywhere in her nightshirt.'

Whilst Marina collected a track suit, socks, shoes and a coat, Angelos watched the police as they photographed the knife where it lay before lifting it by the tip of the blade and placing it inside a plastic bag which they sealed and signed. There was blood on the blade and Angelos wondered just how seriously the man had been wounded.

'What happened to the window?'

'I don't know,' admitted Angelos. 'I assume it was broken during the altercation.'

The policeman photographed the window from inside and out, along with the broken china that lay beneath it. 'I presume you wish to accompany the lady to the medical centre and then the police station?'

'I certainly do, and I think the lady who was first on the scene should also accompany us. She also saw the man and can describe him.'

Angelos, Natasha and Marina squashed themselves into the back of the car with the police in the front seats.

Marina took Natasha's arm and helped her to walk into the centre. They took seats at the side and one of the policemen stood beside them whilst the other went to the reception desk and explained that the lady needed to be seen immediately and declared fit enough to attend the station and make a statement.

'The doctor has a patient at the moment. I'll make sure you go in next.'

Natasha sat with her head in her hands, still shivering. She was frightened. Would the police believe that she had acted in self defence?

A man exited the doctor's surgery and the policeman placed a hand beneath Natasha's arm. 'Up you get. You'll be going in now.'

Natasha rose stiffly and drew in a sharp breath that made her clutch at her side again. 'That's him,' she said. 'I'm sure that's him.'

The policeman looked at the man she was indicating and shook his head. 'You must be mistaken. That is Detective Inspector Graphides.'

Manu averted his eyes and hurried from the building. He had not expected the girl to call the police or go to the medical centre with her injuries.

Marina clutched at Angelos's arm. 'I don't care what that policeman says. I'm sure he was the man I saw.'

Angelos nodded. 'I am willing to believe you, but I don't think now is the time to try to identify him. Accompany your friend into the doctor whilst I make a telephone call.'

The receptionist spoke to Angelos sharply as he took out his mobile 'phone. 'The use of a mobile is not permitted in here.'

Angelos walked outside the door. He needed to speak to Mr Iliopolakis urgently.

Vasilis listened carefully to Angelos as he described the assault that had taken place on Natasha and how the girl had defended herself, adding that they were at the medical centre where she was being treated. 'A man was in with the doctor when we arrived. When he came out both girls recognised him as Natasha's assailant. The police said he was a detective, named Graphides. Is that right?'

'Speak to the doctor when the girls come out and ask the doctor the nature of the man's injuries. He could be visiting for an ongoing complaint.'

'Medical information is confidential,' Angelos reminded Vasilis.

'Tell them you are a lawyer. Imply that you are working on his behalf if necessary. 'Phone me back as soon as possible.'

Angelos returned inside the medical centre and waited until Natasha emerged from the doctor's surgery. Quickly he passed her and slipped inside the door, his credentials in his hand.

'I'm sorry to bother you, doctor. The man who was here before your last patient, are you able to tell me the reason for his visit? I believe he was involved in a stabbing incident and will probably be pressing charges.'

The doctor frowned. 'It is unethical to discuss medical details without the patient's permission.'

'I should have come in with him so you could have told me then. Can you just confirm that he has a stab wound? I don't need any details.'

The doctor nodded. 'It is only a flesh wound. A few stitches were necessary but there was no real damage luckily.'

'Thank you.' Angelos did not like to press the doctor for the patient's name. If he was supposed to be representing the man he should certainly know the name of his client.

Kostas Yianides read through the report from the detective who had interviewed Natasha in the presence of Angelos Spanides. Kostas was surprised that his neighbour had been retained as her lawyer at such short notice. The girl had made a statement confirming that she had been attacked and defended herself with a carving knife. The medical certificate confirmed that she had suffered two broken ribs, along with a broken nose and cheek bone. He had a degree of sympathy with her, but to fight back with a knife was unacceptable. He had been prepared to propose bail, but Angelos had insisted she was taken into custody. Marina had also made a statement and been told she was free to leave, but would be called as a witness when the case went before the court.

'Why can't I go home?' asked Natasha. 'I don't want to spend the night in a police cell.'

Angelos requested a few moments alone with the girl. 'I feel you are far safer here. There is no guarantee that he will not return tonight and you are certainly not in a position to defend yourself.'

'That policeman said he was a detective.'

'I know, but I also believe he could be the man I was making enquiries about. You're absolutely certain he was your attacker?'

'Positive. Marina recognised him as well.'

'Are you prepared to press charges against him?'

'Is that what you want me to do?'

'I need to make a telephone call. When I have done that I'll speak to you again about a prosecution. In the meantime try to get some rest.'

Angelos telephoned Vasilis a second time, confirming that the man who had attended the medical centre was a detective known as Emmanuel Graphides and he had been treated for a stab wound.

'Ask for him to be brought in for questioning about today's incident. Tell him the girl is going to press charges against him. You say you know the chief of police well so he should listen to you. Let me know the outcome later.'

Kostas was surprised when Angelos reappeared in the police station and requested a formal meeting with him. He was even more astounded when Angelos asked for Emmanuel Graphides to visit the station immediately and account for his movements that day.

'The man called in sick.'

'We saw him at the medical centre. The doctor confirmed he had a superficial stab wound and both girls saw him and identified him as the attacker.'

Kostas shook his head. 'I know the man has rather a quick temper, but I can't believe what you are telling me. He could have resembled the assailant. I understand the victim was suffering from shock; she may well have been confused. Her friend would back her up anyway. Those girls always stick together.'

'The knife that was found at the scene was collected by your men. According to the girl her attacker pulled it from his jacket and threw it on the floor. His fingerprints should be on it. You will have Mr Graphides prints on file as a matter of course so they can easily be checked. Assuming they match with those on the handle of the knife you have the identity of the assailant.'

'It will take a while for that information to be returned from Athens. I really do not see that I can do anything before I receive their report.'

Angelos withdrew papers from his briefcase. 'I have copies of the statements here from the woman he attacked and her friend who went to her aid. The young lady is placing charges against Emmanuel Graphides for assault. As her lawyer I am insisting that you bring him in for questioning immediately. I am also requesting that you place a restraining order on him forbidding him to enter the Old Town as a matter of public safety. He may well return to the area and cause injury to one of the other girls.'

Kostas pushed back his chair. 'You really do not leave me any choice.'

Manu sat nervously before the chief of police. He had been shocked when a police car had arrived at the chemist's shop and he had been requested to go to the station. At first he had refused, saying he had called in sick earlier in the day and as such was not on duty.

Patiently and quietly the policeman had explained that he was not wanted for duty, but the chief would like to question him about an incident that had happened earlier in the day. At first Manu was going to declare he had not been out, then realised there would be a record of his visit to the medical centre that could be checked and he was sure the girl had recognised him. He would deny all knowledge of her, of course and hope that would be the end of the matter.

'So, Detective Inspector Graphides, I hear you are unwell. What is the nature of your complaint? Nothing catching, I hope.'

'Just generally under the weather, sir. Bit run down.'

'So run down that you needed to visit the medical centre?'

Manu bit at his lip angrily and did not answer. The police had seen him there and that girl must have identified him. He would definitely deal with her later.

'As I understand it you have a superficial stab wound.'

'I was attacked,' muttered Manu.

'Where were you when this attack happened to you?'

'In the Old Town.'

'That's usually a pretty peaceful place. Whereabouts?'

'Near the San Francisco Gate.'

'Not the most salubrious area, but we don't usually have any trouble up there. Why were you there?'

'I wanted to ask someone if they knew where my wife is hiding.'

'I thought you had declared your wife to be a missing person. Has she now turned up alive and well? That's good news.'

Manu gritted his teeth. 'She never has been missing. She's been living somewhere all this time, probably under an assumed name.'

'So who did you speak to?'

'I went to her grandmother's shop.'

'According to my information the shop is closed at present. Where did you go to make enquiries after that?'

Manu did not answer. Kostas obviously knew exactly where he had been.

'I believe you went up to the red light area to speak to the girls who live there,' continued Kostas.

'I don't know any of those girls.'

'I was not presuming that you knew them. Did you threaten the lady you questioned?'

'Of course not,' Manu spat the words out.

'According to the lady's statement you punched her in the side, breaking two ribs incidentally; you then punched her in the face causing a broken nose and cheek bone. You also damaged her property by throwing a large china bowl through her window; both the bowl and the window are broken, of course.'

'Rubbish. It is a tissue of lies.'

'I realise it is her word against yours, but her injuries are clear for all to see. She would hardly have inflicted such damage to herself. In her efforts to escape you she took a carving knife with the intention of threatening you so you would leave. When you attacked her further she used the knife to defend herself.'

'She attacked me.'

'In her statement she claims self defence.'

Manu thought quickly. 'I was the one acting in self defence. I only hit her to prevent her from using the knife on me a second time.'

'So you do admit to using physical force on her?'

'It was necessary.'

Kostas sighed. A clever lawyer would certainly get the man acquitted of the charge.

'Why didn't you 'phone in a report of the assault?'

'I saw no need. I was not seriously injured.'

'Any assault on a member of the police force is a serious matter. You failed in your duty, Detective Inspector.'

'I'm sorry, sir. It won't happen again. May I leave now?'

'Yes, but I am placing a restraining order on you with immediate effect. You are not to enter the Old Town for any reason. I am also relieving you of your duties.'

'You mean I am suspended?'

'From active duties temporarily whilst this enquiry takes place.'

Manu left the police station and entered the nearest bar. He could not believe it – suspended from active duty. He was going to be stuck in the office all day typing up reports from the other members of the force. The girl had attacked him with a knife. Now he had to wait for the result of his blood test to make sure she had not transmitted any disease to him. He would ignore the order forbidding him to enter the Old Town. She would regret refusing to give him the information he wanted and daring to bring a prosecution against him. By the time he had finished with her she would be only too willing to withdraw her accusation. He felt the blood rushing to his head and ordered another glass of whisky.

April – July 2010

Vasilis considered the information Angelos had imparted to him. Monika had a right to know the events that had taken place. He called Monika into his office and asked her to take a seat. She immediately looked concerned and he smiled at her.

'There is nothing for you to worry about. I have spoken to Angelos and I wanted to update you on events in Rhodes.'

'Has Manu been served with my divorce petition?'

Vasilis nodded. 'As I understand it, after Manu received the notification he went up to the Old Town planning to ask your grandmother where you were. When he found the shop was closed he went up to the street where the girls live. He did not believe the lady he spoke to and decided to use force to gain the information.'

'Oh, no. Who was it? Is she badly hurt?'

'I believe her name to be Natasha and she won't be working for a while due to her broken ribs and some very unsightly bruises to her face.'

A tear ran down Monika's face. 'I never wanted anyone else to get hurt because of me.'

'You must not blame yourself. Your husband obviously has an ungovernable temper. The young lady did not succumb to her beating without a fight. She stabbed him.'

'Oh!' Monika's hand flew to her mouth. Was Manu dead? She crossed herself for having such a wicked thought.

'It was whilst he was at the medical centre receiving treatment that the injured lady arrived. Both she and her companion recognised him as her assailant. The policeman with them said his name was Detective Inspector Graphides.'

Monika let out a breath of relief.

'Angelos had also accompanied the ladies. He telephoned me with this information and I told him he must report the facts to the police chief and ask for a restraining order to be placed on Manu. This has been done, but I think now is the time to present the chief of police with the medical evidence that is included in your divorce petition. May I have your permission?'

Monika nodded. 'Of course. Manu cannot be kept under constant surveillance and the girls should not be intimidated by him.'

'Thank you; I hoped you would agree.'

Vasilis telephoned Angelos and instructed him to proceed with Monika's divorce petition along with revealing her medical records.

'Impress upon Kostas Yianides that her statement should be taken into account along with the current assault charge. I don't want to hear that an astute lawyer has managed to get the prostitute's case dismissed.'

'Her profession goes against her. They are more likely to believe the version a detective gives. There are no witnesses to the actual attack.'

'That is why the assaults on his wife need to be taken into account. The more evidence there is against him the less credible he becomes. How long is this going to take? Have you any idea?'

'Some months I expect,' answered Angelos cautiously. 'The medical staff will have to be interviewed and their statements verified. The background of the prostitute will be investigated to see if she has been in trouble for assault at an earlier date. All this takes time.'

'What about Monika? Will her background be investigated?' asked Vasilis.

'Undoubtedly. Is there anyone, apart from yourself, who can vouch for her character?'

'My staff; they all get on well with her.'

'What about her previous employer on Rhodes?'

'The librarian was contacted for a reference by Mrs Planatakis when Monika first applied for work here. She spoke very highly of her.'

'Send me her name and address and I'll speak to her. Incidentally, has Miss Kokanides had any time off sick whilst working for you?'

Vasilis frowned. 'Not that I know of. I can ask Mrs Planatakis, why?'

'Some young women have a bad habit of self harming to draw attention to themselves. I need to ensure that she does not have this problem.'

'I think it most unlikely. I'll e-mail you the librarian's name. Assuming she has not retired you should be able to find her at the library in the Old Town.'

Once again Angelos visited the police station and sat in Kostas's office.

'Have you had the result from Athens regarding the fingerprints on the knife?'

Kostas nodded. 'Two sets were identifiable. Manu was obviously telling the truth when he claimed he was attacked by the girl.'

'I don't think anyone is disputing that fact. It is the reason behind the attack that should be under investigation.'

'He would hardly stand there and allow her to stab him. Of course he was going to defend himself.'

'Mr Graphides is a big man and physically fit. I understand he attends the gym regularly. With his knowledge of disarming criminals it should have been relatively simple for him to remove the knife from the girl's hand without resorting to physical violence.'

'He claims he hit her to prevent her from stabbing him a second time.'

Angelos looked down at Natasha's statement, although he was conversant with the details. 'So how do you account for him removing the knife from his coat and throwing it on the floor? He was then in possession of the knife so she would be unable to stab him again. Is he still suspended from active duty?'

Kostas nodded. 'I'm sure he will be reinstated once the case has been heard.'

'I hope not.' Angelos withdrew the papers from his briefcase. 'I have a sworn statement here from his wife. She is petitioning for a divorce on account of his unacceptable treatment. There are medical records to back up her claim. His wife was so frightened of him that she actually left Rhodes. She has lived in constant fear that her mother or grandmother would be attacked, consequently keeping her address a secret even from them. It is only now that her relatives have left Rhodes that she has had the courage to sue for a divorce.'

'So that was why you were asking me about him. I thought we were just having a neighbourly chat. Where have they gone?'

'I am not at liberty to disclose their location. I will leave these papers for your perusal and you will probably wish to speak to Mr Graphides regarding their veracity. I am proposing to lodge these papers with the court today. I think it would be advisable if Mr Graphides was kept in custody. I would not want him disappearing before the hearing or harassing witnesses. Assuming the outcome is in his wife's favour she will be pressing for compensation to be paid to her immediately.'

Once Angelos had left Kostas read the reports through carefully. Before the case went before the court he would need Manu to be examined by the police psychiatrist. There must be an underlying reason for the man's unreasonable behaviour.

Manu entered Kostas's office eagerly expecting to hear that the charges against him had been dropped. 'Am I able to return to active duty?'

Kostas shook his head. 'I'm afraid there is another matter that has been brought to my attention. I understand your wife is petitioning for a divorce. She is citing unreasonable behaviour on your part, using physical violence against her to the extent that she became so frightened of you that she left the island.'

'She was always bumping into things and bruising herself,' muttered Manu sulkily. 'She had a miscarriage and it affected her mentally.'

'The report I have received from her employer states that there has never been any indication of mental instability.'

'I'm sure a psychiatrist would have a different opinion.'

Kostas shook his head. 'I am in possession of a copy of her hospital reports. She was given a brain scan to ensure there was no cranial damage after her fall and subsequent concussion. She was also given counselling after the loss of the child and it was determined that she was of completely sound mind. The report lists the injuries she sustained at the time and a note was made of bruising to her body that had obviously happened at an earlier date.'

'I said she was always bumping into things.'

'There were two other occasions when your wife attended the medical centre,' continued Kostas. 'The first was when a tin hit her in the eye and the second was when her elbow was chipped. How do you account for those injuries Mr Graphides?'

'The tin fell out of the cupboard and the front door slammed back on her arm.'

'I have a statement from the lady who was her employer at that time. She confirmed that she often saw bruises on your wife's arms. Whilst making a hospital visit your wife admitted that you had thrown the tin at her and slammed the door deliberately on her arm.'

'Lies. That woman at the library was always trying to interfere.'

'So you are prepared to plead innocence on all counts?'

'Of course.'

'In that case I have no choice but to instruct the lawyer acting on behalf of your wife and the girl who was attacked to proceed with the prosecution against you. You will have the opportunity to prove your innocence in court.'

'What!' Manu sprang to his feet. His eyes were bloodshot and a pulse was throbbing in his temple. 'They have no right to accuse me.' He banged on Kostas's desk. 'My wife is a liar. She told me her mother worked in a bar and then a shop. She was a prostitute. She's put that girl from the red light area up to this. She'll regret it when I get hold of her again.'

Kostas listened to Manu's outburst impassively and pressed the bell beneath his desk requesting a uniformed officer to enter.

'Please escort Mr Graphides to a cell. He needs some time to calm down.'

'You mean lock him in?'

'Yes.' Kostas sighed wearily. The man must certainly be referred to the psychiatrist.

'You can't do this to me,' shouted Manu. 'I'm a detective.'

'That does not mean that you are above the law.'

'You'll regret this. I'll sue you. I'll have you drummed out of the force. I will be the chief of police once you have been removed; then there will be some changes made.' The vengeful look on Manu's face made Kostas shiver.

Manu sat in the police cell. He could certainly not complain about his treatment compared with many of the others who were in custody. He had been allowed his own clothes; a policeman had visited the chemists' shop and waited whilst his mother made up a bag, including his toiletries. To her acute embarrassment the policeman had unpacked it on the counter and checked every item. His nail file, scissors and a belt were returned to her.

Manu spent long hours sitting in his cell, thinking of the two women who deserved punishment for their actions and how he would wreak his vengeance upon them. He spent as long as he was allowed in the gymnasium each day, determined to keep fit and venting his anger on the punch bag. On two occasions it had been necessary for the guards to physically separate him when fighting with other inmates and a number complained that he had threatened them. They now tried to avoid associating with him and the guards watched him carefully, alert for any incidents that might arise and warning him that if he caused any more trouble his privileges would be withdrawn and he would remain in his cell for most of the day.

His blood test had been returned as positive and he raged against the result when it was given to him. At first he tried to claim that the result was incorrect. It had to be; he did not feel ill.

The prison doctor explained how the disease was transmitted and the current treatment that was on offer. 'There is no reason why you cannot live to a healthy old age. It is not the killer disease from thirty years ago. Medicine has moved on and new treatments are proving very successful.'

'Monika must have transmitted that to me,' Manu insisted. 'She was probably infected by her mother. I'll make them pay. Her, her mother and her grandmother, they'll all regret making me sick.'

Manu's father had employed a lawyer on behalf of his son and no time limit was put on the length of their meetings. Filippos found it hard to contain his irritation with the young man; pertinent questions went unanswered; Manu would sit in a sulky silence or bang his hands on the desk insisting he was innocent and would get his revenge on those who had accused him otherwise.

Filippos spoke to Mr Graphides about his concerns. 'I'm not sure I'm the right man to represent your son. He is most reluctant to give me any information. I need to be able to hold him up as an exemplary policeman who would not dream of molesting anyone.

I need to find flaws in the prosecution's evidence. I cannot do that unless he talks to me about the incidents and controls his temper.'

'There's nothing to talk about. He's innocent and it's your job to make sure he is exonerated. That's what I'm paying you for.'

Filippos shrugged and sighed. The father was no easier to deal with than his son. He had spoken to Kostas, requesting Manu was given bail, but Kostas had refused.

'I cannot keep the man under surveillance twenty four hours a day. The prosecution lawyer is concerned that he will ignore his restraining order and go to the Old Town and intimidate the girls. I certainly cannot consider bail until I have received the psychiatrist's report. I fear there has to be something seriously wrong with the man.'

Vasilis had told Monika that Manu was being held in custody and she waited nervously to hear he had been released. She had not told either her mother or grandmother about the attack on Natasha, not wishing to upset or worry them, but they had been relieved to know that Manu was in custody.

'What have they charged him with?' asked Litsa.

Monika shrugged. 'Threatening behaviour I believe. I can't ask for any details.'

'How long will they keep him locked up?' asked Monique.

'I've no idea.'

Monique puffed out her cheeks in disapproval. 'So we could go back home and I could reopen the shop.'

'That wouldn't be very sensible, Grandma. You would only have to leave again when he is released. Mr Iliopolakis might not be so willing to help you a second time.'

'We don't really want to be here longer than six months,' said Litsa. 'We'll have to start paying rent then.'

'I hope you're saving towards it. I don't expect Mr Iliopolakis can claim it to be a sanctuary indefinitely. You both have work so you would be expected to pay your way.' By being frugal Monika had managed to save a few Euros each week and she did not want to have to subsidise her relatives' rent, subsequently delaying her dream of driving lessons yet again.

When Vasilis called her into his office the next time she was expecting to be told that progress had been made and a date set when her divorce petition would be heard.

Vasilis shook his head. 'I have no further news at the moment. I am sure Angelos will advise me of any events. I really wanted to tell you that Cathy and I are going away for a week or so. We're going down to Elounda to a big birthday party. The old lady is going to be a hundred.'

Monika looked puzzled.

'I believe Cathy has mentioned to you that we have friends down there. They are a large extended family; the oldest member will be a hundred this year. They have invited relatives from America to come over and join in the celebrations and Cathy has suggested that you might like to come down with us.'

Monika blushed. 'I am not part of their family.'

Vasilis smiled. 'Cathy thought you might be willing to come in a working capacity. Marianne will organise most of the catering, but on the day it could be very useful to have an extra person to hand the food around and ensure there are enough clean plates and cutlery. I'm sure Giovanni could arrange for you to stay in one of his self catering apartments in exchange for your help. They had a serious fire down there a couple of years ago and they have just about finished rebuilding. Once the party is over you could have a few days to yourself to explore the area and then we will drive you back to Heraklion. A change of scene could do you good. Cathy remarked on how pale and edgy you seemed on your last visit.'

'I'm just worried that somehow Manu will find out where we are. He can't be kept in prison indefinitely. Even if he is convicted for the assaults his sentence will be reduced due to the time he has already spent there. He could still come looking for me in ten years' time.'

'You mustn't think like that, Monika. At the moment you and your family are perfectly safe. I'm sure your mother will be pleased to know that you are going to have a week away from working at the hotel. Can I tell Cathy you are coming?'

'I would love to,' answered Monika.

Monika was surprised when Vasilis asked her to sit in the front seat of his car. 'Cathy is more comfortable in the back,' he explained. 'She is able to sit with her legs up, besides you will be better able to see the scenery from the front seat. She has seen it many times before.'

There seemed very little to see as Vasilis drove through the outskirts of Heraklion and Monika settled back in her seat. She was unable to carry on a conversation with Cathy without turning around and she did not like to distract Vasilis from his driving. They turned onto the road that led through the mountains and Vasilis waved his hand.

'If you keep a look out on each side you'll probably see some sheep and goats. They all belong to someone, but they are allowed to roam as they wish. Watch the sky as well; there are usually some eagles to be spotted soaring on the thermal currents.'

'We had eagles in Rhodes up at the Cross in Filerimos, but I've never seen any in Crete before.'

'They wouldn't come down into the town unless they were quite desperate for food.'

'Do they catch the sheep and goats?'

'If the opportunity arises. They can only manage the lambs and kids. A fully grown animal is too heavy for them to carry away.'

Monika looked at alternate sides of the road and then up at the sky until she felt quite dizzy. 'Look,' she said finally, 'There's an eagle.' She watched the bird dipping and soaring, hovering low over a lamb that rushed to its mother for shelter. She gave a little shiver.

'Are you cold?' asked Vasilis.

'No,' Monika smiled. 'I just feel a bit like the lamb, wanting protection from the eagle that could swoop down at any moment and carry me off.'

Vasilis laughed. 'I think you are rather larger than a lamb. An eagle would not be able to lift you.'

Monika smiled back. She had been thinking how vulnerable she was if Manu was released.

'We will stay on the new road,' announced Vasilis. 'It is considerably quicker as we do not have to drive through the centres of Malia or Hersonissos. 'Once we take the turning to Elounda I will tell you to look out again; until then just look at whatever interests you.'

Everything interested Monika. She had walked over Monte Smith many times, but the sprawl of the New Town could always be seen in the distance. Here much of the land was given over to agriculture with people working in the fields and no buildings in sight. Monika realised she had never truly been out in the countryside before. The most exciting bus journey she had ever taken with her mother had been to Lindos.

Monika sighed. 'Is there anywhere like this in Elounda?'

Vasilis shook his head. 'Elounda is a small town. You can walk along the road by the sea as far as Plaka or walk up to the old villages at the base of the hills. Some of the visitors spend every day out walking whilst others spend their time lying on the beach. In the evening they will be in the bars and tavernas regaling their friends with their exploits of the day.'

'That must be very exciting if they have spent the day lying on the beach,' remarked Monika dryly.

'Even those who usually spend their time on the beach eventually feel the need to see something other than the sea and will visit somewhere a friend has recommended.'

'It's not warm enough yet for the beach, but I would like to walk around and probably visit the old villages. What else should I see if I have the time?'

'Spinalonga, of course. I do not know if the boats will be running yet, but I'm sure John would take you over.'

'What about Yiorgo?' asked Cathy from the back seat and Monika realised she had been listening to their conversation.

'I don't know if he has the boat ready for the season yet. I can ask Vasi. It would be better for Monika to go with John as he would be able to tell her the history; Yiorgo only gives a general spiel to the tourists. Now, we are turning off towards Elounda, Monika. You will see glimpses of the sea and when I get to a certain place I will draw in and you can look at the most beautiful view in the world.'

Monika enjoyed her ten days down in Elounda. She had been introduced to all the members of the family, but found it difficult to remember how they were related; then to her consternation more arrived from America. Marianne had assured her that her help had been invaluable on the day of Annita's birthday party.

'It was such a relief not to have to worry about refilling plates. I knew Marcus would deal efficiently with the bar, but I wasn't so sure about the ladies I had asked to come in and help. They are cleaners, not waitresses, and spoke no English.'

Monika smiled to herself. She was also a cleaner.

John had taken her over to Spinalonga and related the history of the island to her whilst she listened spell-bound.

'Is that all true?' she asked when he finished speaking.

'Absolutely.'

'It isn't really the same as the book I read.'

'That was a make believe story, not the factual one. They are making a television series of that book at the moment. Most of the filming is taking place in Pano Elounda. They have constructed temporary facades to make the village look like Spinalonga and you can walk up and watch them provided you keep out of their way. My little girls have been taking part.'

Monika looked at him in surprise. 'I don't remember any mention of twins.'

John grinned. 'They use just one of them at a time. Being identical no one watching the series will know that two babies have been used.'

'I suppose being here with you and seeing the houses and you actually having had relatives here makes everything seem more real to me. You told me facts that I didn't know before. You are so lucky to be able to look out and see it every day of the year.'

'I don't think the occupants considered themselves lucky when they looked across at the mainland. You have to remember they were prisoners. You should buy a copy of Old Uncle Yannis's book; that will tell you the true history. Uncle Yannis has copies in his shop.'

Monika shivered. Manu was a prisoner and she doubted if his surroundings were as beautiful as the island where she stood.

She had walked up to Plaka and been fascinated by the goods Uncle Yannis had on display in his shop. 'These are the same as the pots in the museum,' she remarked.

'They are authentic copies,' Yannis had informed her with pride. 'Everything in the shop is labelled with its place of origin. You will not turn anything up and see "made in China" stamped on the bottom. If you want cheap souvenirs then visit Saffron. Her items are of a good quality, but they are not certified copies.'

'I can't possibly afford anything like your pots, but I would like a copy of the book that describes life on Spinalonga. John told me his great great uncle lived there.'

Yannis nodded. 'I was named after him. I remember visiting the island on many occasions to see him. My sister,' he indicated Marisa, who bobbed her head at Monika, 'was married over there. Spinalonga is a very special place for us. Have a look at the sketches before you leave. They were done by Old Uncle Yannis's adopted daughter.'

Monika looked through the sketches eagerly and then turned

her attention to those displayed on the walls. 'Were those done by her also?'

Yannis shook his head. 'Those were the sketches my mother made before she died. They are of the family when they were out working on the farm. She never visited Spinalonga.'

Monika studied the sketches with interest. Had she not been told differently she would have happily accepted that they were all by the same artist.

Clutching her book, Monika had been surprised when she entered the shop two doors further up. It was crammed with every souvenir of the area you could imagine along with jewellery and T-shirts. Saffron smiled at her interest.

'I wanted a shop where people could afford to purchase a gift to take back home. Uncle Yannis's shop is amazing, but the prices are exorbitant and then there is the cost of shipping. Here a child can spend a few Euros and take a brooch or dish back for their grandmother. I make sure my items are of a better quality than those in the town.'

'I know Mr Iliopolakis refers to his friends as "the family" and I really understand why now. You all seem to be related in some way.'

Saffron laughed. 'Related or connected. I had no idea I had any family until I came here. I then found I had a sister, cousin and grandmother along with other members.'

Monika looked wistful. 'I wish I had a lot of relatives. There's only my mother and grandmother.' She selected postcards showing the area to take back with her and was embarrassed when Saffron insisted that she should not pay for them.

By the time she returned to Heraklion with Vasilis and Cathy she felt she knew the area well. She had read Old Uncle Yannis's book, hardly able to put it down, and once finished she asked John if he would be willing to take her over to Spinalonga a second time.

'You don't have to stay with me. You could arrange a time to collect me.'

John smiled at her enthusiasm. 'I'm always willing to take visitors to Spinalonga. I'll be happy to stay over there with you. You may have some more questions for me to answer.'

She had walked up to Kato Elounda and on to Pano Elounda and watched the filming that was taking place there. The set that had been built was convincingly like the village on Spinalonga. The old buildings in the villages reminded her in many ways of those in Rhodes Old Town and she felt a pang of home sickness. As she had walked past Vasi's hotel on her way to the Causeway she gazed at it enviously. What must it be like to stay there? She had no complaint with the self catering apartments, but Vasi's hotel was in a different class. Cathy had insisted that Monika should be taken up to the house Vasilis had built for her when they were first married and was now lived in by Vasi and Saffron.

'You can understand how impractical it would be for me to try to live here now,' said Cathy and Monika had agreed. She would certainly not want to live that far from the town and up the steep hill without having a car. She thought again about her driving lessons. Once she was back in Heraklion she would make enquiries and find out exactly how much they would cost; maybe by this time next year she would have gained her licence. She would then be able to bring her mother and grandmother down to the beautiful area.

The thought brought her out of her day dream abruptly. Anything could have happened by this time next year.

Monique and Litsa listened avidly to her account of Elounda and the party that had been held for the old lady. She described her visit to Spinalonga with John and Monique shook her head sadly.

'That was a bad time. I knew of five people from the Old Town who were taken away. We were all fearful that we may have caught it from them. They never returned.'

'John told me his great great uncle was a sufferer and sent to the island. He was one of the fortunate few who survived the war and eventually went to the hospital in Athens. I bought a copy of his book and it is full of information. You can borrow it if you wish.'

Litsa looked at the thickness of the book and shook her head. 'Why don't you just tell us about it?'

'One day I'll take you down there so you can see everywhere for yourselves,' promised Monika, but she did not disclose her desire to have driving lessons, although determined now that she would learn. There must be many more beautiful places on Crete that she would like to see and the only practical way of visiting them was by car.

At first Monika found driving through the traffic in Heraklion intimidating but she was determined to overcome her fears. Once her instructor took her to a quieter area on the outskirts of the town she felt more confident. Learning the road signs was easy and each evening she would study the Highway Code so she would know the answer to any questions she was asked. She could not afford to fail when it was time to take her test. The lessons were gradually swallowing up most of her savings and driving was more difficult than she had envisaged.

Her grandmother continually mentioned her desire to return to Rhodes, but Monika was adamant that she should stay on Crete until the outcome of the prosecutions against Manu was known. Monique grumbled that now they had been living in the apartment for six months they would have to begin to pay rent. Monika did not like to ask Vasilis for an extension to the arrangement and spoke quietly to her mother.

'Mamma, I am expecting Mr Iliopolakis to start charging you rent from the end of this month. If it is too much for you to afford I will help you look for somewhere more reasonable.'

'Your grandmother should be able to afford it. She has her pension along with her wages. She has more each week than either of us. She just misses Rhodes and her shop.'

'You won't let her return to Rhodes, will you?'

'I can hardly stop her, but it would be foolish to return until we know how long Manu will be kept in prison.'

Monika did not like to pester Vasilis and ask when the court case would take place, but she was relieved when he told her a date had been set for November.

'Will I have to attend?' she asked nervously.

'I think it very unlikely. According to Angelos the assault case will be heard first. After that has been dealt with, provided they find in Natasha's favour, it will add credence to your divorce petition which will then be presented. Angelos will ask for your divorce to be finalised as soon as possible due to the evidence against your husband.'

'What happens if Manu is cleared of the charges to Natasha?'

'Your petition will still go ahead, with a claim for compensation and your expenses, but you may well have to wait two or more years for it to be finalised.'

Monika shook her head. 'Even if I am granted a divorce I cannot see Manu paying me any money.'

'He is bound by law to pay you whatever amount is decided by the court. It has to be in cash and paid immediately. All the time it is unpaid he will be kept in prison.'

'If he has to pay compensation to Natasha as well as me how will he find the money? If he is given a prison sentence he will not be working.'

'That is his problem, not yours. He will have to apply to the bank for a loan. I expect his father would stand as a guarantor unless he has enough savings to pay his son's debts outright.'

'I feel sorry for Mr and Mrs Graphides. I was not very fond of either of them. I felt they disliked me, but they were never actively hostile.'

August – November 2010

Kostas studied the report the psychiatrist finally presented to him. It made both interesting and disconcerting reading.

Reading through the account of his encounter with Natasha showed discrepancies. According to Manu he had called at her house to ask if she had any information. He had not intended to go inside. Natasha had insisted it was too cold to stand and talk on the doorstep as she was still in her nightclothes. Once inside she had propositioned him and when he refused her advances she had drawn the knife and threatened him. In defending himself he had hit her; it was self defence. He claimed not to know how the window came to be broken and suggested the girl had caused the damage herself after he left.

Again Kostas made a list of the variations between Manu's description of the interview and the sworn statements of Natasha and Marina.

When asked about the incidents Monika had reported he had become enraged. He declared that she frequently disobeyed him or ignored his instructions and had lied about her parentage to him. He was certain she had no feelings towards him, but married him to gain respectability and in doing so had infected him with the HIV virus.

The psychiatrist had summarised his conclusions at the end of the long report by saying that Emmanuel Graphides wanted to be in control, not only of situations but also to dominate those people around him who were unable to defend themselves adequately against him. He frequently deluded himself that he was the victim in each case and not directly responsible for the injuries either woman had suffered at his hands.

Angelos read the report through and e-mailed a copy to Vasilis with a covering letter.

I note the psychiatrist has not recommended any treatment at this stage. Mr Graphides has had a brain scan and there is no underlying medical problem there that could explain his behaviour. His childhood is being investigated; he may have been physically abused as a child and that has given him the desire to control others. Physical violence would give him the delusion of power.

Please ask Miss Kokanides to contact me as I need her confirmation that she did not lie to her husband on any occasion. I also need her to be tested for the HIV as Mr Graphides has been declared positive and is convinced that she transmitted it to him.

I wish to use the psychiatrist's report as evidence against him.

He is still being held on remand and bail has not been granted.

Vasilis did not show the report to Monika, but he did ask her to contact Angelos and confirm that she had never lied to Manu.

Monika dropped her eyes. 'I cannot do that.'

Vasilis looked at her in surprise. 'Did you lie to him? That would be excusable if it saved you from a beating.'

'I told him my mother was working in a bar.'

Vasilis frowned. 'Where was she working?'

'In the street as a prostitute,' whispered Monika.

Vasilis swallowed. He would have to be very tactful here. He would never have suspected that Litsa had worked at such an unsavoury occupation. That accounted for her being on such friendly terms with the girls in the street.

'You kept this hidden from Manu?'

'I couldn't tell him. I was in love with him at the time. I thought he was a good man who upheld the law and kept us all safe and I was frightened he would leave me if he knew the truth. My mother told me she worked in a bar when I was too young to understand where she went each evening. Once we were married my mother moved back to live with my grandmother and found some shop work.'

'I see. So how did Manu find out that you had kept this information from him?'

'A man who lived in the street with one of the girls was murdered. The police interviewed everyone and one of the girls said my mother used to work there. He told Manu. That was when Manu threw me against the wall and I fell down the stairs.'

Vasilis rubbed his hand across his forehead. 'Did you lie to him about anything else?'

'I told him my father had been in the navy. My mother had told me he was a sailor and had an accident. I repeated that to Manu, but I don't know if that is true or not. I don't know who my father was.'

Vasilis shook his head sadly. Manu would probably claim mitigating circumstances that meant he lost control of his temper on that occasion. 'You will have to tell Angelos the same as you have told me and he'll probably ask you for a sworn statement.'

'You won't hold this against my mother, will you?' asked Monika anxiously. 'She only worked up there so she had sufficient money to provide for me. I never wanted for anything and then she paid all my University fees.'

'Your mother never mentioned being ill with any infection she had caught from her – her – customers?'

'Never. Mamma went to the clinic regularly to be checked. All the girls do. They know the risks.'

'Have you ever had a test, Monika?'

Monika shook her head. 'I had my blood tested when I was pregnant to ensure I was not deficient in iron or anything, but not the kind of test you mean. Why?'

'Manu had a blood test after his encounter with the girl in the street. It has come back positive.'

Monika looked at Vasilis in horror. 'You mean he may have infected me? How would I know?'

'He is actually claiming that you infected him having contracted it from your mother. I think it more likely that the girl who attacked him passed the infection on. Angelos is contacting her and asking for her latest medical record.'

'But how? He didn't have a sexual encounter with her.'

'According to the report he hit her and made her nose bleed. If he had an open wound on his hands he could have become infected that way. If he touched the wound in his side before he had cleaned his hands he could have transmitted it to himself. You have to be very careful about bodily fluids these days. This is why we make sure there is always a plentiful supply of gloves for you to wear whilst you are cleaning. Do you have any problem with going to the local clinic and asking for a blood test?'

'No problem at all. I don't think there is anything wrong with me, but I would like to be certain. Please don't tell my mother until after I have the result.'

'I wouldn't dream of it. Is there anything else that could be detrimental to your case that you have not disclosed?'

Monika shook her head. 'Nothing.'

'Then I will ask you to speak to Angelos now. Here is his number. You may use this telephone in my office. I will be in reception when you have finished.'

'Thank you, sir.' Monika had expected to have to use her mobile 'phone and she was unsure if she had sufficient credit for what would probably be quite a lengthy call.

Vasilis sat in an armchair well away from any visitors and took out the report from Angelos again. He would have to study it further and speak to the lawyer when Monika finished her call. He was only a short way through when his mobile 'phone rang and he saw it was Cathy calling him.

'Are you alright?' Cathy only phoned him at the hotel if she had a problem.

'I'm fine. I've just had a call from Vasi. He said the old lady died last night.'

'Old lady?' For a moment Vasilis was confused. 'You mean Annita?'

'In her sleep apparently.'

'A lovely way to go at her age. We'll drive down this afternoon. Ask Vasi if we can stay with him and then we can find out if the family need any help with the arrangements.'

'Are you able to get away at such short notice?'

'Of course; there's nothing of any importance happening here.' Monika's problems fled from Vasilis's mind until he saw her exiting his office.

She smiled shakily at him. 'I have to make a written statement and send it to Angelos. He said he would only produce it if necessary. I also have to make an appointment at the clinic.'

Vasilis nodded distractedly. 'I'm sure you can deal with it. I will give you his telephone number and you can e-mail your statement to him. He can then send a typed copy to you for your signature if necessary.' Vasilis wrote the numbers on the reverse of a business card. 'Cathy and I will be away for a few days, but if you need me urgently please call my mobile number. The old lady in Elounda died last night. We have to go down for her funeral.'

'I am so sorry. I only spoke to her briefly, but everyone seemed to love her and hold her in high esteem.'

'She was remarkable. Bryony is probably the person who knows her history best. You must ask her to tell you one day.'

Monika nodded. She could not remember which of the various ladies she had met was called Bryony. 'Have a safe journey.'

That evening Monika sat and began to compose a statement for Angelos. Having admitted to Vasilis that her mother had worked as a prostitute she could hardly claim ignorance of the fact to the lawyer. She confessed that she had not been strictly honest with Manu when describing her parentage as she had been worried that if Manu knew the truth he would terminate their relationship. She assured Angelos that her mother had given up the work some years previously and had never had any issues concerning her health. She added the date she had been given by the clinic for a blood test and that as soon as she had the result she would contact him and give permission for the clinic to send him a copy of the report.

Having read it through a number of times Monika wrote it out as neatly as possible. She signed it and addressed an envelope to Angelos. Without Vasilis at the hotel to give her permission she did not consider that she had any right to use his office and his computer for her private business, nor did she want whoever was on reception to send it on her behalf. They would undoubtedly read it. It was better to post it and telephone Angelos to say her statement was on the way to him.

Monika waited anxiously for the result of her blood test and when it came back telling her that she was clear of HIV she drew a breath of relief. Not only was she healthy, but Manu could not blame her for his own infection. She sent the results on to Angelos and also told Vasilis the good news.

'I'm pleased to hear you have nothing wrong. I have some interesting information from Angelos. I think we can be fairly certain that Natasha transmitted it to him.'

Monika frowned. 'If she gave it to Manu will that mean her evidence cannot be used?'

'I think it is unlikely to have any bearing on the case. She could still be awarded damages for her physical injuries, but Manu could counter claim for the infection she appears to have given him. Of course, had he not assaulted her he would not have been injured or infected.'

'Poetic justice,' murmured Monika. 'What a mess that man has made of his life.'

'A mess of his own making. You have nothing to blame yourself for. I know Angelos is in receipt of your statement regarding your mother's circumstances at the time of your marriage. He will only produce that if it is strictly necessary. I understand he has been making enquiries at the school Manu attended as a child. He is remembered by the staff who are still there as a bully. Apparently he often had bruises evident on his arms and legs and it was thought they were caused by his father. Mr Graphides insisted he never laid a finger on him and they had occurred whilst the boy was playing football.'

'Very likely,' agreed Monika. 'I know Mrs Graphides was rather in awe of her husband. She seemed quite a timid woman, but that doesn't mean he ever hurt her.'

'Now, Monika, there are two other things I need to talk to you about. The first is the rent for the apartment your grandmother and mother are occupying. I have spoken to my accountant and he says I cannot extend sanctuary. I will have to charge them rent from the beginning of September.'

Monika's heart sank. She should not have spent so much of her savings on her driving lessons. It was very likely she would have to subsidise her mother and grandmother to allow them to continue to live at the apartment and that was more important than passing her driving test that was booked for October.

'I understand that your mother has been promoted to the position of cashier and her salary has increased. I have also given your grandmother an extra Euro an hour for her work. They should be able to manage two hundred Euros.'

'Two hundred a week!' The sum was greater than Monika had ever imagined.

'No, two hundred a month and they are still responsible for their utility bills.'

'Oh!' Monika felt limp with relief. 'They should be able to

manage that between them and my grandmother receives her pension. If they have a problem I can always work some extra hours to help them.'

'That comes to the second thing I wanted to talk to you about. Would you like to train as a receptionist?'

Monika sucked in her breath. She had planned to approach the library service to see if she was able to obtain work with them once the court case was over, but to become a receptionist at the hotel would be equally rewarding.

'I would like that very much, Mr Iliopolakis.'

'Good. That saves me from having to advertise the position and spend time interviewing applicants. Davros is retiring at the end of the year so you will have plenty of time to become proficient. You will also be earning double the amount you are paid at the moment.'

Monika's face reddened. Her first thought had been that she would be able to complete her course of lessons and take her driving test.

'I really do not know how to thank you, Mr Iliopolakis. You have been so good to me.'

Vasilis smiled. 'Cathy continually reminds me that someone who has a University degree in languages should not be working as a cleaner. This will stop her from worrying away at me.'

Monika found the work expected of her as a receptionist was interesting and varied. Davros was patient with her, explaining how the booking system was recorded and the details she would need from a customer who telephoned to make a reservation. It was certainly not as difficult as she had originally envisaged. Pleased to finally be rid of the blue overall that she had worn whilst cleaning for so many years she treated herself to two straight skirts, a pair of black trousers and four toning blouses along with a new pair of shoes with low heels. They would probably make her feet and legs ache at first, but she could not wear her trainers whilst working on reception.

She spent a sleepless night before her driving test. She was pleased she had told no one about her forthcoming ordeal. She would not have to admit to having failed. She was elated and relieved when she was told she had passed. At last, she could drive. She could hire a car and go wherever she pleased, taking her mother and grandmother with her. Had it not been for the impending court case against Manu she would have been completely happy.

The next two weekends Monika rented a small car and drove cautiously out of Heraklion; before she took her mother or grandmother out she wanted to feel confident that she was able to drive safely unaccompanied by a qualified instructor. Finally satisfied that she was competent she told her mother and grandmother that she had her driving licence and planned to hire a car at the weekend and take them down the coast to Kokkini Hani.

'Why Kokkini Hani?' asked Litsa.

'It is not too far and I understand it has a lovely sandy beach. I thought we could take a packed lunch, go for a swim and later have a look around before we returned.'

'I don't want to eat my lunch sitting on a sandy beach,' protested Monique. 'Sand gets into everything.'

'In that case after I have had a swim we could walk into the town and find a taverna. I really do want to have a swim,' answered Monika with a smile. 'I loved going to the beach in Rhodes and there really isn't anywhere at Heraklion. If you go to the outskirts there are hotels everywhere and their beaches are private and can only be used by their guests.'

Litsa looked thoughtful. 'I'd quite like to go for a swim. I haven't been in the sea for years, but I don't have a costume.'

'Wear and old T-shirt and shorts and bring a change of clothing with you.'

Litsa nodded. 'I suppose I could.'

The visit to Kokkini Hani was a success in Monika's eyes. Whilst her grandmother sat on the beach she and her mother had enjoyed the cool water, lying in the sun for a short while afterwards. They had walked to the tavernas at the top of the beach and finally selected the most inexpensive meal.

'We should have brought a packed lunch,' said Litsa as she eyed the prices. 'We could have sat in the car and eaten it.'

'We'll go somewhere else next week,' Monika promised her mother and grandmother. 'Have a look at the map and see where you think might be interesting.'

It became a regular routine for Monika to hire a car and drive her mother and grandmother out for the day, usually along the coast road and stopping for a swim before finding somewhere to sit and eat the lunch they had taken with them. As Monika's confidence grew they were able to go further afield until she finally decided she could manage the drive to Hersonissos.

Monika swam at Hersonissos and came out of the sea shivering. 'That's it. I'll not go in the sea again; it's far too cold now. Next week we'll drive to some of the inland villages; then I won't even be tempted to swim.'

Angelos telephoned Vasilis and assured him he would do his utmost to have Manu convicted of assault on Natasha and the girl consequently exonerated from his accusation that she had attacked him and he had only acted in self defence. She was no longer working in the street after being confirmed as HIV positive some months earlier and was attending the clinic regularly for treatment.

When Vasilis told Monika the trial was to commence the following day her spirits dropped. There was no guarantee that Manu would have to pay her any compensation and although she was saving as much as possible from her wages she doubted that she would have sufficient to pay the lawyer and the court costs without approaching the bank and asking for a loan. She would have to ask Mr Iliopolakis the procedure as she did not have a bank account. She should not have squandered her money on driving lessons.

Manu sat before the magistrate in the criminal court, Filippos on one side and his father on the other. Angelos sat further away with Natasha and Marina. He had insisted they appeared with him.

'Manu could claim something that has not been covered in your statements. I would then have to verify the information with you. We do not want to have the case adjourned time and again whilst I track you down and ask for a further sworn statement. Sooner or later the magistrate would throw the case out and say we were wasting his time.'

Angelos presented his accusation on behalf of Natasha, describing the events that had taken place that morning in the Old Town. Manu continually muttered "not true, not true" until both the magistrate and his lawyer asked him to keep silent until he was asked to present his own version.

'I'll not keep quiet. Why should I be treated like this? I am the injured party. That girl stabbed me. She could have killed me. Everything she says is lies.'

Mr Graphides took hold of his son's arm, telling him to calm down and Manu shook it off.

'I'll not calm down,' he shouted. 'You know I came back to the shop with blood all over me. Not satisfied with injuring me I now find she has infected me. She should be in jail.'

Filippos looked at Manu's statement and asked to confer with his client. 'You didn't mention in your statement that you were "covered in blood". You said you placed a temporary dressing on the wound before going to the medical centre. If you were bleeding so badly why didn't you go straight to the hospital as an emergency?'

Manu shrugged and scowled. 'That's my business.'

Filippos looked at Manu's father. 'When your son returned to your shop did you see any sign of blood on him?'

Mr Graphides looked from the lawyer to the magistrate and

back to his son. He was not sure if he was under oath. Manu glared at him. Slowly Mr Graphides shook his head. 'I didn't know he had been hurt.'

Angelos smiled complacently. 'This is the first discrepancy. I am not saying Mr Graphides is deliberately lying about his condition. I am saying he is exaggerating. A small amount of blood looks alarming to someone who is not used to dealing with injuries.'

The magistrate nodded understandingly. 'What other discrepancies do you wish to bring to my attention?'

Angelos cleared his throat. 'Mr Graphides gave a statement to Kostas Yianides, the chief of police, about the events of that morning and was relieved of his active duties whilst an investigation took place. I advised Mr Yianides that the young lady who had been assaulted was planning to proceed with a prosecution and that Mr Graphides wife was also going to petition for a divorce on the grounds of physical abuse.'

Manu jumped to his feet. 'She's a liar. They are both liars.'

Filippos and Mr Graphides pulled Manu back down into his seat. 'If you keep interrupting the magistrate will ask to have you removed and the case will be heard in your absence,' Filippos advised him. 'Sit down and keep quiet.'

'Does the application for divorce have any relevance to the assault on either party?'

Angelos nodded. 'It has a direct bearing on the events. Mrs Graphides suffered a miscarriage at her husband's hands and was so frightened of him causing her further injury that she left Rhodes and went into hiding, living under her maiden name.'

The magistrate raised his eyebrows. 'Where is she now?'

'I am not prepared to say in front of Mr Graphides. I will write down an address where she can be contacted and pass it to you. She was too scared of her husband to bring divorce proceedings against him until she had arranged for her grandmother and mother to join her in a place of safety. Her divorce petition is due to be presented at the conclusion of this case.'

Angelos wrote down the address of the "Central Hotel" and passed the information to the magistrate who raised his eyebrows. 'Please continue Mr Spanides.'

'In an effort to find his wife's location Mr Graphides visited the Old Town and tried to beat the information of her whereabouts from this lady sitting beside me. She stabbed Mr Graphides in self defence after he had broken two of her ribs, her nose and cheek bone and blacked her eye. She had no intention of doing him a serious injury; she just wanted to avoid any further brutality from him. She is claiming compensation for the injuries she suffered.'

The magistrate looked at Natasha who was sitting demurely beside Angelos, her eyes downcast.

'When Mr Yianides confronted Mr Graphides with the information that he was to be prosecuted for assault he became so aggressive and threatening that Mr Yianides had no choice but to have the detective placed in a cell. He has been detained since on a charge of threatening behaviour and ordered to undergo a psychiatric assessment. When Mr Graphides was interviewed by the psychiatrist he gave a different version of the events from the one he had given to Mr Yianides originally. In the opinion of the psychiatrist Mr Graphides suffers from a need to dominate those around him. If he does not have his own way he then becomes physically abusive.'

'You're useless.' Manu turned to Filippos. 'Why aren't you defending me against these charges? You should be contesting every word that man says. It's libel,' shouted Manu.

'Please be quiet, Manu. Shouting will do you no good. I will defend you when the magistrate asks me to present your version of events.'

Manu banged on the table in front of him. 'Don't tell me to be quiet. You're not the one that is being blamed by these women. They've made it all up between them. I'll make them regret it.'

The magistrate regarded Manu sternly and signalled to the police officers who were standing behind him. 'Please remove Mr Graphides from the court so we are able to proceed without these continual interruptions.'

Manu bunched his fists. 'If you touch me you'll suffer,' he threatened; a wild look in his eyes.

Ignoring his threat the police officers seized Manu's arms and began to drag him towards the door, whilst he continued to struggle and protest. Angelos put his finger to his lips and shook his head at the girls beside him.

'I suggest we have a short recess, once the situation has calmed we can proceed.'

Filippos and Mr Graphides hurried from the court room; once outside Filippos shook his head. 'I cannot represent your son. He is being completely unreasonable.'

'You have to,' snapped back Elias Graphides. 'You have to get these ridiculous charges against him dismissed.'

'I'm afraid Mr Graphides has probably convicted himself due to his behaviour. He has demonstrated before the magistrate that he has a violent temper and if released I fear he would have no hesitation in attacking the lady a second time. I am withdrawing my services immediately.' Filippos walked away leaving Elias Graphides feeling distinctly worried.

As soon as the magistrate re-entered and Manu had been brought back into the court Elias Graphides was on his feet.

'I am requesting an adjournment; my son's lawyer has had to withdraw from the case for personal reasons.'

'Does he not have an associate who could act on his behalf?'

'I'll be my own lawyer. I know all about the law and my rights,' shouted Manu.

'In that case, Mr Graphides, you should know that until the prosecution has finished presenting its case you should remain silent. Please proceed, Mr Spanides.'

Angelos ran his hand through his hair. 'I am presenting Mr Graphides as a man who constantly deludes himself about the veracity of a situation. He has a desire to dominate every situation and he believes he has the right to use physical power to obtain whatever he wants or to vent his anger if refused. I am requesting substantial damages to be awarded to the lady known as Miss Natasha and any assault charges against her to be dismissed.'

'She attacked me. She should be paying me compensation.' Manu was on his feet again with his fists clenched.

The magistrate sighed. 'Do you have anything sensible to say in your own defence, Mr Graphides?'

'She's a prostitute. I'll make her pay for her lies.'

'Please calm down, Mr Graphides. Have you anything to add that will have any bearing on the case?'

The magistrate waited, giving time for Manu to present an argument in his favour. When none was forthcoming he continued.

'I have read the sworn statement given by the lady who claims to have been assaulted and also that of the lady who went to her assistance. I have read two versions of your statement of events, Mr Graphides, and I do not find either of them plausible. I am therefore sentencing you to four years for common assault. The amount of damages to be awarded will be decided later and you are liable for all the court costs. Whilst you are detained you will undergo a course of psychiatric treatment and anger management counselling.'

Manu clenched his teeth. 'You can't sentence me. I'm a detective. You have no right to call yourself a magistrate; you have no idea what you're doing, you stupid old man.'

'Mr Graphides, you have just added a further six months to your sentence for contempt of court. Please take the prisoner away. We will now adjourn for half an hour.'

Angelos sat back with a sigh of relief. Manu had very effectively convicted himself. Had he waited for his lawyer to present his defence it could have been a different outcome and unlikely that Natasha would have been awarded any damages.

Natasha looked at Angelos. 'Did I understand that he has to pay me compensation for my injuries?'

Angelos nodded. 'I have no idea how much you will get.'

'Thank you. Whatever it is I will be grateful. I've managed

to find a cheap room but now I can't work any longer I'm living on my savings. What happens next?'

'You and Marina may go home and I will contact you when the amount of damages has been decided. I have to stay here and present Mrs Graphides divorce petition to the civil court.'

'Poor Monika, fancy being married to a monster like that! She was such a sweet girl. Will she be receiving any compensation?'

'That remains to be seen.'

Angelos sat outside the civil court waiting for his name to be called. The magistrate who had dealt with the earlier case saw him waiting there and raised his eyebrows.

'I thought the prosecution against Mr Graphides had been dealt with. The compensation amount has not been decided as yet.'

'Yes, thank you, sir. I am now waiting to present the divorce petition on behalf of Mr Graphides's wife. Mr Graphides acted violently towards her on a number of occasions causing actual bodily harm. I have her medical records with me to confirm the injuries she sustained.'

The magistrate held up his hand. 'Are you talking about the same man as I sentenced earlier?'

'Yes, sir.'

'I'll have a quick word with the presiding lawyer. It could save his time and yours.' The magistrate walked on and Angelos continued to wait patiently.

It was more than two hours later when Angelos's name was finally called and he entered the lawyer's office and passed Monika's petition to him. Angelos waited for the lawyer to read through the document.

'Has Mr Graphides presented any evidence why a divorce should not be granted?'

'Not that I know of, sir.'

'I understand Mr Graphides demonstrated his quick and uncontrollable temper in court today. As he has not submitted any defence I don't think this application needs to be discussed.' The lawyer placed the official seal on the paper and signed it. 'I will see that the necessary documents are drawn up. I understand you are acting on behalf of the lady and all communication should be addressed to you. Is that correct?'

Angelos nodded. 'The lady wishes to continue to conceal the address where she is residing at this time. I would also like to ask for compensation for the lady, not only for her injuries, but also for having to leave her home, family and place of work. For five years she has worked under her maiden name as a cleaner in a hotel. Her previous job as a trained librarian was considerably more remunerative so I believe she also deserves compensation for her loss of earnings over that time as well as the expenses incurred by my employment.'

The lawyer frowned. 'I will have to consult my financial advisers regarding the final sum. The differential between the wages of a cleaner and a librarian will need to be calculated. The final figure is going to be a substantial amount and Mr Graphides will be ordered to pay immediately. If he does not have the money available he will have to come to an arrangement with the bank.'

'Thank you, sir. I will wait to hear further from you.'

Angelos telephoned Vasilis and relayed to him the events of the assault trial. 'I've never heard anyone speak to a magistrate in such a way; so rude and disrespectful. He told the magistrate he was a stupid old man who didn't know what he was doing.' Angelos chuckled. 'That earned him an extra six months for contempt of court.'

Vasilis listened patiently. 'I'm pleased the girl was given compensation, but what happened about the divorce petition? Was that granted?'

'That went straight through. The magistrate had a word with the lawyer and Mr Graphides had not entered any plea of defence. It's just a question of completing the official paper work and deciding upon the amount of compensation the lady should receive along with her expenses. It should be finalised within three months. Will it be in order if I send my final account to her at the hotel? Of course, if she is not able to pay immediately and has to wait for the money to come through from her ex-husband I will be forced to charge interest.'

'I'm sure there will be no problem with your payment.' Vasilis would pay the lawyer's bill himself and allow Monika to repay him at a later date rather than incur interest. 'Any communication for her should be sent to the hotel and she will receive it promptly.'

'There's just one other thing,' continued Angelos. 'I assume the lady has a bank account where the money can be paid in directly to her?'

'I'm sure she has. I'll ask her to send you the details.'

Vasilis asked Monika to come to his office and she entered nervously. Had she made a terrible error when booking some conference rooms?

'There's no need to look so worried, Monika. I have just had a telephone call from Angelos. I am pleased to tell you that your divorce had gone through and will be finalised in three months.'

Monika exhaled deeply. 'That is such a relief. I thought the defence lawyer might say I had left it too long before taking proceedings.'

'I don't know the whole story, but according to Angelos Mr Graphides behaved very badly before the magistrate. He has been sentenced to four years for the assault on the lady along with a further six months for contempt of court. He has to pay Natasha compensation along with her lawyer's fees. You will also receive compensation and I understand it will be worked out on the salary you would have received from the library over the previous years and the amount you have earned whilst working for me.'

Monika frowned. 'That is going to be a lot of money. I was earning fifteen thousand Euros a year when I left and I would have had an annual increment of five hundred Euros until I reached the top of the scale.'

'I would say approximately one hundred thousand Euros once your cleaning wages have been deducted.'

Monika gasped. 'As much as that!'

Vasilis smiled at her reaction. Cathy received more than that each year in royalties from her deceased father's books and he certainly earned considerably more from his investments.

'Angelos's expenses will be added to the amount, but, of course, you will have to pay that back to him. He will send his bill here and if you do not have sufficient to pay him in full at that time please speak to me. You do not want him to be charging you interest on the outstanding amount.'

'Thank you, Mr Iliopolakis. You must also tell me how much I owe you and as soon as my compensation money comes through I will pay you.'

'As far as I am aware you owe me five hundred Euros for the interview Vasi had with Angelos and his subsequent visit to the girls in the street.'

'Is that all? What about the flight and the hotel?'

Vasilis waved his hand airily. 'I told you, that was a failed business meeting. Angelos would like you to send him the details of your bank account so the money can be transferred directly to you.'

'I don't have a bank account,' admitted Monika. 'I've always kept any savings I had in a box beneath my bed.'

'You will need to put a small amount in the bank to officially open the account. It is a very simple procedure. I will come with you and act as a reference for you.'

'Suppose I want some of the money out to spend?'

Vasilis smiled at her ignorance. 'You will be given a bank book that tells you how much money is in your account. When you want any money out you tell the cashier how much you want and hand him the book. He will give you a form to sign and the money will be deducted from the balance in your book by the computer and you will be handed the notes.'

April 2011

The first time Elias Graphides was allowed to visit Manu in prison he sat awkwardly at the table with guards hovering in the background to ensure he did not pass anything illegal to his son.

'How are you? Are you being treated decently?' he asked.

Manu shrugged. 'What do you think? I shouldn't be here. That magistrate wouldn't listen to me and the lawyer you employed was worse than useless.'

'He was recommended to me. I'm sorry he wasn't suitable.'

'Sorry,' sneered Manu. 'That's all you people ever say. If he had presented my case properly I wouldn't be here now.'

'You dismissed him, Manu.'

'Because he was useless! Why does no one listen to me? I'm a detective, not a criminal.'

'You committed a criminal act and then you were foolish enough to be rude to the magistrate.' Elias sighed. 'I tried to knock some sense into you when you were a boy and got into trouble at school because of your temper and using your fists. I thought when you joined the police force I had been successful.'

'That girl who attacked me with the knife will regret it when I get out of here. I'm not paying her compensation. She should be paying me. She gave me her disease.'

'Had you not hit her and got her blood on your hands you would not have become infected,' Elias tried to reason with Manu.

'It's no great problem now if you are positive. The treatment has improved and provided you follow the doctor's orders there's no reason for it to develop further.'

'What do you know about it?'

'I'm a chemist, remember. I hand out prescriptions for it all the time; some of the recipients have been having medication for years now. Put that to one side at the moment; there are other things I need to discuss with you.'

'Such as?'

'The compensation money for both the women and the court fees. How much money do you have in the bank?'

'That's my business.'

'Manu, I am trying to help you. You have a bill for over three hundred thousand Euros. Do you have that amount of money in the bank?'

'Of course not.'

'You know the law, once compensation has been agreed by the court it has to be paid in full immediately. Where are you going to get the money from? I cannot see the bank being willing to give you a loan as you are in prison with no regular income.'

For the first time Manu looked concerned. 'They can't keep me here indefinitely. I ought to have my sentence reduced due to the time I spent in custody before the trial.'

'Had you behaved sensibly and not threatened Mr Yianides you would probably have been granted bail. I'll approach the bank and see if I can get a loan, but I need to know how much to ask for, so tell me how much you have on your account.'

'My book is in the drawer by my bed at home.'

Mr Graphides nodded. He had already found the bank book, but had hoped that Manu would have some money elsewhere. There was certainly not sufficient in his bank account to cover even the court fees.

Elias Graphides left the bank feeling depressed. To obtain the large loan he required to cover the costs and compensation Manu had been ordered to pay he had needed to sign his chemist's shop and the living accommodation above over to the bank as a guarantee of repayment. It was a worry. If anything happened to him the shop would have to close down and his wife would have no income. The bank would reclaim the property and she could end up homeless. All because Manu had an ungovernable temper.

Monika bought a bottle of wine as she hurried to her mother's apartment. Her decree nisi had finally arrived at the hotel, along with a statement saying how much money she had been awarded by the court. She could not believe the sum and kept looking at the figures thinking there must have been a mistake. Her loss of earnings over the years had been taken into account, along with her medical expenses for her arm and eye, the court fees and another five thousand as compensation for the trauma she had suffered at Manu's hands. Even deducting the amount Vasilis had paid on her behalf for the court fees she was looking at a sum in excess of two hundred thousand Euros. She had thought herself rich when she had managed to save almost a thousand Euros in the past.

'I've had to open a bank account,' she said to her mother. 'I can't keep that amount in a shoe box under my bed.'

'I should think not,' replied Litsa. 'Besides, it wouldn't be safe to carry all that cash back to Rhodes.'

Monika frowned. 'I can't come back to Rhodes yet.'

'Why ever not? Mrs Ethanides should be due to retire next year and you could have her job.'

Monika shook her head. 'Someone else will be better qualified than me by now. Besides, Manu will be released from prison once he has served his sentence. He could easily come looking for me again. Mr Spanides said he was very aggressive in the court and made further threats against Natasha and myself. I can't possibly leave at the moment anyway. Mr Iliopolakis is relying on me for the summer season. I cannot let him down after all he has done for us.'

'Your grandmother wants to go back and re-open her shop.'

'I don't think that would be wise. That would be the first place Manu came looking for me and I don't trust him not to hurt you. Do you really want to open up your shop again, Grandma? I thought you were enjoying spending your time with the ladies in the sewing room.'

'I can't leave it closed indefinitely. I need to go back and make sure a water pipe hasn't burst or the roof isn't leaking.'

Monika nodded. 'I understand that, but why don't you sell it?'

'Sell it? Sell my shop? If I did I'd not have anything to leave to your mother.'

'You would have the money.'

'Money doesn't last forever. A building kept in good repair lasts and appreciates in value.'

Monika sighed. 'I can't stop you from going back, but please don't plan to stay there. You could ask Mr Iliopolakis for a week off and Mamma could ask the shop for the same. I'll buy you return tickets for a flight,' she promised rashly. 'You'll be there in an hour or so and won't have to travel by ferry to Piraeus and back to Rhodes. Please, will you do that for me? Check all is well at the shop and then return to Crete.'

'And leave the shop closed up again,' grumbled Monique. 'I'll lose all my regular customers.'

Monika did not remind her grandmother that her customers would have had to find somewhere else to shop whilst she was in Crete. 'The building will still be there and you'll know there aren't any problems. Do you want to go back to Rhodes to live, Mamma?'

Litsa shrugged. 'Not particularly. I have some work here. If I went back to Rhodes I'd have to look for another job.'

Monique looked pained. 'I don't think I could live at the shop on my own.'

'No one is asking you to, Grandma. You and Mamma will just go for a visit. If I am willing to pay your flight expenses I want a promise from both of you that you will return; no changing your mind at the last minute and deciding to stay. We can always discuss returning permanently at a later date.'

Monique sighed heavily. 'I've never flown in an aeroplane.'

'You'll enjoy it,' Monika assured her grandmother. 'Whilst you're there I'd like you to visit Mrs Ethanides and apologise to her for me leaving so abruptly without giving her proper notice or an explanation. I'd also like you to call on Natasha and tell her how sorry I am that Manu hurt her.'

'What do you plan to do with your money?' asked Litsa curiously.

'At the moment it is going to sit in the bank. I can't really believe that it is all mine. I keep expecting to be told to pay it back.'

Although both her mother and grandmother had given her their word that they would return to Crete on the flight she had arranged for them she was concerned that her grandmother would refuse and stay at the shop. She almost hoped the building would have fallen down and her grandmother would be unable to live there. Such a possibility was most unlikely as the buildings in the Old Town had survived earthquakes and the ravages of war.

Monique looked at the exterior of her shop. It looked no different from when she had left it, which was a relief to her. She turned the key in the padlock and pushed open the door. It grated on the stone floor where it had dropped on its hinges and it needed both her and Litsa's strength to push it wide enough for them to enter.

Inside smelt damp and musty due to being closed up for so long. The stock still sat on the shelves, some of the labels peeling off the tins, and others showing signs of rust. There was an air of dereliction and neglect.

Litsa walked through to the back room and wrinkled her nose. The bedding had black mould spores and the whole room smelled of damp.

Monique gave a heavy sigh. 'I knew I should have returned earlier. Now it's going to cost a lot to get the place up and running again.'

Litsa eyed her mother sternly. 'We promised Monika we would return to Crete next week. We'll just have to throw all of this away.'

'It's wicked to leave a nice house like this to fall into disrepair,' grumbled Monique.

Litsa looked around. She had never been critical of the home she had grown up in, but now she compared it with the apartment where they had been living. These rooms were small, dark and dismal. They had always smelled of damp when it rained heavily during the winter despite keeping a fire lit continually in the back room. She gave a shudder. She certainly did not want to return here to live.

'We'll walk into the New Town and find somewhere cheap to stay. It's too late today to start to think about doing any clearing out. I'll take the bedding to the rubbish bins tomorrow. Once we've got rid of it all we can open up the windows and give the place an airing.'

Monique looked around sadly. She had been looking forward to returning and had expected the house to look just as she had left it.

Litsa place an arm around her mother's shoulders. 'Don't be too unhappy, Mamma. It will be fine again when we leave.'

'Only to fall into disrepair again,' said Monique despondently.

Litsa made two bundles of the damp bedding from her mother's bed. 'I'll take this to the rubbish bin and return for the other one.'

'I could help you.' offered Monique.

'You stay here. You could start putting those rusty tins down on the counter. They'll all need to be thrown away.'

'That's my stock,' complained Monique.

'You couldn't possibly sell it the state it's in. The contents could be bad and people would end up poisoned.'

'We could open some up and see.'

'No, Mamma. It is all going to be thrown away.' Litsa spoke firmly. 'Put it on the counter and when I've thrown the bedding I'll come back for it. If we get rid of the rubbish today we could visit Mrs Ethanides and Natasha tomorrow. You can always come back here later and see if there's anything you want to keep.'

Litsa made numerous trips to the rubbish bins, filling them up and then placing further rubbish at the side.

'Where are we supposed to put our rubbish, you selfish person?' asked a woman from behind her.

Litsa flushed and turned around. 'I'm sorry. We're turning out. Why, Marina, I'm pleased to see you.'

'Litsa? What are you doing here? We thought you'd left for good.'

'We've only come back to sort out my mother's shop. We're not actually stopping.'

'She isn't going to open up again, then?'

Litsa shook her head. 'It isn't practical.'

'Shame. It would be convenient again for us.'

'How are you all? I heard Natasha was ill?'

Marina shrugged. 'She's doing fine, but can't work, of course. She's trying to find something decent to do, but all she has at the moment is road sweeping. Just about pays the rent, but there's not a lot left after paying for her medicines.'

'Is she still living in the street?'

Marina shook her head. 'She couldn't stay there without her regular money coming in. She's found a small room down by the wine distillery. It's hardly more than a cupboard and stinks of wine.'

'I have a message for her from Monika. Would you be able to take me there?'

'When? Now?'

Litsa considered quickly. 'If that suits you and you think she'll be at home. I'll have to go back to the shop and tell my mother where I'm going.'

'Why don't I 'phone her and ask her to meet you at the shop?' Marina pulled her mobile from her trouser pocket, after a short conversation she turned back to Litsa with a smile. 'She'll be with you in about half an hour. Can you wait for her?'

'Of course. Come back with me and say hello to my mother. She'll be pleased to see you again.'

Litsa placed two chairs outside of the shop, hoping they would still be sturdy enough to take a person's weight. 'You are not to tell Marina where we are living,' she warned her mother. 'Let her think we are in Piraeus with Monika.'

Monique sighed. She felt miserable and depressed by the condition her property had fallen into during her absence.

Natasha arrived and Litsa scrutinized her. She looked well, despite being thinner than she remembered.

'We'll have to stay out here and talk, everywhere inside is damp and smelly,' she apologised.

'Why don't we go to a taverna?' suggested Monique. 'We've not had anything to eat or drink since we arrived here.'

'We can't possibly go to a taverna until we've at least had a wash,' remonstrated Litsa.

'You can come back to me and wash,' offered Marina and Litsa smiled at her gratefully.

Monique and Litsa made themselves as presentable as possible before thanking Marina and accompanying Natasha out through the San Francisco gate to a small taverna. Litsa ordered a meal for all of them and smiled at Natasha when she protested.

'We can't sit here and eat in front of you; besides it will save you from having to make yourself a meal this evening. Monika was most insistent that we saw you. She wanted to thank you and also to apologise for Manu.'

Natasha shrugged. 'It's over now. I'm just concentrating on my health. I've been told that provided I keep taking the medicine and go for regular checkups I could stay healthy for years.'

'Have you received your compensation money?'

'Yes, that will be a great help. Working as a road sweeper hardly covers my costs. I've certainly made some inroads into my savings.'

'You could move away from the wine distillery to somewhere better.'

'I wish! The rent for anywhere decent is extortionate. Tell me what you have been up to? How is Monika? Is she working in a library?'

Over their meal Litsa explained that Monika had been a cleaner at a hotel for some years and was now working as a receptionist there. 'They have been so good to her that she refused to ask for time off to come here with us.'

'Has her ex paid her compensation?' asked Natasha.

'Everything is settled and finalised, thank goodness.'

'How does she plan to use her money?'

'She hasn't decided yet. I think she'll buy a car,' smiled Monique. 'We've had some lovely days out with her when she has hired one.'

'Where have you been?'

Litsa shot her mother a warning glance. 'Just out of the town and into the countryside mostly.'

'Are you all coming back to Rhodes?'

Litsa shook her head. 'My mother would like to open up the shop again but it isn't practical. Everything we had left behind was damp and mouldy, even the tinned goods. She would have to spend a considerable amount on new stock.'

Natasha looked thoughtful. 'So what will you do with it?'

'Close it up again.' Monique sighed heavily. 'I expected to work in that shop until my dying day.'

'You're not going to sell it?'

'It's family property. When I go it will belong to Litsa and then Monika. I can't possibly sell it.'

'Would you consider renting it?' asked Natasha.

'Who would want to rent a little shop in that area? If it was in the main tourist area it would be a different matter. Someone would snap it up and probably open it as a boutique or for souvenirs. It's only suitable as a general store. I never made a fortune, but it was sufficient for my needs.'

'Would you consider renting it to me?'

'To you?' Litsa looked at Natasha in surprise.

'What would you do with it?' asked Monique suspiciously. 'I wouldn't want it used by the street girls.'

Natasha shook her head. 'I wouldn't do that. It would mean I had somewhere decent to live and if you were agreeable I'd open up the shop again.'

'I've told you it would cost an awful lot to stock it up again.'

Natasha leaned forward. 'If you let me rent the property at a reasonable price I'd be willing to buy new stock. I could use my compensation money and have to take it slowly. I would need to have an agreement from you saying that the goods and any profit from the shop belonged to me. It would give me somewhere decent to live along with an income. I know the girls would support me and spread the word that the shop was open again.'

Litsa looked at her mother. 'It's worth considering, Mamma.'

'I don't know. I'll have to think about it.'

'Why don't Mamma and I discuss it tonight and meet you again tomorrow? You could have a proper look inside then. We're planning to visit Mrs Ethanides at the library tomorrow morning; then we'll be up at the shop to continue removing the rubbish.'

Litsa considered the idea Natasha had put to them. It could be the answer. Her mother would continue to own the shop and have a rental income from it. The alternative was to leave it closed and it would become derelict. They could probably ask Angelos, the lawyer who had acted on behalf of both Natasha and Monika to draw up an agreement.

Litsa's immediate concern was money as she did not have a bank account. She had brought a considerable amount of Euros with her, knowing that the utility bills would have to be paid, but she had not accounted for a hotel bill as she had expected to stay at the shop. If they agreed with Natasha's proposal there would be the additional expense of a lawyer's fee. She would have to discuss the idea with Monika and ask if she could pay the lawyer's expenses.

Monika was enthusiastic about the idea of Natasha renting the shop. 'You must certainly consult a lawyer and have a legal agreement between you. Go and talk to Angelos. He'll know what needs to be done or he'll send you to someone who can help. Even if the shop fails Natasha must agree to continue paying the rent and utility bills whilst she lives there. In the event of her health failing and she cannot run the shop as a business it will be her responsibility to sell whatever stock she has. All the time she can pay her expenses there is no reason why she shouldn't live there.'

'Suppose she became really ill and had to go into the hospital?'

'You'll have to ask Angelos to write in a clause that covers that eventuality. She obviously could not be held responsible for the rent if she was unable to live there. Grandma will have to be responsible for any repairs that are needed to the building, but if Natasha causes any damage she will have to pay for that. I'll give you Angelos's address and telephone number. Have you got a pen and paper?'

Litsa wrote down the details Monika gave her for Angelos. She hoped they would be able to arrange an appointment with him the following day. Suddenly there seemed a lot of work to complete during the short time they were going to be spending on Rhodes. She was thankful Monika had arranged flights for them both ways and they would not have to spend two days travelling by ferry to return to Crete.

Monika met her mother and grandmother from the airport in the early evening and took them by taxi back to her apartment.

'It's a bit of a squash, but I have a meal prepared for you so we can sit and talk. How was Mrs Ethanides?'

'Very pleased to know you are safe and well; but sorry to hear that you are not working in a library.'

Monika shrugged. 'At least I have a decent job and I do enjoy it. Did you arrange everything satisfactorily with Angelos? I've spoken to Mr Iliopolakis and he is arranging for Angelos to send the bill for his legal expenses in drawing up a contract with Natasha to him. As soon as he receives it I'll pay him back so there's nothing to worry about there.'

'I'll repay you when I get the rents from Natasha,' promised Monique and Monika accepted her grandmother's offer.

'I felt quite guilty not coming over with you and helping so I thought you both deserved a treat next weekend. How would you like to drive down to Elounda? If we start at a reasonable time we should easily be there by lunch time and we could go over and visit Spinalonga. Would you like that?'

Litsa nodded eagerly, but Monique looked doubtful. 'I'm not sure I want to see somewhere that has such sad memories.'

'When John took me around he gave the impression that once his great great uncle had managed to get them organised it became a village no different from any other on the mainland. I think you would find it interesting, Grandma. There's certainly nothing nasty over there. If you wanted we could drive up to the other little villages and you could have a look at them.'

'Have you bought a car?' asked Litsa.

Monika smiled and shook her head. 'It's far more practical to hire one. We didn't go anywhere during the winter months and we only have the weekends available whilst we're working. Most of the time a car would be sitting there doing nothing.'

Despite her initial misgivings Monique enjoyed her visit to Spinalonga. Monika had bought a guide book printed in English and with that to aid her, along with her memory, she was able to walk through the throngs of visitors and give her mother and grandmother relevant information.

'I should have tried to contact John and asked if he would come over with us. He could have told you far more than I have. He makes the island seem so alive; you expect to see an original inhabitant walk around the corner any minute.'

'I hope not,' muttered Monique and crossed herself.

'I'm sure there are no ghosts left here now, and if there were they wouldn't be interested in us,' Monika assured her. 'We'll catch the boat back to Plaka and have a wander around the shops. I can show you where I stayed when I came down here for the birthday party and stop at the taverna there for a drink. They do serve meals, but cater mostly for the tourists. I've heard there's an excellent taverna up in the village of Mavrikiano and I thought we could go there for a meal before we drive back.'

'What's wrong with the tavernas down in the village?' asked Litsa.

'Nothing. I had some really nice meals in them, but I have heard that "The Hope" is very special.'

Landing back at the quay at Plaka Monika led the way up towards Saffron's shop. 'You don't have to buy anything, but I ought to just pop in and say hello to her. She is Mr Vasi's partner and I've often met her when I've been visiting Cathy. You can see Uncle Yannis's shop; he has some wonderful museum copies of artefacts, but I don't know if he will be open.'

'What is the point of having a shop if it isn't open?' asked Monique.

Monika smiled. 'He has a notice on the door with his telephone number and he will come and open up especially for a customer or you can ask Saffron to contact him. His goods are very expensive and I imagine he became bored sitting in there all day without any customers.'

'Who is the artist?' asked Litsa, waving her hand towards Ronnie.

Monika frowned. 'She looks vaguely familiar, but I don't know her. Do you want to stop and look at her work?'

'No, if we stop she'll expect us to buy something.'

'We just say "no thank you" and walk away. Come on, let's have a look. She wasn't around when I was down here before.'

Monika looked at the picture clipped to Ronnie's easel and was surprised how well the artist had captured Spinalonga with the sun lighting one side whilst the other was beginning to be in shadow as the sun moved around. More paintings were displayed on a board at the side, each one of them differing slightly from the other.

'She's certainly very talented,' remarked Litsa. 'Do you think anyone actually buys them? They could take a photograph.'

'True, but hundreds of other people would have the same photo. All her paintings appear to be a little different from each other so you would be the only person to have that particular view.'

'I'm not buying one,' said Monique firmly. 'I'd rather go and have a look at that shop you mentioned.'

Uncle Yannis's shop was closed and when they had looked their fill at the artefacts on display in the window they moved into Saffron's shop where Monika waved a greeting to Saffron. To Monika's surprise there were a variety of paintings of Spinalonga in transparent polythene envelopes. She looked through them and approached Saffron when she had finished serving a customer.

'Are these paintings done by the artist sitting down by the quay?'

Saffron nodded. 'She was at my great grandmother's birthday party.'

Monika wrinkled her brow. 'I don't remember her.'

'She kept a low profile. She was here as the partner to one of my distant cousins. The relationship folded and she decided to return here and see if she could make a living as an artist.'

'That was brave of her. Is she succeeding?'

'She appears to be. She returned to America for the winter but came back here a couple of weeks ago and is planning to stay for the summer. Her pictures sell well with the tourists.'

Monika sighed. 'I wish I was an artist. I would love to live here rather than Heraklion.'

'I agree. I'm pleased Vasi's father and Cathy decided they would buy his Heraklion apartment. If we were living there I wouldn't have my relatives all around me or my shop. You'll have to ask Vasi if he needs a new receptionist.'

'I would feel very guilty if I did that after the way Mr Iliopolakis has been so good to me.'

Saffron shrugged. 'I'm sure he would understand if you wanted a change of scene.'

Monika hesitated. 'It would only be for the summer, wouldn't it? What would I do in the winter months?'

'Go back to Heraklion. It's very quiet down here once the tourists have left.'

'Would Mr Iliopolakis be willing to take me back just for the winter?'

'You'd have to ask him. Shall I tell Vasi you would be interested if the opportunity arose?'

'I'd need to think about it. I have my apartment in Heraklion. If I was down here I would need to find somewhere to live and then have to look for a new apartment when I went back to Heraklion.'

'You could live at Giovanni's self catering apartments. I'm sure if you were going to live there for the whole season he would make an arrangement with you as he has for Ronnie and there are always apartments available in Heraklion,' smiled Saffron.

Monika nodded. The idea was certainly worth considering. 'Let me introduce you to my mother and grandmother, then I must take them up to the taverna to meet John. I've promised to drive them to Kato and Pano and on to Mavrikiano for a meal. We mustn't leave it too late as we still have to drive back to Heraklion.'

Saffron frowned. 'Have you booked at "The Hope"? You could arrive and find they are already full.'

'Really? I thought this early in the season it would be easy to get a table.'

'I suggest you 'phone and tell them the time you plan to arrive. I have their number.' Saffron handed Monika a business card advertising the taverna. 'Do your mother or grandmother want to buy anything? I'll give them a discount.'

'I'll ask them. I want one of Ronnie's paintings. Should I buy it from you or ask her?'

'I can't discount that. We have an arrangement to always sell at the same price so we don't rival each other. All I can say is that we have a larger selection at the moment than she has available. She will only have those she has completed today.'

Monika looked through the selection of paintings again and finally selected one that showed Spinalonga bathed in sunlight. 'This is always the way I picture it in my mind.'

'Pay us a visit during the winter and it will look very different.' Saffron rolled the painting carefully and sealed it inside the polythene bag. 'Enjoy the remainder of your day.'

May 2011 – August 2012

Monika left her money sitting in the bank. Her mother suggested that she bought herself a larger apartment in Heraklion but Monika refused.

'I'm quite happy where I am.' Monika did not confide in her mother that she was seriously considering any offer Vasi might make for her to move to his hotel in Elounda.

During the summer she made frequent visits to the area, renewing her acquaintance with the various members of the extended family who lived there and also getting to know Ronnie. Her mother and grandmother were always willing to accompany her, and they often drove up into the hills to the other small villages and sampled the food on offer at their tavernas. They would return to the coast for Monika and her mother to swim and even her grandmother would now hold up her skirt and dip her feet into the cool water.

As the summer season drew to a close Monika asked Vasilis Iliopolakis if she could have a week's holiday as she wished to visit Rhodes with her mother and grandmother. Monique wanted to return to her shop and see if Natasha had a thriving business and also the condition of the property. With Angelos's help Natasha had set up a bank account and sent her rent promptly. Monika had insisted that her grandmother also opened a bank account to enable her to receive it.

At first Monique had resisted. 'I'm used to having money in my hand.' Now Monique enjoyed watching the amount recorded in her bank book growing, but it was not as satisfying to her as when she used to count her notes and add them to the box she kept in her back room.

Monika, her mother and grandmother landed at the airport on Rhodes and took a taxi to Martiou Street, just outside the Old Town, and Monika booked them into the hotel on the corner. She felt almost as nervous this time as previously. Suppose, unknown to her, Manu had been released early? She had planned their timetable for the three days they would be there and she hoped nothing would occur to disrupt them.

Although her grandmother was anxious to visit her shop Monika insisted they waited until the following morning before they walked into the town.

'If we walk along to the Milon Gate I could call in and see if Rebekah is there,' said Litsa. 'You could go on to the shop and I'd catch you up later.'

'That's the long way round,' protested Monique. 'We ought to go through the Navarhiou Gate and cut up through the roads.'

'It's just as far whichever way we go,' argued Litsa.

'Why don't we enter by the Navarhiou Gate and you continue on to see if Rebekah is at home? Grandma and I can go up to the shop and you can meet us there later. Alternatively you visit Rebekah tomorrow when I go to see Mrs Ethanides.'

'And what am I supposed to do whilst you're visiting your friends?' asked Monique waspishly.

'I'm sure that when you have visited Natasha today you'll think of many things you need to ask her and you'll also want to have a look inside and see if there are any problems. I want to pay a quick visit to Mr Spanides to thank him for all his help and then the following two days we could hire a car and drive down to Kallithea. I've never been there and I hear it has been magnificently restored. Then we could go on to Lindos. I remember you took me there once by bus.'

Litsa smiled. Monika was always so organised. She knew that when she had talked to Rebekah for a while they would have nothing else to say to each other; their lives had diverged so differently. She certainly did not want to spend hours sitting at the shop talking to Natasha, discussing stock and customers, but a drive down the coast sounded most attractive.

Although Monika knew that Manu was still in prison she avoided going anywhere near their old apartment, the chemist's shop or tavernas where she knew his friends spent their evenings. She also knew that whatever inducement she was offered she would not want to return to Rhodes to live permanently

Mrs Ethanides understood when she broached the subject to Monika.

'There are too many unpleasant memories here for me and I would be frightened that Manu would come looking for me.'

'Are you planning to apply for a place at the library where you are living now?' asked Mrs Ethanides. 'I know you are not divulging your address, but I would be willing to give you a reference.'

'I'm very grateful that you vouched for me when I applied for work at the hotel. I was fortunate. I became friends with the owner's wife and they have been exceptionally good to me and my family. I'm happier now I'm working as a receptionist for him and have no plans to leave at present.'

'Are you keeping up with your languages?'

'English mostly, but I use my German and French occasionally and still read in those languages.'

Mrs Ethanides sighed. 'If life had worked out differently for you, Monika, you could have been a chief librarian by now and attending conferences worldwide. I feel that your talents have been wasted.'

Monika shrugged. 'We can all look back on events in our lives with regret. At least I am free from Manu now.'

'Do you have a new man in your life?'

Monika shook her head. 'I've not met anyone, but I'm not sure I would want to marry again. Suppose I made a bad mistake a second time?'

Mrs Ethanides smiled. 'You are older and wiser now. I hope you will meet someone one day.'

Litsa had already arrived at the shop by the time Monika joined them. She had been right about her surmise, after enquiring about Rebekah's boys there seemed little to say apart from the usual pleasantries about each other's health and how they passed their days. With a promise to call when she was next in the area Litsa walked up the hill to her mother's shop. As she rounded the corner she could see her mother sitting outside, wearing her coat to ward off the chilly wind that was blowing, Natasha beside her.

'Why don't you sit inside out of the wind?' she asked.

'Natasha has been painting. It smells,' explained Monique.

'If I had known you were visiting this week I would have delayed painting until next week. It has become very quiet now so I thought it an ideal time to give the inside walls of the shop a fresh coat of paint. Come and see what you think, Litsa.'

Litsa followed Natasha inside and looked at the stock piled against one wall whilst the other three were being painted.

'Are you doing it yourself, Natasha?'

'I'm quite enjoying it, provided I take it slowly and don't wear myself out. I did the back rooms first before I opened the shop. I wanted to be living somewhere decent again. I talked to the girls and asked which goods would be most popular with them and then I bought small quantities. They were pleased to be able to shop here again rather than having to walk into the centre or the New Town. I'm actually beginning to make a small profit.' Natasha smiled proudly and led the way through to the back room.

The old stone walls had been painted white, making the room look larger and brighter. Natasha had placed a bed with a pink cover in the corner along with pink curtains. She had simply repeated the decor she had enjoyed when she lived up in the street.

'I really appreciate having a small kitchen area rather than just a sink and a hot plate. It means I can cook proper nourishing food for myself. I've been told that is important to help me stay well.'

'I'm impressed, Natasha. You could easily use your illness to excuse you from keeping everywhere clean and tidy. You didn't know we were going to call on you this week and everywhere is immaculate.'

Natasha smiled. 'I always made sure my room was clean and tidy when I lived in the street. If a customer came into a dirty room they might think I was dirty in my person and go away.'

'You don't do any work like that here, do you?' asked Litsa warily.

Natasha shook her head. 'I was told I shouldn't work now I'm sick. If I did so and the authorities found out I'd be in trouble. Thanks to your mother I can manage to live here, close to my friends and have a small income from the shop.'

'Once Monika arrives I think we should leave. My mother's getting cold sitting outside.'

'I did invite her inside,' insisted Natasha.

'I know, but she's a stubborn old lady and would not have felt comfortable sitting in your back room and seeing your bed and the pink accessories. She probably used the smell of paint as an excuse.'

Natasha shook her head sadly. 'She always did have the wrong idea about us. We have always been a group of decent girls, you know that. We just made our living in a dubious way. I can't say I miss the life, only the money it brought in.'

Litsa smiled in sympathy; she knew exactly what Natasha meant.

Although Monika had enjoyed driving her mother and grandmother to Kalithea and Lindos, relieved to be away from the town, she was not sorry when it was time to take a taxi to the airport and return to Crete. She could have seen Mrs Ethanides, visited Mr Spanides and checked on Natasha and her grandmother's shop all in one day had she been there alone. If her mother and grandmother wished to visit at a later date she was sure she could make an excuse not to accompany them.

The winter months passed slowly, after some days of pouring rain the sun would suddenly shine and everyone's spirits would be lifted, only to be accompanied by a cold wind that penetrated the warmest clothing. Monika did not hire a car at the weekends as there would be no pleasure in driving to any village and finding the local taverna closed, or even worse, that there had been a fall of snow and they were stuck on an icy road.

Most weekends they spent in one or the others' warm apartment, occasionally visiting the cinema or attending a concert. Monika still visited Cathy regularly and was always interested to hear any news of Elounda and the family. When Saffron and Vasi called whilst she was there she was fascinated to hear that Ronnie had inherited an old house in the village of Kastelli and that John was engaged in tracing her ancestry.

'I thought she was an American.'

'She is,' smiled Saffron, 'but her great uncle was taken over to the States by his family when he was a small boy. He knew he was born on Crete and had only vague memories of living here. By chance they visited Kastelli and he recognised an abandoned house as his childhood home. He was the only living descendent so it was legally his. He gave it to Ronnie.'

'Gave it?' Monika's eyes opened wide. No one gave away their house.

'He said he was too old to uproot himself from America and deal with repairs and renovations so he transferred the ownership to Ronnie. She's been staying at our house now Giovanni's apartments are closed for the winter and she spends her time there turning out all the rubbish that has accumulated inside.'

'Will she go there to live?'

'I don't know her final plans. The walls are sound, but the roof has fallen in over the years that it has been neglected. It will take a considerable amount of time and work to make it habitable.'

'When the weather improves we'll drive to Kastelli and have a look. Will we be able to find it easily or is it tucked away in one of the village streets?'

'You'll find it easily enough,' said Vasi. 'It's the big house on the corner as you enter the village.'

Monika gasped. 'That one! I thought you were talking about a cottage.'

Vasi shook his head. 'The family must originally have been quite rich and influential. It will be interesting to see what John finds out about them.'

Monika thought about the conversation as she walked home. She knew nothing about her ancestry. Her mother had told her that her grandfather had died in a road accident, but she had no idea about her great grandparents and had never asked. At the weekend she would question her grandmother and ask her to tell her all she could remember about her antecedents.

Monika was busy at Vasilis's hotel throughout the winter months with conference arrangements. Various members of staff were off sick with colds and chest infections and Monika finally succumbed to the germs. She stayed in her apartment until the worst of her coughing and sneezing was over, refusing to visit her mother and grandmother not wishing to pass on her cold. Despite her precautions a few weeks later they had caught the infection that was affecting so many people.

Litsa recovered quickly, but although Monique was no longer sneezing, her cough persisted until Monika insisted on a visit to the chemist to ask for a remedy, despite her grandmother's protestations that it was due to the traffic fumes in the city. She had never suffered a day's illness whilst in Rhodes.

The chemist agreed that the pollution did not help, but he

also wanted to know what materials Monique was working on at present with the other ladies, believing she could be suffering from an allergy due to the fibres.

'What rubbish,' exclaimed Monique, but she did not refuse the linctus he prescribed for her. 'I've only been sewing new hooks onto some curtains. We've all been doing the same work and the other ladies are not ill.'

Although Monique took the linctus regularly, returning to the chemist to ask for another bottle, her cough persisted. When she suffered a particularly prolonged or violent bout she would press her hand to her chest.

'It must be a chest infection,' declared Monika. 'We'll have to go to the doctor. He'll probably give you an antibiotic to clear it up.'

The doctor sounded Monique's chest and frowned. 'You're certainly very wheezy. I'll give you an antibiotic and I'd like you to stay away from the curtains you say you're repairing. They could be aggravating your condition. If your cough hasn't lessened by the end of the week come back to me and I'll send you for a chest X-ray.'

Monique grumbled. 'It's only a cough. You're both making such a fuss.'

Litsa shook her head. 'If it was only a cough you would be feeling considerably better after taking the linctus the chemist supplied. We'll see how you are when you have finished the course of antibiotics.'

To Monique's annoyance she did not feel any better after finishing the antibiotics. She continued to cough and there was a feeling of discomfort in her chest. She tried to make light of it to her daughter and Monika, but she was beginning to worry that there might be something more seriously wrong with her and did not refuse to return to the doctor and keep her subsequent appointment for a chest X-ray.

Litsa sat with her mother hoping they would not be kept

waiting for the result for too much longer. She had taken the day off work and wanted to have an hour or so wandering around the shops looking at the special offers they were advertising. She had nothing particularly in mind, but it was a good opportunity to look at their summer stock and see if anything attracted her. Monique coughed again, discreetly wiping the phlegm into a tissue. As if the sound had reminded the doctor of her presence his door opened.

He regarded them gravely. 'I'm afraid you could have something more serious than a chest infection, Mrs Kokanides. There is a definite shadow on one of your lungs.'

Monique clutched Litsa's hand. 'What is it?' she whispered.

'I'm not prepared to make a definite diagnosis without the results from further tests. Are you coughing up phlegm?'

'Sometimes.'

'I will give you a sputum container and the next time you cough something up please spit it into the container. I will send that off for analysis this afternoon. I will also make an appointment for you to have a blood test tomorrow and if you return to me in two days' time I should have the results and that will give me a clearer picture of your complaint and I will be able to suggest the relevant treatment.'

Monique looked at the doctor uncomprehendingly. 'So it isn't a chest infection?'

'I need to find out exactly what is causing the shadow to show up. There can be many reasons for a shadow; a past infection that has left a scar is a prime example. I'm sure that whatever the problem is it can be dealt with effectively.' He wrote Monique's name on a label and stuck it on the sputum container and handed it to her. 'Go to reception and they will make you an appointment for your blood test. Leave the container with your sample at reception and they will send it for analysis. Make an appointment to return for the results in two days' time.'

He helped Monique to her feet and smiled at her. 'I'm sure we can soon get you feeling more comfortable.'

When Monika visited Cathy she asked after her grandmother. 'How did you know she was not well?'

'Vasilis told me. Is she feeling any better?'

Monika shook her head. 'I'm really worried. The doctor has told my mother that he suspects lung cancer and he has referred my grandmother to a specialist at the hospital.'

'Oh, no, I hope he's wrong.'

Monika shrugged. 'So do we. We haven't told Grandma about the doctor's suspicions. There's no point in worrying her unduly until the diagnosis is confirmed.'

'Do you have insurance? Medical treatment can be so expensive otherwise.'

'No, Grandma always said it was unnecessary as she was never ill.' Monika sighed. 'I should have insisted that she had it now I have some money.'

'Has your grandmother any savings?'

'A little from where Natasha has paid her rent for the shop.'

Cathy wrinkled her brow. 'I believe the Government is willing to help people who do not have enough money to cover all their medical treatment.'

'You mean like Natasha? She goes to the clinic for her check-ups and prescriptions and pays only a small amount for her medicines.'

'It could be worth your while to make enquiries. If your grandmother signed the shop over to your mother she would no longer be receiving the rent so her savings would not increase. I'm sure your mother would keep the money to one side just in case your grandmother did need it.'

Monika looked at Cathy doubtfully. 'Would that be legal?'

Cathy shrugged. 'If anyone asks your grandmother tells them that once she became ill she felt she could no longer cope with dealing with the rent and repairs so gave the premises to your mother. Provided an agreement was drawn up with a lawyer no one can dispute it.'

'It would be a weight off my mind. If it is a cancer the treatment is very expensive and Grandma might need hospitalization at times. I don't know if the money I received from Manu would cover everything until she was well again.'

'Wait until you have seen the specialist and have a diagnosis and hear the treatment he recommends. In the meantime I'll speak to Vasilis and ask his advice about signing the shop over to your mother.'

Monika tried to choke back a sob. 'I can't bear the thought of Grandma being really ill. I lived with her until I married Manu. It was like having two mothers.'

Cathy patted Monika's shoulder. 'Cry if you want. There's no one here except me and I'm going to make you a cup of English tea. That is what everyone in England always does when they have a crisis to face.'

Cathy placed a box of tissues beside Monika and walked slowly into the kitchen. She still felt the death of her own mother keenly, but at least she had died peacefully and not from an illness.

The specialist confirmed that Monique was suffering from lung cancer and advised an operation to remove the affected part of the lung.

'Will that cure her?' asked Litsa.

'After the removal she will be given a course of chemotherapy to ensure there have been no cells left behind. The treatment is not pleasant, but by the end of the year your mother should have recovered from the ordeal and be able to enjoy a healthy life style again.'

Grudgingly Monique signed over ownership of her shop in Rhodes Old Town to her daughter. 'I shall want it back when I'm better,' she said firmly and Litsa promised that she would keep her mother's money separate from her own.

'I will only use the rent money to pay for your treatment and your share of the rent. I'll keep all the receipts and you can check them when I transfer the money back to you.'

Slightly mollified Monique agreed to enter the hospital the following week and Litsa spoke to her employer, requesting two weeks off so she could spend the time at the hospital attending to her mother.

Monika explained the situation to Vasilis. 'Is it possible for me to work less hours? My mother is going to spend all day with my grandmother, but she needs some rest. If my schedule could be arranged so I can arrive later in the morning I would be able to spend the night at the hospital.'

Vasilis agreed to Monika's request readily. 'If you need any extra time off let me know and I will arrange for reception cover. When your grandmother first returns home she will still need care.'

'My mother has said she will give her notice in at the shop if necessary. When she knows how my grandmother copes once she is home she is hoping she will be able to leave her during the day and go into work, at least for a few hours.'

Monique returned home after her operation feeling weak and depressed.

'Just rest and you'll soon feel better,' Litsa assured her. 'You've had some major surgery. It takes time to recover from the anaesthetic and the bruising inside your body.'

'I expected to feel better once they had operated,' grumbled Monique.

'Be patient, Mamma.' Litsa knew that once her mother had returned to the hospital for an X-ray and commenced chemotherapy she would not feel well for some months, but it would not help to warn her of the effects the treatment would have. 'Now the weather is better Monika will be able to take us out for a ride into the country and that will help you. You're not used to being indoors all the time.'

'I'd like to return to work. I get bored sitting here and doing nothing. I miss chatting with the ladies whilst we're sewing.'

'Would you like me to ask them to visit you? Just one of them at a time and not for too long so you do not become over tired?'

'Despina might be willing.'

Monique felt exhausted for the first few days after her fortnightly chemotherapy sessions, but by the time the next appointment arrived she always felt considerably better and would complain that she had to attend again.

By the weekend she would have recovered sufficiently for Monika to drive her to a local village or coastal resort during the afternoon and attend church on the Sunday morning. The following week she welcomed a visit from one of the ladies whom she had worked in the sewing room with before reluctantly returning to the hospital for her next treatment. Both Litsa and Monika began to relax, feeling that the worst of the ordeal was over.

Cathy asked after Monique each time Monika visited and was relieved to see the girl looking happier.

'Grandma has asked to go down to Elounda. I am going to work some extra hours so I can have the whole of Saturday off. She must be feeling much better to be able to contemplate such a long drive. Although I have been taking her out we haven't gone very far as I didn't want to tire her. We can always stop half way if it appears to be too much for her.'

'If it wasn't the height of the season I'm sure Vasi would have arranged for you to stay at his hotel over night. Maybe you could stay up at his house? Would you like me to ask him?'

Monika shook her head. 'Thank you for the offer, but if Grandma decides she can travel no further than Hersonissos it would be putting them to a lot of trouble for nothing. I'm sure Saffron is busy at her shop and wouldn't want to have guests just at the moment.'

As Monika drove down the hill to Elounda she caught her breath as the view of the bay with Spinalonga spread out before her. Although Cathy had relayed the news of John's investigation into

Ronnie's ancestry, finding that her great grandmother had been born on the island, she was hoping she could spend some time with her and find out how her house was progressing.

Monika settled her mother and grandmother at the taverna in Plaka and insisted they had a light meal. 'Afterwards you can order some drinks and I'll go down to see if Ronnie is in the square and call in at Saffron's shop. When I return I'll order a drink and you can go for a wander, Mamma. That will mean that Grandma can stay here and rest before we drive back.'

Monika was disappointed when she saw no sign of Ronnie sitting at her easel and walked back up the hill to Saffron's shop. She noticed that the gift shop belonging to Uncle Yannis was still closed with a notice on the door with his contact details.

Saffron greeted her with pleasure, asked after her grandmother, and between serving customers answered her query about Ronnie's whereabouts.

'She's probably up at her house. It's nearly finished and she wants to have it completed by the time her relatives come for a visit. It's at the decorating stage and she wants to check the colours she has chosen for the walls are as she envisions. It can be hard to tell when you just look at a colour swatch.'

'Provided my grandmother continues to improve the next time we visit I'll ask Ronnie if we can visit her house. I'd love to see inside.'

'I'm sure she would be happy to show you.'

'I see your uncle's shop is still closed,' remarked Monika.

'He's finding it very difficult. His wife has dementia. A good deal of the time you would never know there was anything wrong, but she becomes very confused. She wakes poor Uncle Yannis up in the night and demands to be taken to visit her mother. As soon as he thinks he has calmed her down she starts asking again to be taken. She obviously doesn't remember that her mother died years ago and has no conception that it is the middle of the night or early hours.'

'Oh, the poor man. How does he cope?'

'During the day it is not so bad. There is usually someone around to keep an eye on her and make sure that she doesn't do anything that could harm her. That gives Uncle Yannis a chance to have a sleep, but it's not the same as having an undisturbed night.'

'No wonder he doesn't want to spend all day sitting up in his shop. It's a shame, as he has some beautiful items in there.'

Saffron smiled. 'Each week I bring something into my shop and try to sell it on his behalf. Sometimes I am successful, but it is often difficult convincing the customer that it is an authentic museum replica, although it has the official seal and certificate. I hope he will be able to return one day and open up full time.'

Monika nodded sympathetically. It had often been difficult dealing with her grandmother when she was suffering from the effects of the chemotherapy, but at least her mind had not been affected.

Monika returned to her mother and grandmother, checking that Monique was still happy to sit at the taverna whilst Litsa walked around down in the square.

'The next time we come down you should be feeling well enough to at least visit Saffron's shop and we could also drive up to Kastelli to see Ronnie's house. Saffron says it is almost finished.'

September - November 2012

Monika related to Cathy how much her grandmother appeared to have enjoyed their visit to Elounda. 'I think she may have found the journey a little too much to cope with. She insisted that she had enjoyed the visit but slept all the way back. It may have been partly the heat, of course. I'll wait until it has cooled down a little in September before we go down again. I'm hoping Ronnie's house will be finished and she will take us up there so we can see inside.'

'That will depend upon Kyriakos. He has a broken ankle so he's finding coping with the taverna rather difficult. Ronnie is running backwards and forwards with the customers' orders until he can walk properly.'

'How did that happen?'

'There were two young men going around robbing the tavernas; as they tried to make their escape Kyriakos was run over.'

'When was that?'

'Last week. I'm sure Kyriakos will love to tell you all the details. Apparently they were apprehended by a beer bottle.'

Monika looked at Cathy in surprise. 'A beer bottle?'

'A customer threw it and hit the pillion rider. In turn he fell forwards and threw the driver off balance and that was when they ran Kyriakos down.'

'How awful. Thank goodness he wasn't badly hurt.'

'According to Saffron, Ronnie was in an awful panic. She thought Kyriakos was dead, but it was only a concussion fortunately. I'm sure Ronnie and Kyriakos will tell you all the details.'

'I thought I'd arrange a visit for the weekend after this. I'll have to ask Mr Iliopolakis if I can work some extra hours so I can have the whole day off again.'

'I'm sure that will be no problem. Vasilis is planning for us to go down sometime soon. As Uncle Yannis hardly has his shop open any more Vasilis thought he might be willing to sell some of his very large items to him at a good price. He says he could use them in the hotel.'

'Where would he put them?'

Cathy waved her hand airily. 'In reception I expect, where people can see them; or the conference rooms. Before we do that I want to go up to Chania to check on the memorial my father had built there. We always try to go at least three times a year just to see that all is in order and speak to the village priest.'

Monika nodded. When Cathy had told her more about her first visit to Crete and meeting Vasilis she had also related how her father's first wife and son had been massacred by the retreating German forces.

'What happens in between visits?'

'Vasilis gives the local church a donation each year and the villagers make sure it is well tended.'

'You'll have to give me directions. I'd like to see it.'

'It's quite a long drive. If you're planning to take your grandmother it would be better to wait until next spring before the tourist season starts. The roads are less congested and it would be cooler.'

'I'll bear that in mind. Grandma should be quite well enough to make the journey by then.'

Monika approached Vasilis with a request to work extra hours and have the following Saturday free.

'That is no problem,' smiled Vasilis. 'I will rearrange your schedule. You don't have to work extra hours to enable you to take time off. Just let me know in advance when you do not want to work.'

'I know I don't need the money any longer, but I feel it is taking advantage of you and disrupting the other receptionists. They could have plans made for their time off.'

'If that was the case I'm sure they would tell me. They know your grandmother has been ill and you have needed some time off to tend to her.'

'I feel a bit of a fraud now she is well again.'

'You are still giving her attention and I'm sure she appreciates that you give up your time to take her out. Where are you planning to go?'

'Oh, Elounda, of course. Both my mother and grandmother love going down there. I'm hoping Ronnie will be able to take us up to see her house. It must be almost completed.'

Vasilis frowned. 'You obviously haven't heard. There's been a fire and her house is ruined.'

'A fire? How? When did that happen? How awful for her.'

'Well, they are sure it was done deliberately and the police are investigating.'

'I'll certainly not ask her if I can visit her house. She must be quite devastated; first the robbery at Kyriakos's taverna and now a fire at her house.'

There was no sign of Ronnie in the square and Monika walked into Saffron's shop to see if she knew where she was.

'If you want to see Ronnie you'll have to go up to Kyriakos's taverna. She's still helping him at the moment. He's not using his crutches any more, only a stick, but it makes it difficult for him to carry more than one plate of food at a time.'

Ronnie was surprised when they arrived at the taverna. 'How did you know I was here?'

'I asked Saffron when I couldn't find you in the square. She told me Kyriakos had a broken ankle and you were helping out up here.'

'Did she tell you what happened?'

'Only that there was a robbery and Kyriakos had been hurt as they tried to get away. Mr Iliopolakis told me there had been a fire at your house. I'm so sorry.'

Ronnie shrugged. 'Come and sit down with Kyriakos. Give me five minutes to get you some drinks then I'll let him tell you about the events that took place up here. Now it is all over and he has nothing worse than a broken ankle we can laugh over some of it. You should have seen the man throw a beer bottle at the boys on the scooter. He was a terrific shot.'

'We mustn't stay too long. We have to drive back to Heraklion and my grandmother has not been well.' Monika walked into the taverna with Ronnie.

'Saffron told me. She certainly looks thinner than I remember her last year. How is she now?'

'Very much better. She has to return to the hospital for regular checkups, but all seems well at the moment.'

'Are you still working at Vasilis's hotel in Heraklion?'

Monika nodded and Ronnie pulled a face. 'I can't think why you stay up there. You ought to ask to come down here and work for Vasi.'

'If it was all year round work I'd consider it, but I also have to think of my mother and grandmother. I wouldn't be happy leaving them up in Heraklion. After all I asked them to come over here so we could be together.'

Ronnie smiled and loaded their drinks onto a tray along with some nuts and olives. She knew if her mother ever decided to come to Crete to live she would feel that she must live close to her.

They listened to Kyriakos's account of the robbery, how the two young men had been systematically driving around the island and helping themselves to the money from shops or the local tavernas. When he finally finished recounting the story Monika turned back to Ronnie.

'Tell me about the fire? Is there an awful lot of damage?'

'Apparently the exterior, being stone, is structurally sound, but the fire went up through the roof and gutted the interior. It is going to cost a good deal to have it repaired a second time. At least there was very little damage to the extension. At first the police accused me of doing it.'

'Why on earth would you burn down your own house?'

'They said it was to get insurance money, but I haven't any insurance on the house. I saw no need until it was completed. Now they are trying to say it was the builder from the village who did it out of spite as he wasn't asked to do the work originally.'

'That's a bit extreme.'

Ronnie nodded. 'That was what Giovanni thought and he invited that lawyer friend of his over from Athens. He's looking into it on my behalf.'

'I suppose it wasn't the men who attacked Kyriakos?'

'They were in gaol at the time and they wouldn't have known who owned the house. Old Kassie who lives in the house opposite saw the man who set the fire and I'm sure it was the building inspector. The police are disinclined to believe her and are still convinced it was her son, the village builder.'

Monika translated the information for the benefit of her mother and grandmother who sympathised, adding in an undertone 'Now you see why I would not go to the police and report Manu. I was sure they would not believe me.'

'I had wanted it all finished ready for when my mother and great uncle visit,' continued Ronnie. 'Now I've had to arrange for them to stay at Vasi's hotel.'

Monika smiled. 'I'm sure it's no hardship to stay there.'

As Monika drove up the hill from Elounda she drew in at a convenient spot and looked at the view. How she would like to wake up each morning and see the bay with the island of

Spinalonga at the far end, rather than the apartments that were opposite her. She would have to see if she could have another weekend to herself next month and make a visit before everywhere closed down for the winter.

When Litsa left the hospital after her mother had attended for her regular appointment she was feeling most unhappy. Whilst Monique dressed the specialist had called Litsa into his room and shown her the X-ray of Monique's lungs that had been taken earlier.

'You see the new shadow that is developing?'

Litsa nodded; a hollow feeling in the pit of her stomach. 'Has the cancer come back?'

'We knew it could happen, despite her operation and subsequent treatment.'

'So she will need to have some more treatment?'

The specialist nodded his head. 'We will try a further course of chemotherapy and hope that will halt any further deterioration.'

'She seemed so well,' said Litsa miserably. 'Are you sure chemotherapy will work this time?'

'I can't give you any guarantee, but I am hopeful.'

'Why don't you take out the part that is affected?'

'We have to halt the spread of the disease. We cannot keep taking out more and more of your mother's lungs. They do not grow back even if we are able to make them healthy again. Do you want me to talk to your mother or would you prefer to tell her the bad news yourself?'

'I'd like you to talk to her; explain why she needs chemotherapy again. Suppose she refuses to have the treatment?'

'That would be most unwise, but we cannot insist. I hope I can rely on you to persuade her that it is in her best interests. Speak to her now and we can make her first appointment.'

In silence Litsa and Monique made the taxi journey back to their apartment, Litsa clutching her mother's hand tightly.

Monika was equally distressed when she was told the bad news. 'I'll speak to Mr Iliopolakis. I'm sure there will be no problem about me having time off. You can't stay in the hospital with Grandma all day and night.'

'She should only need to stay in for twenty four hours each time. They will give her the drugs intravenously and monitor her during the evening. They will only keep her in overnight as a safety precaution in case she has an adverse reaction. I should be able to manage that,' said Litsa positively.

'You still have to look after Grandma when she comes home. You stay with her during the day and I'll stay overnight. That way you can get some proper sleep. I can ask for the morning off and have some sleep before going in to work in the afternoon.'

Monika approached Vasilis and he agreed to rearrange her work schedule so she did not need to go to work until later in the day when Monique had received her treatment.

'Are you sure you wouldn't like a whole day off each time? It can be arranged?'

Monika shook her head. 'That shouldn't be necessary. I can make up my hours on the Saturday as I don't think Grandma will feel like going out and visiting for a while.'

Monique's treatments seemed to be going well with only the expected side effects of a feeling of weakness and lack of appetite due to the strong drugs that had been given to her. Both Litsa and Monika felt encouraged, although they were both aware that if the second course of treatment was unsuccessful the cancer would spread and they had not dared to ask the specialist for his prognosis.

The following week when Monika walked into work in the afternoon she was handed a message from Vasilis.

"I did not like to telephone you as you would either be at the hospital or sleeping. Cathy and I have driven down to Elounda for a funeral. We should be returning on Monday and provided all is well with your Grandmother we will look forward to seeing you as usual."

Monika read the brief message a second time, wishing Vasilis had told her whose funeral they were attending. It was probably someone from the village whom she did not know. She pushed the message into her pocket and thought no more about it. Cathy would no doubt tell her when she visited.

Cathy immediately asked after Monique when Monika visited her.

'She feels weak and nauseous most of the time. Just as she begins to feel a little better she has to go for another treatment. Her hair is beginning to come out again.' Monika sighed. 'Provided the treatment is successful that is a small price to pay. I just wish she would stop grumbling about it. There's nothing we can do to prevent it. Mr Iliopolakis left me a message at the hotel to say you had gone down to Elounda for a funeral. Was it someone you knew from when you lived down there?'

'It was Uncle Yannis's wife, Ourania.'

Monika gasped. 'The one who had demetia?'

Cathy nodded. 'It was unexpected. She had an aneurism during the night and Uncle Yannis found her dead in the morning.'

'What an awful shock for him.'

'It was, but in many ways it was also a relief. Her mother suffered from a form of dementia and became very violent. She had to be taken into care during the last months of her life. Uncle Yannis dreaded that Ourania would have to go away eventually.'

'At least he has his large family around to support him, he's not alone.' Monika was not sure how much sympathy she should show for the man she had only met once. 'Have they found out who set fire to Ronnie's house?'

Cathy nodded. 'The lawyer Giovanni asked to come over from Athens investigated far more thoroughly than the local police. Ronnie had been quite right to suspect the building inspector. He's in custody and the accounts at his office are being looked into. From the little I've heard he and that awful Alecos had become adept at making people pay time and again for visits and certificates.'

'How did they do that?'

'They would claim the work was faulty and needed to be done again so they could charge for another visit. The builders would ignore the order to do it again and call him back a week later. The original work would be passed, but the customer would be charged for two visits. Either that or he would withhold completion certificates and charge the customer a large sum saying that was the only way to go to the head of the queue and have them passed.'

'Who was responsible for passing them?' asked Monika curiously.

'He was. There was no queue. If the work was completed when he visited the certificate could have been signed on the spot.'

'On the spot?' queried Monika and Cathy smiled.

'An English saying that you are obviously not familiar with. It means immediately in this case.'

'Oh,' Monika felt foolish. 'I was thinking of a spot like you have on your face.'

Cathy laughed. 'I like that. I can just imagine the builders walking around with signatures written all over their faces. I'll tell Vasilis tonight.'

'Please don't. He'll think me terribly stupid.'

'Vasilis's English is not perfect. He will probably think it means the same as you did. I'll think up some English words that can be used in different contexts and we'll have a quiz one night between you and Vasilis and see which one of you has the better knowledge of the language.'

'I remember how confusing I found it when I first started to learn the language. The same words having different meanings and often those that were spelt the same way being pronounced differently.' Monika shook her head. 'That seems a long time ago now.'

'Well I'm pleased you persisted with your lessons. I should have persevered with my Greek, but it was far easier to speak in English with Vasilis. I've never pretended to be a linguist. We learnt French when I was at school and that was a struggle for me.'

Yannis drove up to his shop in Plaka accompanied by Marisa. He looked around at the neglected premises and stock.

'I hardly know where to start,' he said.

Marisa looked around. 'Take the notice off the door for a start. Then remove everything from the shelves on that wall and stack them over here. I'll wash the pots whilst you wash the shelves. When we return tomorrow the shelves will be dry and you can put the pots back. We can complete a section each day and then you can decide if you want to open up any of the boxes where you have stock stored and change the display.'

Yannis shook his head. 'Better to leave things as they are. There are only a few more weeks of the tourist season. The walls need to be repainted so everything will have to be put away. Just dust the pots off for the time being. They can be washed next year.'

Marisa pulled out a grubby duster from beneath the counter. 'I'd better start on the top shelf. Can you help me get the step ladder?'

'Are you sure you'll be safe up there on that? Maybe I should go up.'

'I haven't had a hip replacement,' replied Marisa scathingly. 'Just hold it firmly at the bottom so it doesn't wobble and I'll be safe enough.'

The dust that had accumulated on the pots on the top shelf made them both cough and choke as she disturbed it.

'How long is it since you cleaned up here, Yannis?'

'Last year, I think.'

Marisa looked at him disbelievingly.

'Well, it may have been the year before.'

'More like the year before that! It's inches thick. Go and get me the dustpan and brush and I'll try to sweep up the worst of it; stop it from flying everywhere.'

Yannis stood and held the step ladder whilst Marisa removed as much of the dust as possible. 'Is there any point in putting these pots back up here? They'll all need to be taken down for the walls to be painted and the shelves need to be washed. You fetch some boxes from the back and I'll hand them down to you.'

It was a slow and laborious job dusting each pot and then handing it carefully down for Yannis to place in a box and when the top shelf was cleared Marisa regained the ground and declared she had done enough for one day. Yannis was disappointed that no one had entered the shop and enquired about any of his goods; and he was extremely bored having spent most of his time steadying the step ladder for his sister.

'We'll come back each day and do some more,' Marisa assured him. 'By the time you open up again next season everywhere will look clean and attractive. Everything just looks old and dingy at the moment.'

Monique continued to attend the hospital for her chemotherapy but she was not sure if it was beneficial. She was still short of breath after the slightest exertion and if she coughed her chest hurt. Litsa tried to encourage her by saying that it was all part of the treatment and when the course was finished there would be an improvement.

'You only have two more sessions. Then you will be able to relax and concentrate on getting your strength back.'

'If the doctor says I need more treatment I shall refuse,' stated Monique. 'I feel far worse now than when I was first diagnosed.'

'If you had not had the treatment you would probably not be with us.'

Monique eyed her daughter balefully. 'Might have been a good thing. I'm just a nuisance to you now.'

'Mamma, you must never think of yourself as a nuisance. I wish you had never been taken ill, but I am only too pleased to be able to look after you and help you all I can.'

Monique sighed. Neither Litsa nor Monika ever complained about having to sit in the apartment with her or attend the hospital.

She hoped Litsa was correct when she said she would feel well again when her treatments were over.

As they entered the hospital, Litsa pushing Monique in a wheelchair, a young man held the door open and Litsa looked at him in surprise. 'It's Kyriakos, isn't it? What are you doing up here?'

Kyriakos gave her a beaming smile. 'I needed some tests taken. Nothing to worry about.'

'Your ankle has healed?'

Kyriakos nodded happily. 'Everything is now well with me. How is your mother?'

'She has two more treatments. We are hoping the specialist will be able to give us good news when those are finished.'

'I am just about to drive back to Elounda. I will tell Ronnie I have seen you.'

Litsa would have liked to have asked about Ronnie's house, but knew that once they became involved in a conversation it was likely to make her mother late for her appointment.

Kyriakos drove down to Elounda with a feeling of euphoria. He did not have leprosy. He had Vitiligo. The doctor had explained to him that the condition in itself was nothing to worry about; just patches of white skin would appear on his body where the pigment was lost. Further tests had been taken to determine whether the condition was caused by a thyroid disorder, the onset of diabetes or if he had pernicious anaemia. The results would be sent to the hospital in Aghios Nikolaos and appropriate treatment given if necessary.

He parked near the square at Plaka and went in search of Ronnie. He remembered that her relatives were visiting and she could well have taken them out for the day. Due to the destruction of her house she might be down at Vasi's hotel where she had arranged for them to stay. He would look for her there before he went to make his peace with his mother.

Kyriakos saw them sitting on the waterfront, chatting whilst they ate their meal and hurried across the road.

'I am returned,' he said quietly and Ronnie looked up.

A look of delight crossed her face and she sprang to her feet and flung her arms around his neck. 'Where have you been? I've been so worried. I left you at the hospital and then you just disappeared. No one knew where you were.'

Kyriakos hugged her to him. 'I could not tell you. I could not come near you in case such an awful thing was true.'

'What do you mean? You only went to have your plaster removed. Did you think they were going to amputate your leg?'

'No, no, that would have been nothing to me, just an inconvenience. I found out about my grandfather. He lived on Spinalonga.'

Kyriakos waited whilst Ronnie digested his words. 'You mean, he had, he was ....?'

'He had leprosy. My mother did not tell me and when tests came back clear time and again she decided there was no problem. I asked the doctor to give me a thorough examination and he queried the white patches of skin on my arms and my back. I thought they were the result of the motor bike accident, but he was not so sure. He sent me to Heraklion for tests. That is where I have been.'

'Why didn't you tell me?'

'I could not come near you. If leprosy had been confirmed I would have asked to be admitted for treatment. I would not risk infecting you.'

'Would you have told me?'

Kyriakos shook his head. 'No. I would have written you a letter to say I no longer loved you. After a while you would have met someone else and been happy with them.'

Ronnie drew Kyriakos's head down and kissed him, passionately. 'I don't want anyone else. I want to be with you.'

'You have not asked what is wrong with me.'

Ronnie drew back, her eyes wide with alarm. 'There is something wrong?'

'I have Vitiligo. It is nothing to worry about, but means I have patches of white skin. It is not infectious or contagious.'

'Can it be halted with a cream or something?'

'It depends upon the cause. They have taken tests and I have to go for the results next week.'

'I am coming with you,' said Ronnie firmly. 'I am going to sit outside the doctor's room in case you decide to run away again.'

'I will not run away from you, except for a short while now. I need to go home and speak to my mother. I also need to have a shower and some clean clothes. I lived in my car for three days. I feel very dirty.'

'You will come back?'

'Of course I will come back. I have to speak to my chef and arrange to have the taverna open again. Where shall I meet you?'

'You don't have to spend the evening with us,' Charlene assured her daughter.

Ronnie looked at her mother and great uncle. 'Shall we ask Vasi if he is willing to close his dining room tonight and we all meet here? Saffie could bring her mother down and the family could come along.'

Kyriakos shook his head. 'That is not a good idea. Vasi may have diners already booked and Nicola would be unable to come because of the children. It is better if I speak to Giovanni and ask if we can all meet there.'

'Do you think he would be willing?'

Kyriakos shrugged. 'Why not? He owes me a favour for allowing Saffie to use my kitchen. If there is a problem I will ask if my chef would go to help.'

'Will your mother come?'

Kyriakos considered. 'I do not think that is a good idea. I need to talk to her. I do not think she would enjoy a meeting at the moment.'

Although Monique had completed her course of chemotherapy she felt no better and she was dreading her follow up appointment with the specialist where another X-ray of her lungs would be taken. She would not consider that she had been cured if she continued to be short of breath and had chest pains whenever she exerted herself. Litsa no longer needed to stay at home to look after her and had returned to working in the shop during the afternoons. Now she felt lonely and neglected. She wished one of her sewing companions would come to visit, but when her chemotherapy had sapped all her energy she had refused them. Now she regretted being so hasty. Provided the prognosis from the specialist was good she would ask Monika to tell them and request a visit when they had the time.

Litsa listened gravely to the specialist as he explained to her that the shadow on her mother's lungs that was the tumour was no smaller than when the treatment had commenced.

'I am sorry. We have done the best we can,'

'Have you told my mother?'

The specialist shook his head. 'It will not help her to know. I have told her that she is progressing as expected. Encourage her to meet with her friends and go out with you when she feels fit enough. All the time she is able to enjoy her days and believe her health will improve with time it will help her.'

'How long are you talking about, doctor?'

'I cannot say with any certainty. I would estimate probably four months, maybe longer.'

Litsa left the consulting room and made her way rapidly to the ladies' toilet. She locked herself into a cubicle and cried, choking sobs that eventually abated. She rose and washed her face and hands at the sink. She must return and face her mother, pretending all was well, and take her home.

2013

Each day Monika waited for a phone call from her mother asking her to go to the hospital immediately. Three times her grandmother had been taken into hospital and placed on an oxygen machine to help her breathing, only to be sent home when her condition showed some improvement. Now she was in hospital again and both Litsa and Monika knew that it was only a matter of time before the oxygen no longer helped the the frail body that lay beneath the sheet.

Monika had spoken to Vasilis and he understood that she might have to leave the hotel at a moment's notice and ensured there was always a receptionist working with her. She explained to Cathy that she would be unable to visit on a regular basis as she would be relieving her mother at home so she was able to get some rest or spending the evening and night at the hospital beside her grandmother's bed.

Cathy was sympathetic and offered any help they were able to give, but after thanking her Monika assured her there was nothing anyone could do and it was just a matter of time.

It was with a feeling of dread that Monika took a taxi to the hospital and hurried to the single room where her grandmother lay. She sat beside her and held her hand, talking quietly and telling her how much she loved her until the oxygen machine gave a warning signal that it was no longer working.

Litsa rang the bell for the nurse who appeared remarkably quickly and took in the scene at a glance.

'I'll call the doctor.'

Monika and Litsa looked at each other. They knew there was nothing the doctor could do; it was just a formality to call him to confirm that Monique was no longer breathing.

They sat together in silence waiting for the receptionist to tell them the death certificate was ready for them to collect, along with any belongings that were still in Monique's room.

'I'll get them, Mamma. There will only be her toiletries so I'll only be a few minutes.'

Monika looked at the empty bed, already stripped and ready to be made up for the next patient, and she felt the tears dribbling down her face. She brushed her hand across her eyes and sniffed as she bent to remove the meagre contents of her grandmother's locker. She hoped her grandmother had been able to understand how much she loved her.

'Have you got everything?' a voice behind her asked.

'I don't want to take anything home with me. Is there somewhere I can throw them away?'

The orderly shook her head. 'We have to insist that you take all her personal possessions with you. You can dispose of them later if you wish. You may change your mind once you get home.'

Monika lifted down the dressing gown from behind the door and wrinkled her nose. The smell of the chemotherapy drugs clung to it. She placed it over her arm and picked up the carrier bag of toiletries. They would all go into the first rubbish bin she saw on their way home.

Vasilis insisted Monika had a week away from work. 'You will need to spend some time with your mother and also arrange for her funeral. Let me know the details and I will tell the ladies who sewed with her. I know they will be upset that she will not be coming back to join them.'

Monika was surprised when she took her place at the front of the church with her mother to see so many people already there. The ladies from the sewing room were sitting at one side, along with Ariadne and three other employees from the hotel; the owner and one of the assistants from the shop where her mother worked had taken time away from their duties and their neighbours from the other apartments had joined them. Sitting by the side of the women was Cathy and opposite with the two men was Vasilis. Monika felt the tears spring into her eyes. She had expected the congregation to consist of her mother and herself.

The service over, Vasilis touched Monika's arm as she left the church. 'I have arranged for us to return to the hotel and have some refreshment. You and your mother can travel with Cathy and myself. It will be better to have some people around you for a while. Other employees at the hotel want to give you their condolences.'

Monika smiled at him gratefully. 'We kept telling her that she was looking better. I think that was more us being hopeful. We knew she was deteriorating gradually. I have to be glad for her sake that the end has come, but we will miss her so much.'

'Of course, that is only natural. You will always miss her, but the pain of parting will lessen.'

Although Monika knew the truth of Vasilis's words her mother seemed sunk in depression. 'It's so lonely here without Mamma. I come home and there's no one to speak to.'

'I come each day when I have finished work,' Monika reminded her mother.

'That's not the same. You come and stay for an hour or so and then I'm on my own again. I'm not used to being alone.'

'Are you trying to say that you would like me to come and live with you?'

'Would you? That would make all the difference.' Litsa's face lit up with hope.

'I'll think about it.' Monika was not sure that she wanted to live with her mother again. She had become used to spending her evenings alone and amusing herself when she left Rhodes. She felt guilty that she had not agreed readily to the suggestion when she saw her mother's face fall.

'I would have to speak to Mr Iliopolakis. This apartment belongs to him, remember. He might not want you to continue to live here.'

'He wouldn't throw me out?' Litsa looked horrified at the thought.

'I'm sure he wouldn't, but he might want to let to someone else at a higher rental.'

'Can you speak to him? If you came here to live with me we could pay him some extra rent if that is the problem. You earn good money and I have the rent that Natasha pays. I suppose that all belongs to me now?'

Monika nodded. 'It was good advice for Grandma to sign the shop over to you when she first became ill. It saves you from having to return to Rhodes and deal with legal papers.'

'I'd like to go back. I don't like Heraklion and I miss my friends.'

'You have other friends here. To return would be foolish. Manu would be bound to find out where you were and pay you a visit.'

Monika approached Vasilis and asked if he would agree to her sharing her mother's apartment.

'There is no reason why you shouldn't. You could buy your own apartment, of course.'

Monika shook her head. 'I don't feel ready. Suppose I bought somewhere and then found I did not like living there? I might have a problem selling. No, I'll wait until I'm certain that I'm investing wisely. I've never had so much money before and I don't want to waste it.'

Although Monika had declared that she did not want to buy

an apartment she looked as she walked around the streets. Those that had a notice to say they were for sale were above shops in the centre or so far out that she would need to buy a car for her and her mother to get in to work each day. She wondered if she should ask Vasilis if he was willing to sell his apartment to them, but she was not sure she would want to live there for the remainder of her life. It was not a bad area, but the only views from their windows were the apartment blocks in front and behind them or down to the busy road.

Now she had moved into the apartment with her mother, Litsa appeared happier. Monika allowed her to talk to her heart's content whilst they prepared and ate a meal together, then Monika would declare her intention of retiring to the bedroom so she could sit and read whilst her mother watched the television. At first Litsa had grumbled, but now she accepted that Monika needed time alone.

'Are you going to hire a car again this year?' asked Litsa as they washed and dried the dishes together.

'I thought I'd wait another week or two until the weather is more reliable. Is there anywhere special you would like to go?'

Litsa shrugged. 'I don't mind where I go provided I can leave the town behind for a few hours. At least on Rhodes you could walk down to the sea or up on Monte Smith and down the other side. Here there is just the commercial port and some parks.'

'I'd quite like to drive up to Chania at some time and see the memorial that Cathy's father had built for his first wife and son. Before we think about Chania I'd like to go down to Elounda and see what has happened with Ronnie's house. Once the season starts we'll make that visit a priority.'

Under Yannis's direction John and Marcus moved into the shop and began to paint the walls. Yannis began to bring the boxes out from the back room and John stopped him.

'You can't start to put stock back out until the walls and shelves are completely dry. If the pots ended up with paint on them you'd be cross and it could damage them if we tried to remove it. Leave them in the back room for the time being. They'll only get in the way when we have to move the ladders.'

Yannis sighed. Although he realised the sense of John's words he hated seeing his shop bare of goods. He wished he and Marisa had completed the cleaning last year and she had not insisted that the walls needed to be repainted.

'What can I do whilst you're working?' he asked.

John thought rapidly. His uncle really was in the way and he wished he would go home and leave them to complete the job.

'Why don't you start making out some new price labels? If you bought new stock I expect the price would have increased. You ought to check out the catalogues and change your old prices accordingly.'

'I sold those pots to Vasilis at the original price. Maybe I should have asked him for more?'

'Too late now. At least you sold some.' John decanted some more paint into a smaller container and climbed back up the ladder.

'What's the problem?' asked Marcus.

'Uncle Yannis is in a hurry to get everything out and on the shelves. I think he would have preferred us to paint around them.'

'I'll come up next week with him and he can tell me exactly where he wants them. I'll try to make sure that whatever he wants on the top shelves is relatively small and light.'

'They are usually the items that sell more readily,' remarked John.

'He may have duplicates that he can keep in the stock room and sell those. I don't think either of them should be climbing step ladders at their age.'

'Try and stop him! Have you finished that section? I can't do any more until we've moved the ladders along.'

Giovanni and Marianne were pleased. Bookings had come in and the self catering apartments were almost full for the beginning of the season. Giovanni had insisted that repairs and decoration up there and at the taverna took priority over the refurbishment of his uncle's shop.

'I hope letting an apartment to Kyriakos and Ronnie won't be a problem.'

'Why should it be? Ronnie's never been any trouble.'

'I don't want Kyriakos coming in after he has closed his taverna at night and disturbing everyone else.'

'I'm sure he won't. You're looking for problems that don't exist. It should be easier this year as we don't have Aunt Ourania to watch over.'

'Until Nicola has the baby.'

'Why should that cause a problem?'

'Well, the girls could be jealous of him and Nicola will want to spend some time with her parents when they come over.'

Marianne shrugged. 'John will be able to help out properly this time and I'm sure Bryony will be delighted to either have the girls or the baby to herself for a few hours each day. I do hope Nicola's latest scan is correct and he is going to be a boy.'

'That will mean John spoils him. At least it isn't twins again.'

'Giovanni, what's wrong with you? They would be delighted if they had twin boys to go with the girls.'

Giovanni sighed. 'I just feel that everything is going rather too well at the moment.'

Marianne squeezed her husband's hand. 'Then enjoy it before disaster strikes.'

'What disaster?'

Marianne shrugged. 'I don't know; the one you seem determined to bring about.'

Saffron was feeling pleased with herself. She had repainted the walls of her shop, resisting Vasi's proposal that he would ask Mr Palamakis and his grandsons to do the work.

'I can manage the inside. I'd be grateful if they would paint the woodwork outside, though. Maybe Uncle Yannis would like his woodwork painted at the same time? They'd probably manage all of it in two or three days.'

'I'm not sure if they have finished Ronnie's work. I had to insist they left her to come to the hotel. She won't be very pleased if I then ask them to paint your shop.'

Saffron shrugged. 'In that case I'll just paint the sills and the rest will have to wait until this time next year.'

Knowing the tourist season had started Monika suggested to her mother that they visited Elounda at the weekend.

'When we arrive we'll have a drink in the square and I'll see if Ronnie is around,' said Monika. 'I promise I'll not spend hours talking to her. Then we can visit Saffron and see if she has any new stock this year before we go up to see John. Cathy has told me that he and his wife are expecting another child this year.'

'Couldn't we stop in Elounda before we drive on to Plaka? I'd like to go into the church there and light a candle for your grandmother.'

'Of course. I understand that Yannis has opened his shop again. It could be interesting to have a look in there, but I'm not intending to buy anything.'

Litsa nodded agreement. She would be pleased to be away from Heraklion for the day. She tried to convince herself that it was no different from living in the Old Town in Rhodes, but there was not the same atmosphere in the large town.

Monika drew into the car park close to the church. 'Let's walk over and have a quick look at the sea. That is what I miss so much.'

They strolled across to the waterfront where the boatmen were advertising the visits to Spinalonga and walked a little further along to where the fishing boats were moored. The tourists to the area walked amongst them, but there was none of the congestion there that was everywhere in Heraklion.

Litsa drew in a deep breath of the sea air. 'It's so peaceful here.'

Monika linked arms with her mother. 'Do you want to walk on further or shall we go to the church?'

'I'm thirsty. Couldn't we stop here for a drink before we go on to Plaka?'

'Of course. Anywhere you particularly fancy?'

'They all look much the same. Why don't we go to that one by the church?'

They turned into a small area and took seats at the table, watching the waiter as he waited for a break in the traffic to hurry across the road to take their order. Monika felt guilty when she only asked for a frappe for her mother and mango juice for herself.

'You would like something to eat?'

Monika shook her head. 'No, just drinks, please. It is too early to eat.'

'It's not that early,' protested Litsa as the waiter made his way back to fulfil their order.

'We'll eat when we get to Plaka. We don't really want to be sitting here for hours. If we see Ronnie she's bound to know if Kyriakos is open and we could eat there.'

Litsa finished her frappe whilst Monika was still only half way through her large glass of mango juice. 'You go on into the church. I'll finish this and meet you in there.'

'Be careful crossing that road to pay.'

'I'll just raise my hand to the waiter and leave the money on the table. Have you enough change for a candle?'

Litsa nodded and made her way along the path to the church. She knew Monika had been drinking her juice slowly so she could have a few minutes to herself and say a prayer for her mother.

Monika joined her mother and after a few minutes Litsa lifted her head and smiled. 'I haven't lit a candle yet. I was waiting for you.'

Litsa and Monika lit their candles, each saying another prayer for Monique as they began to burn down.

As they turned to leave a lady entered the church from a back room carrying an ornate display of flowers.

'They are beautiful,' remarked Litsa and the woman smiled.

'I enjoy arranging them. I am sure our Heavenly Father loved flowers or He would not have put them on this earth. It is good to put them in His house.' Her Greek was stilted and accented.

'You are not Greek?' remarked Monika before she could stop herself.

The woman smiled. 'No. I live here, but I am not Greek. I come from England.'

'Your Greek is very good. Your husband is Greek?' Monika reverted to English

The woman shook her head. 'No, I visited Elounda and fell in love with the area and the people. I decided I wanted to live here rather than England. Did you live there to learn your English?'

'No, I learnt my languages at school. Do you arrange fresh flowers every week?'

'Usually. When I am able I collect wild flowers and in the winter time I use leaves and berries to make a display. For the special church celebration days other ladies usually join me either in the fields or to help arrange them. It is a shame you were not here at Easter to see them. Would you like to see a photograph?'

From the pocket of her apron she withdrew a mobile 'phone and scrolled down until she found the photographs. She handed the 'phone to Monika.

'Just scroll down and you will see them.'

Monika and Litsa stood together and admired the collection of photographs. 'They are magnificent. Were you a florist in England?'

'No, I just love flowers. I always have some in my apartment.'

'The next time we are down here we'll come in and admire your latest creations.'

'You are not stopping in Elounda?'

'We only came into the church to light a candle for my

grandmother. We are actually on our way to Plaka to visit our friends there.'

'Your friends live in Plaka? It is a small place I am sure to know them.'

'Well, they don't actually live in the village. They have self catering apartments, shops and a taverna.'

The woman smiled. 'Of course I know them; they must be the family who have the twin girls. When you see them say that Brenda says hello.'

'I will,' promised Monika. 'This is my mother, Litsa and I am Monika.'

'It has been a pleasure meeting you. When you are here again ask for Brenda.'

'I like that idea,' said Litsa as they walked back to the car. 'It must be lovely to go out and collect the flowers from the countryside. In Heraklion the church buys the displays ready made up from a florist. I'm pleased we met her.'

'She seems a very nice lady,' agreed Monika. 'We'll look for her again the next time we come down.'

They found Ronnie sitting in the square at Plaka painting.

'What has happened about your house?' asked Monika.

Ronnie smiled happily. 'The main house is still a wreck, but the extension I had altered to make a self contained apartment. Kyriakos and I lived there throughout the winter and it was very comfortable.'

'It's quite a distance for you to have to come and paint,' observed Monika.

'We've come to an arrangement. We live up there during the winter and have one of Giovanni's self catering apartments during the summer. That way I can get up when the sun rises and paint leaving Kyriakos asleep. I usually go back about ten when he is up so we have some time together. He goes off to the taverna and I return here to paint or stay at home for a siesta. Some evenings

I go up to the taverna and help out for a while or stay down here to touch up my paintings. It was a little difficult at first working out our own schedules, but it's fine now.'

'Will you rebuild the main house?'

Ronnie shrugged. 'Eventually, but there's no rush. After it was burnt down I felt like abandoning the whole project. Had it not been for Kyriakos I would very likely have gone back to America. As it happens it has turned out for the best. It has provided us with somewhere to live. I was adamant that I was not going to live with his mother. She was quite horrible to me when Kyriakos disappeared.'

'He disappeared?'

'He found out his grandfather had suffered from leprosy and asked the doctor to examine him when he had his plaster removed. The doctor sent him up to Heraklion and he didn't tell anyone where he was going or why.'

'Oh, we met him when we were taking my grandmother for her treatment. He was just leaving. Did the doctor say anything was wrong with him?'

'He has Vitiligo. It causes white patches of skin where the pigment has been lost. Absolutely nothing to worry about and although they've taken other tests they can't seem to find out the cause in his case. He's a bit self conscious of the patches on his arms and says he'll wear a long sleeved shirt all summer. I say he's stupid. They could be where his arms were scraped when he had the motor bike accident. If he lets the sun get to them they could soon darken up. Anyway, what are you doing down here?'

'We fancied a change of scene from Heraklion now the weather is better. I want to see Yannis's shop now he has it open again, visit Saffron and also call in on John. Cathy told me he is going to be a father again.'

'He's over the moon. The scan reckons it will be a boy so he is delighted.'

'What about the girls?'

'They're preparing them, letting them feel the baby kick and explaining that Nicola is looking after him until he is big enough to be born, the same as she did with them. They won't lack attention when he arrives.'

Litsa shuffled her feet and looked around, making it clear to Monika that she wished to move on.

'We'd better go and visit Saffron. My mother is getting restless.'

Ronnie grinned. 'You'd better go and see Uncle Yannis next; then she can talk to him in Greek.'

Monika and Litsa looked through the windows of Yannis's shop. Marisa sat with a magazine open in front of her and Yannis was sitting staring blankly into space.

'I don't think it is a good idea to go in,' said Monika. 'Let's speak to Saffron first and ask her opinion.'

Saffron pulled a face when they spoke to her. 'I think Uncle Yannis thought freshening the shop up would bring him customers again, but it hasn't happened. People stop and look, occasionally someone will go in, but when they know his prices they leave without buying anything. He's very down hearted.'

'What about you? Are you doing well still?'

'I can't complain, although it's early in the season. I'll be only too pleased if I'm rushed off my feet in August. Have you seen Ronnie?'

'We were talking to her a short while ago. I understand she and Kyriakos are together.'

'About time. The poor man has been besotted by her ever since she first arrived here. He was too shy to declare his intentions and she was too involved with her house to notice.'

'We're going up to see John and then we'll go and see if Kyriakos is open for a late lunch. By the way, we met a lady at the church in Elounda called Brenda. She appears to know the family and asked us to say hello.'

Saffron nodded. 'Nice lady. Since she has come over here to

live she has made both Greek and English friends. She seems able to mix with the two cultures very happily. Sometimes the other nationalities who come here to live keep very much within their own little group. The Greeks don't like that. It makes them feel like second class citizens in their own country.'

Yannis sat in his shop and watched the tourists walk past. They would look at his window display and point at various items before moving on. During the previous week he had only had three customers walk in and show interest in his goods. When he told them the price they shook their head and walked out. People no longer had the money available to spend as they had in the past. He was rapidly losing his original enthusiasm for reopening. It was not the same without Ourania.

If trade had not picked up by the end of June he would close. He was wasting money on electricity for the lights. It would be too late in the season to let the shop to anyone else. He should have made the decision earlier and not reopened.

Marisa was no happier than her brother. She used to enjoy being in the shop with Ourania where they read magazines and discussed the various articles. Yannis was not interested and hardly spoke to her. He seemed disinterested in the business and she wished she had not offered to be in the shop with him each day. At least if she was back at the house she could talk to Marianne or Bryony and help them with the meals or cleaning.

As the summer wore on Monika began to notice the oppressive heat of Heraklion. The apartment did not have air conditioning and even having an electric fan running and all the windows open during the evening did nothing to cool the air. Due to the traffic noise and fumes they often closed the windows early and depended solely on the fan.

Litsa would return from the shop hot and exhausted. Her clothes damp with perspiration and her hair limp. She would take a cool shower, but no sooner had she dried herself than she was perspiring again. They had not had air conditioning in the Old Town, but the stone walls of the shop had kept the heat at bay.

Tentatively she suggested to Monika that she should approach Vasilis and ask if air conditioning could be installed, but Monika refused.

'He has done far more for us than we could ever have expected. I cannot ask him for anything else.'

'You could offer to pay him for the installation. We could share the cost between us.'

'If the apartment belonged to us I would obviously have it put in, but it would be a waste of money if we moved elsewhere.'

'Are you thinking of moving?'

Monika sighed. 'No, but Mr Iliopolakis could always ask us to leave. He might decide to sell the apartment. Property prices have risen.'

'I thought he had plenty of money.'

'He has, but he is a business man. He could receive an offer that was too good to refuse.'

Each weekend Monika hired a car and they drove to one of the beach resorts further along the coast, looking for somewhere that the tourists had not invaded where they could cool their hot bodies in the sea. For once Monika was glad that her grandmother was no longer alive; she would not have been able to cope with the heat after her treatment.

'I'm tired of going to the beach and sitting there for hours. There's nothing to do,' complained Litsa.

'So what would you like to do?' asked Monika patiently; she was quite happy to sit on the beach and read.

'Why don't we go down to Elounda next weekend? We could visit John and he would be sure to have some photos of his baby boy with him. We might see that nice lady again that we met at the church and we can wander around the shops at Plaka and you could talk to your friends.'

'I thought you would find the journey too long in this heat that's why I haven't suggested a visit.'

'You could hire a car with air conditioning; then it wouldn't matter how long we drove for.'

'I'll see if the hire company has one available. The visitors may have taken them all.'

'If they have you could book one for the following weekend.'

Monika sighed. Hiring a car with air conditioning would be more expensive and her mother never thought to offer her any money towards the petrol.

It was pleasant driving down to Elounda in the cool interior of the car, despite the traffic congestion on the outskirts of Heraklion. Once on the main road Monika was able to increase her speed and began to look forward eagerly to their visit. Cathy had told her that Nicola had given birth to a large and healthy baby boy and they had called him Yannis. Monika felt envious. She had not mourned for the loss of her unborn baby, but she would like to think that she would become a mother at some time. Provided she met someone soon it would not be too late.

Plaka was as busy as ever when they left the car and walked up to the square. Ronnie was surrounded by tourists admiring her painting and again Monika felt envious. If she was a talented artist she would sit on the waterfront at Elounda and paint. A boat had just returned carrying passengers from Spinalonga and they hurried up the hill to Saffron's shop.

'We'll sit and have a drink before we go to see Saffron. She'll be far too busy to talk to us until this crowd has dispersed.'

Litsa looked around, every shop had someone looking in the windows and discussing the items on sale except the one that sold the museum replicas. 'I see he's closed again,' remarked Litsa.

'What a shame. With so many people around you would have thought he would have been as busy as everyone else.'

They sipped their drinks, whilst Monika kept an eye on

Saffron's shop. As soon as the tourists began to hurry towards the car park for their coach she rose.

'You stay and finish your drink. I'll go and see Saffron before the next boat lands.'

She hurried across and Saffron greeted her with a smile. 'Just the person I need. Watch the shop for me for a few minutes. I really do need the toilet.'

Monika stood there by the counter. It must be quite exciting to have your own shop, to be in control of the goods you sold and at the end of the season know you had made a good profit. She felt envious again and shook her head impatiently. Why did everyone in Elounda and Plaka seem to have such a happy and successful life? She must stop feeling envious; she had a good deal to be grateful for now.

Saffron reappeared. 'Thanks. It's always difficult if I'm here alone. I either have to leave the shop unattended or close up. If people see I'm closed they don't usually come back.'

'I see Yannis's shop is closed again.'

Saffron sighed. 'It just didn't work out. He was sitting there all day long and not selling anything.'

'Will he open again next season?'

'I doubt it. He'll probably rent it out to someone. I hope whoever takes it won't open another gift shop like mine.'

'That would be rather foolish, wouldn't it?'

'Some people seem to think they can undercut the shops who are already established. They usually fail and it's another empty shop again. We need something different to attract the tourists.'

'What are you thinking of?' asked Monika.

Saffron shrugged. 'I don't know. Oh, here they come again. Would you like to stay and help me?'

'What do you want me to do?'

'Just wrap the goods and keep an eye out for pilfering.'

It was more than half an hour later when Monika returned to where her mother was sitting patiently waiting for her.

'You were gone a long time. I've ordered myself another drink. Do you want one?'

Monika nodded distractedly. She wanted to think.

'What were you talking to Saffron about for so long? She seemed very busy.'

'We didn't actually talk much. I was helping her with the customers, wrapping their purchases.'

'That's the kind of job I would like,' said Litsa. 'Working in a nice shop like that rather than a grocers.'

'Mmm.' Monika hardly heard her.

'Well, wouldn't you prefer to be working there than in the grocers where I am every day? The air is cleaner up here and you'd see so many different people. If it was quiet there would be the other shop keepers to talk to and .....'

'Mamma, hush a minute. I'm trying to think.'

'What's to think about? Did you charge someone the wrong price? If so you ought to go back and tell Saffron.'

'Mamma, please, just let me think for a few minutes.'

Litsa compressed her lips; Monika was not usually this impatient with her. She must have made a serious mistake when helping Saffron.

Monika sat staring across the square. It could be possible, and she would certainly not impinge on Saffron's business.

'I need to speak to Saffron again,' she said.

'Tell her what happened. I'm sure she will understand. You're not used to working in a shop.'

Saffron looked surprised when Monika returned so quickly. 'I thought you were going up to see John.'

'We will, but I wanted to ask you something first. Do you think Yannis would rent his shop to me?'

'You? What would you do with it?'

'I'd open a book shop.' Monika smiled broadly.

Coming Soon

A continuation to Monika's story will be the next novel in the series, due for publication in December 2017. A taster is included here.

Crete 2013

Driving from Elounda back to Heraklion Monika forced herself to put her idea of a bookshop out of her mind and concentrate on driving. She wanted to be back at the apartment, shut herself in the bedroom and try to think of the practicalities such an undertaking would mean.

As soon as she returned to the apartment after depositing the car back at the garage her mother began to chatter to her about their day.

'I'm sorry, Mamma. I just need a little bit of peace and quiet for a while. I'll take a drink and go into the bedroom.'

'Have you got a headache from the sun? Maybe we should not have driven so far, even though the car had air con. Next week we won't go out for so long. Driving is probably tiring for you after a week at work.'

Monika shook her head and drew a glass of water from the tap. 'We'll talk about next week later.'

'You go and lie down. Do you want some Dupon? I have some in my bag?'

'Thank you, no, I don't have a headache.'

Litsa frowned. 'What is wrong then? Did one of your friends upset you when we were in Elounda or Plaka?'

'No, Mamma, please, just let me go and sit in the bedroom quietly for a while. I need to do some thinking.'

'What about?'

'Nothing for you to worry over.'

'You didn't damage the car when you were taking it back?'

'No, Mamma.' Monika went into the bedroom and closed the door firmly behind her. This was when she wished she still had her own apartment where she could escape from her mother's incessant talking.

Monika took a notebook and her bank book from the drawer beside her bed. She propped the pillows up behind her and picked up her pen, headed a page as "Important Questions" and sat back. The first thing she needed to know was if Yannis would rent his shop to her the following season. If so, how much was the rent? How much could she expect to pay for utilities?

She turned the page and wrote down the amounts she had calculated as being the maximum. She turned another page and headed it "Questions". She would need shelving and have to pay someone to fix it. "Measure for shelving", "cost of shelving", "cost of fixing". A computer would be a necessity to allow her to look at the brochures from book wholesalers and publishers, see which books they were offering, which ones appeared to be the most popular and the cost of transporting them from their warehouse.

Another page was turned and she wrote down price stickers, receipt book and bags. She would not consider purchasing a computerised till in the initial stages; customers could be given a hand written receipt. Ideally the bags should have the name of her shop printed on them as an advertisement and she smiled wryly. She had not thought of a name.

On a fresh page she wrote down a brief summary of her expected expenditure, added the figures up and increased the total by a thousand Euros.

Monika chewed the end of her pen thoughtfully. She would have no regular income. She was sure her mother would want to join her in Elounda which would mean leaving her shop work in Heraklion. More income lost. They still had to pay to rent an apartment and they were unlikely to find one in Elounda or Plaka with such a low rent during the season. Monika gave a deep sigh. There was so much more to her idea than she had realised when it first came to her.

She looked at the balance in her bank book. It looked a magnificent sum, but would it be sufficient? She felt a moment of panic. Did she dare take the chance? If she used all her money and then the shop was not a success she would have nothing.

Monika picked up her mobile 'phone. She would ask Vasilis Iliopolakis for advice. Half way through pressing in the numbers for the telephone at his house she stopped. She had no right to disturb him on a Sunday evening. She would speak to him at the hotel the following day and ask if she could call and talk to him about her idea and discuss the financial implications with him.

Vasilis was surprised when Monika asked if she could visit him and Cathy that evening.

'Only if it is convenient,' she assured him. 'It is to ask your financial advice as a business man.'

'Of course you may come over, unless you would rather discuss it with me now?'

Monika shook her head. 'I think Cathy could also be helpful to me.'

'Cathy does not have any business knowledge,' smiled Vasilis.

'I'm sure she would be able to give me some help.'

Monika returned to the reception desk, leaving Vasilis to ponder her request. If she wanted information about investing her money in stocks and shares he could only tell her the possible risks and refer her to a reputable broker.

'I need to go out this evening to visit Mr Iliopolakis and Cathy,' Monika informed her mother. 'I don't know what time I will be back so can you leave me some supper, please?'

'You usually visit them on a Wednesday. Why are you going

this evening?' asked Litsa.

'I need to talk to Mr Iliopolakis about something.'

'Have you got a problem at the hotel? Surely he could sort that out for you when he goes in next.'

'No, Mamma. I don't have any problem. Everything at the hotel is fine.'

'So why do you need to see him this evening? There's a film on the television that I thought we could watch together.'

'You enjoy the film and you can tell me about it tomorrow. I'm just having a quick shower and changing into something casual then I will be off.'

Monika closed the bathroom door before her mother could ask her any more questions. She had no intention of divulging her idea to Litsa. Her mother loved to gossip and Monika knew she would immediately tell her co-workers at the shop, who would tell their relatives and friends; before she knew it word would have got back to the staff at the hotel.

Now wearing cotton trousers and a T-shirt Monika checked that she had her notebook in her bag. She felt incredibly nervous. If Mr Iliopolakis advised against the venture she would be bound to respect his opinion, but she would also be desperately disappointed.

Vasilis opened the door to her and led her through to the small patio at the rear where Cathy was sitting at the garden table, an almost empty glass in her hand.

'I'm pleased you've arrived,' she smiled and held out her glass towards Vasilis. 'I'm just ready for a refill. White for you, Monika? I have a chicken salad ready for later, so I thought white wine was more appropriate.'

'I'd love a glass of wine, but I don't expect you to feed me. I asked my mother to save something for me for when I returned home.'

'Nonsense. There's far too much for just the two of us and the salad will be limp and uneatable by tomorrow.'

Vasilis handed a glass of wine to Monika and refilled Cathy's glass. 'I have already had half the amount of wine I am allowed in one evening so I will wish you good health with a glass of water.' He raised his glass and took a seat at the table. 'Now, what is it that you wish to discuss with me?'

'Well,' Monika hesitated, 'I drove my mother down to Elounda and Plaka on Sunday. I visited Saffron and she told me that Uncle Yannis is hardly ever at his shop and he is thinking of closing it next year and renting the premises out.'

'You want to take over his business?'

'Oh, no, I want to open a bookshop.'

'A bookshop? Why?'

'Because there isn't one down in that area. The nearest one would be in Aghios Nikolaos. Do you think he would allow me to do so?'

Vasilis shrugged. 'If he agrees to rent his shop to you he cannot stipulate the goods you sell. There are some items that would be unacceptable, but I hardly think you would consider opening a shop that sells sexual aids and toys as some do in Heraklion.'

Monika blushed. 'I certainly wouldn't.'

'What would you do with the stock that belongs to him?' asked Cathy. 'You wouldn't want it around or stored in the back room as it is now.'

'I have no idea how much stock he has. I know Saffron usually displays an item and replaces it with another if it is sold. I would be willing to do that.'

'You would have to come to an arrangement with Yannis. I cannot advise you there.'

'I realise that. I will have to make an appointment to speak with him. I need to know how much rent he is likely to charge and whether I would be able to afford it, along with the utility bills. I wanted to ask you if you thought my idea was viable.'

Vasilis shrugged. 'I don't see why a bookshop should not be a success. If you stocked books in Greek I'm sure the locals would be grateful and tourists often want a book to read whilst they are lying on the beach.'

'Would tourists be willing to purchase new books? Most hotels seem to have a book shelf where they can help themselves.'

'They have, but the self catering accommodation does not.'

'I have money that I could invest in more shelving suitable for books and also book stock, but if I was not successful I will have lost everything.'

Vasilis smiled sympathetically. 'You will be no worse off than you were before you received your compensation money.'

Monika shook her head. 'I will have no work and my mother and I will be without a home.'

'Your mother will still have the rental income from her shop on Rhodes.'

'Even if the bookshop was a success during the season would I have made enough for us to live on during the winter? I couldn't expect my mother to use her money to subsidise my idea. She might need it later for medical expenses.'

'Provided you only agreed to renting the premises from Yannis for one season and if you found you were running at a loss you could close and he would have to rent to someone else. You would have lost your original investment but you could return to work at "The Central" as a receptionist.'

'Thank you, Mr Iliopolakis. I would certainly be very grateful to know I was able to come back and work for you.'

'I would not be able to help you with accommodation again. I do not want the responsibility of becoming a landlord to people I do not know. If you left I would sell the apartment. There is always someone who is looking for good tenants and I would give you and your mother a reference.'

Cathy frowned. 'You are both jumping ahead. Would Yannis's shop be large enough for a book shop? It is only half the size of Saffie's and books take up a lot of space. Would you have enough shelves?'

'I doubt it. I would have to ask permission to add some more, and they would have to be firmly fixed to the walls so they could not fall over. At least once they were installed I would not have to buy them again. I wanted to ask you about books, Cathy. Do your father's books still sell well?'

'Are you planning to cater for children?'

'Children and adults, but I need to know which books are popular. I cannot afford to buy a hundred books and have ninety still sitting on the shelves at the end of a season.'

'I will ask Vasilis to unearth last year's royalty statement that I received. That will tell me how many of my father's books sold. I'm afraid I take little notice of the number.'

'When I worked in the library we had catalogues stored on the machine and if we wanted to order a book we looked up the author or title. Do you know if it is possible for bookshops to obtain computerised lists?'

Vasilis shrugged. 'I expect so, but I am not the person to ask. Saffie should be able to give you that information. I know she has computerised catalogues from suppliers for the gifts she sells.'

'Do they quote the cost of having the goods sent to her?'

'They would have to. No one is going to place an order and find it has cost more to have it delivered than the price of the goods. Are you going to sell only new books?'

Monika frowned. 'I hadn't really thought that far ahead. I could have a section of second hand books; ones a customer had read and no longer wanted. I could buy them back for one Euro and sell them on for two provided they were in good condition.'

'You could take some from the shelf in the hotel,' offered Vasilis. 'You know we throw away those that have loose pages or where someone has spilled their drink. I wouldn't expect you to have those. There could even be a box of books in the cupboard below.'

'Is there?' Monika looked at Vasilis in surprise. 'I had no idea. I've only ever helped myself from the shelf and not looked in the cupboard.'

'What do you think, Mr Iliopolakis? Will my idea work?'

'I cannot say with any certainty. I think the thing you need to do next is speak to Yannis. You cannot really make any firm plans until you know if he will let the premises to you and allow you to add extra shelves.'

'You don't think it's a stupid idea that's bound to fail?' Monika looked from Vasilis to Cathy anxiously.

'I think it is a good idea,' said Cathy firmly.

Vasilis nodded. 'Provided you do not become too ambitious in the first instance and find you have run out of money before you have opened. You do not want to go to the bank and ask for a loan if that can be avoided. The interest rates are extortionate.'

'I will be very conscientious about my expenses. Once I have found out the details from Yannis and the cost of shelving I will put aside an amount for purchasing books. I have to remember that I will also have to rent an apartment. I thought I should divide my savings in half to start with, one half for the bookshop and the other for living expenses. At least I won't have any wages to pay to anyone.' Monika gave a nervous laugh.

'What does your mother think of the idea?' asked Cathy.

'I haven't told her yet. Until I know for certain that I can go ahead I don't want her fretting that she will have no work and we won't have a home. If I'm unable to go ahead with my ideas she would have had all that worry for nothing.'

Vasilis picked up the bottle of white wine and refilled Cathy and Monika's glasses. He looked at the amount that was left and tipped it into his own glass.

'It might be a rather generous measure, but I'm sure a little extra will not hurt me.' He lifted his glass and touched Monika's. 'Here's to your success.'

To be continued ......

ROMANCE OPTIONS

First published in 2022 by
The Dedalus Press
13 Moyclare Road
Baldoyle
Dublin D13 K1C2
Ireland

www.dedaluspress.com

ISBN 978-1-915629-01-2 (paperback)
ISBN 978-1-915629-00-5 (hardback)

Dedalus Press titles are available in Ireland
from Argosy Books (www.argosybooks.ie) and in the UK
from Inpress Books (www.inpressbooks.co.uk)

Printed in Ireland by Print Dynamics.

Cover image: Olly Kava / Shutterstock

The Dedalus Press receives financial assistance from
The Arts Council / An Chomhairle Ealaíon.